A Bit Of The Dark World

by

Toni V. Sweeney

Published by
CLASS ACT BOOKS
121 Berry Hill Lane
Port Townsend, Washington 98368
www.classactbooks.com

ISBN: 978-1-938703-47-8

Credits

Cover Artist: Bev Haynes
Editor: Sherry Derr-Wille
Copy Editor: Anita York

Printed in the United States of America

Dedication

To Dirk Mosig for opening his Lovecraft library to me and
sparking the idea for this novel;
To the late William Rex Tutor for our brief but memorable
acquaintance in 1973, which led to his becoming Drex's model;
And to Emma Carranza who became Martha

There was a crack in his head and a little bit of the dark world came through and pressed him to death.

Rudyard Kipling
The Phantom Rickshaw

Chapter 1

Godalmighty, what a night!

Daniel Walker, MD, was a big man though not a particularly clumsy one, but there was nothing graceful about the way he reeled through the door of his office after stubbing the toe of his Croc on the threshold. Wavering to catch his balance and prevent crashing into his desk, he staggered around it and fell into the big executive's chair, then jerked open the center drawer, searching frantically for the pack of cigarettes he kept there.

…Gotta have that smoke…lemme at it before I have a nicotine fit. He was acting like a true addict and admitted it. *Found it.* As if discovering water in the desert, he extracted one, snapped open the lighter lying inside the drawer, and flicked it into life.

The tobacco flared, the tip of the cigarette glowed, wrapped paper curling blackly. Raking one hand through his coarse black hair, he leaned back, hungrily gulping in smoke. *Ahhh…*He closed his eyes, exhaling in a long, slow trickle. He'd been trying to quit, was doing pretty well too, what with that *Nicorette CQ* patch and all, but now? Hell, after tonight…he'd ripped the little piece of drug-soaked adhesive off his shoulder. *The way I feel right now, I'd smoke a whole damned carton if I had it.*

He'd never seen anything like it. As if God Himself had battered down the Gates of Hell and set free total calamity. Cracked ribs, broken arms, fractured legs…ambulances and police cars swarming and wailing…was there anyone left in Temple and surrounds in one piece?

A bit of an exaggeration perhaps. It was August and there was a full moon. Everyone knew those two things separately were bad news but together they spelled disaster. The heat and the moonlight made all the loonies—and they didn't call them *luna*-tics for nothing—even crazier, while the sane ones bore the brunt of their madness.

Whatever…the violence kept him busy. Once he'd realized he wasn't going to see anyone upright and conscious, he had the desk nurse call his office, deciding there was no need to make his patients sit and wait. They probably had better things to do. Not *Yours Truly,* however. Along with the other surgical teams, young Dr. Walker was the *Man of the Hour*, and he'd been proving it since nine o'clock that morning, stepping out of the surgery arena only long enough to take a leak when the urge became overpowering. Wouldn't do to piss into his socks and hold up surgery while they sanitized the OR.

It was now late in the evening and the realization he'd had neither lunch nor dinner was sinking in, accompanied by the demanding, twisting growls of his long-empty stomach. He wished he'd squirreled away a couple of candy bars in his desk. Who was he kidding? He was too damned tired to think about eating. *Have to throw together a sandwich when I get home.* At the moment, he didn't care if he ever ate again. A slug of whiskey…maybe. Too bad he didn't keep a bottle in the desk drawer, too.

Heat close to his knuckles made him glance at his left hand. The cigarette was nearly burned to the filter. *When did that happen?* Had he been sitting there, half-asleep, holding a lit cigarette? *Guess it's a good thing I'm not in bed.* He glanced at his watch. The digital numbers blinked eleven o'clock. Not exactly the time of night to drift into a doze while pondering the *Meaning of Life*, but he wanted—no, *needed*—to think about what happened. Relive it. Try to figure out why.

Lean back. Relax. Think…and don't fall asleep!

~ * ~

Most of the cases were simple enough, in spite of all the pain involved. Barely the expected amount of danger to the patient. It was almost assembly-line: Roll one in, put him back together, roll him out. *Next, please.*

Then they brought in the girl…

Woman. She was a woman, not a girl.

At that precise moment, he hadn't been thinking about his patients. In a brief pause in the action, he was wondering why he hadn't become a peanut farmer instead of an orthopedic surgeon. God knows, the hours would've been better.

He'd stepped out of OR, wanting a breath of air not laden with the scent of blood and anesthetic, making a bee-line for the Exit and passing through the emergency room waiting area…

…where they were bringing her in, rolling in the gurney. The EMT, seeing him standing there trying to decide which way to go, began reeling off her vites.

Funny how the mind can latch onto trivial details. He'd turned to look at her and…froze.

The most beautiful woman he'd ever seen. Even with the blood and the pain. All he wanted was to take her in his arms and tell her everything was going to be all right. He, the Great Physician, would save her.

He didn't move. Couldn't.

No bells. No thunderclaps. Just a flood of emotion so raw and stark it shocked him with its ferocity. He felt vulnerable and exposed, as if he'd been stripped naked for the entire ER to see. Actually looked around to make sure certain no one was staring.

"Doc?" The tech was the only one looking, still talking. He put a hand on the scrub-clad shoulder as if to get his attention.

"Go on." His voice was calm in spite of his internal tremors. "I'm listening." He may have said more, he didn't remember. A lot might've happened but it was forgotten because von Dorff came crashing through the ER doors, raving like the psycho he was.

"Where is she? What's being done?"

Seeing that rich bastard was something to be avoided on a good day. It took all his control to keep from smashing his latex-covered fist into that island weirdo's face. That would've been the perfect ending to a shitty day…breaking his hand hitting that freak.

A tired smile flickered. *Who takes care of the orthopedist's broken bones? Could the physician truly heal himself?* Good question.

He'd settled for barking an order at a nurse, "Get that bastard out of here," while silently praying, *Five minutes, Lord. Just let me have five minutes with that scumbag and to Hell with what happens to my hands.* Still shouting, Von Dorff was hustled out of sight.

Why was he there, anyway? What was she to him? Why had she been on the island? How could she be anything to that...that... He couldn't think of an obscenity vile enough. *God, I must really be tired!*

That's what he got for being the only orthopedic surgeon in this little town, a place where he wouldn't be practicing if he hadn't been born here. If his mother's people hadn't lived in Temple, Georgia, since Time Immemorial. He was certain such a color-conscious little Deep South hamlet wouldn't otherwise accept a halfbreed doctor, not even in today's Politically Correct world.

Sometimes, especially after late-night sojourns like this, he tried to imagine where he'd be if he were all white. Probably in a big city hospital somewhere, overworked, underpaid, and popping pills or shooting up to keep himself going. But here? He might be overworked, maybe a little underpaid, but all in all, things weren't so bad, and he'd never felt the need for anything stronger than his cigarettes. Still, if more nights like this one came along...

~ * ~

The cigarette burned itself out. Stubbing it into the ashtray, he got to his feet, dragging his jacket off the coat tree by the door. Pulling it on over his scrub smock, he started out, switching off the lights. Dictation on tonight's circus could wait until tomorrow.

Better head home and get some rest. His patients would expect Dr. Walker bright and early, following-up on the repairs he'd done tonight. If he hurried, he might catch a couple of hours sleep before then.

No choice, of course. He *had* to be there. They needed him. In case *she* needed him…

~ * ~

In the deep, they huddled, hearing the human's faraway thoughts and welcoming them.

It has begun…the thoughts rippled through the water, rising to the surface.

Except for an initiated few, the world had no knowledge of them, though they'd always existed. Long before Earth, they came into being in the thick and formless darkness beyond the point of the farthermost star. When the great cosmic cloud began its spiraling descent into the swirling mass of stardust whose explosion became the birth of the Earth and its siblings, they were sucked into the vortex and flung onto that infant world.

It was glorious…now they had a place to rule, and when the creature to be called Man evolved enough reasoning to acknowledge their power, there were slaves and worshipers at their eldritch shrines.

Eventually, as expected, their enemies came, those older, more powerful Others, and the inevitable battle for possession of the little world began. Conquered, they were banished…some exiled to the point in Time from which they began, others imprisoned deep within the darkness of the planet itself or far below the surface of its oceans. Even there, bound as they were, the evil within them still managed to trickle free like tiny bubbles escaping from a sunken ship, bursting and briefly spreading their malevolence once more…to those who waited…

One found his prison in the waters off the coast of the continent known as North America when men overcame enough of their fears to explore. In its southern waters, islands huddled together against the onslaught of the ocean they named the Atlantic. A group of unnamed land projections, these were already marked by mysterious stories and superstitious whispers, further enhanced by their mist-enshrouded shores and the bleak moss-draped terrain. One stood isolated from its companions as if even among themselves, the other islands shunned it.

In later more civilized times, no ship came there because of the danger of rocks lurking below the waterline. Indeed, had the waters been safe, no ship would stop since no settlers, either native or white dared force the islands to offer shelter. Long ago, the native tribes abandoned the area because of the shadow of the fearful being sleeping beneath the waves, a thing sometimes briefly shaking off its dreadful slumbers and clawing its way to the surface, only to be dragged downward again by its chains.

Thus they waited under the lash of the current, worn by the waves…until a stranger, in flight from certain unnamed acts, arrived in the early years of the first century of settlement.

He purchased the land from the tribe daring claim ownership. They, a remnant of the Yamacraw, an outlawed tribe of the Creeks, gladly relinquished it to one they considered so unstable of mind as to want to live on an island known to be accursed. They traded their birthright for a half dozen iron ax heads, twelve strings of glass beads and a bolt of scarlet cloth and considered they got the best of the bargain.

The foreigner, a secret, reticent man who socialized little with his mainland neighbors and referred to his beginnings even less, built his home, settled his people, and set about ensuring his immortality. Stubbornly conquering their home's harshness, as aloof as the old man himself, his descendants discouraged friendliness. As expected, stories grew up about them. They chose neither to substantiate nor deny the whisperings until eventually the reason for their apartness was as lost to the memory as the stranger's past.

And they lived and went their secret ways and watched and waited...

Chapter 2

Orange pinwheels in a black sky in a shower of shooting stars exploding into burning rain and a blaze of red surging into a pale green void jagged and saw-toothed in a pulsing mass and she lies in its center until it fades to orange pink gray and disappears in a pinprick of light and all is whirling whirling as a face floats into view and I don't know you go away oh Rob where are you?

The pale green nothing becomes a box in a hospital room with pale green walls and a pale green floor and everyone has a pale green face and even their voices are pale green...

If everyone is green why is this one red? Red red red blood red hair red eyes...fire fire...

...and she closes her eyes to shut out the greenness even welcomes the pinwheels when they come back because she hurts too much to think until one day they don't come back and she opens her eyes and decides she's going to live so why fight it?

~ * ~

Lisa woke once again from the dream-that-wasn't-a-dream, and the realization she could finally put a name to her prison. Temple General Hospital. A landmark in the little town. How many times had she driven past the place, barely giving it a glance, blandly uncaring if it was a *House of Pain*?

The first week in the pale green room with the pale green floor inside the House of Pain was never clear. Even much, much later when she tried to remember, it remained mere vignettes linked together by a fragile chain of semi-consciousness.

Today was different. It was her first day of *true* awareness, though she had no idea *which* day it was. She lay motionless in the narrow bed, face turned toward the window, seeing sunlight red against the insides of her closed eyelids as she tried to arrange the most recent events in her life into some understandable sequence. She didn't move. No one must know she was awake, not yet, not until she had a chance to determine in her own mind what had really happened.

Be calm. Take it slowly. *What's the last thing I remember?* Isn't that what they always ask?

The very last thing? Lying on a table of some sort. Looking up at the green ceiling. *Why green?* There was a curtain hiding her from the rest of the room. Noise behind it. Swiftly-moving figures. Soft *pad-pad* of rubber soles.

Someone near her. Only a voice and a pair of hands hovering above her, seizing her arms, turning them this way and that, displaying bleeding gashes to the world. She watched the shining metal hook go in-and-out. *Hey Dude, pretty neat hemstitching! No pain there. Wait a minute…he's sticking a needle through my skin and it doesn't hurt? That's not right… Hey! Quit making me into a human pincushion…*

The hands disappeared as another presence surged closer. She sensed the change. *This one's different. He barks orders. And they jump.*

A voice droned. Did she hear her name? A reply from that forceful entity. Impatient. Brusque. Disturbing in its deepness. She wanted to apologize for being such a bother.

Fingers touching her legs. Pain with it. Whimpering, she tried to pull away, anger wrenched from her at this disturbance of her consciousness. She raised her head, seeing only a green blur. Her arms thrashed out.

"Stand by her!" It was a harsh rasp. "I don't want her falling off the table while I'm doing my exam."

Hands lifted her skirt. She turned her head, protesting with a moan. *Where's Rob? Why aren't you here? Stop them from whatever they're doing to me.*

"Jesus Christ!" Rough with anger now, as if he had pain of his own. "Where'd all that blood come from?"

"She's got multiple lacerations." Someone was defensive. "A compound fracture of the left femur and a possible broken pelvis…and you want to know why she's bleeding? Give me a break, Doc."

"There's too much blood." Did he shake his head? "I'm no OB/GYN but that looks like vaginal blood to me. Good God, she isn't pregnant, is she?"

"How the Hell should I know?" Anger from his companion, as if his ignorance were being pointed out. "She's in no condition to answer and the driver's deep-fried."

"Watch it, you idiot. She can probably hear you."

"Sorry…"

Hands on her ankle. A groan from their owner as if he, too, suffered. "Shit…that leg's broken in three places. Why can't I ever get a clean, simple greenstick fracture to work on? Does anyone know what they were doing on the island? That's private property."

"Speaking of that...von Dorff's in the Waiting Room, raising a ruckus."

"You tell that bastard to take his rich ass out of my hospital."

"Got a good reason? He's the one called EMS. Pulled her out of the car."

"X-rays?" The man called von Dorff was dismissed by the sound of films being shuffled from one hand to another. "Your diagnosis is a little off. Pelvis isn't broken. Get her prepped for surgery. I want a team standing by—*Stat!*"

"B-but—" Someone else spoke up. "Who'll sign the consent forms? You can't op—"

"Later." The curtain was swept aside, footsteps and voice fading away. "Does anybody know who she is?"

No one knew and no one answered and hands pushed Lisa back against the table and held her there. *Other hands had held her, too.* When? Someone else had touched her and hurt her. Was he the one...this man whose voice held so much anger and concern? She could hear yelling, sounds of a scuffle, cursing. *What's happening? Is it Rob? Are they keeping him from me?* She wanted to call out. Couldn't.

Scissors sliced through her skirt, pulling it away, sliding it off her body. Her blouse followed. Cold air touched her skin as her underwear disappeared, leaving her naked and...

She was too tired to fight or wonder and she closed her eyes at this new indignity.

A bell was ringing. The sound grew louder and louder until it became a roar drowning out whatever else was said. Great orange pinwheels began to revolve in the black sky...

~ * ~

Lisa and Robin Chambers were newly-weds, or close enough. They'd been married exactly fourteen months and a week, still so fresh the glitter hadn't yet rubbed off their marriage. They stayed in bed all day on weekends, ate breakfast with as few clothes on as possible and showered together when the sex got them all hot and sweaty, then did it again because showering got them hot and sweaty, too.

Unlike a good many of their college classmates, Rob snared a good job so Lisa didn't have to work. They were starting out seventy-five percent better than most of the kids they'd gone to school with. That was probably due to Robin having graduated first and gotten a job in Temple and being already settled before he and Lisa tied the knot. He'd gone ahead to pave the way, driving back to Athens every weekend where sophomore Lisa was still studying at the University of Georgia.

Rob never missed a weekend for three years, he and his Mustang traveling I-75 until he was certain the car could go the distance by itself. Not because he didn't trust Lisa to spend those two days without him when she wasn't in classes, but because he was so damned in love with her. The fact that they'd have the rest of their lives together after graduation didn't enter into it. He wanted to be with her as often as he could. Now.

Two days after that long-awaited graduation day, they were married. Finally. At the age of twenty-five

13

and twenty-two, they became Mr. and Mrs. Robin Chambers...

...and moved to Temple, Georgia, fully prepared to have a *Happily Ever After* for the rest of their lives, unaware it wasn't going to happen.

~ * ~

When Rob arrived home, he gave no hint he was going to drag Lisa from the house and into the car for an evening drive.

She protested she was getting supper ready. He said he didn't care. There was something more important than food right then. Knowing how much he appreciate her cooking, Lisa wondered about that but he was so insistent, she decided not to argue. They *never* argued, and she wasn't about to break that remarkable record this early in their marriage.

She thought his explanation that they'd been in Temple nearly fourteen months and still hadn't seen much of the town was a little lame. They'd been to the movies and had eaten at several fast food places as well as a couple of restaurants. They'd gone to the beach, even if technically that wasn't *in* Temple. They even attended Mass occasionally.

None of that seemed to matter. Tonight, Rob declared, they were going to see some of the countryside.

Okay, Fine. But why not on a Sunday afternoon? In the daylight. Why now? He was so excited, almost elated, she went with him out of sheer surprise.

Throwing the Mustang into gear, he backed it out of the driveway, speeding away with a squeal of tires. Rob headed the car down the Coast Road, the highway running parallel with the canal opening into the sea. Though Lisa'd never been this way before, he drove as if it were familiar. At least the speed at which the Mustang was going indicated that.

"Don't you think you should slow down?" She wondered if he'd already scouted the area. Sometimes he did that so he'd be familiar with it before they actually went there.

She'd barely gotten the words out before he snapped, "I don't need your help to drive, Lisa."

A little chastened, she remained silent. Rob's mood changed abruptly, his eagerness now replaced by something bordering on anxiety. He pushed the car faster, as if they were late getting to wherever they were going.

Where are *we going?* Casting an anxious glance at her husband, Lisa started to ask, then sat back without saying anything. Rob didn't look in her direction but the momentary tightening of his lips told her he'd seen her expression out of the corner of his eye. Seen and was angered by it. That was upsetting. Rob was usually so easy-going. Not tonight, however. For nearly twenty minutes, neither spoke and the atmosphere within the car became more and more tense.

What's possessed him, anyway? What made him want to go for a drive at this time of night?

Metal flickered in the headlight's glare. A bridge came into view, railings and supports looking fairly new. It stretched into infinity, leaving the mainland and reaching across the ocean. Rob turned the car onto the bridge. The wheels made a *thrumming* sound as they sped over the steel roadway.

It was now so dark the countryside they were supposed to be seeing was only vague shapes crowding the road's edge. Lisa could see the shadowy spikes of a palmetto's fronds and an oleander's long, slender leaves, but nothing more. There was darkness on all sides, only the glimmer of the moon on the water and the soft splash of waves lapping at the girders indicating what was below. The bridge, its silver expanse extended before them, seemed their only link with the earth...

~ * ~

Moving through darkness...

The black sky cleared, the moon morphing into a reflective crescent hanging from a tangle of machinery on the ceiling, a mirror of a spotlight. The table rolled under, taking Lisa with it. She was the star, caught in that circle of light, on her private stage.

Lazily she turned her head, surprised to find both arms outstretched, strapped to extensions of the table. *When did that happen?* A needle and tube ran from one arm to a bottle of clear fluid feeding itself drop by drop into her body. A man in a rumpled green smock hovered over the other, inserting a silver spike into the bend of her elbow. She didn't feel it. Just lay with arms outflung, tied onto the crucifix of the operating table, gazing indifferently at the people gathered at its foot, a faceless group wrapped in green.

*Green, green, the grass is greener...*the words swam through her head...*green grow the lilacs...the wearing of the green...*and they were. All of them. With a vengeance. *Why are they here? Who cares?* She was sick of all that green. *I hope I never see another green thing as long as I live.* She wanted to tell them that. As

16

if he heard, one of the men detached himself from the little group, presenting himself for her pronouncement.

Shifting her gaze, Lisa blinked. She didn't say anything, merely stared, too weary to speak.

He was wearing a scrub suit, loose and ill-fitting—and green, of course. *My, how we do love that color.* His face was hidden by a surgical mask, hair covered by a ridiculous cap looking like something worn in a shower. Even more absurd, it had smiley faces all over it, little yellow globes staring at her with hideous grins. Above the mask, the only visible part of him were the darkest pair of eyes she'd ever seen, almost black, their pupils mere pinpoints in the bright light. She stared into their depths and tried to concentrate, as if looking into those eyes was the most important thing she could do.

I should tell him how important it is. Nothing but a senseless mumble came out. He leaned over her. Not trying to touch her, holding his hands near his chest, fingers curved protectively against his palms. *Good hands, gentle hands,* they *won't hurt.* His gloves were so tight and thin she could see his nails and the creases in his fingers.

"We won't move you until you're asleep, Mrs. Chambers. It's going to be all right."

*I'll take your word for that. Fine with me, Doc. Good show, go ahead...*her mouth didn't want to say what she wanted it to so she jerked her head in a nod and closed her eyes again. *I'm so tired of it all. Especially living. For God's sake, just get on with it.*

She didn't see him nod to the man standing behind her or the others take up their positions around the table. Her body relaxed and the clouds came back but they were pink this time and there were no pinwheels exploding inside her brain…

~ * ~

The island loomed before them and they were on land again, the road narrowing into a snake of a path with a layer of beach soil slithering away from the tires.

Leaving the safety of the bridge, they drove into a dead world. The car was in a tunnel, trees huddling together, overhead branches grasping each other hiding the sky. A low, thin mist hovered, plucking at tatters of Spanish moss. It fluttered in the breeze blowing from the shore.

Lisa looked up through the windshield. Though it was as sticky and humid as only a Southern summer night could be, she felt chilled. Perhaps it was the darkness and the enclosed sensation, as if the trees were creeping closer, slowly entrapping them. The wind blowing through the window onto her damp skin made her shiver. Pressing one of the buttons in the arm rest, she closed the window.

"Cold?" Robin glanced her way. It was the first time he'd spoken since they crossed the bridge.

"A little chilly." She sounded apologetic, voice loud in the stillness. Rob was already turning away, attention once more on the road. His expression was set and urgent. Combined with the speed at which he was driving, that added to Lisa's uneasiness.

As a distraction, she turned her attention outside again. *It's too quiet.* Where were the familiar night noises…frogs, crickets, an occasional bird? In spite of its haven of trees, the lonely stretch of road held no sounds other than the noise of the motor and swish of tires. As if beyond the shadows, all life ceased. Through Rob's open window floated the scent of honeysuckle, thickly sweet and overpowering, mingling with the salt tang on the breeze.

We're lost. She felt foolishly close to panic. *That's silly. All we have to do is turn around and—* "Rob, let's go back. It's dark. We can't see anything." She touched his arm, afraid without knowing why. "Are we going to drive all night?"

For a moment, he didn't answer, merely stared straight ahead. When he did look at her, his gaze was blank and uncomprehending. As if he were waking in an unfamiliar place and not understanding how he'd gotten there. He shuddered, blinked, and startled recognition flashed.

"Okay, sweetheart. Don't know what I was thinking. I..." His attention was jerked back to the road. "What the Hell...?"

Through a parting of branches, a glowing, swollen moon sprinkled light onto the road. From the corner of her eye, Lisa saw it, too. Something running, dark and man-high but shapeless—*are those wings?*—darting in front of the car to the safety of the ditch on the far side.

In the next instant, the creature was forgotten and she fought to keep her balance as Rob slammed on the brakes and jerked the wheel, swerving to avoid hitting the thing. The sandy soil slid away, the car went into a skid. Rob struggled with the wheel, taking his foot off the brake pedal, trying to regain control. They felt the momentary shudder as a tire struck a rock jutting out of the road's shoulder. The steering wheel was wrenched from Rob's hands as the other tire went off the edge of the road.

Lisa's scream hung briefly in the night air as the Mustang plunged down the slope of the ditch. In spite of their seat belts, she and Rob collided against each other with heart-numbing force as the nose of the car hit bottom and bounced up the other side. With a shattering of metal and glass, it dived into the trunk of a tree, air bags exploding from their compartments.

Something went wrong. The bags stayed flat, wrapping around them like yards of elastic. Encased in a rubberized shroud, Rob smashed against the windshield as his seatbelt ripped apart. Lisa's body hurtled out of the seat, fear-stiffened legs striking under the dashboard with a loud *snap-snap-snap!* Fire shot up her right leg. In the aftermath of the impact rocking the car, she bounced back against the seat, and the first of the black clouds descended...

~ * ~

The light's blinding. Lisa raised a hand, shielding her eyes. Someone approached the bed on soft-soled shoes.

"Miz Chambers?"

From the protection of her palm, Lisa peered at the figure.

"Hmm..." She *croaked* the word. *My throat's so dry.* How could she ask all the questions in her mind when she could barely speak? *For God's sake, give me some water!* Her brain felt soft and mushy. The hand over her eyes began to shake.

"Are you awake?" A blue-striped pinafore swam into view, a blue cap atop a mass of curls.

"Unh-huh." All the smart-ass remarks she could've made cowered at the back of her mind. She managed to nod her head up and down, very slowly.

"Good." The woman sounded relieved. "Doctor wanted to be notified when you were conscious."

Conscious? That's a matter of opinion.

The woman turned toward a doorway out of Lisa's sight, then looked back. "Don't go 'way. I'll be right back." Then she was gone.

Doctor? Dr. Who? That's not right. What's the doctor's name? She should know but couldn't remember. *Don't go away?* Lisa felt an absurd desire to laugh. *Who's she kidding? I can't move. How can I possibly go—*Her thoughts tangled as she realized it was true. *I can't move!* Only her hands and arms had any feeling.

She remembered striking the dashboard. That sickening sound which could only be bones breaking. Had her legs been amputated? Her back broken? *Am I paralyzed?*

She knew there was a white expanse of sheet before her but was afraid to look down. Afraid to confirm the absence of the bumps and ridges of feet and legs. *Will Robin want an invalid wife?* She had a mental picture of herself in a wheelchair. Crippled. Useless.

"Oh God!" Putting both hands to her face, she felt the pull of stiff muscles as her shoulders began to shake. "No, no, no."

Her hands were rough, scratching her face. Raising them, she stared at the white bands encircling both hands from palm to elbow. Her wedding ring was gone. And her watch. The edge of a piece of tape had come unraveled and she picked at it, holding her hands close to her face so she moved as little as possible. It was important she not exert herself. *I may need all my strength.*

The door opened and the blue pinafore was back, two other figures following. Lisa flicked a disinterested glance in their direction as one came to the head of the bed.

"Mrs. Chambers?"

She'd heard that voice before. Quiet, deep, faint but audible Southern accent. *Do I know you?* "Huh…?" Strange how thick her tongue felt.

"Do you know where you are, Mrs. Chambers?"

Didn't I say they'd ask that? "Yes," she whispered, plucking at the tape. "…hospital."

"Do you know *why* you're here?" he persisted.

"Sure." She dropped her hands to her chest and winced as pain knifed through her. "Car got in the way of a tree." Had she said this before? Perhaps not. Closing her eyes, she tried unsuccessfully to stifle a giggle. *Really, the whole thing's so absurd. Why else would I be in a hospital? For a hangnail?*

There were no more questions and in the long silence, she felt someone touch her feet. It didn't hurt this time. Nevertheless, she raised her head, fixing a bleary stare on the white-coated figure now at the foot of the bed. She peered across the white field at him. Craning her neck hurt, too. "Hey! You!"

"Yes, Mrs. Chambers?" Without looking up, he took the scissors offered by the nurse, and clipped the strip of gauze he was wrapping around her ankle.

Polite. Just the proper amount of concern, but detached, far enough removed not to be personal. Lisa almost applauded. "Doctor…"

"Walker. Daniel Walker."

"Are you sure?'

That stopped him. Piece of tape in one hand, he paused, frowning at her. It aged his face at least a year. "Am I sure…*what?*"

"You're a doctor?"

For a silent moment longer, he looked at her and then at the tiny name tag pinned over the pocket of his coat, tilting it with his finger.

"*Daniel Walker, MD,*" he read. "Yep, I'm a doctor, all right."

"Just wanted to make certain." She felt she should explain. Leaning back against the pillow, she spoke to the ceiling. "Can't be too careful, you know, what with all the identity theft nowadays."

She made an effort to cross her arms over her chest in what was to be a decisive gesture. Instead, her right arm missed her left and she nearly socked herself on the jaw.

"You're still a li'l uncoordinated," he commented, mildly. His accent seemed to come and go. She wondered if it was for her benefit. An attempt at a little down-homey country doctor air? She wanted to tell him he wasn't succeeding. He looked anything but *homey.* "I suggest you take it easy."

Ignoring that bit of useful advice, Lisa returned to her original subject, stating bluntly, "You don't look old enough to be a doctor."

"I'm old enough."

Oops. She'd struck a nerve. The nurse chose that moment to make some kind of noise…an abortive snicker? She put her hand to her mouth, smothering the sound.

"That's enough out of you, Myrtice." Though he didn't look in her direction, it was as if he'd glared.

"Sorry." She gave another little snort before subsiding into silence. She didn't seem particularly worried she might've angered him.

"Does this hurt?" His hands were on her left foot now, firm pressure against her instep.

"No. In fact, I think that's the only place in my whole body that *doesn't* hurt."

"Not surprisin'…that's prob'ly the only bone not broken."

"What?"

"Relax." At her horrified yelp, he went on, "I'm only kiddin'. You're gettin' along fine. Jus' fine." There was a smile in his voice now.

"You wouldn't lie to an invalid, would you?" Her head was beginning to ache so she closed her eyes.

"Mrs. Chambers, that's the last thing I'd do," he assured her with strange earnestness. He moved from the foot of the bed, coming into full view again.

"Felicia."

"Beg pardon?" At least he didn't ask, *"Say what?"* She hated that phrase. It sounded so phony.

"Not *Mrs. Chambers*. My name's Felicia…Lisa…" It was a sleepy murmur. She could hear the nurse arranging items on the tray. "What's your name? Oh right…Walker. Daniel Walker, MD." She giggled. "Sounds like a TV show…" Opening one eye, she

24

peered at him, rousing herself from the sleep threatening to overpower her. "Hey, Doc?"

"Yes, Mrs. Chambers?" There was so much patience in his voice she wanted to cry.

"You're pretty cute, you know? Yep, downright hunky…hunky-dory doctor…" She dissolved into a stream of giggles subsiding abruptly into a soft snore.

A hand touched her face, turning back an eyelid. A tiny light bore into her eye, forcing her awake again. She tried to blink, ending by glaring at the light. *Go toward the light, Lisa.*

"Look up…now, down…at the window," he ordered and as she obeyed, touched the other eye, repeating his instructions. His hand hovered over her nose. "Can you see my hand clearly? How many fingers do you see?"

Eyes nearly crossing, Lisa squinted. She tried to focus, gave up and closed her eyes again. "Two?" she guessed hopefully.

Somewhere, someone was singing. She listened intently as the doctor kept talking. *Why doesn't he shut up? Can't he hear the music?* She began to hum along with the singer. *Camptown ladies sing this song…doo-dah…doo-dah…*

"Damn, she's going again." His voice was low, intended only for himself to hear. "Better cut back on the sedation. Lisa…? Mrs. Chambers?"

Lisa let the music flow over her, drowning out his voice…

Oh, doo-dah-da-a-ay…

~ * ~

Stunned, unable to move, numbness flowed from body to mind. Her arms were too heavy to lift her hands to the seatbelt and the simple task of freeing herself. *It should be so easy...* She managed to move one hand but it jerked outward, striking the window. For a moment her fingers scraped against the glass. *Why did I shut it?*

Rob hadn't moved. She couldn't tell if he was breathing. There was a strong smell of spilled gasoline. She could hear the car's engine still racing...high-pitched and screaming like an animal in a trap...

Nails scratching the glass, her hand slid down the window and fell into her lap. *Try again...*flap, slap...directly onto the seat belt buckle this time. A weak tug...her head wobbled drunkenly, dizziness washing over her.

There was a faint moan from the driver's side. That encouraged her to try once more but the movement threw a blanket of pain over her. She was surrounded by it. Engulfed. The touch of her fingers on the buckle flange made fire slice through her.

Someone screamed. The gasoline smell got stronger. Over the sound of the running motor, she heard a crackling. *Fire?* Smoke trickled through the dashboard and under the upward-crushed edges of the hood. Flames licked their way free. Lisa coughed as pungent burning-rubber fumes filled the car. *Got to get out. Help.* She didn't know if she said it aloud or not. The pain shot through her again, bringing back the dark...

~ * ~

When she next awoke, it was to look directly into those dark eyes again. He was sitting by the bed, sun gleaming off his white coat. He smiled, and in that moment of first consciousness, she felt wrapped in warmth.

"Welcome back to the land of the living."

"What are *you* doing here?"

"Lunch break." His easy tone indicated he spent little time bothering with such minor items as food. He didn't seem upset by her bluntness either. "I've been waiting for my most important patient to wake up."

"Flatterer." By now she was able to focus her eyes enough to get her first good look at his face, and its youthfulness shocked her. There was an odd familiarity she didn't understand. She told herself she'd probably seen him many times in the past...days...weeks...and simply didn't remember.

"Mrs. Chambers, this is the first time you've been fully conscious and I need to check a few things." The cornball accent disappeared. He was all business now, breaking through the thoughts she'd arranged into a vague semblance of order. They scattered like marbles struck by an aggie.

As he stood, she studied him silently, surprising herself by liking what she saw...and not in a doctor-patient way.

Watch that, Lisa. Remember, you're an old married lady now. Right, but I'm married, not dead. Hadn't Robin said that to her, just the other day? They'd been discussing Angelina Jolie and he'd said how hot she was. Lisa protested that, reminding him he was married. "I sure am," he agreed, kissing her. "To the woman I love. Still I can appreciate other women. Look but don't touch. *Hell, Lisa, I'm married, not dead.*"

Wait'll I tell him that. It'll give him a laugh. She went back to her appreciation of Dr. Walker's looks.

Dark, not like someone often out in the sun but naturally. Almost...Spanish? Cuban? Hair with a definite wave, maybe a little too long, nearly black in the glare from the window. His eyes weren't brown as she'd thought, but hazel, flecked with green and gold in their darkness, and shadowed by the most beautiful lashes she'd ever seen, so thick they looked mascaraed...*man*scaraed. *Bet he hates them.* Out of the pocket of the white coat hung the inevitable stethoscope. She felt there was something about him she should remember but couldn't. That worried her.

'"...check this one and get those bandages off today." He was at the end of the bed now.

From somewhere the nurse materialized. *What's her name? Myrtle?*

"Okay," he ordered. "Wiggle your left foot."

"I can't." That earlier fear pounced again.

"Sure you can. It's your right leg that's in a cast. Your left ankle's only sprained. Just take it easy and move it."

There was something in his tone telling her he wouldn't accept her refusal. Forehead creasing in a scowl of effort, Lisa bit her lip and wiggled her toes. Though it hurt, she welcomed the pain for the mere fact that she could *feel* it. More questions came as he checked the cast on her other leg, elevated on a foam block. Satisfied her circulation was unimpaired under all that plaster, he began to remove the bandages from her arms.

With the intentness of a child watching an adult perform some difficult task, Lisa turned her attention to his face again. A memory came as he lifted her arm from the bed. That dark head bending over the name tag on his coat, reading aloud…

"Daniel Walker, MD," she whispered. She felt very weary and closed her eyes but there were no black clouds this time and she sensed he was smiling.

"You remember."

"I've a feeling I've been very rude." She didn't open her eyes. "If I have, I'm sorry."

"No problem, Mrs. Chambers." His answer was as calm as ever. "Pain killers can sometimes put a person's inhibitions as well as their pain to sleep."

He was busy clipping through the gauze sleeve, hands quick and efficient but still gentle. Dropping the scissors back onto the tray the nurse held, he parted the bandage. It followed the scissors to the tray.

"You had a few burns and lacerations," he explained. "All superficial. There won't be any scars. We felt it best to cover them for your own protection. You got pretty violent a couple of times."

~ * ~

Hands tugged at her shoulders…the car screamed as the door was wrenched open…and so did she, body shattering with the force she was pulled from it.

Solid ground under her back. She was in one piece but that piece was a single burning pain. An eruption of flame propelled an orange spiral into the sky. The ground shuddered, bits of blazing metal spun through the air, striking the ground around her, igniting the grass into little spurts of fire.

Lisa stared into pain-blinded darkness. She couldn't see the owner of those hands. *Where did the moon go? Are clouds covering it?*

29

"Rob? Rob!" All she could hear was the fire's roar.

Hands brushed her shoulders, moving down her hips and legs. Even their light touch sent spasms through her, bursting out in another scream. Cold air fanned her legs and she felt the stickiness of blood as something flung itself upon her...pushing her into the grass...a throbbing, relentless movement driving jagged fiery splinters through her body.

Pain forced her eyes open again. Flames leaped above the trees. Coils of black smoke rent the air, searing the edges of the moon, changing it from bone-white to dark red as the boiling darkness hid it. A single fireball spun away, becoming a red-tinged face with a flaming sheet of hair curling and crackling. The blaze from the car shadowed high cheekbones, curving a mouth laughing at her struggles while its eyes became white glowing mirrors reflecting her bloodied and broken image staring back at her, mouth open in a voiceless scream.

Fiery locks hissed, a flaming medusa sending off sparks as bright cinders gathered, becoming massive and monstrous, a pulsing jelly-like orb with flaming tendrils writhing and groping toward her. The face disappeared. All she could see were the flames and smoke mingling dark and blood-red in the air. Floating in the crimson haze were fire-born things...shapeless blobs circling and giggling and gibbering...while Lisa's mind screamed...

A searing thrust like a burning sword drove into her body. Fire slashed upward, consuming her thighs, spreading through her as she struggled to escape the weight pinning her to the ground. Her hands balled into bloody fists striking out. Her wrists were seized and slammed against the grass.

The agony ended in a final scalding eruption. Lisa flung back her head and shrieked. The flaming face hovered, mouth moving in words she couldn't understand as the night came alive with sounds. Frogs, birds, insects, freed from their silence, a frantic chorus mingling with her own screams. The words echoed into a kaleidoscope of voices swirling around her as the fire danced...faster and faster and faster... There was a second explosion and the smoke billowed upward.

It entered Lisa's head and drove out the words as it filled the corners of her mind with a welcome oblivion...

~ * ~

The other bandage lay on the tray beside the first.

"Funny thing about these cuts. They look like nail marks." He turned her arm, surveying the half-healed scratches. "You must've scraped something when you were pulled from the car."

Lisa looked at the inside of her forearm. Starting at her wrist and moving downward were five small, irregular slashes, one overlapping the other. Each cut was crescent-shaped and deeply-grooved as if something strong had dug in and ripped, and each was now scabbed and red. There were similar scratches on the other arm, too. *He's right. They* do *look like fingernail scratches*. She shook her head, not wanting to think.

It was only after Dr. Walker left that she realized she hadn't asked about Robin.

~ * ~

Just outside Lisa's door, Daniel Walker paused to scribble a note on the blank sheet in the front of her chart. He stared at what he'd written, then reached for the handset of the device attached to the wall. Though it looked like a telephone, it was actually a dictation unit, relaying whatever was said into it to a receiver on the desk of the hospital transcriptionist assigned to prepare his case histories.

While Myrtice waited, he spoke into the mouthpiece, "Case note on Lisa Chambers, Patient identification number..." *Lisa Chambers...Felicia...Mrs. Robin. Widow.* That wasn't right. *She shouldn't be lying in a hospital bed. She should be at home, cooking her husband breakfast.* And he shouldn't be an unidentifiable burnt corpse. *He should be coming through the kitchen door, stopping behind his wife and putting his arms around her waist as she bends over the stove...kissing her ear, nuzzling her throat through her hair as he turns her around, pressing her body against his...* The strident buzz from the handset, indicating too much silence followed his initial words, cut into his thoughts. *Quit daydreaming, Walker. Get on with it.* "Uh...case note on Lisa Chambers. This 23-year-old patient..."

~ * ~

Hear me, O Dark Ones! Crouched on a wave-bound rock, the creature howled his anger to the stars. *I, M'AneseNebh, spawn of many-tentacled Tschenebhua, call upon thee!*

Sea winds stirred salt-matted hair and the hunched scaled shoulders shivered.

How long must I tolerate my brother's existence? Your commands have been obeyed...by me...seen in the green fires of the Star Stone...witnessed by my Dread Lord's minions...the woman is mine. The Mansion and the Key are united...

Talons curved, raking the sky as hackles rose in impotent fury.

*Still   he   opposes   me and...I...would...see...him...die...*He stifled his rage, smothered it into control, lest they think he begged and received his plea with contempt. *In the Name of He who is to Come...Great Cthulu...Azathoth the Mighty...Yog-Sothoth, Sharer of the Dominion...Grant me the promised power.*

His words were seized by the wind and dragged downward. The child's distress carried to the father, sinking to the deep-entombed ocean prisoner who even then stirred and struggled before settling once again amid his chains.

Long after the cries died away, a second figure stood on the porch of the old manor house. Staring into the darkness, he raised his cigarette, watching pale smoke drift across the yard.

So the creature's angered, is he? Whether in his thoughts or spoken aloud, he never hid his scorn for his brother. He studied the glowing tip of the cigarette. *Bleating his despair to our father. As if he can help. I'll always best him. Doesn't he realize it's a game? One he's never going to win? How can he when he's less than human? Poor M'AneseNebh...blessed with the desire but cursed with that deformed body...he may be the Vessel through whom they speak but I'm the Chosen*

One, protected from harm because of my outward humanity. Taking the woman would be so easy it'd be boring if she weren't such a delicious morsel…

Flicking the cigarette into the air, he watched its fiery trail through the darkness. It struck the sand, glowed a moment, then died. Laughing softly, he walked into the darkened house.

Chapter 3

Time gets lost when you can't see the world, when the sun's trapped in a window frame and daylight creeps timidly through half-drawn blinds...when all other light's artificial and even the air's machine-freshened. There's no way to know what day it is or even the month or the year when life's bounded by four pale walls. Time becomes marked by the habits of others, recognizing footsteps instead of faces, knowing who'll be where at what hour. You become a connoisseur of acoustical ceiling tile and window slats because when you're flat on your back, that's all you can see.

~ * ~

Lisa had been in the hospital three weeks, ten days of which she had no memory. On the ninth day, she woke to the greeting of Dan Walker's dark eyes and began the process of healing both her body and her life. Today when he arrived, she found enough courage to ask the question she should've asked long before.

"When can I see Rob?" Taking a deep breath, she blurted its anxiety, causing him to stop in the midst of checking her ankle.

Doctor and nurse exchanged glances before he answered. "Your husband was...injured, too, Mrs. Chambers. He—"

"How badly?" She didn't let him finish. There was too much caution in his reply. She'd caught him off-guard and he took too long to answer. She sensed what he *wasn't* saying.

"Well…"

"Rob's dead isn't he?"

~ * ~

Daniel Walker looked away. The moment he'd been dreading had come, the time to tell this broken and battered young woman she was alone, that only she survived the wreck. He didn't know how she'd guessed but in a way he was relieved. Now he wouldn't have to search for a way to break it to her gently. *Break it gently? How can anyone be told of violent death in a gentle way? What trite and useless words do I choose? I'm sorry for your loss?* He'd come to hate that phrase for its overuse in television dramas. *That's the most unfeeling group of words currently in the English language.* Besides, he lied badly.

So far he'd been lucky. Few of his patients succumbed while under his care, but the loss of those few and the aftermath of facing their families were forever sealed in a hidden corner of his heart, along with the knowledge his skill had failed…that the *God Complex* all physicians possessed to some degree wasn't as infallible as he thought. With her question, Lisa lifted that little weight of responsibility, one less pound of guilt, from him.

Releasing her ankle, he stepped away from the bed.

"Yes." One word. To break her heart.

~ * ~

"I knew it," she whispered, closing her eyes and shaking her head.

"How could you?" he asked. "You haven't mentioned your husband since you regained consciousness."

"Neither have you." She opened her eyes, looking up at him. "No one's mentioned Rob at all. If he'd gotten out of the car, if he were alive, even if he were hurt, someone would've told me, reassured me but no one has, so…"

It was a long speech and Lisa's voice, still husky from disuse, trailed into a silence broken only as muffled movement from the corridor sifted through the closed door. No one spoke. Sitting in her chair near the window, the hospital volunteer was a mere spectator, hands held tightly in her lap. Behind the doctor, Myrtice shifted her weight. The silence held until Lisa spoke again with a thick sob.

"H-how…"

Here it comes! Damn it, no. Anger flared. *Now I'll have a case of hysteria on my hands.* He remembered how she'd fought against Myrtice's restraining hands in the ER. *If she flails around on the bed with her leg casted like that… If she hurts herself…*

Moving to the head of the bed, he motioned for Myrtice to be ready if she tried to sit up. He heard the nurse toss the armful of charts…out of the corner of his eye saw them fall onto the bedside table as she followed him.

"Please. I need to know." Lisa held up a hand, eyes and voice tearless.

"No," he told her. "You don't."

"Don't say that." The upraised hand curled itself into a fist, quivering with abrupt and violent rage. "Don't

37

you dare say that." Her tone changed, mimicking someone. *"Do this, Lisa, it's for your own good. I'm sorry, dear, you can't do that. It's for your own good.* All my life people have been deciding what's good for me and what's not." Both hands clenched, punctuating her last words with sharp little blows against the bed, her voice never rising from that rigidly quiet, too calm, tone. "Don't you dare tell me I don't need to know this."

The fists fell to the sheet as if she'd disowned them.

"All right." He shook his head, not in refusal but as a way of shrugging away the lies he'd intended to say. Smiling in defeat, he repeated softly, "All right."

Pushing down the safety railing attached to the bed frame, he sat on the edge of the bed, something he forbade his patients' visitors to do. Her body rolled toward him as the mattress gave under his weight. Just then she looked very small and very helpless, except for that carefully-controlled bleakness on her face. Her right hand still lay where it had fallen. He slid his own under it, lifting it from the bed. She didn't resist as he pried open the tight little fist so it rested, small and pale in his own.

His hands were large but well-formed. *Good, gentle hands.* Lisa remembered again the skill they held. He touched the backs of her fingers, stroking lightly, calming her. Lisa relaxed.

"Do you remember much about the accident?" His voice was very low, as if in those few seconds he isolated them from everything. He had nowhere to go and nothing to do except sit and talk...just the two of them...his tone idly conversational, as if he were barely interested, not betraying the aversion he had to subjecting her to extra grief.

"Enough."

"Good." He looked relieved. "I won't have to go into that then."

"There was something in the road. An animal. Rob swerved to miss it and… The car went off the road and into a ditch…" She broke off, frowning as she tried to remember.

"That ties in with what Drexl told us."

"Drexl?" Did she imagine it or was there a change of tone saying he wished it were otherwise, that this Drexl was lying?

He nodded. "He pulled you from the car. He was driving from the other direction. Lucky for you. He got there as your car left the road."

"What was he doing there? I don't remember seeing any headlights. Only…" she broke off, shaking her head. *I won't say anything about the flaming face. Or the other things.* Not until she was certain they were real.

"It's *his* island," Dan answered. "What's more to the point is—why were *you* there? You were trespassing, you know. Why did you go there?"

From somewhere a memory jolted into Lisa's mind…he'd asked that in the ER and gotten no answer.

"No one goes to Land's End Island without a direct invitation from Drexl von Dorff himself." This time he didn't hide his dislike, fairly spat the name.

"I-I… R-Rob wanted to go for a drive. We went down the Coast Road and when we came to the bridge, he…simply turned, that's all."

"I see."

She could tell by his expression he didn't believe her.

"Did he often do things like that? Drive onto a bridge with a well-displayed *No Trespassing* sign on it?"

Sign? There hadn't been a sign, she was certain. "Is it a crime to do something on the spur of the moment?" Her anger came out cold as ice. *I don't have to defend Robin to anybody.*

"No, Mrs. Chambers." *It is if it kills you and puts your wife in the hospital.*

"This Drexl. You say he pulled me out of the car? Why didn't he save Rob, too?"

"It happened too fast. He was too busy with you..." Later the irony of those words would haunt him. "The car exploded..."

"Then Rob was burned..." What little expression she had was wiped away, leaving pale blankness.

"No." He said it quickly to stop the horror of the image from forming in her mind. "He was already dead." *Don't think that. You mustn't.* His hand tightened around hers.

"Liar!" She jerked her hand away, refusing to look at him. "Rob was alive. I heard him. That's why I tried to get out..."

"He was dead before the fire," he repeated. "There were massive internal injuries." *Please, let her believe me.* He touched her hand again, forcing her to look at him. "I'm not lying, Lisa. I swear."

"Cross your heart?" she asked anxiously, like a child.

"Cross my heart." He released her hand to perform the childish ritual. Only Myrtice standing behind him, saw him put his left hand behind his back, crossing his fingers in an equally childish gesture negating the power of the lie he was telling.

"I believe you." She sighed, as if it were too exhausting to *not* believe.

He got up, sliding the railing back into place, then glanced at his watch as he picked up the charts from the table. "I'm sorry. We have to go."

"Please. Do you have to? Right now?" She took a deep shuddering breath as if a lungful of air might lessen the pain.

"Well..."

"You're supposed to see Mrs. Cross at eight-thirty, Doctor." Myrtice stepped in with their pre-arranged excuse, planned to prevent delaying his rounds.

"I think I can spare a few more minutes." He handed her the charts and went on, "Go ahead and check on Mrs. Cross. She's supposed to be dismissed tomorrow, so there shouldn't be any problems. Mr. Ray, too. I'll catch up with you."

"All right." Mouth open in surprise, Myrtice took the charts and walked stiffly from the room.

Removing the stethoscope from around his neck and tucking it into his jacket pocket, he pulled a straight-backed chair to the bed and sat down.

~ * ~

Outside Mrs. Cross' room, Myrtice paused to scowl in the direction of Lisa's door. She didn't like what had happened. *And no, I'm not jealous.* Well...perhaps she was a little more proprietary toward her doctor than most nurses were. After all, they were fifth cousins on his mother's side, and in a small town like Temple, where everyone knew everybody else, that made them closer than some siblings.

~ * ~

Myrtice'd had a bad case of hero worship for Daniel Walker since the day he repaired the broken arm of her favorite Barbie doll, gluing the fragments together with household cement and wrapping the injury with duct tape to hold it together until the adhesive dried.

"Gosh, Danny, you're wonderful." She hugged the doll as he placed it in her arms. "She's good as new."

"This was just practice," he announced with twelve-year-old assurance. "When I grow up I'm doing to be a *real* doctor."

"Can I be your nurse, Danny?"

"Sure."

He kept his promise. Myrtice was an RN working the graveyard shift at a hospital in Americus when his letter arrived. He'd graduated, done his internship and was returning to Temple to set up practice with old Dr. Long, and he wanted her with him.

Thinking how a good many doctors married their nurses, she couldn't agree fast enough. She gave notice the next day, fretted out the next two weeks, then packed and headed back to Temple. The marriage hadn't happened, but within a year, Dr. Long was only too glad to retire and let his young colleague take over. By then, Dan was accepted by the townspeople as a returning Temple-ite.

So what if he's young? After all, he's a Temple boy even if his parents did move away when he was sixteen. No matter if he's part-Indian. Why, he's homefolks.

42

Daniel Walker was the only orthopedic surgeon in the little town, though not the only one on Temple's staff since the hospital served all the towns around it. As such, the people in Temple wouldn't let him leave if he wanted to.

They'd had some difficult cases but he always managed that professional detachment. If a patient was particularly possessive and tried to delay his departure that was Myrtice's cue to step in and remind him of an urgent appointment or another patient waiting to be seen, as she had today. This time, though, he ignored her and allowed Lisa Chambers to detain him...and Myrtice didn't like that.

Shifting the charts to her other arm, she sighed. "I hope you know what you're doing, Cousin Danny." She pushed open the door to Mrs. Cross' room.

~ * ~

"Is there anyone you'd like us to call?

"Like who?" She gave him a blank look.

"I don't know...your parents, a brother or sister. We found your husband's wallet. It listed you as next-of-kin but you had no personal identification."

"Rob hurried me out of the house so fast I didn't have a chance to get my purse." She looked as if that fact still surprised her.

"We assumed you were his wife. The police sent someone to your home." As the officer stood at the door, the lady living had across the street rushed out to confront him. "A neighbor, Mrs. Campbell, identified you."

Good old Mrs. Campbell. Busybody extraordinaire...but in this case, a blessing.

"Rob and I are...were...only children," she explained. "Rob's father died a few months after our wedding. He was all alone." She sighed. "Now I am, too."

"I see." He remembered something else, saying it quickly, determined not to let her give in to self-pity. "One of the men at your husband's office is taking care of all the reports and claims to be filed. He said for you not to worry."

"That's good of him." She said it in an offhanded way as if she wasn't really interested in her husband's co-worker's kindness. "Oh my God!" Without warning, she appeared panicky.

" Timothy!"

"What? Who's Timothy?" *Good Lord, not a child?*

"My cat. He's been alone all this time. He'll starve."

"Mrs. Campbell has the cat." The notifying officer told him that but hadn't mentioned the animal's name.

Another silence. From outside came a low and distant grumble of thunder, the weekly summer rainstorm announcing its arrival.

Abruptly her lower lip quivered. "I want my Aunt Allie."

"Who?" It was so like a child's *I want Mommy,* he was startled.

"My Aunt Alice. Alice Townsend. She helped my mother raise me after my father died."

"Tell me where to find her." *Is she the one who tells you what's good for you?*

"She lives in Macon. On High St...Oh God, I can't remember the address." She cried it in sudden shock. "Is it evening yet?"

"It's morning." He frowned, not understanding.

"She won't be home. She'll be at the college. Mercer University. She teaches there."

"Wait a minute." Taking his i-Phone from his breast pocket, he began texting in letters. There was a barely audible *beep*. "Alice Townsend?" Moving fingers paused. "T-O..."

Lisa spelled it for him.

"Macon...Mercer University...What department?"

"She's in the English Department."

"She'll be notified if I have to call her myself," he promised. He tapped *Save* and returned the little unit to his pocket, then stood up. "I have to go. I've a few other patients to visit."

He returned the chair to its place against the wall, watching her as he did so. The reaction he'd expected still hadn't come but he knew it would. Some time, probably in the middle of the night, when she was alone. The knowledge of what she'd lost would strike her and he had to do something to ease that blow as much as possible when it happened. He reached for the chart hanging at the foot of the bed. "I'll order a sedative."

"No." One hand went up, waving slightly. "I don't want one. Not now. The last thing I want to do is sleep." *I need to stay awake. To think. To remember. About the red face. That's important. Later...later, I'll think of Rob...*

He didn't argue, merely nodded, though he scribbled something in the chart. Lisa thought he turned toward the door a little reluctantly. He had his hand on the push plate when she called after him, "Dr. Walker?"

He looked back at her.

"Tell Aunt Allie to hurry."

"I will. I promise." She looked so small and childlike lying there he felt a painful twist in his heart. As he went through the door, he called to the volunteer who'd been sitting through the whole thing. "Martha, could I see you a minute?"

She followed him into the corridor.

Chapter 4

Do you love your husband?

It was an *Inquisition for Two.* An unknown speaker as interrogator, Lisa the accused. The questions were always the same. Only two of them...whirling around and around and coming back to her like swarming gnats, biting and stinging.

Of course, I do.

You're not crying. Why don't you cry? If you love him so damned much, why don't you shed at least one tear?

I don't know.

Prove you love him. Can't you squeeze out just one? One tiny tear? I don't think you do.

Yes, I do. I do.

Why don't you cry?

I don't know. I don't know. I don't know don't know...

~ * ~

Watching Lisa, Martha Carreras tiptoed into the room and settled herself into the chair by the window. Placing her knitting basket on the floor, she pulled out a length of yarn and a six-inch steel crochet hook. While the patient slept, Martha crocheted or knitted to keep herself busy. Though her fingers moved swiftly, it was automatic, wrapping the yarn over the needle's hook, pulling it through the loop. She didn't look at the pattern she was making, keeping her gaze on the still figure staring with dull eyes at the ceiling.

Lisa's quiet bothered Martha. She'd had patients who complained continuously and those in such pain they were constantly sedated, while others talked as if they'd been vaccinated with a phonograph needle, but never one like Lisa Chambers. If she didn't blink from time to time, Martha would've sworn the girl was in a coma.

~ * ~

"It just ain't natural, Chuck," she'd told her husband the night before. "The way she lays there, not talkin', just lookin' at the ceilin'."

"Now, Marty." Carlos Carreras placed calming hands on his wife's plump shoulders as he reminded her, "Remember what they told you when you took that job? *Never get too—*"

"*—emotionally involved with a patient.* Yeah, yeah, I know."

"*Professional distance,* I think they call it." He *knew* that was what they called it. He'd read the hospital volunteer's manual, too, when Martha brought it home. From cover to cover.

"I know, but…" Martha was in no mood to be mollified. "She's so alone. And that aunt of hers…not comin' until the quarter's out at that college…" She shook her head, anger starting afresh.

"It's only a few weeks, isn't it?"

"Three weeks."

"Three weeks then," he amended. "Maybe she feels she can't leave her classes this close to the end of school. What could she do just now, anyway?"

"She could be here," Martha answered. She didn't care if Dr. Walker did say he was personally keeping the aunt informed of Lisa's progress. "It's not fair. That girl bein' all alone…"

She continued complaining and Chuck kept on soothing until all the frustration abated. Now here she was, watching Lisa watch the ceiling, feeling again the irritation at being unable to help.

There was something different about this patient. She'd seen it in Dr. Walker's attitude, and also in the way that man acted, the one who rescued her. Coming to the hospital every day to ask about her when a phone call would've gotten the same results. Daily driving the twenty miles from that island to be told her present condition—*She's holding her own*—and then being turned away because Dr. Walker wasn't allowing her any visitors. At least, not that *specific* visitor.

Maybe a visitor's what she needs.

~ * ~

Stopping in the middle of a row, she asked, "Is there anything you'd like to talk about, Miz Chambers?" Her voice seemed loud in the quiet room, like shouting in church.

"Like what?" The dull eyes moved from their pointless gaze, settling on her.

"Oh, I don't know…your husband?" Immediately she knew that was the wrong thing to say. *Darn it.* She could almost hear the *click* as Lisa's expression blanked out. The white face went whiter and what little life was in her eyes fled as they returned to the green expanse above her.

"No. I don't." With those three words, Martha was shut out. No rudeness, only stubborn determination. *I won't talk about him. Not now. Not yet.*

In a few minutes, however, Martha was surprised to see the tearless eyes move from the ceiling to fasten on her again, studying the steady *in-out-loop* movement of the fingers holding the hook. Lisa's gaze shifting to her face. "Tell me about him."

"Who?"

"The man who saved me. Drexl von Dorff. Do you know anything about him?"

"Well…" Though it wasn't the expected question, she groped for an answer. Usually Martha had a store of information on the tip of her tongue but in this case, she had to admit her knowledge was sadly lacking. Drexl von Dorff's name was well-known in Temple but she'd seen him only once…in the hospital lobby, at the information desk as he asked about Lisa.

At first, seeing the long red hair and faded distressed jeans on the tall figure leaning against the counter, she supposed him to be a transient. Some bum looking for a medical hand-out. When he turned, Martha was literally stopped in her tracks. She didn't even notice the woman bumping into her and muttering in irritation as she went around the plump body blocking her path.

Drexl von Dorff was one of the most handsome men she'd ever seen.

He didn't see *her*, however. She had the feeling she was too far beneath his interest to even be sensed. His gaze swept impersonally over her and the others rushing back and forth through the lobby before he whirled and disappeared through the outer doors as they swung open.

Shaken, Martha continued on her way.

She didn't tell Lisa that, of course. Instead, to hide the feelings the moment still evoked, she said, "I guess he's what you'd call good-lookin', if you like spoiled rich boys." There was a disdainful sniff. "I mean, runnin' around with that long hair and those torn clothes. Of course, with all the money he's got, I 'spose he can look any way he wants."

She broke off as Lisa raised her head, staring at her. *Can she know what I'm thinking?* She blushed, sending a rosy hue through her tanned skin.

"Dr. Walker said he owned that island."

"Oh, he does." She added in embarrassment, "I'll be truthful with you, Miz Chambers. I know as much about that young fella as the next guy, which is precious little. His great-great-great-granddaddy or somebody bought that li'l island before the War Between the States and they've been there ever since. They're not very sociable. Too good, I guess." Her own chin raised a little. "There's money there, you'd better believe it. Business holdings up Nawth somewhere. Noo England, I think. Two or three times a year he comes through on his way to the airport in Macon." It was a long speech for Martha but once started, she couldn't seem to stop. "Sometimes he drives that fancy car of his. Sometimes he has…what do you call it…a driver…?"

"Chauffeur?'

"…chauffeur…drive him. There's only him now. About four years ago…how do you think this looks?" She held up the three attached granny squares in various shades of green and yellow.

"It's nice," Lisa assured her. She waited for her to go on but Martha stayed silent, placing the squares on her lap, smoothing them, studying them with satisfaction. "About four years ago…?"

"Oh, yeah…that was when his daddy died. He came to Temple to get a doctor. That was the last time he was in town, until now."

"What do you mean?'

"When you had your accident. He followed the ambulance and hung around gettin' in everybody's way until Dr. Walker threatened to throw him out. A nurse put him in the waitin' room and he wouldn't leave 'til Dr. Walker assured him you were all right. You've have thought he was your husband or somethin', the way he was actin'…" As Lisa drew in a sharp breath, she realized what she'd said. "Oh, shoot, honey. I'm sorry. I didn't mean that. Dr. Walker's always tellin' me my tongue gets in the way of my eyeteeth and I can't see what I'm sayin'. I guess he's right." Struggling to regain the slender thread of Lisa's attention, Martha chattered on. "Now, if you were to ask me about Dr. Walker, I could tell you a lot more."

Lisa made a noncommittal sound. She had no doubt about the doctor's ability as a surgeon but the slightly irreverent way he'd spoken to her bothered her, as did his good looks. *Especially* those good looks…

"He seems familiar, somehow," she said. "The doctor, I mean. I don't know…his eyes…"

"Yeah." Anxious not to say the wrong thing this time, Martha agreed enthusiastically. "Dr. Walker's one of the best-liked doctors at TempeGen. All he has to do is turn those big beautiful peepers on a nurse and he gets plenty of cooperation." Pink flooded her tanned face. "Oh, darn it...I mean, everyone's so eager to please him. I mean...Well, he's a really nice guy."

Lisa didn't answer.

"You're right about his eyes. Guess they're so interesting because he's part Indian."

"He's Native American?" The political correctness drummed into her by her aunt sprang to attention. That'd explain his darkness, but that wavy hair... Come to think of it, she'd never seen a *real* Native American. Most of those in the movies or on television were usually Caucasians hiding under layers of copper greasepaint. Could some of them have hair that was wavy, or even curly and not stick-straight as the stereotype demanded?

"You don't mind bein' treated by a doctor who's not all white, do you?" Martha remembered a couple of patients who refused to have a Cuban sitter. *Cuban!* That angered her more than a little, what with her born and raised and living all her life not twenty miles north of Savannah and unable to speak a word of Spanish. She'd had a big case of hero worship after Dr. Walker defended her in front of those prejudiced few.

"Of course not." *White. Not white. Do some people still think that way?* Of course they do. In small towns and big cities, and not just Southern ones. "What tribe?"

"Creek, I think. They used to be thick as fleas around here."

Dredging up a history lesson, Lisa remembered the Creeks had peacefully sold their lands to the Georgia government. In spite of that, they'd still joined the Cherokees somewhere in Oklahoma when the governor maneuvered them into several battles with Georgia forces.

Typical treachery. White man speak with forked tongue. Ugh. She tried to envision Dr. Walker in native Creek clothing—moccasins and a loin cloth, hips and legs bare, cowrie shell necklace lying on a naked chest incised with blue-stained tattoos, his head shaved except for a roached strip *a la Mohawk* into which feathers had been stuck. It should've been a ridiculous vision but it was disturbingly sensuous…and as sexy as Hell, shocking Lisa that she could think such a thing about any man with Rob violently dead so recently. Shaking her head, she thrust the vision away, forcing herself to think of Drexl von Dorff instead.

Drexl. What an odd name. Man of Mystery. With a capital M. Chauffeurs… island… He's the only one now. He's all alone, too. That thought spun around in her brain. She could almost see it and she was glad of that. She concentrated on the faceless image of her rescuer. *Anything to keep from thinking about Robin.*

Chapter 5

She could smell a rose. Surely no one dared open a window, actually allowing the scents of the outside world to invade her room? Lisa opened her eyes, looking directly into half-opened pink curls, a single transparent pearl of moisture resting on one of the outer petals. She held her breath. It was too perfect to be real.

Behind the rose, Martha's dark eyes crinkled at the corners. Lisa touched the petal. Like a tear, the droplet rolled onto her finger and vanished.

"Do you like it?"

"It's beautiful, Martha. What's the occasion?"

"It's my wedding anniversary. Chuck, that's my husband, gave me eighteen pink roses. One for each year of our blissful wedded life." She laughed, pleased with the phrase, pleased with Lisa's interest.

"You don't look old enough to have been married that long." Still holding the rose, Lisa watched the volunteer sit and pick up her knitting.

"It's true." There was smug satisfaction in the answer. "Eighteen years and four li'l ones. I was sixteen and Chuck was eighteen. It was pretty hard at first but then he got a job with *Georgia Power* and it's been smooth sailin' ever since. Darn…missed two stitches. Oh, well…" She began to unravel the yarn. "'Course I don't recommend teenage marriage for everybody. We were lucky." She stopped, concentrating on the granny square she held.

Eighteen anniversaries. Eighteen years. Lisa closed her eyes, blotting out the room, allowing the thought to overwhelm her. She'd had little more than a year with Robin. *Fourteen months...*

~ * ~

April, fourteen months before, she stood at the altar in St. Joseph's, watching the priest's hand hover over the rings on the little silver salver, making the sign of the Cross as he blessed them. He held up her ring, Robin repeating the words he told him to say. The ring slid cold and heavy onto her finger.

If anyone can show just cause why these two should not be joined, let him speak...

She waited anxiously. *Silly, who's going to say such a thing?*

"She's mine!" It thundered from the walls, the nave of the church, the altar.

Lisa whirled, her train striking one of the candle stands, sending it to the floor. A candle rolled down the aisle. The crimson carpet smoldered, a burst of flame spouting over the ribbon-bedecked pews. The congregation scrambled, panic-stricken, Aunt Alice and Rob's father falling over each other trying to escape.

"She's mine!" Flames shot outward, forming a pair of fiery arms and she pulled away from Robin, running toward them. They tried to embrace her while behind her, she heard Father Donovan, calling, *"Mrs. Chambers... Mrs. Chambers..."*

~ * ~

Pausing before Lisa's door, Daniel Walker looked at the man standing beside him.

"I want one thing clear before we go in." His voice was hard with a no-argument tone. "I'm letting you see her against my better judgment, so if you do anything...*anything*...to upset her, out you go...and I don't give a goddamn what the Chief of Surgery says."

"I'll make one thing clear, too, Walker." Drexl von Dorff's answer was equally sharp. "I'm not in the habit of begging for what I want. Someday you're going to pay for making me do it. Be warned." His smile held no warmth.

"Like that worries me. I'm glad we understand each other." Daniel Walker pushed open the door.

~ * ~

"Mrs. Chambers?" Footsteps near the bed. "I've brought you a visitor."

Lisa shook herself awake, startled as his words picked blended into her dream. She opened her eyes. At first, the overhead light dazzled her, then something moved between her and the light. Lisa blinked and her eyes focused...

...in a blaze of fire the face from her nightmare loomed over her...eyes glittering, long hair streaming brightly.

She screamed. Covering her eyes with one hand, she thrust the other in front of her as if to ward the thing away. All the pain came back and she was again beside the burning car while that Hell-lit face floated above her.

"Lisa. What is it?" Dr. Walker caught the flailing hand as she shrilled a high, broken wail. "Martha, get the door. The whole hospital'll hear her."

Martha's feet pattered. The door swung shut.

"Don't let it hurt me. Make it go away." Lisa clutched his hand, the other still over her eyes.

"Make *what* go away?" His tone wavered between irritation and concern.

"T-the face. That a-awful f-face." She continued to sob.

"Perhaps I'd better go." Someone else spoke.

"No." The doctor moved as if to stop someone. "Not after all the Hell you've raised to get in here." When he turned back to the bed, his voice was sharp. "Stop crying, Lisa." His left hand pulled from hers, gripping her shoulder tightly. It hurt. He shook her. Hard. Startled, she stopped crying but kept her eyes closed. "What face, Lisa? Tell me."

"The face at the wreck." She swallowed and choked as a ball of air lodged itself in her chest. "Above me. All flaming."

"Lisa, open your eyes." His voice was gentle now. He took her hand again.

"But the face…"

"There's no flaming face. Only Martha and myself and Drexl."

"D-Drexl?"

"That's right. He's been driving the staff crazy asking to see you. So please look at him and give us all a little peace."

She forced herself to drop the hand shielding her eyes. She'd never thought she'd seen anyone look as grim as the doctor did. *Is he really that angry with me?* She was hanging onto his hand as if her life depended on it. His fingers were white she was squeezing so tightly. Out of the corner of her eye, she saw Martha hovering near the foot of the bed and next to her...

She looked directly at the person standing there.

He was very tall but younger than Martha's description made her think, dressed in jeans and a dark sweater giving his hair a fire-lit brilliance. His eyes weren't white and burning but green and filled with concern and his mouth, instead of curling into cruel laughter at her terror, was set in a severe, straight line.

He smiled...and a golden glow filled the room. Lisa felt weak. If she'd been standing, her legs wouldn't have held her up. It was as Dr. Walker said. Drexl von Dorff was only a man, not the demon her pain-filled brain made him. Only a man...but a *beautiful* one.

"Mr. von Dorff, I'm sorry. The last thing I remember was your face lit by the flames from the car. Seeing you now... She dropped Dr. Walker's hand and held out her own to her visitor. "Please, forgive me."

"*I* should apologize to *you*." He stepped around the doctor and took her hand. His skin was cool against hers. "It must've been a shock."

His voice is beautiful, too. As deep and quiet as the doctor's, but there was something strange in the way he spoke, the tone harsh, clashing with Walker's slow, soft drawl.

"I had no idea you'd remember seeing me. Otherwise I'd have asked the doctor to prepare you a little."

"Have you really come to the hospital every day asking about me?" *How could I have been frightened of him?*

"You'd better believe it, and my persistence finally paid off," he assured her. "I knew they couldn't keep me out forever." The green eyes flicked toward the doctor and she saw Walker stiffen. Von Dorff looked back at her, smiling in satisfaction. He released her hand. "I won't stay, but I will come back to see you...if I may?" That was added as if in afterthought as he glanced at the doctor again.

Walker took his time answering and it was given grudgingly. "Very well, but if there's another episode like *this*, I'll leave word at the desk you're not to be allowed back."

"I won't upset her." That was accepted with an ironic little nod. "You'll see." It was said quietly yet sounded like a threat.

What's this? Lisa looked from one to the other. *A mutual hate society?* Whatever the doctor's feelings for von Dorff, it wasn't one-sided, and neither was making an effort to hide it.

Smiling again and including Martha in its radiance, von Dorff disappeared through the swinging door.

"Bastard."

Did she really hear that?

Walker relaxed visibly. "I mean it, Lisa. If he does anything making you have a setback, I'll have him barred from the hospital."

Lisa blinked, not certain what to say but he appeared not to expect an answer, going on briskly, as if to make up for the anger Von Dorff wrested from him, "I'm going to have the physiotherapist work up a set of exercises for you, Mrs. Chambers."

"Exercises? How can I do exercises when I'm flat on my back?"

"Easily." It came out so calmly, she nearly laughed. "Nothing fancy. Just a little ankle rotation, things like that. Can't do much about your other leg until the cast comes off. Like I said, you've only a bad sprain in the left one. We'll get you started on flexion-extension exercises. To keep the muscles in shape."

"Okay." Experimentally, Lisa moved her ankle. It hurt but she agreed he was right. She had to strengthen her muscles so when she could walk again, her legs would hold her up. *I'll be so glad to get out of here and home again.*

"If you're settled down again, Mrs. Chambers, I'll get on with my rounds."

"Doctor?" Why did he sound so abrupt? Really irritated. *What did I do?*

"Uh-huh?" He paused at the door.

"You called me Lisa, before."

"Yes, Mrs. Chambers. I know." He smiled as the door closed behind him.

~ * ~

Damn, didn't mean to slip up like that. He never called patients by their first names. Having von Dorff get the better of him by going over his head to the COS of the hospital plus Lisa's little upset made him forget himself for a moment. He'd lost control, speaking to her the way he thought of her…and that wouldn't do. *Better not let that happen again.*

Chapter 6

The sixth week. What's so special about it?

Lisa awoke with a feeling today was different somehow...*Why?* She let her gaze rove the room, coming to rest on the little fold-up calendar Martha had set on the bedside table. The date was circled with overlapping red lines. *Of course.* Aunt Allie'd soon be here, and...Drexl von Dorff was coming back.

It was now almost three weeks since his initial visit and Lisa had been certain he'd never return. The day before, Martha brought her the message, called in to the switchboard. *Will stop by tomorrow, if I may?*

He was prompt. As if he'd heard her thought, his bright head appeared around the edge of the open door. "May I come in? Walker the Worrisome isn't lurking nearby, is he?"

"The coast's clear." Lisa didn't stifle her pleasure at having a visitor. She even forgave his insult to Dr. Walker. She saw Martha sit up a little straighter, the hand holding the hook stilled. "Come in."

"Five minutes." He came into the room exclaiming, "That's all your hardnosed doctor gave me." His hands were behind his back but Lisa could see the edge of a slim, green box. "Barely enough time for me to give you this..." He held out the box, pushing it into her hands. "And ask how you are."

Lisa pulled off the lid, pushing aside the shiny green tissue paper. *Roses.* "Ohhh. Look, Martha." She tilted the box so the roses leaned out of the paper, then pressed her face against the dark red petals. The volunteer got up, dropped her crocheting on the chair and pattered over.

"I see someone else brought you a flower, too." He noticed Martha's rosebud in its vase by the bed.

"It's one of Martha's anniversary flowers." Lisa pulled her nose out of the roses long enough to say that, then buried it into the blossoms again. *They smell so sweet.*

"Here." Martha deftly pulled box and flowers out of her hands. "I'll take care of these before you sniff all the scent out of 'em." She hurried toward the door.

"Let me know when my time's up," Drexl called after her.

He was wearing another pair of jeans, though these were designer-cut and untattered with elaborate stitching on pockets and seams. The olive-green turtleneck was of some soft stuff shrieking *expensive. A sweater, in this weather?* His hair might be hanging below his shoulders but it had been recently and expertly styled.

"Thank you, Mr. Von Dorff." She shook off her mental appraisal.

"You're most welcome, Mrs. Chambers," His answer was very formal. "However, there's a favor, I'd like to ask."

"What's that?"

"Call me *Drex*. Please. *Mr. von Dorff* was my father. It makes me feel ancient when I hear that." The request was accompanying by a smile meant to win her compliance. "You didn't answer my question." She looked puzzled. "How are you?"

"Better."

"But not well enough to leave this place?" He drew the straight-backed chair back to the bedside, turned it around and sat astride it, arms resting on its back.

"Dr. Walker's going to x-ray my leg soon." Lisa couldn't hide her reaction to what he'd done. Rob had sat that way sometimes, placing his arms on the back of the chair and resting his chin on them. She'd always considered it a masculine affectation. When Drexl von Dorff did it, it looked completely natural. "If everything's okay, maybe he'll take this cast off." She gestured at the white sheet hiding her legs. "Who knows?"

"Who, indeed?" he agreed, smiling.

Lisa was dazzled. "It'll be good to be on my own two feet again."

"I'm looking forward to that, too."

Why did those few words send a shiver through her? Lisa returned his smile, thinking again about his accent. Not the flat, syllable-stretching drawl of a Georgian nor the softer, rounded tones of the coastal-dweller. A little of both with a foreign tinge, something in his pronunciation hinting English wasn't his native language, but hadn't Martha said his people had been here before the War Between the States? She was wondering if it'd be rude to ask him when the volunteer burst back into the room.

"Ta-dah!" With a flourish she set a white vase on the little dresser, demanding, "How do they look? Puts my one li'l flower to shame." Glancing at her watch, she informed Drex dramatically, "Time… Your five minutes are now up."

"Oh no…not so soon." The words were out before Lisa could stop them. "Please stay a little longer."

"I'd better not," Drex's answer was quiet. "Got to follow the Almighty Doctor Walker's orders or I won't be allowed back." He smiled again as if he had a secret neither Lisa nor the doctor knew. "But he won't always be giving the orders, will he?"

With that, he was gone.

~ * ~

In a little while, Martha also left to take her morning coffee break.

Lisa sighed. *It was good to see Mr. Von Dorff… Drex. He really wakes up this dull place. He's so alive…* The thought stabbed through her like a knife. *Right. He's alive. And Robin's dead. What's this dull town to me? Robin's not here…*an old ballad, she'd hummed it often while Rob was at work, never thinking of its real meaning. It was one she should be singing now, instead of enjoying the attentions of this stranger, reveling in his gift of flowers when her husband had died such a horrible death. *No roses for Robin's grave.* She wasn't even certain where it was. Or if there was one. Had there been a funeral? If so, when? Another thing no one mentioned. *You should be in mourning, not laughing. You wicked, heartless, uncaring…*

A tear rolled down her cheek. She wiped it away but another took its place, then another, until she felt she'd drown in the waterfall cascading down her face. That was the way Martha, mellow from the inner warmth of her coffee, found her…with her face in her hands, crying quietly.

"Lisa?" She set down the cup she held. "What's the matter? Is your leg bothering you?"

Lisa didn't answer, just shook her head, swiping at her eyes with her fingers.

"Here." Martha pulled a tissue from a box on the bedside table. "Wipe your eyes and tell me. Shall I call a nurse?"

"No. It's…Oh, it's Rob…" She took the tissue and snuffled into it.

"I should've known." The volunteer's voice dropped sympathetically. "Maybe it's best if you try not to think about him. Mournin' won't help, and—"

"That's just it," Lisa interrupted. "I'm not mourning. I don't feel anything. When I think of Rob, *if* I think of him…nothing." She paused to wipe her eyes with the tissue, then regarded it, chin quivering before bursting out, "What's the matter with me? I thought I loved Rob but I can't even cry for him." A tear rolled down her cheek. "I'm not crying for him now." She said it as if she suddenly realized the fact. "I'm crying for myself because I feel so guilty. He's dead and I'm alive and I'm looking forward to seeing Drexl von Dorff again and that's wrong, too, but I don't seem to care about Rob and…I…feel…guilty…"

"Of course you loved him," Martha ignored the reference to Drex. "All this is natural enough."

"It is?"

"You've been through a lot. Just wait. One day, everything'll get right again. And you'll cry. Properly. You'll see."

"I hope so," Lisa's murmur was tearful.

"As for Mr. Von Dorff, he's a distraction. That's all. Heck, if I'd gone through what you have, I'd look forward to anyone comin' to visit me…even my mother-in-law." She laughed and shook her head. "I'm kiddin'. I like Chuck's mother, but you know what I mean. There's nothin' for you to feel guilty about, honey. Just wait." She said it with certainty, then went on in a brisk tone, "Now, wipe away those tears. You don't want Dr. Walker thinking you're a crybaby, do you?"

~ * ~

That was exactly what Dr. Walker thought.

"What is it with women?" he exploded as she attempted to explain why she was upset. "You cry about everything. You have a visitor, you go into hysterics. You can't cry for your husband, so you cry about that." He took a deep breath. "Does everything have to end in a crying jag?"

"That's not fair." Lisa's estimation of the doctor did a backslide past zero.

"About as fair as you crying," he retorted.

"Look, I explained why I was afraid when—"

"Okay, I admit that was understandable," he conceded. "Still—"

"Dr. Walker." Her interruption was abruptly cold. "Are you married?"

"What? No. Why?" The change of subject puzzled him.

"Ever been married?"

"Not unlucky enough to have had that pleasure, but what's that—"

"A typical bachelor response. Ever lose someone you loved?" There was a flicker of a response, quickly hidden. "Why can't you understand how I feel?"

He thought that over. "You're right, Lisa, and I'm sorry. I've absolutely no idea what you're going through. I can sympathize with the pain from your injuries, but the rest?" He shook his head. "Oh, come on, quit glaring at me. I simply don't want any outbursts preventing your getting well."

She gave him a doubtful stare.

"I'm serious, young lady."

"Young lady?" She couldn't resist a little barb. "You're not that much older than I am...Daniel Walker, MD."

"I'm well aware of that," he answered. "But I'm trying to ignore it and be professional."

"You know," Lisa eyed him critically. "You're a great doctor..."

"Why thank you, Mrs. Chambers." He bowed with dramatic irony, one hand touching his heart.

"...but you've a rotten bedside manner."

"I've a terrific bedside manner," he informed her solemnly. The sudden twinkle in his eyes startled her. "Just ask any nurse around here."

She didn't want to laugh, but the sound bubbled out, part shock, part amusement. *Oh my God...*

"I see you got the exercises." As if to make up for that slip into sarcasm, he scowled and indicated the little sheet of paper on the table, something Lisa hadn't noticed until that moment. "Good. Do them, take it easy and follow Doctor's Orders, and you'll be out of here in no time."

~ * ~

"Exercise time," Martha announced brightly, looking at her watch.

"You don't have to sound so happy about it," Lisa grumbled.

"It's good for you." Folding back the edge of the sheet, Martha lifted her foot. "You've got cold feet." She cradled the frigid appendage in her hands. "Oh well, cold feet, warm heart."

"That's *Cold hands, Warm heart*," Lisa corrected. *Warm heart? Never. Cold as ice. Dead. Dead as my poor dear Robin.* No matter what anyone said, she was determined to punish herself for her lack of grief. Only now, she'd do it mentally.

"Whatever. Ready?" Martha began to count as Lisa pushed her foot against the sitter's hand.

"One...*ouch.* Two...*ouch.* Three, four...hey, I'm getting better. It only hurt to *two* this time."

Chapter 7

Alice Townsend paused for her first look at Macon's Municipal Airport. Behind her, the other passengers waited to leave the plane so she stepped aside, allowing them to go down the ramp and ahead of her into the terminal.

Here I am... anxious and apprehensive, if the sick feeling in her stomach was any indication of her emotional state and not merely latent air sickness. Since the phone call nearly three weeks before, she'd been waiting for this moment. Temple, Georgia...a mere dot on the map, a name mentioned in e-mails and phone calls from Lisa. Not the most important town in the whole world...until now.

News of what happened spread through the department and she was certain some felt she was an unloving relative because she didn't drop everything and rush to Temple then and there. Abandoning her students three weeks before the end of the quarter... What good would that do? Robin was already dead and buried and she couldn't go to his funeral, and Lisa was going to be hospitalized for some time yet. Staying, finishing up, and then taking time-off was the best thing, so that's what she did.

Dodging more debarking passengers, she looked for the man who was to meet her, and saw him...or thought she did. Standing a few feet away was a tall, dark man obviously looking for someone, also. Though he was wearing a suit and not jeans or a sweatshirt, she immediately thought, *He can't be the one. He's no older than my students.*

He saw her and stared. Uncertain. Took a step forward, then stopped. When the crowd around her cleared and she still stood there, he made up his mind and started toward her. Alice didn't move. He stopped in front of her, offering his hand and saying, in the voice she recognized from the many phone calls, "Miz Townsend? I'm Daniel Walker."

~ * ~

"I suppose you're wondering why I came to meet you personally."

They were seated in the coffee shop, facing each other across the minute table. It looked fairly new, made of Corion or something, maybe that one called *Sandalwood*, with a beautiful, beige marble-like finish equaling the real thing. She could see the damp sheen where the waitress had wiped it, felt moisture under her elbows.

"As a matter of fact, I am. Let me say I appreciate your calling me so often about Lisa, but… Do you usually put yourself out like that for all your patients?"

"Not at all. It's not usually a good idea but I wanted a chance to talk to you before you see your niece." He produced a pack of cigarettes, holding it up questioningly. "This is a smoking area." She nodded her permission and he lit one. Then he sat there, puffing on it in short, nervous little spurts as he thought about his latest encounter with Lisa that morning.

~ * ~

"Where was he buried?" No greeting. She simply blurted out the question as soon as he came through the door. "W-we don't have burial plots." There was a ragged laugh. "R-Rob said we were too young to n-need them."

"I…think…" Someone told him. What had they said? One of the older men at Robin Chambers' place of employment owned an extra plot…for a child who'd married and gotten his own elsewhere. He'd offered it so what was left of Lisa's husband would have a final resting place. He told her that.

Lisa didn't answer.

"The…the funeral was a simple one…but nice…as those things go," he went on. Not one for funerals any more than he was for weddings, he'd nevertheless found himself at the cemetery that day, with a handful of Robin Chambers' co-workers, the next-door neighbor, and the priest from Holy Cross. It'd been a closed casket ceremony. "When you're able to walk, you can visit his grave,"

"No," she said. "I won't."

He didn't argue.

~ * ~

Alice held out the ashtray. Wordlessly he flicked ash and ground the cigarette against the bottom of the dish, then immediately lit another, drawing on it viciously.

"Do you always smoke like this?"

"Actually, I was trying to quit…getting along fine, too, using a patch and gum…until I met your niece. Now, every time I see her, I want to light up. So…I tossed the patch, and…She's worrying the Hell out of

72

me." The cigarette followed the other into the ashtray. "Sorry. I shouldn't have said that."

"Young man, I assure you I've heard much worse from my students, as well as on TV." She smiled at him. "Has Lisa gotten worse? Are there complications?"

"Nothing like that," he assured her. "She had a triple compound fracture of the right tibia but it's healing nicely. I'll order new x-rays soon and if everything's as I expect, the cast'll come off. As to her other injuries…her body's healing well."

"And her mind?"

He nodded to show he appreciated her quickness in catching the implication. "She's not adjusting to her husband's death at all and she may be building up to something worse than a six-week hospital stay." He watched the smoke from the cigarette stub curl out of the ashtray. "There's no reason she wouldn't mourn her husband, is there? They *were* happily married?"

"Goodness, yes," she laughed. "They'd only been married little more than a year. They were still newlyweds.

"She's got it into her head that her lack of tears means she didn't love him. One minute she's perfectly fine, the next, she's having an attack of remorse." His expression was serious and worried. "She needs an emotional outburst. A catharsis. Not these confusing bouts she's having but the real thing." His smile was ironic. "Although, to Lisa, I imagine what she's having is genuine enough."

Alice regarded him quietly before she spoke, thinking here was a basically shy young man in an unshy profession and while he could confidently give orders ensuring the welfare of his patients, in a personal relationship he'd probably fall all over himself and fail miserably. She didn't understand why she felt that but she was as certain of it as the fact that he was sitting across from her. *What does this mean as far as Lisa's concerned?*

"I love my niece, Doctor, and I'll do everything I can to help her." She pushed the ashtray out of the way, discouraging him from lighting the third cigarette he took out of the pack.

"That's what I wanted to hear." Taking the hint, he dropped the cigarette back into the pack and returned it to his pocket. "It's quarter to one and I've surgery at four. If you're ready, I'll take you to the hospital." He got to his feet, helping her from her chair. Alice couldn't remember the last time a man held her chair for her...or opened a door so she could go through first, either.

Young man, you are interesting. She took a deep breath. "Let's go."

~ * ~

"You know the first thing I'm going to do when I can walk again?" Finishing her lunch, Lisa waited impatiently as Martha supplied her with a water-filled plastic cup, basin, and a toothbrush with a fluoride-striped ribbon on its bristles.

"What?"

"Go to the bathroom." She said it between brushstrokes, sputtering slightly as foam dribbled down her chin.

"Do you have to go now?" Martha set down the basin and plucked a tissue from the box, handing it to her. "Why didn't you say so? I'll get the bedpan—"

"That's what I mean." Picking up the basin, Lisa aimed a sudsy spray at its center and swabbed her mouth with the tissue. "Do you know how embarrassing it is...telling someone every time I want to...go potty? I never thought I'd look forward to simply *walking* into a bathroom. Besides, it's darned difficult brushing my teeth while lying down." She rinsed, spat, and held out toothbrush and cup.

"Nothing like a major injury to cause instant togetherness," Martha said, taking them from her.

"Or a knowledge of one's most private functions...and that's not exactly the kind I want. When I get out of here I'm never going to ask anyone to do anything for me again. Ever. I..." Lisa stopped as the door opened and her aunt came in. "Aunt Allie?" Immediately she was enveloped in the older woman's embrace. "I'm so glad you're here." The words were muffled as Lisa burrowed her face against her aunt's shoulder, hugging her tightly. "Maybe things'll be all right now."

Chapter 8

"I've missed you," Lisa said. Though he'd been a steady visitor, Drexl was conspicuously absent the previous week. Even as she told herself she shouldn't, she found herself looking forward to seeing him when he arrived the following Monday morning.

"And I've missed you." His eyes held a smile seeming to radiate into her own. He glanced around as if making certain Martha wasn't listening, then whispered as he touched a finger to his lips. "I suppose I shouldn't admit that."

"Why not?" she whispered back.

"Because…" He looked away a moment. "Because you're a woman who's just lost her husband and I imagine some people around here are thinking it pretty strange the way you've got another man…a stranger…hanging around like I've been doing."

That was so close to what she'd been thinking, she stared at him.

"Have I shocked you? If so, I'm sorry." He didn't look sorry. If anything, he looked defiant, as if he'd said something after being told not to.

"Has someone actually said that?" she asked. "Dr. Walker…did he…"

"No one's said anything," he assured her. "But I expect it…small town…small minds…and I'm sure somewhere someone's talking behind his hand about *that young widder-woman and that weird von Dorff character who's allus hangin' 'round her...*" His voice switched into a hillbilly twang as his lips quirked. "*...reckon we all know what* he's *got on his mind.* I've very aware of what they think of me."

That made her laugh. "As long as they're not saying it where I can hear."

"You're not worried, then?" he asked. "That I'm besmirching your good name by continually coming here?"

"Besmirching? Widder-woman? Where do you get these phrases?" She shook her head, though she felt like crossing her fingers behind her back as she said it. "It doesn't worry me, because I know it's not true."

"Isn't it?"

"Of course not." She met his gaze calmly. "After all, I didn't even know you before my accident, and..."

"And...what?" he prompted.

"And...even if it were true, what could we possibly do with me in a cast?" She waved a hand at the sheet hiding her right leg.

"I'm very inventive." His laugh was a deep, secret sound, sending a chill through her though the twinkle in his eyes held only teasing. His hand went over hers, giving it a quick squeeze. "There's one thing to remember, though."

"What's that?" She smiled, thinking he was about to make another joke.

"You aren't always going to be covered in plaster."

There was a good three seconds of silence as she thought about that. It sounded almost like a threat...yet the little twist she felt inside definitely wasn't fear.

"I'm sorry this happened, Lisa…about your husband, I mean." Briefly he avoided looking at her. "I'm sorry it had to happen that way."

It was such an odd way to put it. The twist changed to a chill.

"Was that the reason you stayed away? Because of something someone said?" she asked, to cover the confusion and the accompanying twinge of guilt. "If so, it's really upset my social calendar." She tried to speak lightly, hurrying on to complain how endless the time without her morning visitor seemed.

Becoming more alert each day, she was rapidly getting bored and not looking forward to another dragging week. She'd done some serious thinking during his absence, ending by rationalizing that, as Martha said, she wasn't really interested in Drexl von Dorff as a man but merely as someone distracting her from thinking about Robin and her future life without him. It was only partially working. Lisa felt like someone whistling in the dark…she was telling herself something she only half-believed despite the fact she wanted to believe it wholeheartedly.

"…and I guess I won't see you tomorrow."

"Oh? Are you planning a trip somewhere?" He glanced pointedly at the mound of sheet as if reminding her of her immobility.

"I wish. I'm scheduled for x-ray at eight in the morning."

"No big deal," he shrugged. Somehow he managed to give that bit of slang a foreign intonation. "I can always come later. In the afternoon? What time does the Chief make his evening rounds?"

"He usually comes in about five o'clock."

"I'll be here at four," he promised. "In and out before he knows it."

Once again she wondered why the two men disliked each other so. Though *dislike* wasn't exactly the best description. It was stronger than that, the tenseness...a bilateral enmity... bordering on downright hate.

"Did your aunt get here on time?" he asked, changing the subject.

Lisa nodded.

~ * ~

Aunt Allie was settled in, rescuing Timothy from Mrs. Campbell's too solicitous care.

He's been overfed and over-pampered. That cat's spoiled rotten, she told Lisa.

She came every day after lunchtime to see Lisa, immediately expressing a desire to meet Drex. *I'd like to see this young man who's made such an impression on you. I want to thank him for saving you, too.*

~ * ~

"I'm glad she's here," Drex went on. "That was the real reason I stayed away. I thought you might want a little time with your aunt without an outsider intruding."

"You could never be an in—" Lisa began.

"Nice of you to say, but I've been told that plenty of times."

She wondered who dared say such a thing, then thought she knew...Doctor *Sticking-his-handsome-nose-in-where-he-shouldn't* Walker.

~ * ~

Drex stayed until he was shooed out when Martha brought Lisa's breakfast. She barely had time to finish it when her room was invaded by Dr. Walker, Myrtice, and an orderly pushing a wheelchair

"B-but...I'm supposed to..."

"Change of plans," Walker interrupted. "There was an opening in x-ray today so I asked them to move your appointment." He looked down at her. "I thought you were impatient to get out of this cast."

"I am...but..." Lisa resented the slight smirk she thought she saw on his dark face. "All right...let's get going."

"That's more like it."

The sheet was whipped expertly off her legs and tossed to Myrtice who folded it neatly, handing it to Martha as they began to ease Lisa into the chair.

"Okay, hold up her leg...keep it straight...that's it... Myrtice, help her slide to the edge of the bed...don't let the leg drop." Walker was beside her, an arm around her waist, the orderly on the other side. Together they lifted Lisa, depositing her into the chair. "Easy, let her down gently...that's it..." The orderly stepped back. Walker said, "You can let go now."

"What?" She realized she was hanging on to his upper arm, squeezing tightly. She released it. "Sorry."

Both feet now rested on the chair's metal foot stands, side by side. Her right one felt weightless and heavy at the same time. Lisa looked down at her feet. *Hi, right leg. Hello, right foot. May I re-introduce you to left foot?* Moving her left foot toward the right one slightly, she wiggled her toes. *Hi, there! Long time no see. Care to run a little race?* The right one moved also. *I don't think so. Not yet, anyway.*

Lisa stifled a giggle then glanced around to see if anyone noticed. No? Good. No need to call their attention to that bit of foolishness.

"Where to?" she asked, settling herself as modestly as possible which wasn't easy. The nightgown Aunt Allie brought her seemed much too short. No one bothered to provide a lap robe. She smiled at the orderly, glad he wasn't wearing green.

"X-ray first," Walker said. "Then, we'll see…"

~ * ~

Things proceeded quickly. After the x-rays, Lisa was rolled into the hallway outside the department door and parked there. In a few minutes, Walker came out, stopping to look down at her. She smiled at him, thinking how he and the entire hospital appeared much more pleasant now that she was right-side-up.

"You're getting along better than I thought," he told her. "There's been some early healing. Want to see?'

"Could I?" The invitation surprised her. "I've never seen an x-ray." She added, "Never had one before, for that matter."

"Heck of a way to start, isn't it?" He smiled. "They're your bones, Mrs. Chambers. Who's got a better right to look at them than you?" Stepping behind her chair, he wheeled her back inside.

She frowned as she studied the white-on-black transparencies clipped onto a light panel attached to the wall.

"What's the matter?" he asked. "Not impressed with the Inner Woman?"

"It's not that," she protested. "I've never thought about it before…having a *skeleton* inside me." She nodded at the x-ray and shivered visibly. "It's kind of eerie."

"Don't let it creep you out," he warned. "Be proud of those bones. They're young and strong and you've got good bone structure. That'll treat you kindly as you grow older." He looked down at her as he spoke, nodding as if to affirm something. "You've very beautiful bones…"

His voice trailed away as he studied her face. Yes indeed…high, delicately rounded cheekbones, a square little chin, just enough of a tip-tiled nose with a smattering of freckles…

"Here, look at this." He turned his attention back to the x-ray. His finger traced the dim outline of a fracture then moved to another. She could see the faint shape of her cast, the bones clear and white in contrast. "See those tiny lines?" He tapped three separate jagged but blurred areas. "That's all that's left of your injury. It's almost completely healed." He shook his head, studying the picture as if it still amazed him. "Fractures as severe as those should take longer to repair themselves. Unusual…very unusual…" He looked from the film to Lisa and back again as if comparing the two. "You're a very lucky young lady."

"It's the bone structure," Lisa told him solemnly. She felt she had to say something upbeat though her thoughts weren't so amusing. How lucky is it to become a widow at age twenty-three?

When he laughed, she joined in though the sound was a little hollow.

~ * ~

A little later, Lisa found herself in the Casting Room where the heavy plaster was cut away. With the first high-pitched buzz of the saw, she refused to watch, begging to be assured they weren't removing her leg along with the cast. They didn't, replacing it with an equally strong, but very lightweight splint.

"Why a splint?" She was disappointed. "I thought once you took off a cast, that's it."

"That's definitely not *it*," Dr. Walker corrected. "You're getting crutches today and if you're a good girl, maybe…just maybe…in a few days, we'll talk about your going home."

"This Thursday?" Lisa asked.

"We'll see."

He left her to the mercy of the physiotherapist who fitted her with a pair of Canadian crutches.

"Not so rough on the armpits," he said as he taught her how to use them. Sliding her arms inside the metal bands and grasping the rubber handgrips, Lisa took her first shaky steps, following his instructions. "Steady now…go ahead. Remember, one, two, swing…it's okay…Just think now you've got three legs under you…"

"Three legs?" Lisa grunted. Amazing how heavy her body felt when all her weight seemed to be on her forearms. "Before this happened, I could barely get around on two."

He laughed and cupped her elbows. "I'll catch you if you fall."

She didn't fall. Keeping the leg in the splint slightly bent so it didn't touch the floor, she took that first step. *One, two, swing*…and a second…*one, two, swing*…

Biting her lip in concentration, she made a circuit of the exercise room and back to the wheelchair, panting slightly, face flushed with triumph.

With the crutches across her lap, she was taken back to her room *via* wheelchair but at the door, told the attendant, "Let me out here. I'll go the rest of the way on my own." Grasping the crutches, she hauled herself to her feet, adjusted the arm bands and swung through the door as he opened it for her.

"Hi, Martha...bye, Martha." Before the volunteer could speak, she disappeared into the tiny bathroom to the left of the door. Several moments later, there was a flushing and Lisa emerged, grinning. "You can't imagine how good it feels to do that...on my own. Now you won't have to wait on me so much." Rocking unsteadily, she braced the crutches in front of her. "M-Martha? I-I think I overdid it. Can you help me to the bed?"

~ * ~

Lisa was tired, she admitted it. Why else would she have fallen asleep in the middle of the afternoon, waking only as the dinner tray was brought in? She surveyed it greedily. Chicken casserole...peas...apple cobbler...*Who said hospital food isn't good?*

In the midst of her third mouthful, however, nausea rose so violently she thought she might choke. She could feel her stomach twisting. A hot sickly sensation scalded the inside of her throat and she knew she was going to throw up. Lisa dropped her fork, chewing rapidly and swallowing even quicker. She waited for it to come back up, surprised when it didn't, though the sick feeling persisted.

"Are you all right?" Martha asked.

Lisa nodded and gestured at the tray. "You can take this away. I-I'm too tired to finish," she lied.

~ ❦ ~

Later, she was hungry, of course. *Should've filched the cookie offered as part of the dessert.*

"I'll get you a glass of orange juice to tide you over," Martha offered.

"How about grape juice?" Lisa asked. *Cold grape juice…yes…*she could almost taste it. *Deep, dark, sweetly sour…*her mouth began to water.

"I'll check," Martha promised.

She drank the juice greedily, nearly downing the entire glass in one gulp and splashing some of it on her gown. Licking her lips and savoring the aftertaste, she lowered the glass.

"That was fast," Martha exclaimed. She shook her head as she saw the stains on the gown-front. "I'll have to get you another nightgown to wear." She went to the little dresser, pulling open a drawer and bringing out one of the nighties Aunt Allie brought from home.

Switching the glass from one hand to the other, Lisa pulled the gown over her head and slid on the other. She was thankful her aunt had brought a couple of the modest older gowns Lisa owned before she and Robin married. He'd insisted she get some very sexy ones for their honeymoon, then convinced her sleeping nude was even better and definitely more convenient.

For a moment, Lisa's fingers stilled. Memory of lying naked with Rob, pressed skin-to-skin, how he'd looked with his dark hair falling over his passion-flushed face…

While Martha took the soiled gown to the sink and ran water on it to keep the stain from setting, Lisa bit her lip, determined not to let the tears stinging her eyes fall. She forced herself to finish with the buttons.

Martha hung the gown in the closet. "I'll give it to your aunt to take home and launder next time she comes."

"Could I have another glass of juice?" Lisa held out the glass. She laughed. "Please, sir...may I have some more?"

"Oliver Twist, you ain't, girl," Martha told her, taking the glass and setting it on the bedside table. "Nothing doin'. You'll be needin' to get up in the middle of the night if you drink anymore."

I already do that. Lisa remembered the times in the past week she'd had to ring for the night nurse, even when she hadn't had anything to drink before going to sleep. She didn't tell Martha that.

She fell asleep soon after. Turning off the lights, Martha tiptoed out, leaving only the little nightlight burning in its niche above the roses.

~ * ~

A little later, Lisa awoke, surprised to find herself alone. *Rude of me to fall asleep like that. I didn't even tell Martha good night. Oh well, I'll apologize in the morning.*

The fragrance of Drexl's roses was strong in the little room. *Mmm...*Lisa took a deep breath, immediately cutting it short in mid-inhale. *Something's wrong.* The smell changed, wasn't sweet as she expected, not as they'd been at first. There was a bitter, dusty underscent as if they were dying, but that couldn't be...

She looked at the white vase. They *were* dying. Three of the buds were blackened and drooping, the petals curled and dry. As she watched, one of them fell from its stem, then a second, striking the table top with a whispery rustle. Something dripped from the center of the remaining blossoms, slim scarlet threads stretching and abruptly curling upward, hovering wormlike in the air. They wavered blindly…as if searching for something.

For me… They're looking for me… Lisa's hand went to her mouth, stifling the scream bubbling against her lips. *I have to be quiet. Not a sound.* The worms hesitated…movement stopped, all pointing in her direction. They'd found her…the slender strands would stretch out and reach her and…

A burst of decaying vegetation poured over her. Gagging and choking, Lisa fumbled for the light cord, clutching at it with frantic fingers…

The reading lamp came on…light flooded the room, making her blink. The flowers were where Martha put them, fresh and red and sweet, no dead petals, no blood-red strands…

She slept the rest of the night with the light on.

Chapter 9

My name is Lisa Chambers. I'm a widow. Two months ago my husband died very horribly. I've just learned I'm pregnant with his child. Oh, God, thank you...

~ * ~

She was still having trouble believing that miracle. Even after confirmation by the obstetrician Dr. Walker brought in when he read the nurse's notes of being called to help her to the bathroom several times a night and Lisa's own explanation of that embarrassing morning nausea.

Dr. Bradley Halyard...as different as Walker as night from day. Short, blond, balding. *Mutt and Jeff,* Aunt Allie would've said... He'd asked very personal questions about contraception and the last time she and Robin had sex before he was killed. Tests confirmed his suspicions. Then he spoke the words no expectant mother wanted to hear.

The first to sixth weeks are the most critical for a fetus... several things harmful to your baby... drugs... x-rays...

*Damage...to her baby...*invisible deadly beams cutting through her, burning into her baby...and she never felt it. *I don't want to hear this. I was happy. You're spoiling everything. Go away.* She looked down at the magazine lying abandoned in her lap. *American*

Baby...she'd been reading it, enjoying an article on decorating a nursery...*is he telling me I may not have a nursery?*

It could be born blind...deaf...mentally retarded...Halyard's voice continued in a drone, making her want to put her hands over her ears. *I recommend you have an abortion...*

Both he and Walker waited for her answer.

"No." *I won't kill Robin's baby. Not when I thought he was lost to me forever and now I've gotten part of him back.*

Halyard looked oddly relieved. Walker was understanding, squeezing her hand, telling her he'd sign her dismissal papers.

When Alice arrived, Lisa gave her the news, calmly and unemotionally, as well as her decision. Alice was shocked, then concerned, finally happy for her niece. Telling Drex had been much more difficult.

~ * ~

At her awkward stuttering explanation, he appeared surprisingly delighted. When she told him Halyard's suggestion, he went white, blood leeching from his face so fast she thought he might faint.

"For God's sake, why?" He stepped away from the bed as if she'd struck at him, dropping her hand, his own falling to his side.

"The x-rays. He's afraid the radiation..." she stopped.

"Hell...I never thought about..." He stared at her as if he couldn't believe what she was saying.

"The baby could be blind, or..." She didn't finish, refusing to repeat those other awful things.

As if he didn't hear, Drex turned away, walking to the window. Hands against the sill, he stared out. The morning sun, reflecting off the windshield of a car parked below them, flickered through the blinds, transforming his hair into a mass of fiery waves.

The memory of how the flames from the car had done the same thing rushed through her mind.

"Will you...do it?" His voice was husky. He didn't look at her. The hand gripping the edge of the sill was white against the painted wood.

"Of course not."

"Thank God." It was a bare whisper. He relaxed, shoulders dropping, head bowed as if in sudden fatigue.

"Do you think I could murder Rob's baby?"

"Rob?" The look he turned toward her was blank, eyes glittering in the sunlight. "Who..." Remembrance cleared them. He came back to the bed, shaking his head. "I'm sorry, Lisa. For a minute, I forgot you have...had...a husband. Forgive me."

She felt brief resentment...how could he forget Rob, after what he'd said about gossip and her being a widow?

Without warning, he caught her hands again, saying so fiercely she cringed, "Walker hates me. Don't let him talk you into changing your mind. Promise."

She was startled as she thought she read her own fears of the night before mirrored in his expression. Lisa was touched and frightened at the same time, as well as confused. Why would Walker's hatred of Drex make him want her baby dead?

"Dr. Walker understands." His grip hurt. She managed to pull away her hands without actually wrenching them from his grasp. "I want this baby."

Those words seemed to calm him.

"I'm sorry. I shouldn't act like that but..." He shrugged, his expression holding surprise, as if he'd abruptly realized something. "I never thought about it until now. I must be a closet Pro-Lifer because I definitely believe everything deserves a right to live... Everything and everyone..."

Silence fell between them, his words seeming to settle around her. There was something else she had to say and she didn't want to. She couldn't look at him so she studied the sheet, tracing a nervous circle on its white surface with her finger. "Will this change our friendship?"

"Your being pregnant?" The way he scowled made her think so. "Of course it does. I guess I should admit it." He caught Lisa's hand again, gently this time, as he leaned forward, whispering into her ear, "I don't intend to be merely a friend."

~ * ~

Walker scheduled her dismissal for the next day so she had plenty of time to think about her decision and what it meant. No matter what she thought, however, it always came back to the same thing.

Abortion... Another trip to that surgical arena...tired again to that cross...she'd be drugged...and while she was unconscious, someone would take a knife and cut the slender thread of that fragile life within her, as if he were removing a malignant substance from her body.

But it wasn't malignant…it was Rob's child…and that thread was now her only tie to him.

I made the right decision…no matter how it turns out.

~ * ~

Dr. Walker insisted on pushing her wheelchair to the side entrance where a taxi was waiting. Alice, overnight case in hand, followed.

As they came through the double doors, she saw Drex leaning against one of the granite columns attached to the roofed-over drive-through. He straightened and came toward them, hair bright in the pre-noon sun, eyes hidden by smoky lenses.

"Drex…look, they've sprung me at last." She smiled up at him.

"So I see." He looked from her to Alice, holding out his hand. "You must be Lisa's aunt, the best college professor in Macon."

"Instructor, young man." She corrected, but her smile said his remark pleased her. "I'm not a professor yet."

"What are you doing here?" There was an electric crackle of anger in Walker's voice.

As if noticing him for the first time, Drex turned his attention to the doctor. He did it slowly, one copper brow raised as if discovering something annoying. Though they were the same height, he seemed to look down on Walker. Behind the dark glasses, his eyes were unreadable, though his answer was quiet. "I came to take Lisa home, of course."

Lisa glanced toward the car parked at the curb. It was the sports car Martha had spoken of, a vintage Jaguar with the Leaper—the metal cat—on its hood. Small and powerful and expensive. Lisa remembered reading an article explaining the cat symbol was missing from newer models but this one…it had to be at least twenty years old. Mentally, she shuddered to think how much the car cost. Its finish was a bright copper and she wondered how much vanity was involved in that, since it matched exactly the color of Drex's hair.

"I know Lisa appreciates your taking time away from the rest of your patients like this but I'm here now," Drex went, smoothly. "You can go."

"I don't think so." Walker looked at the Jag, shaking his head. "Lisa's not going anywhere in that. There's not enough room in that thing for her and her aunt. I won't have her squeezed into that copper-colored tin can."

"It *will* be crowded." Lisa admitted it with disappointment.

"She needs to have her injured leg extended…like lying on the backseat of this taxi." He indicated the cab as the driver got out and came around to open the back door.

Drex didn't answer, looking from Walker to the open door to Lisa.

"In that case…" The smile he turned on the doctor held triumph as he bent and scooped Lisa effortlessly out of the chair. He turned toward the cab, throwing over his shoulder, "Better get on with your rounds, Medicine Man. Your other patients are waiting."

Depositing Lisa on the seat, he waited as she slid over so she was resting against the other door, both legs stretched out before her. "Make certain that door's locked," he ordered. "Don't want it opening and have you falling out."

Automatically, she reached behind her and checked as he got her crutches and placed them in the foot of the cab. Then he opened the front passenger door and helped her aunt inside. Once she was settled, he said, "I'll follow in my car," and shut both doors.

Ignoring the fuming doctor, he ran across to the Jag, slid under the wheel, and started the engine.

The cab pulled away, Drex following. None of them looked back or saw Dr. Walker watching, face dark with anger, hands at his sides but tightly clenched into fists. When the cell in his pocket came to life, it was several seconds before he could compose himself enough to answer it.

~ * ~

Drex didn't stay long. After insisting on paying the cab fare and carrying Lisa into the house, he set her in a lounge chair near the fireplace. "I wanted to make sure you got here safe and sound."

With a promise to come back for another visit and stay longer, he disappeared out the door and a few seconds later, they hear the roar of the car's engine as it sped away.

"So that's Drex." Alice sat on the arm of Lisa's lounger.

"What do you think?" Lisa asked anxiously. Alice's opinion was important to her. She also wanted to soothe her aunt. Alice wanted Drex to swing by the cemetery so she and Lisa could see Robin's grave but Lisa vetoed that immediately. *I'm not going there, not now. After the baby's born...we'll go together. The only time I want to see that place is when I take him to see his father.* Alice protested but Lisa looked tearful so Alice didn't argue, not wanting to upset her.

"That's hard to say on such a brief acquaintance, but I get the feeling he's a very unusual young man." Alice seemed to be choosing her words carefully. "Your doctor doesn't like him very much."

"And you don't either." Lisa made it an accusation.

"Did I say that? He's…" Alice shook her head, thinking back to how Drex and Walker had glared at each other, of the way Drex made lifting Lisa out of the chair seem such a victorious gesture. Something about Drexl von Dorff made her uneasy. "It's like looking at a forest in the daylight and seeing the same scene at night. You know what's there but there are so many shadows and hidden places you can't be sure. The only way to find out is to go into it and then it may be too late. Your red-haired friend's full of shadows and hidden places, I'm afraid." Seeing Lisa's scowl, she laughed. "Will you listen to me? I sound like I'm reading notes from my *Gothic Novel* class. Don't worry. I like your Drex, Lisa."

"He's not *my* Drex," Lisa pointed out.

"No? He cares about you and unless I'm mistaken, so does young Dr. Walker," Alice said.

"I doubt that." Lisa looked at her aunt in surprise.

"Where are your eyes, girl? You were there. Didn't you see the way they were acting? Like two fighting cocks, getting ready to square off."

"You're wrong, Aunt Allie. Daniel Walker's a good doctor but he's a little too ill-mannered for my tastes," Lisa argued. "As for his being interested in me? He's probably had very few patients coming into a hospital with automobile accident injuries and leaving two months pregnant."

"Blind. The girl's blind." Her aunt got up and began to pace in front of the fireplace, arms waving dramatically.

Scr-r—i-i-itch...sharp claws dragged down the back door.

"There's Timothy. Would you let him in? I'm anxious to see him." Lisa was glad of an excuse to change the subject.

Her aunt went into the kitchen. As she heard the back door open, Lisa leaned against the lounger, wondering again what the real reason for Daniel Walker's anger had been. He'd truly had the expression of a child losing the attention of someone he was trying to impress. *Why does he dislike Drex so?*

~ * ~

True to his word, two days later, Drex was back and he soon had Lisa out of the house, in spite of her protests that she'd been ordered to rest and stay quiet.

"Sunshine's good for you. Vitamin D, etc. He wouldn't want you getting pale and wan from lack of it." With that, he had her strapped into the passenger seat of the Jag. He also promised Aunt Allie he'd drive at a safe, reasonable speed, winking at Lisa as he said it.

She had to admit she enjoyed the drive and decided she wouldn't mention it on her next office visit.

~ * ~

Drex's visits continued.

Sometimes they sat in the living room, she in the lounger, her splinted leg on the upraised footrest, Drex on the sofa. Usually, Alice made herself conspicuously absent.

They played board games. To Lisa's surprise, Drex proved himself very adept at Backgammon, and also Parcheesi. Whenever they played that game, he insisted they needed a third participant to make it more of a competition. On those occasions, Alice, pretending reluctance, allowed herself to be persuaded to join in.

At last the day came when Drex invited her to Land's End.

"I'd like you to see it once you're out of that thing and back on your feet." He gestured at the splint. "Before winter comes, before…is it crude of me to say it? Before you get any bigger." He squeezed her hand and kissed her lightly on the forehead. "Once your traveling's curtailed, you won't be able to go anywhere."

"I can always wait until after the baby's born," she said.

"You've got to see it *before*," he insisted.

"Why? Is it that important?"

"Yes. Very."

"I don't know if Aunt Allie'll like that. Going unchaperoned to Land's End, I mean. Driving around here's one thing, but…She's so proper."

"And you're not?"

"No, I'm not," she said, a little defiantly. "I'm just…cautious."

"Cautious. Right. I see a challenge ahead of me."

"What does that mean?"

"It means I'm going to have to convert you from being proper to who-the-Hell-cares?"

"You can try. But I don't think twenty-three years of walking the line can be overcome so quickly."

"We'll see," he said. "I'll start when you visit Land's End."

"*If* I go," she said.

"Why wouldn't you?"

"It all depends on your intentions, sir." She said it primly, raising her chin and pressing her lips together.

"My intentions? My, how moral and old-fashioned we sound." He didn't try to hide his laughter. Leaning toward her, he placed a finger under her chin." You're about seventy-five years behind the times, sugar." His voice became mocking, tinged with a whisper of menace. "Seduction can be fun."

The scorn in his tone hurt. In spite of her aunt's admonitions, Lisa never considered herself old-fashioned. Well…maybe she'd stubbornly clung to chastity when she and Rob started dating seriously and he tried to maneuver her into bed, but she told herself she was merely being careful. *Seduction can be fun.* Robin also used that same phrase, laughing as he backed down and accepted her refusal, pushing away his roving hands, and clamping her legs tightly together. Hearing Drex say it jolted her since she was certain he wasn't teasing.

"Come on, Lisa. You know what it's all about. You've got the proof of it right here." He rested his hand on her belly.

Lisa's hurt flared into protective anger. Under his hand, her baby—*Rob's* baby—slept. Safe. Helpless. *And he's laughing. How dare he make light of it?*

She turned her head, not wanting to look at him, making him see he'd gone too far with his heavy-handed teasing.

"Forget I said that. I didn't mean it…" Amazing how quickly he backed down. "Sweetheart…" He tried again, talking to the angry stiffness of her back, softer now, pleading, letting that strange accent give way to a wheedling drawl. His voice became sarcastically Southern. Like Walker, Drex could control his accent when he wished. "I'm jes' so used to havin' mah own way, I plain fuhget mah mannuhs sometimes." He caught her chin in his hand, forcing her to look at him. "Hey, I'm sorry…it's the way I am. I say things and they come out wrong. Forgive me…all right?"

She was ready to say something sharp and caustic, a stab of words hurting him as what he'd said hurt her. Before she could utter the first sound, he leaned over and kissed her.

"Hush, now…" To make sure she did just that, he kissed her again.

For a moment Lisa didn't move. She simply sat very still, but not for long. On their own, her arms raised to encircle Drex's neck. He pulled her close, crushing her against his chest, mouth insistent and seeking against hers.

Soft footpads sounded on the hardwood floor. A silver puff-ball landed in Lisa's lap, wriggling between them, pushing them apart. Lisa looked down at the cat.

"This is Timothy." She stroked the silver head. "He was a wedding present."

"And now he's appointed himself substitute chaperon." Drex leaned over to pet Timothy, The cat looked up, hissed and dodged. He spat, a paw darting out. Drex jerked his hand back, narrowly missing being clawed.

"Timothy, what ails you?"

The cat leaped to the floor, whirling to face them. Back arched, his golden eyes narrowed to angry slits. With a yowl, he disappeared down the hallway.

"Did he scratch you?" She caught Drex's hand, turning it over, searching for telltale red streaks. "I'm sorry. I don't know what's the matter with him. He's usually friendly to visitors."

"Has he been talking to Daniel Walker? He's jealous." Drex was matter-of-fact about it.

"Jealous? Timothy?"

"I imagine he's gotten all of your attention, hasn't he?" Without waiting for an answer, he went on, "You'd better watch him, Lisa. You don't want him pulling that stunt when the baby gets here, because if he does…"

"If he does?" she echoed, thinking it sounded like a threat. She hadn't had time to consider Timothy might be jealous of her baby, or that Timothy would be jealous of anything.

"…that cat and I will have a very serious talk," he went on. He touched her cheek. "Now, where were we?"

The mood was broken however. Lisa didn't allow it to be recovered. When she pleaded fatigue, Drex left soon afterward. She drowsed on the sofa but did very little sleeping. Once more guilt surfaced, this time full force. *What am I doing…encouraging Drex? Allowing him to kiss me…and even worse, responding?* If Timothy hadn't interrupted…*What's wrong with me?*

~ * ~

A few days later, the question changed to *What's wrong with* you? as she sat in an exam room in Dr. Daniel Walker's office and listened to him lecture her about leaving the house.

I shouldn't have told him. At the time, she'd thought learning she was feeling good enough to go for drives with Drex would make him happy. *How could I possibly have thought anything having to do with Drexl von Dorff would make Daniel Walker anything but angry?*

"When I dismissed you, it wasn't to go traipsing all over the countryside," he snapped. "Your leg's newly healed...If you were to bump it by a quick stop in that car...you might end up back in TempeGen again."

"I wear a seatbelt," she said. "It's the law..."

"Doesn't matter, you could still slide forward and hit something. I know how cramped those sports cars are. You need plenty of foot room."

"But I get so tired of sitting in one spot all the time," Lisa protested, a childish whine creeping into her voice.

"You've got your baby to think about now," he reminded her. "Suppose you fell? What if your crutches slipped while you were getting into or out of the car?"

She didn't tell him Drex always carried her to the car. She had a feeling he definitely wouldn't like that.

"Babies grow fast, or so I'm told." He hurried on as if thinking she were about to ask how much he knew about babies. "I want you on two good legs when that little one starts crawling so you can keep up with him."

She didn't answer, letting the image of a miniature Rob scurrying across the living room floor overwhelm her.

"As long as you're my patient, Lisa, I want you to stay put. Please? After that, you'll be Brad Halyard's problem, but right now, your welfare's my business."

"So I'm a problem now?" Her voice rose belligerently. For some reason, she wanted the argument to continue, so she could get in her own two-cents' worth.

"Of course you're not a problem," he laughed, spoiling the whole thing. "A poor choice of words. What should I have said?" He leaned back, tapping his chin and looking up as if searching for something. "Let me see…what word should I use…responsibility? In my care? That sounds good." He caught her hand, patting it. "You're in my care, Lisa…and I don't want you hurt."

"Drex isn't going to do anything to hurt me," she began, hating the warm glow those last words gave her. She wanted to stay angry with him. "He's a good driver…"

"Trust me. Drexl von Dorff can hurt you in more way than you can imagine. From now on, stay put. Please," he went on. "Agreed, Mrs. Chambers?"

"I wish you'd decide what you're going to call me." She didn't answer his question. "Is it Lisa or Mrs. Chambers? Please make up your mind!"

It was such a minor thing but it gave her the satisfaction of having talked back, as well as putting him in his place for daring to butt in where her relationship with Drex—and Lisa realized soon she'd have to face up to the fact that they had a relationship—was concerned.

"Very well, Mrs. Chambers," It was said stiffly, as if she'd insulted him somehow. "I will."

Chapter 10

It was here. At last. The day Lisa was beginning to feel would never arrive. Her final check-up.

Under Dr. Walker's scrutiny, she'd marched barefoot up and down the little hallway outside the exam room, then heard him pronounce her fit and well again.

She'd been walking with the aid of one crutch for two weeks, with both feet on the floor though still favoring her right leg. Today was the first day he allowed her to put full weight on the injured leg. Lisa did it gingerly, and when it didn't hurt, stamped her foot—but lightly—then stood on two legs, grinning broadly. He checked the incision which was now a well-healed scar, nodded with satisfaction, and stared at her thoughtfully for a long moment.

"All right, Mrs. Chambers…you can put your shoes back on. I think you're ready to jump back into the big bad world again with both feet. Stop by my office before you leave." He went out and down the hall.

"That was abrupt." Lisa sat on the exam table and began to pull on her pantyhose. "If I'm dismissed, why do I need to go to his office? Is that like being sent to the principal?"

"He probably wants to give you some last-minute instructions." Myrtice's answer was also short. She handed Lisa her shoes and headed for the door. "You know which is his office, don't you?"

"Last one on the left at the end of the hall." Lisa thought the nurse's attitude left a lot to be desired, too. What happened to friendly manners? The doctors she'd seen when she was a child were always friendly. Was it because she'd been such a problem? Walker's calling her that still rankled a little.

As if aware of what she was thinking, Myrtice gave a grimace of a smile. "Just leave the door open when you leave. 'Bye now." She went out.

Dropping her sandals to the floor, Lisa stepped into them. She got her purse, slung it over her shoulder, and carrying the crutch, left the exam room, heading toward Walker's office. She was a little puzzled. Usually the doctor was so talkative. Too much so, she'd have said, but today…

To her tap on the door, he called for her to come in. Lisa opened the door and went inside.

He was at the mahogany monstrosity he called a desk. It was the size of a small football field, dwarfing the room. Lisa had seen it only once before, on her first visit, but she wasn't surprised to see it still held the same items. There was an odd, transparent clock with no visible mechanism though it appeared to keep perfect time…a small gold-framed photograph of an attractive blonde woman looking nothing like the dark-haired doctor though he identified her as *Dear Old Mom*…assorted papers and reference books…a half-filled cup of coffee sitting directly under the desk lamp—was that mold on its surface or a reflection of the light?—and on one side, a stack of patients' charts balanced on top of the transcription machine.

He'd been dictating when her knock interrupted him, and motioned her to a chair at the side of the desk. "Be with you in a minute."

As she closed the door and seated herself, resting the crutch against the desk, he clicked the switch on the microphone and continued, "Patient is back to full weight-bearing. Fracture appears fully healed. Unless there's further difficulty, she's dismissed this date, to be followed by Bradley Halyard, MD, OB/GYN. Copy to Dr. Halyard, please." Releasing the switch, he returned the microphone to its cradle at the side of the machine. "Congratulations, you're Dr. Halyard's patient from here on."

He breathed an exaggerated sigh that Lisa thought held more than a little genuine relief. She didn't answer. She had a feeling he wanted to say something else. She waited.

"What are you going to do with that?" He gestured at the crutch.

"Stick it and the other one into the ground and use them as a trellis for running roses," she replied. "And hope I never see another crutch again."

She must've sounded a little vehement because he looked surprised.

"I see...well...I...good luck, Lisa." He picked up a chart, flipping through it and studying a page intently.

That's it?

"Thank you, Dr. Walker. Goodbye." She stood and walked out, shutting the door behind her.

~ * ~

When the last patient had been seen and the day's case notes finished, Dan Walker picked up the lone chart still on the desk. Looking at the end tab, he opened it, reading again the words he'd dictated over two and a half months before, after that long night in TempeGen's ER.

Chambers, Felicia (Mrs.) age 23. Patient was brought into Temple General Emergency Room tonight with injuries from an automobile accident. Triple compound fracture of right tibia, multiple contusions and lacerations, concussion. Prepped for surgery. Usual surgical team requested. He looked at that first sentence again. *Twenty-three.* He was almost ten years older than she. Would she think that was too much? *Why the Hell am I worrying about an age difference? She's never given the slightest indication she sees me as anything but a doctor. And God knows I've done nothing to make her like me in any way, shape, or form. All I've done is badger her about von Dorff. Daniel, she's right. You really do have a rotten bedside manner.*

Dropping the chart onto the desk, he reached for the telephone, then held it away from its cradle, listening to the hum of the open line before setting it down again.

That's because I wanted to distance myself from her, he continued his conversation with himself. Argument really, just as he'd argued with himself all the other times after seeing Lisa on his rounds. *I had to keep her at arms-length. A doctor shouldn't get emotionally... romantically... involved with a patient.*

Didn't the *Hippocratic Oath* state just that? *...avoiding any voluntary act of impropriety or corruption, including the seduction of women...*

It can be professional suicide... and I'm definitely not the self-destructive type. But he *had* gotten emotionally involved, whether he wanted to or not. From the first moment he saw her, he was lost and knew it. It had simply taken him this long to admit it.

He remembered how she looked the night the ambulance brought her in, with Myrtice holding her shoulders to keep her from writhing away from his touch. The terrible injuries to her leg...blood streaking the insides of her highs, seeping around the bones jutting through torn skin. He'd thought there was very little bleeding from the wounds themselves for her to be so blood-smeared but there was no time to worry over that minor puzzle. Even then he felt something more than the usual concern for a critically-injured patient and as he scrubbed for surgery, he acknowledged that feeling.

The problem was, he'd let von Dorff see, too. He also let Lisa see his hatred for the islander though she hadn't realized it was his concern for her making him act so stupidly. He wanted to tell her how he really felt. Even when he found out about her pregnancy, it hadn't mattered, except that he wanted to make certain her baby was safe also. *And if that isn't a harebrained idea... a man falling in love with a pregnant woman who's a two-month widow*. Trouble was, he didn't care...not that she'd just lost her husband nor that she was carrying that husband's child. All he knew was he cared for Lisa Chambers, and he had to tell her.

She isn't my patient now. At least I waited that long. Impatient fingers drummed against the phone's base, wanting to pick it up, making no move to do so. *Damn it, she's so vulnerable right now.* She'd lost her husband. Her body was still recovering from trauma...*and now, she's facing the prospect of raising a child by herself, a possibly handicapped child. Von Dorff has his eye on her, too. He'll have no qualms about taking advantage of Lisa's weakness. Maybe do it just to get back at me.* He couldn't let that happen, couldn't allow her to become another of Drex's women. *If she's susceptible to one of us, why not the other? Better me than von Dorff.*

He took a deep breath. *What exactly do I want out of this?* He realized he wasn't certain. Thanks to his actions, she might not want to see him as a potential suitor. All he was sure of was that he didn't want her walking out of his life. Not yet. He reached for the phone again and began to punch in the number typed on the inside cover of the chart.

~ * ~

It rang six times before she answered. When he started to reply to her greeting, his mouth went so dry he couldn't speak.

She'd said, "Hello?" twice more before he managed to get out a sound, clearing his throat frantically, not wanting her to hang up.

"L-Lisa?" Damn, he sounded like a high school kid calling his first date.

"Dr. Walker, is that you?" At least she recognized his voice. "Is anything wrong?"

"No…I…Th-there's something I forgot to ask you when you were here today." *Damn, how lame that sounds.*

"Oh?" She waited and when he said nothing more, asked with a tinge of impatience, "Well? What?"

"I wondered…"

"Yes?"

"I...know it's going to...sound... I wondered if you'd have dinner with me tonight?" There, said in a rush and done with.

She didn't answer. *Forget everything I've said before this moment, Lisa. Please.* "Lisa? Are you still there?"

"I'm still here." Her answer was slow and deliberate. "But...I..."

"Look, forget it." He cut in as her voice trailed away. *Fool. What did you expect?* "It was a stupid idea and I'm sorry I bothered you. Goodbye..." He pulled the handset away, was replacing it in its cradle when he heard her speaking.

"No, wait..."

He had the receiver up and pressed to his ear in time to catch the rest of what she said.

"...because I thought...you didn't...I mean...isn't it unethical for a doctor to...uh...socialize...with a patient?"

"You're not my patient anymore," he reminded her.

"That's...right..." She sounded thoughtful, as if she'd forgotten that fact. "I'm not. In that case..." Her next words were brisk and bright, and very surprising. "I'd be happy to have dinner with you."

"You would?" *Idiot, didn't she just say so?* "I-I mean, great. I'll pick you up at eight-thirty. Is that all right?" He heard a murmured agreement and went on, more to himself than to her, "I'm not on call tonight. I should be through with my rounds by seven if all goes well so I can dash home and grab a quick shower and shave..." He was gabbling. She didn't need to know his personal hygiene habits, not yet, anyway, but he wanted to get it all said before she changed her mind. "We'll have dinner and go dancing...no, not dancing, don't want to tire your leg. You need exercise but not that kind..." He paused for breath, then finished, "Eight-thirty, then..."

"I'll be ready." She was laughing as she disconnected the call. At him, for sounding so stupid, he didn't doubt.

After replacing the phone in its cradle, he sat there smiling. It was several seconds before he realized he was staring at the clock on the desk and its golden hands pointed to six-thirty. Getting up, he went to the nearby closet. Pulling his suit jacket off a hanger, he got his car keys from a pocket. He draped the jacket over his arm and, still wearing his lab coat, went out the door and to the exit, passing his nurse.

"Get a move on, Mud. We've got a lot of patients to see before I take you home tonight." He began to whistle, a surprisingly cheery trill.

Depositing a stack of charts on the transcriptionist's desk, Myrtice hurried to follow him out. She wondered what Danny had to whistle about in this long day which had an even longer way to go before it was over.

~ * ~

For several seconds Lisa stood by the phone. She was still a little surprised...*stunned* might be a better description. *I had no idea he felt that way. Was... oh God... was all that rudeness and anger his way of flirting?* As she dropped the phone onto its base, Alice, who'd been listening unashamedly to her niece's side of the conversation, put in her opinion.

"Do you really think that's wise?" As Lisa gave her a blank stare, she went on, "Having Drex here where you're well-chaperoned is one thing, but going on a date?" When Lisa's expression changed to exasperation mingled with a little anger, she said, "Now, darling, I'm just thinking about you. It's for your own—"

"Stop right there. I don't want to hear it." It was so sharp Alice did just that, giving her niece a startled look. Lisa went on, calmly, "Aunt Allie, I love you dearly but you have to realize I'm not a child anymore."

She sat down. Timothy jumped into her lap and she began to stroke his back, looking at the cat instead of her aunt.

"What I've just done may seem wrong, but..." she sighed. "I know I'm a widow...a pregnant widow...but neither of those facts makes me incompetent. It may be unusual and it may not be exactly what's expected at this particular moment, but I'll make my own decision. It's what I want to do, so Aunt Allie dear..." She smiled so sweetly her next words were a shock. "...butt out!"

"Of course, Lisa." Alice blinked, not knowing whether to nod or burst into tears. She decided on the former. "I didn't mean to..."

"Don't worry." Pushing Timothy to the floor, Lisa got up and put her arms around her aunt, hugging her. "I promise I won't do anything scandalous. Anyway, is going to dinner any different from riding in Drex's car...unchaperoned?"

"I guess not," Alice admitted reluctantly.

"It's merely dinner," Lisa repeated. "Not a prelude to a seduction." *Seduction can be fun*...Drex's words chose that precise moment to pounce into her mind.

"As long as you're not the main course." Alice allowed herself a tight smile. "I'll try not to be such a mother hen. Is it all right if I worry, just a little?"

"Only if you do it quietly," Lisa laughed. She refused to think any more on the propriety of a date with Dr. Walker. Not then any way. It was going to be a pleasant distraction. She told herself that's probably all the doctor planned and said so. "I imagine he simply wants to give me a little change of scenery. You know how worried about me he was."

"Sounds like he's going above and beyond the call of doctor-patient care," Alice muttered, thinking back to his meeting her at the airport. It sounded to her as if Dr. Walker was having a bit of difficulty letting go of this particular patient.

Chapter 11

Lisa opened the door, looking through the screen at the young man standing there. For a moment, she didn't recognize him.

"Dr. Walker?" She didn't intend to put so much disbelief into the words as she stared at the dark suit, dark shirt, and burgundy tie. *My God, take him out of that white coat and he really cleans up nicely.*

"None other."

She pushed open the screen, studying him intently as he took a step toward her.

"Hi." He said it with so much shyness she was startled.

Where did that brusque, brisk, *do-as-I-say* manner go?

Then he smiled.

~ * ~

To say Dan was nervous would've been an understatement. He felt like a kid taking the car out alone for the first time. Somehow he'd managed not to let his patients see how impatient he was to be on his way. He'd even kept it from Myrtice, though he thought he saw her giving him a couple of glances involving raised brows as she followed him down the hospital corridor, nearly running to keep up with his strides. Since she didn't own a car, he drove her home each night and picked her up in the morning but the speed with which he deposited her on the walkway to the little house she rented on Beaumont Street earned him a scowl.

"Are you in a hurry to get somewhere? I was going to ask you if you wanted to come in and share some lasagna leftovers."

"Dang! You know that's one of my favorites, but…" He managed to look apologetic and impatient at the same time. "I can't…" He didn't explain, merely gave her a cousinly peck on the cheek and slammed the passenger door. "See you in the morning."

Getting back into the car, he drove off, leaving Myrtice standing there.

A quick shower, an even quicker swipe of his razor eradicating that five o'clock shadow inherited from his mother's side of the family…he managed to stop before a mirror and straighten his clothes so they didn't look as if he'd thrown them on…which he had…and then he was on his way…

…to stand in Lisa Chamber's doorway, shifting his weight and grinning like an idiot.

~ * ~

"Come on in." That grin was like seeing the sun break through a cloud. She had to smile back. "I'll be ready in a minute,"

"By the way…" He followed her into the foyer. "I've made up my mind."

"About what?" She turned to look at him.

"What I'll call you. Lisa. And you can call me *Dan*."

"Okay, Dr. Dan."

"Nope." He shook his head. "Just *Dan*. Tonight I'm not a doctor, I'm just a guy taking you to dinner."

"In that case, *guy taking me to dinner*, come in and face Aunt Allie while I get my purse."

As he followed her inside, Alice appeared in the kitchen doorway. She was in pajamas and robe, had a book in one hand and a box of chocolate-covered cherries in the other. Lisa picked up her purse from the credenza between the windows but didn't say anything, waiting to see how the confrontation was going to play itself out.

"Good evening, Miz Townsend. How are you?"

Well, so far so good but when did he get so polite? Such a difference from the man at the hospital. If he'd bowed to Aunt Allie it wouldn't have surprised her.

Before Alice could answer, Timothy decided to make an appearance. He headed straight for Dan, stopping directly in front of the doctor. He sat, staring solemnly, golden eyes unblinking. Lisa felt as if the cat and her aunt were in cahoots.

"Hi, cat." Dan bent and held out a hand.

"Careful..." Remembering Timothy's reaction to Drex, Lisa began a warning.

The cat sniffed delicately at Dan's hand, found its soap and antiseptic smell to his liking and present his right ear to be scratched. Dan complied, rubbing both gray-tufted ears and tickling the cat under the chin. Timothy closed his eyes, a rich throaty purr curling out of his chest.

"I'm ready to go." Lisa cleared her throat.

"Sorry, cat." Dan straightened. "The lady's waiting." Timothy glared at Lisa, sniffed, and sprinted back into the kitchen. Dan followed Lisa to the door, holding it open for her.

"Don't keep her out too late, young man." Alice called after them. "Remember, she needs sleep in her condition. Curfew's at eleven."

"For Goodness' sake, Aunt Allie..." Lisa began.

"Timothy and I will be waiting up for you," she went on, settling on the sofa. She opened the book. "*War and Peace*. I've been wanting to read this." She riffled the pages then looked directly at Dan. "There are twelve hundred pages in this thing. I don't want to finish it before my niece walks back through that door."

"Don't worry," Dan said. "I doubt if you'll be into Chapter Five before we get back. It'll take you that long to learn to pronounce the names."

Lisa pushed opened the door and went out. He followed, laughing as he shut it behind him. As he escorted her to the car, he hung back slightly, watching her move effortlessly down the walk. *Now that's a pretty sight.* "Damn, I'm a good surgeon...not even a limp."

"You *are* a good surgeon...and one with no false modesty," Lisa said. "But please, no more doctor talk tonight. Agreed?"

"Agreed." He reached for the door handle and Lisa paused to study his car.

It was a midnight blue Mercedes C63 coupe, gleaming and sleek under the streetlight. Dan pulled open the door. Lisa didn't move.

"I see now why you called Drex's car a tin can."

"Please...no Drex talk tonight either." He gestured toward the car and she got in, settling herself while he slammed the door and ran around, sliding onto the driver's seat.

"Buckle your seat belt." He watched as she struggled to fit together the metal clamp and bracket between the seats. "Here, let me." Leaning over, he pulled the strap, pushing the metal pieces together. There was a click. "There."

His own belt in place, he started the car.

"If you'd had your seatbelt on before, you wouldn't have ended up as my patient."

"I thought we agreed no doctor talk," she said.

"That's not doctor talk," he pointed out. "That's plain highway safety."

"In that case, can we steer clear of anything pertaining to automobile accidents, broken bones, and what happened?"

"Your wish is my command, ma'am." With that, he put the car into gear, sending it shooting away from the curb so swiftly she was glad she was held in place by the seatbelt.

"Anyway, I *did* have my seatbelt on. It came loose, somehow." She paused before adding, "Airbags didn't inflate, either."

"Are you going to sue the manufacturer?"

"Should I?"

"The car's been hauled to the dump. Probably be a little difficult finding out what went wrong in what's left of it...what do you think?"

"I think I just broke my own rule."

"You brought it up." He concentrated on shifting gears.

"Dan...before we go any further, I think there's something I should say."

"That sounds ominous." He didn't take his attention from the road. "What is it?"

"This whole situation is odd. I mean…I'm pregnant, and recently widowed…and you were my doctor, and now we're going on a date…" she paused.

"So far, you've summarized it nicely but not added anything new."

"I just…I feel a little weird about this and I'm certain somewhere along the way someone'll probably make a snide comment and I…I don't want you embarrassed or anything."

"To tell the truth, Lisa…I don't make a habit of dating pregnant women." He still didn't look at her. "And I don't think I've ever dated a widow. They're usually too old."

"How does it feel?"

"So far, perfectly painless on both counts." He managed to look surprised.

"Let's hope it stays that way…oh!" She broke off with a little cry.

"What is it?" He slowed the car to a crawl, giving her a look immediately professional.

"I…the…the baby moved." A look of awe crossed her face. "It startled me, that's all. I wasn't expecting it."

"You shouldn't. Not this early. You shouldn't feel any movement for at least another three months."

"But I did," she protested. She became absorbed in the feeling, wanting it to happen again so she could revel in the life communicating itself to her. "Not exactly a kick, more like a flutter, like wings brushing…I must be farther along than I thought."

"Maybe so." He didn't tell her she'd look a lot bigger, too, if that was the case. "After all, I'm just an orthopod...what do I know about obstetrics? Maybe babies develop faster these days. So you have a little can-can dancer, huh?"

"More like a football player." She placed a hand over her side, wincing as another kick landed. "I think he just batted one over the goalpost."

"You don't use a bat in football."

"Guess nobody told him that." Her eyes were dancing. "Isn't it wonderful?"

"Yes. It is," he agreed. Briefly, his own expression mirrored hers. "Still, it *is* unusual..."

"Quit analyzing it," she interrupted. "You're spoiling things."

Dan shook his head. He thought he'd never seen anyone looking so radiant or so happy and he told her so. "Guess that glow they talk about expectant mothers having really exists. Now we have even more cause to go out tonight."

"Oh?"

"Sure. Baby Chambers has made himself known to the world. That's a *Hallmark Moment* for sure."

By this time, they were pulling into the parking lot of the *Plantation Inn.*

~ * ~

The waiter'd asked, "Your usual place, Dr. Walker?" When Dan nodded, he guided them through the maze of tables and diners to a slightly isolated setting at the rear of the restaurant. After they were seated, he went on, "Your customary drink before ordering?"

Dan nodded and Lisa said, "I'll have a Tom Collins."

"You'll have a Shirley Temple," Dan told her. As she pursed her lips slightly, he made a concession, looking up at the waiter, "Tell Jerry to put two cherries in it, Stan—and an orange slice." To Lisa, he said, "That way you'll get some Vitamin C, too."

"Right, Doc."

"Who gave you the right to tell me what to drink?" Lisa asked as she watched the waiter walk away. "You're not my doctor now, remember?" He'd fallen back into acting so much like his hospital *persona* she hoped their dinner date wasn't going to disintegrate before it even started.

"In Dr. Halyard's absence, I'm appointing myself *in loco parentis*...or in this case, *in loco physician*," he answered, not in the least bothered by her resenting his interference. "Didn't you read any of the pamphlets Brad gives all his new mothers? You know alcohol's not good for either of you right now. One drink per week, isn't that the prescribed limit?"

"In that case, let this be my limit tonight."

His answer to that was a silent headshake.

"We can't get away from it, can we?" she sighed.

"Lisa..." He placed a hand over hers. "If things hadn't happened as they did, your husband would probably be sitting where I am saying the same thing, so..."

The waiter was back, with Dan's drink and a tall frosted glass decorated with two long-stemmed cherries and an orange slice skewered by a red plastic sword. It was filled with ice and pink liquid. Lisa picked up her drink.

"So…you come here often?" Lisa was determined to change the subject. The Shirley Temple tasted as she suspected it would. Seven-Up and cherry flavoring.

"What makes you think that?" He raised his own drink, taking a very careful sip.

"Your usual place…your customary drink?" She repeated what the waiter said. "Which is what, by the way? You also know both the waiter and bartender by their first names."

"Guilty." He shook his head. "I bring all my girls here." He took another swallow, then gestured with the glass. "Gin and tonic. Actually, this is where I have most of my evening meals. I'm a lousy cook."

Stan was back with the menus.

"Order whatever you like," Dan told her. "As long as it's healthful and nutritious, but if you absolutely have to order something fattening…on your next check-up, I'll write Brad an excuse."

"In that case…" Lisa ordered barbecued ribs and a side salad, smiling as he asked for a steak and baked potato with sour cream and cheese. Obviously that *healthful and nutritious* business was a one-sided affair.

"He's a good friend of yours, isn't he?" she asked as the waiter disappeared into the kitchen with their order.

"Brad?" It seemed to take him a minute to figure out who *he* was. "Yup…roomies in college and med school…the whole shebang. Real buds until he got himself hitched." His manner changed slightly.

"Do…did you have a girl?" Something in his tone made her ask.

"Yeah…she married Brad."

"And you never got over it."

He gave her a sharp look before answering. "Sure I did. Took a while, though. After the wedding I decided I had two choices. I could either break up the marriage or bury my jealousy and keep Brad as a friend. I chose my friend. I think I made the best choice."

"How do you mean? Outside of the obvious."

"They've been married seven years now, have three kids. Kathy's twenty pounds overweight and Brad's losing his hair. While I, on the other hand…" He paused to pick up his glass. "…am an eligible bachelor, and have all my hair. And I'm also…" He swirled the liquid in his glass, making the ice clash together. "…having dinner with you."

Luckily, at that moment, Stan returned bearing a tray covered with dishes, saving Lisa from answering. The waiter deftly deposited them on the table, disappearing again. For the next few moments, they gave their attention to the meal but after only a few bites, Lisa sighed and dropped the rib she held back onto her plate.

"Something wrong with the ribs?"

"Not a bit," Lisa assured him, using her napkin to wipe barbecue sauce off her fingers. "It's just that…I can't eat much at a time. Don't seem to have room."

"I imagine it's going to get a lot more crowded in there pretty soon," he said, unsympathetically. Lisa grimaced. She envied the way he was demolishing his steak, leaving only a scrap of baked potato skin. "No prob. We can get a doggie…a kitty bag. You can take it home to whatshisname…your cat."

"Timothy," she supplied.

"Or better yet, take it home and let ol' Timothy watch you eat it. By the way, what were you going to say to me when I started patting his head?'

"Oh, I…" *Should I mention Drex or not?* "I was just going to warn you…" She explained how Timothy had tried to scratch Drex.

"No kidding?" He looked delighted. "That's my kind of cat. Maybe we should give him the ribs after all. As a reward."

On Stan's next pass by the table, he was flagged down and instructed, "The lady has a feline who's a rib connoisseur. We'll take the leftovers with us, but bring me another drink first."

"I hope you remember I'm not the designated driver," Lisa reminded him. "I doubt if I could handle that fancy car of yours."

"Not to worry," he assured her. "I never have over one and a half drinks unless I'm safely at home and not going out again." She frowned. "Ask Stan if you don't believe me."

"It's true, Miss," the waiter said. "He always orders two, then leaves most of the second one still in the glass." He looked at Lisa's drink. "Will you—"

Dan shook his head. "She hasn't finished that one yet." She started to protest. "Too many soft drinks aren't good for you, either."

As the waiter walked away, taking their plates with him, Dan took a slim golden rectangle from his pocket, pressing a button on one end. It opened to reveal a row of cigarettes.

"Mind if I smoke?"

"Is this the point where I remind you second-hand smoke isn't good for expectant mothers, either?" Lisa asked. "Would it matter?" She had a feeling Daniel Walker was good at telling other people what to do but not following his own advice. "Go ahead."

"We're in the smoking section," he said, looking around. With an equally slim golden lighter, he lit the cigarette he'd extracted. "I'll blow the smoke away from you." He did just that. The smoke floated away and didn't bother her.

Stan returned with his drink and the check on a small black tray. They seemed to have a regular routine.

"As a doctor, you do know smoking's bad for your health, don't you?"

"I certainly do." He agreed. He seemed very cheerful about it.

"Then why do you do it?"

"It's a case of *Do as I say, dear, and not as I do*," he quoted.

"You shouldn't, you know." Unconsciously copying her aunt's gesture at the airport snack bar, she picked up the pristine ashtray, holding it out.

"I've no will power." He flicked the beginning ash into the ashtray. She set it down. "Couldn't stop if I wanted to." He didn't mention how far into cigarette-abstinance he'd been before she came along.

"Even though you're probably going to—" *Why don't I shut up? The man's a doctor. He knows what's what. If he wants to kill himself by inhaling carcinogens...*

"Look...when I'm gasping my last, you've my permission to stand by my bedside and say *I told you so.* Okay?" He took a deep pull on the cigarette, then lowered it as he saw the stricken expression on Lisa's face. When he spoke, only a wisp of smoke was exhaled. "Hey...I'm sorry. I shouldn't be so smart-mouthed about something like that." He put a hand over hers. "Forgive me? Look." He stubbed the cigarette into the ashtray. "There...penance."

They both looked at the crushed cigarette, smoke curling from its ashes. Dan sighed, "Damn, if I stick around you for long, I might end up with no vices at all." He didn't sound unhappy however. He picked up his drink, took one swallow, then set it down.

"What other vices do you have?"

"Unh-uh." He shook a finger at her. "Not on the first date. You've got to know me better before I tell all." He glanced at his watch. "Damn, it's nearly ten-thirty. We'd better get a move on if we're going to beat your aunt's curfew."

"You're not serious?" Lisa didn't move.

"I most certainly am." He looked it. "I'd rather have the Chief of Surgery after me than your Aunt Allie." He was on his feet as he spoke, inspecting the check, then dropping a couple of bills onto the tray, and helping Lisa out of her chair.

Stan reappeared with a neatly-wrapped package. "For the connoisseur feline," he said, grinning.

Dan took it, thanked him and stuffed it into his jacket pocket. Taking Lisa's arm, he started out the door, but at the exit, stopped suddenly, putting a hand to his forehead.

"What is it?" she asked.

~ * ~

She's with him? *How can this be?* M'AneseNebh recoiled in surprised and dismay, hackles stiffening along his spine. Paws lifted, he shook them at the sky. *"Old Ones...fathers of my father...help me!*

~ * ~

"Felt dizzy for a minute." Dan shook his head. "Second drink must've been a little stronger than the first."

"Right," Lisa said. "I'm certain that one swallow tipped the scales from sobriety into drunkenness."

"Either that or I merely had a bit of postural hypertension. I shouldn't have gotten up so fast." He pushed open the door. "I'm all right now."

~ * ~

He has magic... he howled the words. *Magic! How can this be? Who gave it to him? How can it be strong enough to shield him from ours?* There was no answer, only the screaming of the wind as it sent the waves crashing over him, drenching his scaly hide and splashing salt-filled water into his slitted eyes. *Where did it come from? When?*

~ * ~

Once back in the Mercedes, Dan turned the car in the opposite direction from her home.

"There's something I want to show you before I again release you into your aunt's custody,' he said in answer to her questioning look. "Have you ever been to Woodland Park?"

"No."

"There's a hill...Lantern Hill...you can see the whole town from there."

He turned the car onto a paved road running through a high iron gate set in a wall made of stacked granite stones. The road ran upward, the car hugging the curves. Parked along the sides of the road were several autos, all looking very empty.

"Is this a parking lot?"

"Nope."

"Where are all the drivers?"

"Probably in the back sets with their dates."

"You mean this is the local Lover's Lane?" Her heart jumped slightly. *Oh, surely he doesn't want to…*

"Uh-huh." He stopped the car at the crest of the hill, pulling over to the curb. Below, Temple lay quiet and peaceful, the lights of the town mirroring the stars twinkling above it. "Take a look at that." He waved a hand. "Bet you didn't know our li'l ol' town could look so durn purty, didya?" His drawn was slow and exaggerated.

"I didn't." She looked over at him. "Thank you for bringing me up here."

"Someday, when you're not pregnant, I'll bring you back." Something flickered in those hazel eyes. "…and not for the view."

"Why doctor." She leaned away from him, hand on her heart as if he'd shocked her. Truthfully, he had. She didn't expect such a frank statement. "Isn't that a trifle juvenile?"

"I'm not exactly ready for Medicare." He looked indignant, brushing a hand through his hair. "No gray, see? Besides, I spent a helluva lot of years studying and working to get that MD after my name. I think I'm entitled to…"

"A few wild oats?" Lisa guessed. "Perhaps, but it might be better to do as the Scotsman said."

"What's that?" He looked suspicious.

"Sow your wild oats in your own backyard so you'll be sure you can reap them." Before he could react, she went on, "And you'd better get another car, too. Unless you know a way of fitting around that center console. I'd hate for you to have that stick shift hit the wrong place."

"Mrs. Chambers. I'm shocked." He didn't look it, however.

~ * ~

As the Mercedes pulled up in front of the house, the sound of the courthouse clock striking eleven floated over the silent air.

Guiding Lisa up the walk, Dan opened the screen door for her. As she fished the keys from her purse, he bent toward her. She raised her face expectantly, only to have him pluck the keys from her hand and insert the one she held into the lock, leaving her standing with lips foolishly pursed. Holding the door open, he stood aside.

Once in the hallway, he peered into the living room, then placed a finger against his lips. "Shh."

Lisa peeped in.

Snoring gently, Alice lay on the sofa, book open on her chest, with Timothy curled into a silver ball on her stomach. The empty chocolate box was on the floor.

Handing Lisa her keys, Dan reached into his pocket and produced the kitty bag, placing it in her hand. Loudly, he cleared his throat. "Ahem...well, Miz Townsend," he called. "Here's your niece, safe and sound."

Startled, Alice snorted and woke, struggling upright. Timothy jumped to the floor and stretched. Lisa giggled. With a smile and a wink, Dan headed to the door.

As it shut, Alice came wide awake, rubbing her eyes. "Did you have a good time, dear?

"I guess so." Abruptly feeling very tired, Lisa sank into the recliner. She heard the sound of the Mercedes pulling away from the curb.

"What does that mean? Either you did or you didn't."

"It means I think I did. It was nice to go out. We talked a bit and drove around a little, but Dr. Walker...Dan...he didn't even try to kiss me."

"A good thing, too," Her aunt stifled a yawn. "That'd definitely be inappropriate." She retrieved her book from the floor. "I'm going to bed. It'd be a good idea for you to do the same." She disappeared down the hall, Timothy behind her, tail waving over his back like a silver question mark.

Lisa sighed. As far as she could tell, Dan Walker had done exactly what she'd predicted. He'd offered a pleasant distraction for the evening. Truth be told, she'd even enjoyed their arguing about her having a drink, as well as his smoking. She'd also gotten a bare insight into his character in that moment when he talked about losing his girl to his best friend...*and then meeting me...How should I interpret that? And that Lover's Lane Remark?*

Depositing the ribs in the refrigerator, she took off her shoes and started to her own room.

I'm too tired to figure it out now. I'm going to copy Scarlett O'Hara and think about it tomorrow...

Chapter 12

I hope you know what you're doing. Why can't you be a proper little widow like anyone else?

Lisa knew she was dreaming. Since she'd had this argument with herself already and thought she'd settled it, she didn't understand why her subconscious was choosing this moment to bring it up again. She struggled to wake up. Nothing happened. She was going to have to let this particular dream continue whether she wanted to or not. She decided to hurry it along by confronting it.

"What does that mean?"

It means someone has to point out the obvious to you, dummy. You've got to make a choice pretty soon. You can't keep putting it off.

"Why do I have to? Who says?"

Do I have to spell everything out for you? I was hoping you'd start facing reality but, oh no, you've still got your head in the sand. All right, here goes... Both those men want you and neither is the type to share.

"Aren't you being a little melodramatic? This isn't *The Vampire Diaries* or something."

If only it were. Then we could ask the scriptwriters to tie up everything before the closing credits. Resolution in 55.27 minutes. Alice was right. You're blind...deliberately. Right now, you're hiding behind the baby and that's keeping you safe enough. You won't always be pregnant, however, and then you're going to have to decide whether you like 'em shy and dark or green-eyed and mysterious.

Lisa made a rude, disbelieving sound. Since she was dreaming, she wondered if it really happened. She thought she felt a tingling in her nose.

I'm warning you. The voice took on some of Alice's overtones. *You're playing with a couple of firebrands…*

"Frankly, I can't see Daniel Walker as a firebrand," she interrupted.

If only you knew…and you may, very soon. That man has depths even his mother doesn't know about, the voice snapped. *I'm afraid you're going to get more than your little fingers burned, sweetie. Definitely.*

Lisa had no answer to that. The idea of Dan Walker's hidden depths made a coiling deep inside her.

Go ahead, ignore me…but don't be surprised when you find yourself flat on your back looking over someone's shoulder and studying his bedroom ceiling.

"That's enough," Lisa took a deep breath. "I'm not listening any more." She turned away. A hand caught her arm. She jerked from its grasp…

~ * ~

…and nearly rolled off the bed.

"Was I dreaming?" Clutching at the bedpost, she pushed back onto her pillow.

All memory disappeared. She couldn't think of a single detail of what had been going on in her brain before she woke up. Why did she feel an odd relief at that? *Probably just as well. I doubt if it was anything important, anyway.* Glancing at the clock, she saw it was nearly eight. *No sense trying to go back to sleep. May as well get up and face the day.*

Hauling herself out of bed, she prepared to do just that. Stirrings downstairs told her Alice was opening the kitchen door, letting Timothy out.

~ * ~

"Thirty-eight…thirty-nine…" Lisa paused, brush against her hair. Hadn't she read somewhere brushing the hair too much wasn't a good thing? *Why did I get into this habit? Anyway, my arm's getting tired.* "To heck with it!"

Tossing the brush onto the dresser, she stood up. *It's getting late. Better hurry and dress.* If there were no emergencies, Dan'd be here at eight.

Whatever guilt she'd had about seeing either man was now buried…deep. *Let the whole town talk,* she thought rebelliously. *I don't care.* She'd rationalized she should enjoy all this attention while she could. *Let's be realistic…*For some reason that made a sudden twinge in her stomach. *…as soon as the baby's born, they'll probably both disappear in a puff of smoke.* They might profess complete devotion now, but the actual appearance of her baby and any hint either was expected to step in and become a surrogate parent would send both running, she was certain. *I'm going to enjoy them while I can…and let the gossip go hang.*

She'd worried about it since her date with Dan Walker. Lisa had given herself a talking-to Alice would've appreciated. She'd come to the conclusion that, though she loved Rob and would always love him, he was gone and nothing was going to bring him back, so she was going to enjoy the attention while it lasted. When the baby was born and both men abruptly found other attractions, she'd settle down to being the attentive mother her child needed...and, if a miracle happened and one decided to stick around...it wouldn't hurt for little Robbie to have a handsome stepdaddy, would it?

She hadn't mentioned this decision to Aunt Allie. That'd be all it'd take to get her aunt started again on how much she disapproved of either of them coming around so often...even Dan, for whom she now showed definite favoritism. *Drex in the morning and Dan at night...what a life. Like night and day...fire and ice.*

~ * ~

Lisa tried to determine why she was attracted to either Daniel Walker or Drexl von Dorff. Since they were exact opposites, she nearly gave up before she started because they were too different for comparison.

After that first night, Dan spoke to Alice, plainly asking permission to see Lisa. A very gentlemanly thing to do...if one were living a century and a half earlier. *Gentlemanly*...it was practically an insult but there was no other way to describe his actions. That word fit him perfectly and she couldn't see him as anything but a Victorian suitor. Asking her aunt's permission...*really*. She hoped he didn't have any of the hidden vices some Victorians were reputed to have. Drex, on the other hand...

Though Drexl von Dorff continued putting in appearances, somehow his path and Dan's never crossed, as if he knew the doctor was also seeing Lisa and when. He had a habit of appearing unexpectedly, occasionally heralding his arrival with a phone call. He was polite to Alice but didn't ask her permission for anything. Drex walked in, told Lisa they were going, and away they went.

Dan's visits coincided with the days he wasn't on call, which were infrequent. He'd never actually said so but Lisa had a feeling until she came along, his entire life had revolved around his practice and the hospital. With a feeling of dismay, she realized he was attempting to fit her into that routine also.

Drex was unpredictable and Dan wasn't and she liked them both...

~ * ~

She'd seen Drex briefly that morning when he stopped by on his way to the airport. Unannounced, as usual.

"Got a business emergency," he told her. "Probably take a few weeks to straighten out but I'll definitely be back by the end of October." He paused before muttering under his breath, "I *have* to be."

"What's so important about October?" she wanted to know. She tried to remember what Martha had told her. Something about his having business holdings up North. Goodness knows Drex never said anything concerning where his money came from.

Instead of answering, he kissed her on the forehead. "Got to go. See you when I get back. Behave yourself."

~ * ~

Lisa was definitely *not* behaving herself because immediately afterward, Dan called and now she was getting ready to go out with him with no feelings of guilt whatsoever.

At first, she'd thought it mere loneliness making her accept Dan's invitations but the more she saw him, the more she was aware of a growing feeling of affection. It wasn't the same as the way she felt about Drex, however. That was more a sensation of excitement, of doing something forbidden. *The Bad Boy Syndrome.* But Dan...? The longer they were together, the more he seemed to unbend, becoming relaxed and...for wont of a better description... uninhibited, though he was nowhere near as outgoing and spontaneous as Drex. She doubted if he would ever be, even if they knew each other a century. *Did I say fire and ice?* If there was anything cold in Dr. Daniel Walker's veins, it was rapidly melting.

Any date they had was based on the assumption no one was going to fall down a flight of stairs or get hit by a car or any of a hundred calamities calling him back to the hospital and leaving Lisa sitting at home waiting. So far, they'd had seven dates, five of which began and ended with Dan appearing at her door and the simultaneous buzzing of the cell phone in his pocket. It didn't pay to be the only orthopedist in town and she selfishly found herself wishing Temple would have a growth-spurt and another specialist would appear, giving him some competition.

She hoped tonight would be accident-free.

Studying herself in the mirror as she slipped out of her robe and reached for bra and panties, Lisa decided she was in pretty good shape for the shape she was in. She was short, barely reaching five-two and she'd always been small-breasted. Rob had once joked he had to have a magnifying glass to find them. They felt so heavy now, veins delicately blue under the skin in contrast to the rosy pink of her nipples. Cupping each, Lisa allowed herself a moment's sadness. *If only you could see them now, Robin. We'd have a good laugh about that, wouldn't we? And then you'd kiss each one, and...* No need to think about that. Not now. She looked at the reflected image of her stomach.

Rounded over the top of her bikini panties, but not overly-large yet. No muffin-top, at least. After all it wasn't quite her third month. Remembering her twenty-three inch waist, she felt enormous. *Should I be showing? Already?* Timidly, she touched the slight swell as if doing so with other than gentleness might shatter the fragile creature within her. *Not too fragile. He survived the car crash, didn't he? One thing's for sure,* she told her reflection. *Neither of them is after your fair and slender body.*

Not right now, anyway.

~ * ~

They drove to Jekyll Island to the *Corsair* where they had dinner.

The only way to the island was by the Sidney Lanier Bridge, one much larger and stronger-looking than the one Robin crossed from the mainland to Land's End Island. For Lisa, it was equally as frightening. In a weird association, she remembered what had happened forty years before.

The sixteen-year-old Sidney Lanier was a drawbridge. As the *African Neptune* headed out of port at Brunswick and attempted to go through the draw span, it crashed against it. Cars stopped on the bridge plunged eighty feet into the water as three sections collapsed.

As she looked down at the black expanse of water on both sides, all she could think of was riding with Robin, how tense everything had been...how quiet...the dark, the water…what if they'd driven off the bridge? What if it had collapsed? For a moment, her stomach quailed as if it could feel that downward plunge…of being swallowed by cold, wet darkness…

Unconsciously, she seized the armrest, fingers gripping it tightly.

"Relax, Lisa." Dan's remark told her he'd seen that frightened movement. "This bridge is completely safe."

"What makes you think I'm afraid?" *It's safe all right… as long as no ships are around.* Ten people died and many of the bodies were never recovered while others washed up on Jekyll's beaches. He had to know about that.

"Because you're hanging onto that armrest as if it's a life preserver."

She jerked her hand away, dropping it into her lap.

"Guess I didn't think this out too well," he sighed. He also remembered when the ship rammed the bridge, one of the few times Brunswick hit the national newscasts. He hadn't thought Lisa would know about it and somehow link it to her own memories of what happened to her and her husband. "Do you want to turn back? If you're…"

"You can't very well do a U-turn on a bridge, can you?" She tried to keep her voice light.

"When we reach the other side, we can turn around."

"It's okay. I'll be all right. I can't avoid bridges all my life just because they remind me of what happened." She wondered how many people had done just that, especially after the *Ziemia Bialostocka* also struck the bridge in 1987.

"That's true, but we can avoid this one tonight, if you want."

"I don't. After all, the bridge we were on didn't collapse." She made the statement decisive. *Dan's driving slowly. There's no danger. I'm being silly. This is perfectly safe.* "Besides, I'm hungry and I'm looking forward to eating at the *Corsair*."

"Ah, the appetite wins out every time." He laughed.

Dropping her hand to her side where he couldn't see, she clenched it into a fist, making herself join in his laughter, pretending interest by asking, "Is this still a drawbridge?"

"Not now. The old bridge was replaced in 2003 with a larger, cable-stayed one," he answered. "That eliminated the need for a drawbridge." It also made it safer for large ships to enter the port.

Leaning back, Lisa smiled at Dan. She didn't relax, however, until they were off the bridge and on the island itself. Only then did her fist loosen and her fingers open.

~ * ~

Afterward, as the car swung back onto the Coast Road once more, he asked, a little too casually, "Want to stop by my apartment?"

"Sure." She made her answer just as casual. "As long as you're not planning a seduction. I don't think I need to point out I'm not exactly in the shape for it right now." She patted the little bulge of her stomach. She always made a point not to sit with her hands folded over it, thinking nothing uglier than a pregnant woman with her hands clasped around her belly Humpty Dumpty-style. "Which I just did, didn't I?"

Giving her such a long and thoughtful stare she began to feel uneasy, he agreed with an extravagant sigh of disappointment, "Yes, I can see seduction's out of the question...tonight."

He turned the car onto the street running to the Seacrest.

Number 6, Seacrest. Lisa knew his address. While in the hospital, she'd made a point to find out, having Martha look it up in the directory at one of the pay phones in the lobby. She still didn't know why she'd wanted that bit of information. Just curious? Maybe.

Drex wasn't listed, of course...or perhaps he had a private number.

The Seacrest was part of Temple's claim to fame, a very expensive, very exclusive condo complex. Martha had been sarcastic as she said that because Temple possessed so many features out of place in such a small town, Temple General and the Seacrest being two of them. The reason was because it was the site of several businesses. The hospital was a well-equipped one, and many doctors from surrounding larger towns, including Macon, Brunswick, and Savannah were also on the staff. Dan might be the only one of his specialty in Temple but TempeGen's doctors were a well-diversified lot.

Dan parked the car in an adjoining lot studded with live oaks and flowerscaped medians. Tucking her hand against his arm, he led her to the front of the long structure which looked more like an office complex than an apartment building. A man in the dark uniform of a security guard opened the glass door. "'Evening, Dr. Walker."

"Hello, Sam." Dan nodded as he and Lisa came inside. Except for the guard's console holding a dozen closed circuit computer screens, the interior was completely bare...no chairs, no potted plants, not even an elevator...only two hallways leading right and left and double glass doors at the back. "Quiet tonight?"

"Isn't it always?" The man smiled at Lisa. "'Evening, Mrs. Chambers."

Giving him a wordless smile, Lisa waited until they were crossing the lobby-like expanse before she whispered, "How did he know who I am?"

"Small town, remember?" Dan patted her hand. "By tomorrow, I imagine all the old biddies will be gathering around their morning coffees exclaiming how that young doctor and the pregnant Widow Chambers had a wild evening in his bachelor digs."

She stifled a nervous giggle as he opened the double glass doors before them with a key card. "We're going back outside?"

"I can see you've never been to the Seacrest." He gestured and she looked out.

The building they were in formed an enormous rectangle, built around eight smaller buildings appearing to be cottages. Lights shone from the windows of one, the others were dark. Behind the cottages was a long bare area. Space for future residents?

"Now this is interesting." She stepped through the doors, waiting as he pulled them shut and joined her.

"The surrounding building houses management, maintenance, and security, with apartments for all personnel," he explained. "This is probably one of the safest places in Temple. Like there's so much potential for danger around here." He took Lisa's arm again, gesturing. "Mine's in the second row."

They went down the steps and through a little park, walking on pink marbled flagstones. Every six feet was lighted by a lantern-shaped lamp so trees and shrubs were plainly visible. The park gave way to a short street leading to the first three condos. A small stake driven into the soil had an arrow affixed to it. On the arrow was written in white paint, *Pseudo-Millionaire's Avenue.*

"One of my neighbors has a sense of humor." Crossing it, Dan turned right, walking toward the condo at the end of the row. "None of us have anywhere near a million dollars...yet."

"Kind of puts a lie to the idea of doctors being underpaid, doesn't it?" Lisa remarked.

"Compared to some places, *I* am." He gave her a sideways glance. "But who's complaining?"

Though they all looked alike from the outside and the backyards were encircled by stone walls, each condo had its own landscaping and outdoor furniture in a variety of styles.

Using the key card again, Dan opened the front door and stepped back, allowing her to enter.

"Give me that shawl and I'll hang it up for you." He was busily punching in a code to the security system by the door.

"Stole," she corrected.

"Stole, shawl, whatever...give me that thing you've got around your shoulders."

Relinquishing it, she started into the living room.

"Watch your step," he called, and she looked down to see two short steps. She walked down them and glanced around.

Set at right angles to each other, a crimson sectional divided by a table and lamp dominated the room. Matching slatted-armed Morris chairs faced them across a slate-topped cocktail table. No television was visible but there was an elaborate sound system in a carved cabinet in the same style as the rest of the furniture. Behind the sofa, a heavy buffet served as a bar, with crystal decanters filling the hutch.

"It's in the bedroom," he said, shutting the closet door and tossing his own jacket onto the sofa.

"What is?" She looked back at him.

"The television…a 48-inch flat screen which I rarely watch because I usually fall asleep. Don't know why I even have one." He came down the steps and stopped beside her. "Well, what do you think?"

She studied the room. The carpet had a Moorish design, crimson and gold, matching the deep red of the upholstery perfectly, just as the pale gold of the walls and the decorative border encircling near the ceiling reflected the floors also. Whoever decorated the room definitely had Dan in mind, she thought. The rich hues complemented his dark coloring perfectly.

"What style is this?" She touched the top of the intricately carved end table, a squared, bulky piece with lattice-work openings at the top of the door. "It looks familiar."

"Mission style," he answered. "You can see it in any *Zorro* movie."

"Of course," she agreed. "I recognize it now. Especially *that*." She gestured at the trestle table in an adjoining room, six straight-backed chairs gathered around it. It was lit by a chandelier consisting of three rectangular lanterns hanging from chains attached to a wooden base.

There was a tapestry on the wall to the left of the dining room. On closer examination, she saw it was a Navajo blanket, Large pieces of pottery were in the armoire holding the stereo, as well as several smaller ones displayed on the end tables.

"Those are beautiful."

"That one was made to hold cornmeal." He pointed at a large round pot with ochre and crimson designs. "The one with the double neck..." He gestured. "That's a wedding vase. It's Acoma. Lucy Lewis."

The name meant nothing to Lisa. She decided it must be the name of an artist well-known to anyone having a knowledge of Southwestern pottery. "You sound as if you know a little about it."

"I spent the summer in Arizona and New Mexico before entering med school. Got that big pot while I was there."

"Is it expensive?"

"I got it cheap. Now it's probably worth a couple of thousand." He said it off-handedly, adding, "The love and work put into creating it makes it priceless."

"I like it...the whole place." She nodded. "These deep rich colors suit you. But why a California Mission theme? I mean, I can understand the Native American influence." She paused, wondering if he minded any reference to his mixed background, then went on, "But …"

"You can thank Mom for the décor. She's an interior decorator and I was told, rather severely, that since I've a very talented relative who'd do it for free, I wasn't going to pay anyone to set up this place for me. Mama's Little Boy, however, had ideas of his own about how he wanted his place to look, and he wanted it to show off his *treasures*. This…" He waved a hand. "…is our compromise."

"Are you really Mama's Little Boy?" she couldn't help asking.

"She likes to think so."

"There's something I'm wondering." She was glad he'd halfway given her an opening for her next question.

"What's that?"

"Do you have an Ind…a Native American Name? *Daniel* has such a Biblical ring to it."

"Of course, I do. My father made certain I was registered as a Native American when I was born…but I can't tell it to you."

"Why not?"

"It's secret. Tell a man your name and he has power over you."

"I'm not a man," she pointed out. "So that doesn't count."

"I'm afraid *man* in this case means *anyone not Creek*. I'll tell you my great-great-great-great-grandfather's name, though. Since he's long gone I don't think it'll matter."

"Okay…what was it?"

"Hviketv-Kats-al-Ka."

"My God, that's a mouthful. Did they call him all that?"

"I think it was shortened to *Katsal-Ka* by the whites. It means *Crawling Panther.*"

That gave Lisa a mental picture of a man edging silently through the brush, a giant black cat creeping up on its prey.

"He was Yamacraw, *Katca'lgi*," Dan went on. "The Panther section of the *Kowakatcu'lgi*, the Wildcat Clan. They were Red Sticks. That meant they were ready to fight when necessary." He smiled. "He was their *hilis haya*, their healer, so I guess being doctors runs in our family."

"How does one get *Walker* out of *huh-ee-ket-tuh khats-all-cah*? She tried to say it the way he had and knew she mangled it terribly.

"One doesn't." He laughed at her stumbling attempt. "My grandfather decided to anglicize the name into something acceptable in the white man's language but he refused to be known as *Panther*. *Crawler* didn't sound so great either, so he stretched it a bit and made it *Walker* instead."

"If he hadn't, you'd have been *Daniel Crawler*?"

"Sounds pretty bad when you put it like that."

"What would you call me...if I were Native American? What would be my secret name?"

"I don't even have to think about that," His answer was so quick she thought perhaps he *had* thought about it. At great length. "*Catē hv·se hok·tē* ... "*Red Sun Woman*."

"You sound as if you know a lot about your...Katsal-Ka." *Red Sun Woman, huh?* He'd definitely not pulled *that* out of thin air.

"When I was younger, my class got the genealogy bug...I was especially hooked. I found out everything I could learn about him. Nearly drove my Grandpa and Grandma Walker wild with my questions." He laughed. "Got an *A* on my report, by the way." He fell silent, looking at her as if making a decision. "Would you like to see something belonging to him?"

"I'd love to see it." She turned toward the armoire, looking at the items on the shelves. "I imagine it's pretty fragile, isn't it?" She envisioned a minute scrap of rawhide from a moccasin, or a bit of beaded blanket. "Which is it?"

"It's not in there." She turned to look back at him. He was unbuttoning his shirt.

"What are you...?"

He reached through the open shirt front, drawing out something on a silver chain. Resting it on his palm, he held it out for her to see. Lisa cupped his hand in hers, staring at the object he held.

A flat disk about the size of a silver dollar. It was fashioned of clay, covered with a dark red glaze. A hollow piece of metal had been pressed into the unfired clay, forming a narrow trough. After it was fired and glazed, crushed shells mixed with mortar were pressed into the hollow, forming the shape of a leaping cat.

"Grandma gave it to me when I graduated from high school," he explained. Lisa touched the disk. It was smooth and cool. "She said since I was the only one in the family since Katsal-Ka who was going to be a healer, I had the right to have it. It's supposed to keep me safe from the evil things causing sickness and help me vanquish them."

"Guess it's working, isn't it?" She smiled and released his hand.

"Would you like a drink?" He tucked the medallion back inside his shirt, closing the three buttons.

More out of surprise than because she wanted one, Lisa nodded. He disappeared through a swinging door on the other side of the armoire, giving her time to think about what he'd said.

There was the sound of a refrigerator opening and closing, the clink of ice and of liquid being poured. When he reappeared, he held an ice-filled highball glass in one hand and an opaque ruby-colored crystal goblet in the other. He held out the goblet.

Taking it, she looked at its contents and began to laugh. It was filled with milk. Shoulders shaking, she sat on the sofa.

"What's so funny?" Dan perched on the edge of the coffee table, facing her.

"This." She held up the glass. "It surprised me when you offered me a drink, and when I saw the size of this goblet, I thought, *if he expects me to drink all that, he must want to get me drunk*, and…it's milk…" She began to laugh again, leaning forward to place a hand on his knee. "I should've known."

"You'll get no alcohol from me, young lady." Slipping his hand under hers, Dan lifted it to his lips. That stopped her laugher. She looked at him, startled. If he'd been Drex, she wouldn't have been surprised…but

Dan doing such a thing? "I hope you've noticed I haven't lit a cigarette all night."

"I did." Knowing what a chain smoker he was, she was touched. "Thank you."

"Don't worry," he broke off with a grin. "I can stand it for a few hours without going into withdrawal."

"If you start shaking and rush me out of here, I'll know you're lying." She smiled again.

"That's better." Setting down his drink, he caught her hand between both of his. "You've been so quiet this evening, I was afraid I'd done something to make you angry, and I swear I'm trying to behave."

"I've been thinking," she began, wishing he *would* misbehave, just a little.

"Better watch that," he cautioned. "If you think too much, your baby'll be born all red and wrinkled."

"There was a minute right after you called, when I almost changed my mind about coming with you tonight," she told him, gently extricating her hand. She took a sip of milk, lowering the glass to trace around the rim with her forefinger, not looking at him.

"Not getting tired of me, are you?" His tone was light but in that moment, they both became serious.

"I had another of those *Why don't you act like a widow* moments," she sighed, looking up at him. "But I wanted to go out and be happy and…" Her voice trailed away. She studied the glass again, hearing Dan raise his own drink, ice cubes clashing together.

He didn't answer and she couldn't tell if that was encouraging or not, so she went on, "I think the whole problem is…I don't feel pregnant. I mean, I know I am…I've had morning sickness and I've felt the baby move, but..." She stumbled to a halt, trying to put into words once and for all the way she felt.

Dan's silence wasn't helping. She looked up to find him staring at her. He set his glass on the table but still didn't speak.

"A man and a woman make love, then she starts feeling a little sick and goes to the doctor and it's *Congratulations, the rabbit died.* She goes home and says, *Guess what, dear? I'm pregnant.* But that didn't happen with me. Our car hit a tree and I was knocked into the middle of three weeks later to wake up with a broken leg and Robin dead...and six weeks after that, I'm pregnant." When he nodded as if he understood her long-winded rambling, she felt relieved.

"Cause and effect," he said quietly. "That's understandable. Too much trauma happened between the last time you and your husband had sex and you finding out about the baby for you to associate the two."

Getting to his feet, he went to the bar. He replenished his drink but the real reason was so she wouldn't see the jealous flush darkening his face as he realized even though the dead man had been her husband, he didn't want to think of someone sleeping with her...unless that someone was himself.

"Guess it's a good thing you found out before you went home." He splashed Scotch into his glass.

"Why do you say that?" She was making short work of the milk. Her speech had made her thirsty.

"Can you imagine how it would've looked if you found out you were pregnant *after* being released from the hospital? That'd really give the wagging tongues something to talk about."

"I'll probably give them more than that before I'm finished because I refuse to hole up in my house like I've done something wrong." That made him sorry he'd said it. She shrugged. "In fact..." Her chin lifted. "I think I'm absolutely finished with this subject."

"That's the girl." Leaving his drink on the bar, he sat in the chair opposite her. "And I'm going to do my part to keep you out of that house as much as I can."

"In that case," she grinned. "You'd better keep Dr. Halyard's number handy...in case you keep me out *too* long."

"I'm a doctor, too, remember? I can boil water with the best of them. Got clean towels and a queen-sized bed in the other room, too." He was on his feet, retrieving his glass and raising it to hide his expression as he decided if he ever got Lisa into his bed, it'd be for something other than delivering her baby. The directness of the thought startled him, as did the one following it. *She's the one. Oh my God...*

In spite of what he told Lisa, and had been telling himself for eight years, he'd never really gotten over the blow to his ego when Kathy Connor married his best friend. He'd had women before and afterward. He'd gotten serious about one other, also, lost her, too, but neither she nor any of the others affected him as quickly or completely as Lisa had, though he'd refused to acknowledge it. With a suddenness leaving him stunned, he knew she was going to be the one to forever drive the memory of any other woman from his heart. In that instant, Kathy and the rest were gone and he didn't regret it a bit.

I went out of my way to get involved and by damn, I'm involved with a vengeance. Any uncertainty was gone. *Damn it, love at first sight* does *exist.* Now he understood the emotion he felt when he first saw Lisa. He wanted her desperately. If she were willing, he'd make love to her this very minute... *No, I wouldn't.* There'd be no affair with a woman who still loved her dead husband, even if she was with another man right then. The way he felt for Lisa was more than serious and if it were in his power, he was going to make it permanent. *And, being who you are, you'll probably never say any of this to her, and you'll lose her, you idiot.* Stunned by that revelation, he lowered his drink, staring at it and thinking he must be crazy or at best merely a fool.

Unaware of his turmoil, Lisa got up, walking to the windows looking out over the backyard. Around the edge of the patio, lanterns flickered over bordering plants and shrubs.

Dan planted himself behind her, putting a hand on her arm. She looked up at him and smiled but didn't move away. Her hair hung over one shoulder, leaving the side of her neck bare. He wanted to kiss that pale spot but forced himself to stay where he was.

"You'll be a good father, Dan." She turned back to her contemplation of the night outside the window.

"What?" He shook off the daze of emotions to stare at her.

"The way you worry about me. Making sure I eat properly when we go out...the milk..." she gestured at the glass sitting on the coffee table. "Always caring about my welfare..."

"It's very important for this particular child to be born as healthy as possible." *Not just for you but for me, too, Lisa.* Taking one of her hands, he clasped it tightly. "When this is over and you hold that baby in your arms, I want you to be completely happy. Brad and I are going to do our best to make certain that happens."

Lisa looked away, not wanting him to see the gleam of tears his words brought to her eyes.

"If you think I'll be such a great father," he went on. "What do you suppose my hypothetical child's mother will say? Think I'll be a good husband?" *Your husband?* He didn't say that.

"You will," she told him. "If you treat her as you do me."

"It may take more than that." He shook his head. "If there's anything more difficult than being a doctor, it's being a doctor's wife. She'll have to be extremely understanding."

"Wasn't Kathy Halyard understanding enough?" The words were out before she could stop them, making her wish she'd bitten her tongue.

"Sure." He sighed but didn't look particularly distressed. Not now. "She simply had the wrong doctor. Once she switched from orthopedics to obstetrics, everything was fine. I—"

His cell began to buzz. He fished it out of his jacket pocket. "Excuse me a minute."

He disappeared into the bedroom, pressing the Speed-Dial button connecting him to the on-call switchboard.

"Dr. Walker…When? Okay, get him to x-ray…I'll be there in fifteen minutes…" He came out, picking up his jacket. "Perfect example of what I'm talking about. A twelve-year-old who thinks he's Evel Knievel. He tried to ride his bike across the top of a brick wall. I've got to go."

As he was talking, she retrieved her stole from the closet.

"What do you think my wife would do now?" he asked, shrugging into his jacket.

"She'd sigh and tell you to get going." *As I've done all those other times*. She wrapped the stole around her shoulders before he could help her.

"I'll take you home, and…"

"That's not necessary," she protested. "Just call me a cab."

"Okay, you're a cab." They both laughed.

"I can wait here until it comes. That security guy…Sam?…can let me know when it arrives. You go on to the hospital. That little boy's more important than your taking me home."

He didn't argue, instead phoned the cab company. As he replaced the receiver, he hurried over to the security grid, punching in four numbers. "When you go out, hit 5. That'll set the lock." He opened the door. "I'll tell Sam to call you when the cab gets here." He tapped the inter-com above the grid. "Hit *Receive* to listen, *Send* to speak."

By now, he had the door open, then stopped and came back to where she stood. Catching her face in his hands, he kissed her. It was a hard little kiss, no more than a peck on the lips but the passion behind it startled her. His hands slid to her shoulders and then, he pulled away, hurrying through the door which shut after him.

~ * ~

The Human beguiles her. Faraway, M'AneseNebh growled in anger. *While I'm not there to free her from his web.* A clawed fist clenched in fury. *Father, far-reaching Tschenebhua, watch over her from your prison. Send forth your magic to quell his own, I beg you...*

Chapter 13

"There's something I'd like to talk to you about before we go," Dan said as he came through the door.

"Okay." Following him down the hall, she watched the movement of his shoulders as he walked ahead of her. He seemed to fill the little foyer. *When did he get so tall or have I been completely unobservant?*

Once seated on the sofa, he began, "Lisa, I want to—"

Timothy caused a minor interruption. Coming through the doorway and seeing his favorite doctor, he launched himself at Dan, giving a yowl of welcome.

"Hi, Timothy." Dan gave the silver head a perfunctory caress and placed the cat on the cushion beside him. "As I was saying…" Timothy insinuated his fluffy body under Dan's arm, butting him in the chest. A thick rumble rolled from his throat as he cuffed Dan's hand, rubbing his head against it. "Go on, Tim. I'm busy." He brushed the cat off his lap.

Timothy landed on his feet, blinking as if he couldn't believe he was being ignored.

"That cat's worse than a maiden aunt," Dan said with irritation, adding, "No offence to Miz Townsend. This is difficult enough to say as it is, without—"

Undaunted, Timothy tried once more. He crouched, leaped, and landed on Dan's knees where he balanced on his hind legs, a paw reaching up to tap the doctor's chin.

"I give up." With a rueful laugh, Dan looked into Timothy's eyes. The cat blinked. "Okay, Tim, you win." He began to scratch the cat's ears as he stood up, Timothy in his arms. "Guess we'd better be on our way."

"What were you going to say?" Lisa asked.

"Never mind, it'll keep. Until a time when your whiskered chaperone isn't around." Setting the cat on the sofa, he took Lisa's arm. "Maybe he's trying to tell me this isn't the right time to say it anyway."

Timothy meowed a farewell as they went out the door.

To break the sudden silence, Lisa asked, "How do you like my new dress?" She moved away, whirling in front of him. "I know I'm not quite ready for maternity clothes but my old ones are getting a little tight and it gave me a good excuse to go shopping."

"I'm not too knowledgeable on women's fashions." He'd never truly paid much attention to such things unless they were too absurd. Frankly, he liked his women out of their clothes. "All I know is I know what I like." He stepped back, studying her critically. The dress was sleeveless and flared slightly, made of some soft material. He guessed it was what was called a shift. The color almost matched her eyes. It had just enough of a hint of green to make her hair gleam like a new penny. Dan took a long time answering because it was such a damned pleasure looking at her. At last he said, "I like it."

"Whew…that was close." She wiped imaginary sweat off her forehead, then leaned toward him, whispering, "Like I was really worried."

He opened the car door and waited until she was settled before asking, "Ever been to St. Simons and Fort Frederica?"

"Robin promised to take me." There was only the slightest hesitation as she spoke her husband's name. "But we never got the chance."

"You're going to get it today," he promised.

~ * ~

They drove over another silver bridge and down another soft and sandy moss-hung road. This time Lisa didn't look at the water or allow herself the slightest tremor.

~ * ~

Fort Frederica was built in 1736 to protect James Oglethorpe's *debatable land*, as Georgia was known, from Spanish invasion. It was named for Frederick Louis, then-Prince of Wales. Once the Spanish were driven out at the Battle of Bloody Marsh in 1742, the Garrison was disbanded, and the soldiers, in the form of the 42nd Regiment of Foot, departed. The colonists followed soon after and by 1758, the island was abandoned, staying that way until 1900 when interest in excavating the area arose. By 1942, the fort and surrounds had come under the Georgia Park Service.

~ * ~

Lisa delighted in the little gray stone museum with its miniature cannon which was fired hourly by one of the rangers. She crossed the bridge under the high cedars, wandering down the path to the area where the town had stood. Running ahead of Dan, she called back to him like a child, urging him to "Hurry..." Leaves crackling under his feet, he followed behind her into the marked-off area where the foundations had been excavated.

This year, fall was late in coming to the islands. Though some of the trees were already losing their leaves, the flowers were still in full bloom. In the muddy ditch running under the bridge, alliums displayed purple balls of blossoms on tall green stalks, profuse in the damp and shadowy trench. Wisteria hung in grape-like lavender bunches while brilliant orange trumpet creepers twined and draped themselves through the branches of thick-trunked cedars.

The sea breeze blew past them, did an about-face under the bridge and swooped into a pile of leaves a groundskeeper had neatly raked to one side of the footpath. They sailed into the air as the wind bounced off a live oak and curled toward them again. It caught Lisa's skirt, lifting it about her knees then reached up to tangle her hair over her face.

Laughing, she brushed back her hair while the other hand clutched at her skirt. She gave up trying to hold her hair, catching at the skirt with both hands, and Dan stood still, unashamedly admiring the unhampered view of her legs. He had a glimpse of a slender thigh before the wind tired of its game and dashed away. *I really did a good job. The scars barely show.* The rest of his observations were completely unprofessional, wholly personal, and a sensual fantasy...

In dark coolness, Lisa danced toward him on those slim legs, arms outstretched, body beckoning...he felt his cock jerk, Oh God, woman, I want you by me always…

"Hey, daydreamer." A warm hand slipped into his. "Come on." Tugging on his arm, she began to run. Dan allowed himself to be pulled down the path.

At the little promontory jutting into the sea, she looked at the black iron cannon and the sea-eaten shell-mortared husk remaining of the original outpost, the barrier the colonists built against the attacking Spanish. The wind puffed up again, making her shiver.

"Oh look." She pointed at something on the slope below them.

Crabs…hundreds of them, sunning on the sand-bagged bank which was the only thing keeping Fort Frederica from slipping back into the waves. Tiny pink disks, none over three inches long, each with an overly-large and unwieldy claw.

"Fiddler crabs." He laughed and tried to catch one. It skittered across his shoe to safety. "Fast li'l buggers, aren't they?"

Together they walked down what had been the main street, where the barest edges of stones rose from the dirt to show where the houses had been. She leaned against him and her body was warm and soft and he liked that.

They stopped before one excavated area where a door stoop, the remnants of a fireplace and a large square divided into two rooms were embedded in the ground. *The Tavern,* a nearby sign explained.

"It's so small. How could very many people crowd into that little space for a mug of ale on a Saturday night?"

"Maybe they had curb...carriage service," he suggested.

"It's interesting, but so sad." She shook her head. "All these people, risking so much to come here and settle this place. And now...they're gone."

"Not gone," he answered. "They're still here."

"What do you mean?" She looked around as if expecting to see the ghosts of long-dead settlers surrounding them.

"Somewhere, maybe not here, perhaps not even in Georgia, but somewhere in the world, their descendants are alive, and those long-dead colonists still live in them."

"I never thought about that." She sat on the low wall of a nearby house, looking up at him, hand shielding her eyes. The wind was beginning to blow from the water again and it fluttered her hair about her shoulders. He pushed back a wisp curling around her cheek, fingers brushing her face.

"You should." He became very serious, pressing one hand against his chest. "We're all someone's immortality, Lisa. Think about it. My great-great-great-great-grandfather died over two hundred and fifty years ago but because I'm alive, he is, too." He studied her expression, misinterpreting it. "I suppose you think that's pretty weird."

"Not necessarily," she surprised him with her answer. "I should've known it. It's been with me all along." She touched the rise of her stomach. "Robin's immortality. I just never thought about it."

Selfishly, that hadn't occurred to him either, so he didn't reply.

"These people were living when Katsal-Ka was." That made her remember that Drex's ancestors had been here about the same time. "Why do you hate Drex so much?"

The question, seemingly coming from nowhere made him go still. With a sigh, he looked out over the water. "Don't spoil a nice afternoon, Lisa."

"I'd like to know. You don't try to hide it so what am I supposed to do but wonder?"

There was a sugarberry growing near the wall, hacked down and cut back until it was little more than a shrub instead of a tree. He pulled a leaf from a thin branch, shredding it into tiny green flakes. "Know much about the Native Americans who lived around here?"

"Nothing other than what you told me the other night."

"Then you already know more than most. Here's what you don't know. Katsal-Ka opposed the sale of Land's End Island to Drex's ancestor." Throwing the bits of leaf to the ground, he went on, hoping to get it said and make the subject die once and for all. "He felt it was wrong to let anyone, much less some stupid white man, settle on land the gods had cursed. That it'd cause greater evil."

"Why did they think the island was cursed?"

"They believed an evil god, something they called a *cetto thlot-lo*—it roughly translates to *snake-fish*—lived there. In fact, the island's original name was *Cetto-cuko, Snake House*. And the man who bought it became known as *Cetto-Hanhkv, snake monster man*."

161

Dan looked across the lawn at the stone markers breaking the green expanse like little tombstones. Again, he touched his chest in that same spot.

"Katsal-Ka always hoped the Yamacraw would get it back but before that could happen, all the Creeks were driven from Georgia."

"And you hate him for that?" She looked at him in amazement. "For something neither of you had any control over?"

"The wind's changing." He ignored her question. "Look at those waves." They were splashing against the sandbags. "Want to go for a walk on the beach?" He held out this hand.

She took it, allowing him to change the subject.

~ * ~

They drove to the end of the island where the Coast Guard Station was housed. Beyond that point, a wild tangle of palmetto and sea oats fought for supremacy against the sand. At the edge of the beach a boundary of rock lay tumbled into a high mound, bleak and dark against the water. The beach was deserted and the only lights were those from a little motel several hundred yards away.

Taking off her sandals, Lisa wiggled her toes into the soft white sand. The tide was out and they walked between swaying clumps of sea oats to the water's edge. A deep dip in the beach had filled with water as the tide receded and in it a trapped fish splashed waiting for high tide.

Behind them the lighthouse rose tall and white.

"It's so quiet. So…isolated."

"I hope they never develop this area." Once more, Dan's hand brushed his chest. "They'll ruin it if they do. I'd hate to see it end up as overcrowded as Savannah Beach with wall-to-wall bodies." He let his hand drop.

"That's the third time you've done that," Lisa said.

"Done what?" His look was so innocent she wondered if he didn't realize what he'd been doing.

"Touched your chest. Right there." She pointed just under his collar bone, not seeming to notice how he started slightly. "Back when we were at Fort Frederica. You've done it three times, rubbed that same spot, then let your hand fall."

"Oh." He gave an embarrassed little laugh. "My medallion. I'm not wearing it. The chain broke, and...I keep forgetting. It feels so odd, because I've worn the thing for nearly thirteen years now and suddenly...I'm without it and I feel...strange...like part of me is missing." He touched the spot where Lisa's fingers had brushed. "I touch there, then remember. Sorry." To change the subject, he caught her hand, swinging her around. "I didn't bring you here to talk about my good luck charm. I thought we might hunt for seashells or something."

"Okay." Lisa looked around. "Look, there's one." She bent to dig something out of the sand, a half-curve of an angel wing. "Oh, it's broken." Disappointed, she tossed it into the water. It sank with barely a splash. Three gray, v-shaped silhouettes glided lazily above the water. She pointed upward. "Look, Dan, seagulls!"

He didn't answer. Eyes on the circling gulls, Lisa felt his hands on her shoulders, turning her toward him. She looked up at him.

"What…"

The rest of her words were stifled by Dan's mouth coming down on hers. She leaned against him, allowing herself to be held tightly. Soft. Pliant. *Lisa, my darling*…he raised his head to whisper the words, then kissed her again. Her arms came up, touching his neck, encircling it. Lips touching her throat, he raised a hand, brushing against her breast…

Don't touch my woman. The voice was so loud it sounded as if shouted into his ear. Dan jerked back.

"Don't…" With surprising strength, Lisa pulled away, whispering frantically, "Stop."

"What is it?" Startled by that shout as well as her abrupt rejection, he released her so quickly she nearly fell, staggering backward a few feet before regaining her balance.

"I thought I could trust you." Her face held a look of complete betrayal. "I should've known better."

"Trust me?" He didn't understand. *What the Hell…? Who yelled?* "Of course you can trust me."

"Su-u-ure I can." *Why am I angry?* Back stiff with fury, she whirled and stamped across the sand to where the car was parked. "And I can trust your roving fingers, too!"

"Wait a minute." He caught up with her, seizing her arm and spinning her around. He was rougher than he intended and she stumbled, jerking away as he attempted to hold her. "What does that mean?"

"I might've known the first chance you got you'd start pawing me." Eyes flashing, she faced him. *That's not what I want to say.*

"Pawing you?" Emotion darkened his face. "That's crazy. I didn't—"

"So I'm crazy now, am I?" *What's happening?* She was frightened but not by Dan.

"Listen, if I wanted to paw you, I've had plenty of opportunities, and…"

She whirled, resuming her march across the sand. This time he got in front of her, blocking her way. She stopped, hands on hips, demanding, "Do you have something to say?"

"All right…" It came out desperately. "So…maybe I was wrong. I let the sun on the water and the atmosphere get to me and I kissed a very pretty woman I like very much. Maybe I wanted to touch her, too, but, my God, you're blowing this all out of proportion. I thought we were friends…"

"So did I, until you did *that.*"

"What do you take me for? You act as if I were going to rape you or some—" He broke off in disbelief. "Come on. You can't mean…is that what you think? Is it?"

"I'll never trust you again." Lisa glared at him. Dismayed, she heard herself say, "I think you've behaved disgracefully, Dr. Walker." *No, I don't mean that.*

"Very well, Mrs. Chambers." His own voice was cold with both insult and hurt. "If you feel that way, then perhaps we should just…"

Don't say it. He was going to. He could feel the words bubbling out. He was going to utter the words separating them forever and he couldn't help himself. He felt like a puppet, saying what he was told to say. Lisa was staring at him as if she couldn't breathe. Mouth

165

open, eyes wide. *Goddamn, she looked as if she's suffocating.*

She actually began to shake.

"No!" She flung both the word and her body at him so violently he staggered backward. Throwing her arms around his neck, she dragged his head do as she pressed her mouth against his. Whatever else he was going to say was muffled against Lisa's lips.

She felt him stiffen in surprise, then relax as he hesitantly returned the kiss. Lightly, his hands touched her waist. They stood that way for several moments, neither moving, locked together.

When she released him, he gasped and laughed shakily. "Does that mean you aren't mad anymore?"

"I'm sorry." She shook her head "It was silly…crazy…whatever you want to call it. I don't know what happened." She was gabbling, trying to get the words out before whatever happened took control again. She thought she could feel it hovering around them, furious and waiting to pounce. "I don't know why…"

"Shhh." He put a finger to her lips and an arm across her shoulders, hugging her against his side. "Come on. Let's go home."

As they walked back to the car, Dan felt battered, as if he'd been in a brawl…and he didn't understand why.

Behind them, the wind screamed like a disappointed banshee.

~ * ~

Why didn't your magic work? You broke the chain…he was without the shaman's protection…she should've rejected him… With a frantic fist, M'AneseNebh pounded the rock on which he stood, sending bits of stone flying into the water. The ocean here was much harsher than at home, the waves stronger. He'd thought the things sleeping beneath their surface as powerful as his sire, but obviously not. The others convinced him to ask them for help, not continue calling on Tschenebhua. *He's so far away,* they said.

This is my punishment... I may lose her. Father, forgive me... I must get home...

~ * ~

Turning the switch on the hobnail colonial lamp by the bed, Lisa welcomed its warm glow. Timothy, curled between the pillows, raised his head with a sleepy meow.

She was tired, felt as if she'd walked for miles, instead of that short trek across the beach. *Is that what being pregnant does. Saps one's strength?* Maybe she'd done too much today. Everything started off so great, and then that argument with Dan...*What was that about, anyway?* How long had she been wanting Dan to kiss her, and when he did...*of all the silly, stupid...*she still didn't understand why she reacted so. It was as if someone made her say those things.

She didn't blame him for getting angry. When she realized he was going to say they shouldn't see each other again, she knew she had to do something, but she couldn't move. She felt as if someone held her...Throwing herself at him had been the only thing she could do. It was like breaking a spell of some kind.

At least it worked.

Kicking off her sandals, Lisa stripped off her dress, dropping it to the floor. Bra and panties followed. She got her nightgown from the closet and slipped it over her head. At the bed, she stopped, one hand on the coverlet.

"Move, Timothy." The cat looked up at her, blinking sleepily. "I want to go to bed." Timothy didn't move. Between the pillows was a cozy place. "I'm in no mood to argue with you," Lisa told him. "I'm too tired."

The truth was, as soon as she was in Dan's arms, seemingly breaking free from whatever held her, she felt exhausted. Seizing the edge of the bedspread, she flipped both it and the cat into the air

With a thump and a surprised yowl, Timothy landed on the floor. He stared at Lisa, tail twitching, then with extreme dignity, jumped back onto the bed and settled himself in the same spot again. Sighing, Lisa got into bed, rolled onto her side and fell asleep.

~ * ~

She was dreaming and knew it but as before, there was no way to escape except to see the dream through to its end.

She was at Temple General, walking down the pale green corridor. Her legs were heavy and she moved awkwardly, which was understandable, consider her advanced pregnancy. *God, I must be eleven months pregnant!*

A man in a lab coat stood in front of her. She called out to him and he turned. "Dan?" She was so relieved she felt faint. "Oh, Dan…"

"I beg your pardon?" He frowned. "Do I know you?"

"Of course you do. It's Lisa." There wasn't a spark of recognition from him. "Dan, don't you recognize me?"

"Oh…it's Mrs. Chambers, isn't it?" His expression changed. "How are you?"

"I'm pregnant," she said bluntly and when she got no response, asked the question she really wanted to know. "Where's my husband?"

"How should I know? Can't you keep track of him?" Brushing past her, he walked away. "He's not my concern. I only treat living patients."

"Come back. Tell me where he is. You know. I know you do." He continued down the hall as if he didn't hear her. She stumbled after him.

A car blocked the hallway, a white Mustang, its front crumpled and dented, hood bowed up and smashed into the engine block. A man with long red hair was tugging on the half-open door. He looked up as he heard her shuffling steps.

"Do you know where my husband is?" She thought she knew him but when he frowned at her, she decided she was mistaken.

"What does he look like?"

"He's tall and has dark hair."

"Weren't you talking to him?"

"That was Dr. Walker."

"Sorry, haven't seen him." His gaze went to her bulging stomach and he sneered. "Hope you find him fast, lady. You look like you need a husband." He turned back to the car.

Try the door.

"Who said that?" Lisa looked around.

Try the door. She touched the knob of the nearest door leading out of the corridor. *That's right. What you want is in there.*

She went in.

The center of the room was filled with a glowing misty light. As she watched, the haze swirled and rose until it formed a vague human shape. She saw Rob's face and started toward him.

"There you are. I've been looking everywhere..."

He backed out of reach. There was a bright flash and flames burst from the floor. Before Lisa could cry out, they flared, died, and Rob was gone...but something stood in his place...

A foul thing...purplish like a giant sea anemone, stubby appendages weaving and squirming against a fat, thick base. It floated toward her, body stretching, arms elongating into slender tentacles darkening to a deep crimson...Lisa waited for it to touch her.

The tentacles wrapped themselves around her, encircling hips, waist and shoulders. As the thick body pressed itself against hers, even when two tentacles brushed her face, she didn't move, though she was afraid. The suctions on their undersides touched her cheeks and forehead, warm and gentle as tiny kisses. She closed her eyes, a wave of hunger and longing engulfing her...

~ * ~

Lisa came awake. The soft strokes against her face continued...*pat*...*pat*...Opening her eyes, she stared directly into Timothy's, and began to laugh. As she hugged the cat to her chest, ruffling his fur, she glanced at the clock.

Midnight? That can't be.

Switching on the bedside lamp, Lisa squinted at her wristwatch. Its tiny face read two o'clock. "Guess Aunt Allie unplugged the clock again." Her aunt had a habit of doing that, thinking Lisa would sleep longer if she didn't know the actual time. Rolling over, she said, "Let's go back to sleep. There's a lot of night left."

Chapter 14

Dressed in the quilted satin robe Robin gave her for her last birthday, Lisa enjoyed being alone without her aunt hovering. This morning, she'd awakened earlier than Alice and was busy being domestic. With bacon sizzling, she listened to the rhythmic *whoosh-whoosh* of the *Mr. Coffee* plugged in at the kitchen counter. As she was placing the last strip of bacon on a paper towel to drain, she heard a soft thud as something struck the front door, rebounding onto the porch.

Hurrying through the house, she opened the screen and bent to retrieve the morning newspaper. As she straightened, she saw a car parked at the curb, an easily-recognizable copper convertible with a just as familiar red-haired figure in the front seat.

"Drex? What are you doing here?" As she watched, he unfolded his body from the small car, stretched, and loped across the lawn to where she stood. "How long have you been out here?"

"All night but that doesn't matter." He gave her a grin. "I just learned the hard way a Jag isn't built for sleeping...or much else." He touched his back, rubbing it and grimacing with exaggerated pain.

"When did you get back, and why didn't you let me know?"

"Late last night and I didn't want to wake you."

"So you slept in the car? Come on in." Newspaper in hand, she went back into the house.

He followed into the hallway, catching her arm. "Have dinner with me tonight." He spun her around as he said it. "It'll make me feel better."

"Can't."

"Got other plans?" One brow went up. "With who?"

"Whom," she corrected but didn't explain.

"Never mind. I think I know." He didn't look happy. "The Big Chief."

"Drex…"

"Looks like I've got my work cut out for me. Guess that'll teach me to go away and leave him to beat my time with my girl." He touched the satin-trimmed edging around the collar of her robe, idly rubbing it between his fingers.

"I'm not your girl." Lisa shivered slightly. She moved away, extricating the collar from his hand.

"Yes, you are." He took a step closer so she had to tilt her head to look up at him. Too close…too close for comfort. *Danger, Lisa Chambers, danger!*

"Since when?"

"Since always." Obviously their time apart meant more to him than she expected. "I want you, Lisa, and I always get what I want."

His words sent a little chill through her as did his half-expected kiss. The newspaper was forgotten, clutched in her hands. She felt Drex's fingers brush her breasts before he seized her by the shoulders. *Why don't I react as I did when Dan touched me?* She didn't move. He pulled her body against his.

"Lisa? Are you downstairs?"

They moved apart with guilty haste.

"I'm getting the newspaper, Aunt Allie," She was breathing too quickly, face flushed. She could feel the thrust of her breasts against the bosom of the robe, nipples peaking, excited by Drex's touch. As her aunt came down the stairs, Lisa folded her arms across her chest, the pink in her cheeks becoming more pronounced. Drex smirked, *damn him.* "Guess who's here…"

Her voice trailed away as Alice appeared carrying Timothy. She was wearing her scruffy old chenille robe, looking dumpy and frowzy with sleep but she wasn't looking at Lisa. She was staring at Drex. Timothy fell from her arms as she gave an exclamation of dismay.

"Oh my God, why didn't you warn me? I look like a rummage sale." Whirling, she fled back up the stairs, her heelless slippers making a loud *slap-slap* on the carpeted steps.

Timothy picked himself off the rug, looked in Drex's direction, arched his back and hissed, and fled after her.

"Didn't change his attitude while I was gone, did he?" Drex's comment sounded mild but she sensed anger behind it.

"I don't understand," Lisa said. "He seems to like…" She stopped. No use mentioning Timothy's preference for Dan.

"Don't worry about it. It's the cat's problem, not mine." He didn't seem to hear her half-statement. Timothy's behavior didn't appear to worry him, either. "Guess you can tell animals don't like me."

"I'm sorry."

"Don't be. I'm certain Timothy's owner can make up for his lack of manners." He began to nuzzle her on the neck, the warmth of his lips sending little chills down her spine. His laugh was a low, breathy chuckle. "Mmmm. Delicious." He pushed aside her collar, nibbling against her shoulder.

"Stop that." Half-heartedly she slapped his hand away. "She'll be back any minute."

"You're right." He laughed again and raised his head. "You'd better compose yourself."

"Compose my…" She started to answer, then thought better of it. He was right. She was the one looking excited…and guilty. Except for the light in his eyes and that smug, lazy smile, Drex didn't appear affected by the moment's bit of *make-out* at all.

Footsteps on the stairs announced Alice's reappearance. She'd brushed her hair and changed into something Lisa recognized as a caftan. *Where'd she get that?* She'd also applied a dab of lipstick.

"Please excuse me, Drexl." She extended her hand graciously. He took it in his own and with a sideways wink at Lisa, raised it to his lips.

"Were you cooking breakfast, Lisa?" Alice's eyes widened. "You should've let me do that."

"I wanted to feel useful for a change." She'd never seen her aunt look so flustered. Beside her, she felt Drex draw in his breath. Before he could say anything, she added, "You do too much around here."

"In that case…" Alice looked at Drex. "Would you like to join us?"

"My dear Miss Townsend, thank you…but no. I have to get home. Although…a cup of coffee before I go would hit the spot..." Still talking, he followed Alice into the kitchen, leaving Lisa standing there.

~ * ~

Later, as Lisa watched the Jag squeal away from the curb and disappear around the corner, the phone rang. She could hear Alice talking as she entered the kitchen.

"Yes, Clara? Really? No, no...it was a friend. Uh-huh. Bye." She returned the phone to its cradle. "That was Clara Campbell. She says that young man was parked in front of the house all night, asleep in his car."

"Did she stay up all night making sure? " Lisa asked. "Maybe take him a pillow and a blanket?"

"Of course not." As Alice appeared to take her question seriously, Lisa rolled her eyes. "But it definitely shows determination...camping out on your doorstep all night."

Aunt Allie, you don't know the half of it. Lisa picked up her coffee cup and smiled into it and didn't answer.

The kitchen phone rang again. Lisa glanced over at the *Caller ID...Dan Walker...*She looked away with complete indifference as Alice reached to answer it. "Don't, Aunt Allie."

"But it's Dan." Alice checked the *ID* also. The phone rang again, insistently this time.

"Let it ring. It'll go to voice mail." Abruptly, she didn't want to be bothered by Dr. Daniel Walker. "I don't feel like talking to him right now."

"All right..." Alice went back to get her coffee.

The phone rang once more, then stopped before voice mail could activate. For a long moment, Lisa stared at the phone. *Why don't I want to talk to him? I've always looked forward to Dan's calls. Why didn't I this time?*

~ * ~

Twice more during the day the phone rang and twice more, Lisa refused to answer it.

The last time, Alice protested, "That's the third time you've..." Lisa looked up from the magazine she was reading, stopping her with a glare. "Lisa, is something wrong between you and Dan?"

"Of course not." *So what if I ignored his other calls? Don't I have a right to?* "I don't want to be bothered right now." She went back to the magazine. As far as she was concerned that settled it.

~ * ~

It was evening when the doorbell rang. Lisa was out of her chair and at the entrance to the foyer before skidding to a halt. Instead of going to the door, she turned and headed for the stairs. The bell sounded again, just as the phone had a half hour before, an urgent tone to its buzz.

"Aren't you going to get that?" Alice looked up from her book.

"Nope." Lisa sauntered leisurely to the stairs as whoever was outside once more pressed the button...three buzzes, short and impatient.

"Then *I* will."

"Whatever." She went up the stairs, pausing at the landing to call down, "If it's Dan, tell him I'm resting and can't see him." She didn't go into her room, however, but hovered out of sight as Alice opened the door.

"Dan, how good to see you."

"Hello, Miz Townsend. I'm sorry to stop by like this but I'm worried about Lisa."

"Why? There's nothing wrong."

Lisa imagined her aunt grimacing as she said it and conveying with the gesture her own opinion.

"I've called her three times today—and she didn't answer. I thought I'd better stop by and…"

"Daniel, I assure you, Lisa's fine."

"May I see her? May I come in?"

"I don't think that'd be a good idea." She could almost see Alice glancing up at the stairs and back at Dan.

"Oh?" His voice went up slightly.

"She…she's resting. I don't think she's been sleeping well."

Don't say that. Silently Lisa beat her fist against the newel post. *Now he'll insist on seeing me, and…*

"Why? Has she been having nightmares again? Maybe I'd better…"

"Dan." She was certain Alice placed a hand on his arm, patting it gently. "It's nothing to worry about. I imagine all expectant mothers have trouble sleeping until they adjust to the changes taking place. Now, why don't you run along…"

"Well…"

"I'll tell Lisa you called, I'm sure she'll get in touch with you tomorrow."

Oh no, I won't. That's where you're wrong. I don't want to see Dan Walker again. She had no idea where that thought came from and it shook her a little but it didn't make her change her mind.

~ * ~

Returning to his car, Dan sat a moment looking back at the house. *What the Hell's going on?* A vibration from his pocket told him his phone was ringing. He dug it out. "Lisa?"

"This is *Kerner's Jewelry*," a woman said. "Dr. Walker?"

"Yes?" He didn't try to hide his disappointment.

"I wanted to let you know we've repaired the chain on your charm. You can pick it up any time."

"It may be a few days." His answer was a little brusque. The last thing he wanted to think about right then was Katsal-Ka's medallion. He'd finally become accustomed to it not being around his neck. "I'll stop by as soon as my schedule allows."

"I'll make a notation so we won't bother you again," the woman answered. "We're open from nine to four-thirty."

As he returned the phone to his pocket, he thought, *Maybe I'd better go ahead and get it. Grandma always told me it'd give me luck, and I have a feeling I need all I can get right now.*

~ * ~

That night, it was difficult getting to sleep. Whether it was the autumn heat or Drex's return, neither the air conditioner nor counting sheep helped. Whatever the reason, it was nearly midnight before the restlessness ceased and Lisa was able to doze…

…and found herself in another nightmare…the fifth in as many days…

~ * ~

Fog like a gray velvet cape. A light shining through it. She'd find help there.

Someone walked ahead of her, his body blocking the light.

"Wait…wait please."

179

He didn't slow his pace or turn around.

You don't want to see him, was whispered from the fog. *You aren't ready to see his face.*

"What do you mean? I need his help." Hands on her arm held her back. Not Dan's gentle hands. *The Other's* hands, those hurting hands.

You aren't ready.

Pulling away, she ran after the man, reached him and clutched at his arm, spinning him around. The burning face of her nightmare stared at her. Lisa fell back, screaming. As she turned to run, his laughter echoed in her ears.

*I warned you...*the whisper was smug. *You aren't ready...*

~ * ~

Lisa opened her eyes. Daylight. She stared at the sunbeams streaming through the window, concentrating with fierce determination. The half-remembered terror of her dream faded.

"I'd better get up," she told Timothy as the cat rose from the foot of the bed and stretched. "My appointment with Dr. Halyard's at ten. I may as well start getting ready."

Chapter 15

"Young lady, you need more sleep," was Dr. Halyard's first comment as he entered the exam room.

Wearily, Lisa agreed. She recounted her dream, ending with, "They're not all frightening. Just disturbing. Enough to make me not want to go back to sleep because I'm afraid I'll dream it all over again."

"Lisa, I'm not trying to get rid of you but I think you need to leave here." The doctor looked serious. "Do nothing for a week or two. Have someone wait on you. Lounge around, be lazy."

"I do that now," she protested. "My aunt does almost all the housework, and—"

"That's not what I mean," he interrupted. "You should get away from Temple completely, the people, the memories…everything. Don't you have friends somewhere you can visit for a while?"

I want you to see Land's End. Hadn't Drex said that? Was Dr. Halyard telling her to go?

"I've had an invitation to visit someone," she admitted.

I always get what I want. Drex had said that, too.

"Accept it," Halyard ordered with a smile. "I can write you prescriptions for vitamins and mild sedatives to help you sleep, but a vacation from all this will do you more good. Accept that invitation." As far as he was concerned, it was settled. "When I see you again, I want those eyes not to have circles under them."

I always get what I want…

Always.

~ * ~

"Lisa…hey, wait up!"

At the sound of Dan's voice, Lisa stiffened so sharply it looked as if she'd been struck. She didn't turn around, instead waited for him to reach her. *Why couldn't I have gotten away before he saw me?* A flush of anger swept over her. *Why does Dr. Halyard have to have offices in the hospital itself?*

"Hey…little lady. I'm glad to see you. I've been worried about you."

"Oh? Why?" She struggled to make it warm enough not to sound unfriendly.

"Mainly because you seem to be avoiding me. I haven't seen you in almost two weeks now…as you very well now." His tone was still light though bordering on concern. "Every time I've called, you haven't answered…or returned my voice mail."

"I didn't realize I was obliged to answer the phone every time it rang." Lisa's tone held slight petulance. "As for not seeing you…blame your patients for that, not me."

"What's the matter?" He scowled. "You sound… as if you don't want to talk to me."

"Maybe I don't." She looked away and even as she did, she wondered, *Why? I'm not angry with Dan. Why shouldn't I want to talk to him? I like seeing him, being with him.*

"Then I think I've a right to ask why not?" He appeared ready for an argument. "You certainly seemed to be enjoying my company until recently." It was an accusation rather than a statement.

"I think we were going a little too fast, Dr. Walker." She'd swear she saw him flinch as she used his title. "Perhaps you were reading something into my seeing you that wasn't really there."

"Was I? I thought…"

"Don't think so much. It may lead you to some fairly inaccurate conclusions," she snapped, and got very busy hunting in her purse for her keys, avoiding his eyes. "Now if you'll excuse me, I have to go home and pack."

"Pack?" The word might've been a signal. He immediately bristled, like a guard dog on alert. "Where are you going?"

"Away. Doctor's orders." *Damn, why did I say that?* "Dr. Halyard suggested I get away from Temple completely for a while. And Dan…" He looked up, confusion in his eyes. She felt a pang of sympathy before it was wiped away. "While I'm gone, don't call Aunt Allie or stop by to question her about me. Because where I go is none of your business."

With that, she turned and walked to her car, leaving him standing there.

Chapter 16

The Jag sped down the coat road toward Land's End Island. The late October sun was shining and the wind blew Lisa's hair in vivid streamers. Once or twice, she found Drex watching her, forehead wrinkled in a slight frown. Both times, he appeared on the verge of speaking.

"Is something the matter?"

He didn't answer right away, simply looked as if he were thinking about something. Finally, he shook his head. Lisa felt a brief *frisson* sweep over her. It was too much like the night she and Robin drove this same route...the silence, the scenery speeding by...except the unbearable tension wasn't present as it had been that night.

They came to the bridge. It looked different in the daylight. She had a bare glimpse at the sign as they sped past. Perhaps it *had* been there before and Robin didn't notice it. She tensed slightly. *Will we see where it happened?*

"We'll go through the village." He said it before she could ask, as if he sensed what she was thinking. "We won't go that way."

She hadn't noticed the fork in the road before. They turned left onto one even narrower and sandier, one almost like a cattle path. Once again, Drex frowned.

"What is it?"

"Nothing."

"Big nothing. You've been looking worried since I got into the car." *Is he having second thoughts about inviting me?* "Look, Drex, if you've decided you don't want me…"

"*Want* you?" Those green eyes seemed to send out sparks. She'd swear to it. "I want you all right." There was no mistaking his meaning. "It's just…I…damn it, Lisa. I'd better tell you before we get there." Slowing the car, he pulled it onto the shoulder, switching off the engine.

"Don't tell me we're out of gas." Now that he was about to say what was bothering him, she attempted lightness. "That line's positively antiquated."

"Be serious." Drex didn't respond to her teasing as she hoped. "I've been putting off telling you this—"

"I knew it…" she exclaimed dramatically, wanting to make him smile. "You've got a wife and six kids locked in the cellar."

"The Manor doesn't have a cellar." He didn't change expression.

"Sorry." She'd never known him to look so worried and that surprised her. From all she'd seen so far, she'd have said Drex was the most confident person she ever met…except for Dan, whose self-assurance as a doctor was off-set by his shyness as a person. "Is it that bad?"

"There's something you have to know about life on Land's End."

"Then tell me."

Taking a deep breath, he didn't speak for several more seconds. "My great-great-great-great-grandfather was some kind of very minor aristocrat in Europe." At that, she started to say something facetious, but his expression made her keep quiet. "In 1734, he brought to this island the ancestors of the people now living here. They were servants but he treated them like slaves. He *used* them, Lisa."

"Used them? I don't understand."

"He…You know what I mean. *Droites des noblesse* or some shit like that." He hesitated before bursting out. "It was the mid-eighteenth century. He considered them his property…to do with as he pleased, and he damn well pleased himself with the women."

She wasn't prepared for that anger. It was startling. Drex, who'd teased her so, hinting at what he wanted to do to her…apologizing for a long-dead relative's behavior? In an effort to cover the embarrassment she imagined he was feeling as well as to ease his anger, she said, with unconvincing nonchalance, "Things like that happened back then. Don't worry about it. This is *Now*…That wouldn't work nowadays."

"Wouldn't it? You're such a naïve little thing." He shook his head as if pitying her ignorance. "It may be 2013 back *there*." He nodded behind them toward the bridge and by extension the mainland. "But here…? Land's End village is filled with living proof of my ancestor's lack of control, Lisa. Not just Old Heinrich, but everyone since." Again, she was startled by the bitterness tingeing his anger. "Thanks to him, his son, and all who followed…" He looked away. "They were nothing but a bunch of undisciplined libertines…pulling women out of the houses, dragging them back to the Manor…"

"Drex…" She felt she should say something but had no idea what.

"There's a whole herd of wood colts running free and when we get there and you see them…"

"You think I'll be so shocked I'll want to leave," she finished for hm.

"If you don't, I'll be the one who's shocked." He laughed but the sound held no humor. He looked away. "And I won't blame you."

"Hey…" She touched his cheek, turning him back to look at her. "Maybe I'm not terribly sophisticated but I don't think I'm as prudish as you make me out to be. I'm not going to blame you for something your however-many-greats grandfather did…" *Not like Dan's doing.* "And I'm not going to blame your relatives on the wrong side of the blanket, either. This is the twenty-first century…live and let live."

Awkward as it was with the console in the way, she leaned toward him, pulling against the seatbelt. What she'd said to Dan flashed through her mind. *Kissing in a Jag isn't much easier than kissing in a Mercedes.* Somehow she managed it, but Drex didn't move. He continued looking at her as if waiting for something.

"I must've done something really good to have been given you."

"Start the engine," she said as she straightened. That statement and the look in his eyes *did* shake her. "Let's go."

~ * ~

The village was little more than a row of houses and a couple of stores facing each other across a five-yard open space. The cottages were made of tabby, the mixture of seashells, sand, and mortar used in construction of most buildings along the coast. They were small, with neat picket-fenced yards. Smoke drifting above the pines told her other houses, apparently very primitive and without heating, hid from sight in the woods. She wondered how cold it got on the island in winter.

The few people about were on the little boarded street, moving slowly in the warm autumn sun. Though they wore modern clothing, Lisa felt they would've been more appropriately dressed if the women had on long skirts and carried parasols. A young girl in jeans and tee-shirt stood on a stepladder, washing the front window of a small building looking as if it were a general store according to the merchandise on display.

A truck rumbled down the street, stopping before it, a new Ford F-150, finish still shiny-bright and not yet pitted by the salt-laden air. Apparently the islanders were fairly solvent. Lisa was aware of the cost of such a vehicle because Robin had teased her about buying one and even priced them. A tall, middle-aged man got out. He looked like a farmer, in overalls, shirtsleeves rolled up, a red bandanna hanging from his hip pocket. He called to someone inside the building and another man came out.

A hunchback.

Lisa managed to swallow her gasp, hoping Drex didn't hear. It wasn't the man's deformity shaking her. He moved easily in spite of being unable to stand erect and was agile as he proved by unlocking the tailgate of the truck and climbing inside. Lifting one of the sacks stacked there, he lowered it to the other driver.

What shook her was his hair…bright copper, Drex's hair…and the handsome face on that grotesquely-bent body. *Is this what he meant?* She didn't look at Drex. Couldn't.

As the car passed, the two men stopped and turned, each bobbing his head in greeting. The girl at the window set down her sponge and pail. From her perch on the ladder, she copied their action.

Drex ignored them, the young lord disregarding peasants.

At the end of the street was a small service station with a shed-sized garage and a single gas pump. Drex pulled the car into the yard and stopped it by the pump. He got out. "Isak?"

A man appeared in the doorway of the station shop. He was a little older than Drex but just as tall. He had the same bright hair and…Lisa looked away so he wouldn't see the horror on her face. His otherwise good looks were marred by a deep, curving harelip.

Drex and the man began to talk. At least Drex did. Isak didn't speak though he made several confirming noises. He probably couldn't with that much of a cleft lip, not intelligibly any way. It didn't sound as if Drex was speaking English. German? That would explain the contradictions in his speech patterns if they spoke another language on the island.

Nodding, Isak set to work, filling the gas tank, checking under the hood. He appeared to know what he was doing for in several minutes, he slammed it shut, muttered something Drex seemed to understand and went back into the shop. Still talking, Drex followed him.

Watching the shop entrance, Lisa unbuckled her seatbelt and stretched slightly.

"Lady?" Behind her, a child spoke. Something touched her shoulder, butterfly-light. "Pretty lady?"

Lisa turned, looking up at the man standing by the car. He was even taller than Drex but heavy-bodied and clumsy-looking. Lank red hair, that same shade of copper, hung over his face in an unkempt mass. Green eyes regarded her dully through the uncombed strands. There was something around his neck, a small leather strap with a buckle. A woven cloth strip was attached to it, dangling against his chest. Lisa stared. *It looks...is that a leash?*

"Pretty lady. Pretty hair." His big hand touched one of the locks falling over Lisa's shoulder. Thick fingers lifted a curl.

Lisa shrank from his touch, immediately regretting the action. She wasn't afraid, just uncomfortable with Drex's distorted image looming over her. *Why doesn't Drex come back?*

"Lady want get out?" He misunderstood her movement. Big hands slid under her arms. "Ah he'p." She was lifted off the car seat, legs dangling.

"Hansi, put the lady down." Drex came out of the shop, running to the car.

"D'ex." Over Lisa's head, the man looked at him, recognition in his eyes. He shook Lisa, making her sway like a doll in his hands. "Lady get out?"

"No," Drex said firmly. "Put her down. You're scaring her, Hansi. Put her down *now*."

"No scare." His hands opened. Lisa fell back onto the seat, landing with a jolt making her teeth click. "Sorry."

He had such an angelic expression on his beautiful vacant face she smiled back at him as she caught her breath.

"Isak!" Drex glared at him. Hansi continued to smile, not understand his anger. "Get your brother." Hansi looked toward the shop as Drex shouted something else in that strange language, breaking into English as Isak ran toward him, slobbering an answer. "Get him inside. I've told you not to let him run lose."

Catching at the cloth strip, Isak pushed Hansi toward the shop. He threw an apologetic slurring of sounds over his shoulder as he tugged on the leash and led his brother away. Hansi went with him obediently, turning to wave at Lisa. Automatically, she raised her own hand.

"Make sure he doesn't get away again," Drex warned. Turning, he saw Lisa's upraised hand and slapped it aside. "Don't encourage him." He got into the car and started the engine. "Did he hurt you?"

"He startled me." She rubbed her fingers. They stung where he'd struck them. "I didn't expect to see him standing there. Isak…he led him away, like he was a dog."

"He probably be smarter if he were." Drex twisted the wheel, sending the car squealing away from the station, sand flying as it turned onto the road again.. "Isak's been warned to keep him locked up but he can figure out how to open the heaviest lock. That leash is a joke." He shook his head.

"Is it so bad if he's free?" she asked. "I mean, surely everyone here knows about him, and…"

"Hansi's got a child's curiosity. He likes to *explore*." The emphasis he put on that word sent a shiver through

Lisa and she didn't know why. "One of these days, he'll manage to cross the bridge, and then we'll all be in trouble."

At this end of the street, there were fewer people about but the ones who were got out of the way as if accustomed to the Jag roaring through town. A dark-haired girl crossing the street was the only one who didn't. She walked directly in front of the car and stopped. She had a straw basket on one arm while the other hand clasped that of a small carrot-topped child of about four.

"Look out." Lisa gasped the word. She put a hand against the dashboard.

"Aura!" Drex skidded the car to a halt three feet from her. Not looking the least bit shaken at nearly being run down, she walked over to the driver's side. The child immediately hid behind her. "It's good to see you."

Is that all he's got to say? Lisa realized if she'd been driving, she'd have yelled at this Aura, calling her an idiot for stopping in the middle of the street as if daring him to run over her.

"Hello, Mr. Drex." She spoke softly, eyes lowered in an attitude of subservience Lisa thought blatantly false. Her voice also had that odd accent.

"This is Lisa Chambers." Drex nodded at Lisa. "She's going to be a guest at the Manor for a few days."

Aura glanced at Lisa but didn't answer. Her eyes flicked across Lisa's waistline and back to Drex.

She knows about my baby and she hates me for it. Why? Lisa felt a tremor twinge through her.

"I guess you're already aware of that, aren't you?" Their gazes seemed to collide. "You do know I might've not been able to stop in time." When she didn't answer, he went on, "How's Joshua getting along? How's his leg?" He ignored her glare.

"Better. He's doing better." She met his look, the one she gave him so exposed, so naked, it made Lisa turn her head.

She loves him. As much as I do. That startled her. *Where did that come from? Since when do I love Drex?*

"Come out from behind your mama, Joshua." Drex turned his attention to the child. "Let's have a look at you."

One eye peeped at them from behind Aura. She caught the little boy's arm, jerking him roughly around her.

"Oh, don't…" Lisa bit off whatever she was going to say as Aura gave her a wordless glare.

"How are you?" Drex asked.

Joshua didn't answer, just stuck a finger into his mouth and stared. Aura shook his shoulder, making him force out a soft, "Ah'm okay."

"Are you doing the exercises the doctor gave you?" The child nodded. "Good." Drex's hand ruffled the coppery curls, then touched the little boy's cheek. It was an awkward caress, as if he wasn't certain how to treat a child…or was afraid to show how he really felt. He looked at Aura and said something odd. "Looks like I was wrong and that doctor was right."

"Thank you, Mr. Drex." Briefly her eyes sparkled. It was as if she'd been given a compliment, seizing the statement and hugging it to herself. *Like a dog thrown a scrap.*

Turning the key, Drex started the car again. Aura and the child were dismissed. She stepped back, pulling the boy with her as the car roared away. Glancing back, Lisa saw her continue across the street, head bowed, shoulders slumped. Joshua ran along behind her. Before the road curved and cut them from sight, Lisa saw that the child limped slightly.

"Here we are."

That made her turn around. The car was pulling into a deep curving driveway, stopping a few feet from the wide front steps and broad porch of Land's End Manor.

Her mental picture was wrong. She'd expected something along the lines of the houses in Brunswick and Savannah...Creole with wrought iron and stucco. The house was long and high, two stories of gray stone and tabby. A verandah ran its front length, bounded by a balustrade and massive banisters lining the stone steps. Long narrow windows reflected the sun. All in all, it was unattractive, rough, and primitive-looking. At the door, a woman in a gray dress and spotless pinafore apron waited.

Drex helped Lisa out of the car and guided her up the steps.

"Ursula," he greeted the woman. "Where's Rustin? Why are you opening the door?

"Rustin had some errands to do for me, Mr. Drex," she explained. "There were a few things the store didn't have."

"This is Lisa." His arm went around her as if displaying a prized possession, as he explained, "Ursula's my housekeeper."

"Mrs. Chambers." Ursula nodded in greeting.

"Hello." Shrinking into Drex's embrace, Lisa forced herself to straighten. She was glad the housekeeper didn't offer to shake hands. There was something odd, almost reptilian, about the woman and it repulsed her.

She was tall, towering over Lisa though nowhere near Drex's height, and extremely pale. Her lack of make-up and dark hair pulled into a bun at the nape of a thin neck emphasized the pallor of her narrow face. Ursula smiled and Lisa thought it a slow secretive expression, as if her strangely slanted eyes could see into her mind and the revulsion she was attempting to hide.

"Ursula's been tending the Manor since my mother died," Drex explained. "How long has it been now? Fourteen years?"

That made Lisa look at him in surprise. *He doesn't remember how long ago his mother died?* She remembered exactly when she'd lost her own mother. To the minute. January 12, 2002, at six-thirty in the afternoon. It was a Sunday. She'd just gotten home from Bible Study and she and Aunt Allie were getting ready to go to the hospital when the call came.

"Sixteen, sir." The housekeeper's voice was soft and sibilant as she went on, "I was expecting you a little later. I'd thought to prepare a cold supper because of the weather, but it's not quite ready…"

"No problem. Just set it on the sideboard. I want to show Lisa the house." Dropping the keys into her hand, he went on, "Have Rustin put the car away when he gets back, and bring up Lisa's bag." He pulled Lisa into the Manor's foyer. It was a large area with doorways opening into it. Against one wall, a mahogany credenza stood under a gilt-framed mirror. Across from that, a staircase interrupted the flow of the walls.

"Yes sir." With a slight bow, she followed them into the house, shutting the massive door Drex carelessly left ajar.

"We'll start with the upstairs. That way by the time we get to the dining room, supper should be ready." He shot Ursula a look saying plainly, *It had better be*. Her expression didn't change. Taking off his jacket, he dropped it over the newel post of the staircase and caught Lisa's hand. "Is it all right for you to climb stairs? Because if not, I'll carry you up."

"I think I can manage." For some reason, she didn't want the housekeeper seeing her in Drex's arms.

"Then come on, and I'll give you the Grand Tour." He sounded eager, like a child showing off his toys.

Lisa wondered how many other women had come to Land's End and if he displayed this much excitement when he showed them around. Out of the corner of her eye, she saw Ursula pull Drex's jacket off the post. The housekeeper clutched it against her chest, stroking the fabric as she watched them go up the stairs. *Did Ursula and Aura make them feel as uneasy as they do me?*

Chapter 17

The upstairs of the house was as impressive as the little bit she'd seen from the foyer. There were a dozen rooms, each furnished with dark furniture and four-posters in an unidentifiable antique style. *The kind of bed I'd imagine Dracula sleeping in when he wasn't using a coffin,* Lisa decided. Thick carpets covered the floors, their design matching the heavy draperies closed against the afternoon sun. Drex gave her a bare moment to see each before dragging her down the hall toward a door at the end.

"This…" He pushed it open. "…will be your room."

Unlike the others, it was light and airy, with four windows, their shutters open behind white organdy curtains. The furniture was also different, of some light-colored wood…a wardrobe, dresser with a mirror, and the tallest bed she'd ever seen. The headboard itself was nearly seven feet high, carved and decorated with scrolls and vines. A white satin comforter spread smoothly over gleaming sheets.

"I hope you like it. It was my mother's room." His voice went soft as he watched her stop in the center and spin around.

"I love it." Even if she hadn't, after learning whose room it had been, she'd have said so. She had a feeling in spite of his saying he didn't remember her death date, Drex had been very close to his mother. That change in his tone spoke volumes. "Are you sure you want me to sleep here?"

"Why wouldn't I?"

"If it was your mother's room..."

"I believe she'd have liked you, Lisa, so I don't think she'd mind you staying in her room."

"Wasn't this your father's room, too?" She didn't know what made her ask that. Perhaps it was the complete absence of anything masculine in sight. Everything, from the translucent curtains to the pink-flowered rug by the bed suggested the only inhabitant had been female.

"Separate bedrooms. That's another little custom my ancestor brought with him...one of the milder ones." He indicated a door in the wall by the dresser. "The master bedroom's through there. Mine. It's locked, so you can sleep in safety." He reached over and pulled a key from the lock, holding it up.

"I didn't..." She began but he interrupted.

"Look, you can see the ocean from here." He tossed the key onto the dresser as he nodded toward the windows. In the distance, beyond a stand of amber sea oats, Lisa saw dark waves capped with foam. "In the evening, you can watch the sun setting on the water."

He touched her arm, stroking fingers down it. She shivered, pulling away to keep him from feeling the tremor. She looked back at the bed.

"That is the most fantastic piece of furniture I've ever seen. It's beautiful. Is it hand-carved?" She hurried to the bed, touching the headboard, fingers following the curve of a vine. They formed a Celtic-appearing design, like eternity knots. In the center of each knot... *Is that a face?* It was so grotesque she couldn't tell. Perhaps merely an elaborate curlicue her imagination made into features...like seeing something in the clouds.

"I imagine so." Drex's answer held disinterested. He touched a bedpost, stroking the amber wood. Lisa's shiver returned as she realized he was touching it as gently as he'd touched her. "You know...the last four generations of my family were conceived and born in this bed." He looked up as she dropped onto the comforter, testing the mattress. "I hope my own children will be, too."

Lisa stopped bouncing, stilled by his expression. "Drex, I..."

"Lisa..." He leaned toward her. "At last I've got you where I want you."

She closed her eyes, felt rather than saw him push her backward. The smoothness of the satin cradled her shoulders. His lips touched her throat, tracing a trail of gentle kisses across it, making her shiver before they reached her mouth. A hand slid under her hips, pulling her against him while the other slipped under the edge of her skirt, brushing against her thigh. His body was heavy, pressing her into the coverlet. She felt a ridge of insistent flesh rising...

The door opened.

Drex jerked away from her, turning to glare at Ursula. "You know you're never to enter a room without knocking."

"I did, sir. You didn't hear."

"What is it?" Clearly angered, he made no move to hide either his displeasure or the half-erection pressing against the zipper of his jeans. Trying to bring as little attention to herself as possible, Lisa pushed down her skirt.

"I've set up dinner for you, sir." Ursula's gaze flicked down his body and back to his face. "I wanted to see if there was anything else you needed before I went to my room."

"I've everything I want." Lisa expected him to look at her as he said it but he continued staring at the housekeeper as if making an effort to control his anger. With a sigh, he succeeded. "Go on to bed. You can clear away the dishes in the morning."

"Yes sir." She disappeared into the hall.

"I'll show you the downstairs." Drex caught Lisa's hand, pulling her from the bed. "Then we'll have supper."

As they came into the hallway, Ursula wasn't to be seen.

~ * ~

Dinner was quiet. Apparently Drex hadn't quite gotten over Ursula's interruption, if his sulky silence was any indication. Though Lisa threw a barrage of questions at him, attempting to get him to talk about the island and the man who'd settled it, he successfully evaded most of her questions.

"After what you said before we got here, the least you can do is tell me more. Come on…give…inquiring minds want to know the low-down on the Master of Land's End." She laughed. "Sounds like an Anne Rice novel, doesn't it?"

"Believe me, the von Dorffs could run circles around Anne Rice when it comes to weird tales. Bram Stoker, too. It's taken over two hundred years for us to make our history," he answered. "And you want to know it all in one night?"

"You said *us*. So you're including yourself? With the rest of the island's Addams Family look alikes?" She hoped he realized she was teasing and didn't take offense.

"Addams Family? Which one am I?" He quirked a copper brow. "Gomez? Uncle Fester? Wait, I know…" He ran fingers through his hair, lifting a handful. "Cousin Itt!"

As she laughed, thinking Ursula would make a good Morticia, so that meant the absent Rustin was probably Lurch, he went on, "I suppose I could give you the *Cliff Notes* version, or… You can wait and learn as we go."

"Do I have a choice?" she said. "I mean…you don't intend to tell me anything, do you?"

"You're not as dumb as I thought." He leaned forward and tapped the end of her nose, then kissed her lightly. "Thank God."

"Have I just been insulted?"

That made him laugh. "If you've finished, what say we go onto the porch and watch the sun set?"

Chapter 18

In the faint gleam from the streetlight shining through the bedroom window, Myrtice raised herself on one elbow, studying the profile of the man sleeping beside her.

~ * ~

While they were on rounds that night, she knew something was wrong when Dan didn't speak to her except to give patient orders. He'd been chatty enough with the patients but between times, he didn't say a word, and once or twice, when he didn't realize she was watching him, he looked positively grim. They finished up, signed out, and walked to his car in the gathering twilight.

They'd gotten through early for a change. Dan was still silent. It was only as she slid onto the passenger seat that he spoke. "How about a drink before we go home?"

"Sure." That was nothing new. Often, they went out for a drink after work, a few times even had dinner. That was BL, of course. *Before Lisa.* Once Lisa Chambers entered the picture, any night he had free belonged to her, and Myrtice got the polite equivalent of a bum's rush when Dan drove her home. Surprised and wondering if his silence had anything to do with the young widow, she decided to take advantage of the situation. "How about *Tomachichi's?*"

"Sounds good."

~ * ~

They'd done more than have a drink. They'd had several, or rather, Dan did. As soon as they sat down, he handed her his keys. "Designated driver, Mud. I've got a load of misery, and I want to drown it."

Nodding, she took the keys, placing them next to her purse. She sipped her own drink while Dan tossed down his first, second, and the third, then slowed to hover over the fourth…and in a voice so quiet she could barely hear it above the music, he told her.

Lisa Chambers—*that little bitch*—had dumped him.

Myrtie was furious and let it show. If Lisa had been present, she might've found herself a return guest in TempeGen's ER within a few minutes. Myrtice never felt such fury before. She seemed to take it as a personal insult, letting it replace the simmering jealousy she'd felt when she realized Dan was dating Lisa—or attempting to—since she was aware how most of those dates ended before they began because of his patients. She'd been pleased about that, especially since she made herself available whenever he was called back to the hospital, attempting as always to show how devoted to him she was and how dedicated a nurse. She'd spent more time with him during those abortive dates than Lisa had and that made her feel as if she'd won some odd victory. At this particular moment, all she wanted to do was gather Dan into her arms and comfort him.

Instead, she let him talk…and talk…and continue to drink, until by the time they were ready to leave, he was too drunk to drive even he'd had the bad judgment to try.

With Dan lolling in the passenger seat, she backed the Mercedes out of the parking space. Dan had let her drive the car a few times and she was always nervous because it was so expensive, and tonight was no different. For a moment, she wavered between driving him home and keeping the car, then picking him up in the morning, or simply taking him home with her. Myrtice had been to her cousin's condo often and was well aware of the security they'd have to go through to get inside. She didn't want anyone seeing Dan as he was at the moment, not even a security guard. Her house had an empty garage where the Mercedes could be hidden from curious eyes.

Dan needed sympathy, and she was going to give him exactly that...and more. While he was wallowing in drunken self-pity, a plan was forming in Myrtice's mind. All she had to do to put it into action was get him to her home. It was easy. At the moment he was dozing, so he didn't realize where they were going, waking only as she stopped the car inside the garage.

It was a struggle getting him out of the Mercedes. He'd now passed into that stage where he was slightly belligerent and wanted to be left alone, wanted to sleep. She managed to drag him through the door into the kitchen where he fell onto one of the stools at the breakfast island. Immediately, he put his arms against the counter, forehead on them.

While he dozed, she poured coffee and set the cup in the microwave, thankful she'd made a fresh pot that morning. She waited impatiently, watching Dan and making certain he didn't awaken, lose his balance, and do a face-plant on the floor. He was going to feel bad enough in the morning without something like that happening.

The microwave *dinged.* She got the coffee, shook him awake and thrust the cup into his hands, leaving him with orders to drink it, while she hurried into the bedroom. In that moment, she wanted nothing more than to get out of her uniform and into something more feminine and appealing.

Kicking her nurse's oxfords into a corner by the dresser, she hurried to the closet, pulling it open to stare at the garments. Which one? She was so intent on making a choice, she didn't hear the step behind her, didn't realize Dan was in the room until his arms encircled her, hands cupping her breasts.

With a squeak of fright, she whirled.

"'Smatter, Mud...di' I scare you?" he laughed, a soft slurred rumble deep in his chest.

"A little...you..."

She didn't get a chance to say more. He caught her in a bear hug, lifting her off her feet, overbalanced, and they both fell onto the bed. The bed shook. Bodies bounced. The framework groaned. Myrtice was certain it'd collapse. Instead, they settled and she struggled out of Dan's embrace, pulling him upright as he laughed again and sputtered, "Oops, din' mean t' do that..."

"Come on, let's get you out of these." Getting to her feet, she loosened his tie, dropping it over the bedroom chair. As she turned to get him out of his jacket, however, he caught her wrists, stilling the hands tugging at his sleeve.

"No."

For an instant, she was dismayed. Surely he wasn't *that* sober...was she going to be disappointed again? *It isn't fair*. When he didn't move, making no effort to get to his feet and leave, she understood. She was being too business-like. *Danny, bless your heart, you blasted romantic*. Simply stripping a man of his clothes wasn't the way he wanted it done. There had to be tenderness and affection...or he wouldn't respond.

He caught her face in his hands, kissing her on the mouth, started to stand, then realized he couldn't, so he simply sat there, arms wrapped loosely around her, pressing his face against her breasts. "Help me, Mud...help me forget..."

Without speaking, she slid out of his arms and sat beside him, leaning forward to press her forehead against his shoulder. She felt his lips brush her temple as his arms tightened around her. They stayed that way for several minutes before one hand crept to her shoulder and from there to the top button of her uniform.

She didn't move as he kissed her on the cheek, then pressed his mouth against hers, fumbling between them until the button came open and so did the next. He pushed her away.

"Need a li'l assistance, Mud...damn it...fingers won't work..."

She moved away, finished unbuttoning the uniform and stepped out of it, dropping it to the floor. When she'd dressed that morning, she'd been seized with a sudden whim to wear her laciest bra and the skimpiest thong imaginable. Myrtice had felt crazy when she bought it. This morning, it seemed as if she were compelled to ditch her pantyhose and wear that sexy little set. As she saw the way Dan was watching her, she was glad she had.

The bra opened in front. She unsnapped it, adding it to the clothing on the floor, drawing a deep non-constricted breath which raised her breasts in a way she hoped was enticing. She pushed his jacket off his shoulders, tossing it away,

The suddenness with which he seized her didn't startle her as much as the soft kiss he gave her. *Relax, damn it. You've finally got him where you want him…even if you've waited fifteen years. Thank God I've been on a diet…*a confusing and frightening wave of anxiety swept over her as she remember the last time Dan had seen her naked…

~ * ~

They'd been teenagers…too old to go skinny dipping together but that hadn't stopped them. Dan had been pretty casual about the whole thing but she'd expected something other than actually happened. Apparently she'd seen it as more important than it was. He'd touched one of her adolescent breasts, tweaked it gently and laughed, *Hey look at Mud…Miz No-tits…* He hadn't realized she was offering her fifteen-year-old self to him, her adored cousin…all he'd seen was a skinny little girl with barely budding breasts, shivering in the cold river water. She couldn't even remember how his own body looked or if he'd become aroused at all…

Nothing happened and soon after Dan went away to school and out of her life for the next ten years…but he was never out of her thoughts…

~ * ~

Dan lurched to his feet. He placed a hand under her breast, brushing his thumb across the nipple. His touch was as light as it had been fumbling before. "Hey there, Miz Some-tits."

He remembered those flat adolescent breasts. She laughed and he joined her and kissed her again, on her mouth, her throat. Hands caressed her back as he bent to take her nipple into his mouth and tease it with his tongue. His hands tightened on her buttocks, bared around that wisp of a thong, pulling her body against his.

She never remembered him undressing, just heard him murmur, "We've both waited a long time for this, Mud..." as his body covered hers in the darkness.

For a while there was nothing but the two of them...and the pleasure. She must've cried out, for he raised his head, asking, "Did I hurt you?" and when she shook her own, he lowered himself again to continue what he was doing. Sometime he slid into her and began to thrust against her, belly brushing back and forth against her own. She gasped her climax, gripping his shoulders tightly, digging in her nails. *Did I scratch him?* As he collapsed against her, she brushed hands over his back, searching...No marks, but...*What's this?* A tiny red oval against the side of his neck. *A hickey? For God's sake, I gave him a hickey?*

Kissing the spot, she smiled. As Dan rolled off her, settling beside her with a sigh, she echoed it. *I'm so happy.* In the morning, he'd be full of remorse and God knew how much guilt, she was certain, but for now... *He's mine. If I have to use that guilt to keep him, by damn, I will.* She might even have whispered that as he pulled her close before he fell asleep.

She had him now and she was going to keep him.

Chapter 19

"There's still some daylight left, why don't we go for a walk instead?"

To Lisa's surprise, Drex agreed, leading her down the steps and around the house to a little path cut into the sandy soil. It wasn't long before she was running ahead of him, looking at the wildflowers growing between the trees. There didn't appear to be much landscaping at the house itself. Though the area around it was free of weeds, it was also bare of cultivated plants and blossoms. Lisa thought that a pity. The Manor needed something bright, like azaleas, to make it a little more attractive. Beach soil filled the yard and sifted into the woods. Perhaps nothing would grow in sand except gaillardia and sea oats.

Most of the trees were stunted and bent as if a strong wind had battered them while young, twisting the trunks. With Drex trailing behind, Lisa wandered across the sandy path dotted with wiry clumps of beach grass until she eventually came to a low tabby wall with an open iron gate.

At the entrance, she hesitated. From the waist-high weeds filling the pathway going through the gate, it looked as if no one had been inside in quite some time. A look at the worn stones protruding from the weeds told her this was the island cemetery. It was behind the manor at the end of the island where the land was rocky and high so there was no danger of the sea undermining the graves and washing them away.

"May I go in?"

"If you want to." He appeared indifferent. "Though I don't know why you would. There's not much to see. Just some crumbling headstones."

Without answering, she made her way through the weeds, pushing them aside or stepping over them. They crackled under her feet, cockleburrs and beggar lice scratching at her legs as if to impede her progress. She drew in her breath as she felt a sharp sting against one ankle, didn't react any more openly because she was certain Drex would tell her to come back, perhaps even pick her up and carry her away. That thought made her more determined to see the cemetery, with the stones containing the names of those long-ago von Dorffs, the possessors of all that rampant, unbridled lust.

Some of the markers appeared fairly recent within the last century, others old and worn, the carvings on them nearly washed away by wind and rain. Like the gate, the cemetery itself was filled with weeds and the smaller markers difficult to see, almost hidden in the plants twining around them. Lisa parted leaves and stickers, peering at the inscriptions. Behind her, Drex followed. When she stopped, so did he.

"There." He pointed. "Isn't that the one you're looking for?"

In the center of the graveyard, a high stone protruded out of the soil. It was a small obelisk, a chunk of crudely-carved needle, with letters so large she could read them from where she stood. Surprisingly, they hadn't been erased by the elements since being placed there nearly three centuries before.

Heinrich Wilhelm von Dorff.

Lisa approached the marker cautiously, as if Heinrich might erupt from it and accuse her of trespassing, demanding she leave. There was no mound under the obelisk, nothing to show the dirt had ever been disturbed and then replaced. Even after all this time, she thought there should be some evidence of the gravedigger's shovel. There weren't any crushed oyster shells scattered over the gravetop as was the custom on the coast. That could only mean...

She stopped, looking back at Drex.

"That's right." He nodded. "It's not really a grave. There's no body buried there."

"Where..."

"He disappeared one night. The Indians were unhappy after they sold him the island, especially their shaman. He actually convinced them to buy it back. Heinrich refused, so... Probably they murdered him and buried his body in the woods." It sounded as if he were completely disinterested in what he was saying.

Indian Shaman...does he mean Dan's great-great-great-great-grandfather? Could Dan's relative have killed Drex's? He'd said they were Red Sticks. That meant they were predisposed to violence.

"It didn't make us leave, though," Drex went on. "We stayed...they were the ones who left."

Not wanting to think about that, or the bleak marker covering nothing, Lisa looked at the other stones. "*Marianna Charlotte, first wife of Heinrich...*" she read. "*First* wife? How many did he have?"

"Four, in all." Drex was still detached. "Women were…fragile…in those days."

Fragile? An odd way to put it. She looked around, searching the stones. "Where are their graves?"

"They weren't Land's End people. They were sent home for burial." His answers were clipped as if revealing facts he didn't like to remember.

Set to one side of Heinrich's stone was a newer marker. Being careful not to step on the mound of oyster shells atop the grave, she peered at the writing. "Elizabeth Anders von Dor—"

"My mother," Drex interrupted. He held out a hand. "Let's go, Lisa."

"Is your father buried here, too?" She didn't move, wondering why there wasn't a second fairly new grave beside Elizabeth's. Hadn't Martha said his father died four years before?

"He hated her when she was alive. Why should he be near her in death?" He sounded so bitter Lisa spun around to stare at him.

"You mean he isn't buried here?"

"He wished to be buried at sea, so like a dutiful son…" His voice was heavy with irony. "I obeyed his wishes. I tossed the old man into the drink." At that irreverence. Lisa winced.

*Full fathom five thy father lies…*what was that from? Shakespeare? *Ariel's Song* about Ferdinand's drowned father. She shivered. He saw it.

"The wind's coming in from the water." There was no wind, and he knew it. "You'll get a chill." He was impatient to leave. "Aren't you ready to go?"

"Wait," she persisted. He'd given out more information than he intended, and she wanted him to tell her more. With that opening, she had to find out all she could before Drex withdrew and closed the door again. "What about these?" She pointed to a group of smaller stones seemingly huddled together in spite of being arranged in neat little rows. "Who were they? Why aren't there any last names on the stones?"

"You already know about them." He gave her a pitying stare. "They shared our blood but had no right to the name. This was the least their fathers could do."

"You mean…"

He nodded. "All von Dorff bastards."

"But there are so many." She didn't mean to say it so loudly. One of two illegitimate children in a generation was one thing, but this… "There must be three dozen. And…" Her gaze swept down the first row. "None of them lived more than a year?"

"I told you my ancestors were undisciplined." He sounded defensive. "They enjoyed it. What if a child died? They'd just make another. Children were even more delicate than women back then."

She knew that, had read enough histories and historical romances to be aware of the dangers of childbirth to both mother and child, but this…There was one small stone set apart from the rest. It didn't bear a name, merely the words, *Stillborn son, 2007.*

2007? That means…

"He didn't even live to breathe the air in this miserable world." Drex looked at the letters.

"Is that how you think of it?"

"Once. Not now." His eyes were thoughtful as he looked at her. He didn't seem to realize she was watching him with a new awareness. "Not since I met you."

"Who was he?" Who was this child who never lived? Whose son was he?

He didn't answer, giving her a very sad look and shrugged, as if accepting defeat. "Let's go back to the house. I guess a little soul-baring's in order."

Turning, he stalked back through the weeds to the gate, leaving her standing here. Lisa ran to his side, but this time, he didn't take her hand.

~ * ~

Drex didn't speak on the walk back to the Manor. On his way upstairs, Ursula stopped him, asking if he wished tea. She got a snapped refusal but didn't react, making Lisa think she was accustomed to rudeness on *the master's* part.

The study was quiet, its walls lined with books. From above the whitewashed brick fireplace, the portrait of a man watched over the room, his red hair and green eyes as well as his stance marking him as a von Dorff. He wore the clothes of the early eighteenth century, wrapped cravat and high collar hiding his throat, hair pulled back and tied at the nape of his neck. The end of a ribbon showed over his shoulder. There was something in the direct gaze of his eyes making them appear more than mere layers of paint on a canvas. On the hand clasping a gold-headed walking stick, an ornate green ring was visible.

Lisa stared at the portrait, waiting for Drex to speak while his own gaze followed her glance toward the picture.

"Contrary to what the mainlanders think, he wasn't German. He came from a little village in Austria that doesn't even exist now. Not that it matters."

"You said the Indians killed him...how do you know that...if his body wasn't found?" *Why do I want to know?*

"The Yamacraw believed a sea god was imprisoned beyond the shallows."

Lisa tensed. Hadn't Dan said the same thing? A *cetto-thlot-lo*...a snake fish...some kind of sea serpent?

"The villagers swear it carried Heinrich away." The look he gave the painted image held glittering hatred. "I used to wish it were true. It'd be fitting for what he did to us."

"What did he do?" His words weren't making sense. What did Heinrich von Dorff's death have to do with all those little graves? "Why should you hate one of your own family so? Is that what you wanted to tell me?"

The look he gave her said he'd forgotten what he said at the cemetery.

"You said you had something to say," she reminded him.

He nodded, walking over to stand directly under the portrait. *They're so alike. Too alike. Just as the men in the village are like Drex. What's that old saying, about breeding true? Von Dorffs really do. But why are they all misshapen and he's perfect?*

"Don't stand over there." She moved over, patting the place beside her on the sofa, wanting him near her,

216

wanting to re-establish the closeness they'd had. It had begun to fade as they drove through the village, at the moment felt non-existent. Why? The villagers were merely people, no matter who they were related to and none of them were to be feared, not even big, lumbering Hansi.

"I can't be serious if I'm close to you." A spark of the old Drex glimmered in his quick smile.

"Sit down, and let's talk."

"All right." His smile fell away. He sat, taking one of her hands. She pulled away, clasping them together in her lap. He didn't protest. "I think it might be better if you ask questions. That way you'll learn what you really want to know."

"Very well." She took a deep breath. "That unmarked headstone. He was your son, wasn't he?"

"Yes." He didn't attempt to deny it. No hesitation, none of the excuses she expected, simply *Yes*.

"Who's his mother?"

"Aura. He was Joshua's brother."

My God. No wonder she hates me. She and Drex had two children and one of them died? And now he's bringing another woman here? Lisa's hands tightened in her lap.

"I'd like to explain."

"Please do." She didn't intend to sound sarcastic but her answer would've seemed that way no matter how she said it.

"It's going to be difficult for you to understand…for anyone who doesn't live as we do."

"Just tell me." Again her voice took on a tone she didn't intend. "Simply come out and say it. This isn't a scene from *Jane Eyre* and we aren't characters in some Gothic novel. We're two people in the twenty-first century who…care about each other. At least I think we do. I want to know about you and your family, Drex, good or bad, so…" She made a helpless gesture. "…tell me."

"Easier said than done." He gave a short mirthless laugh, looking down at his own hands. "I'm not sure where to begin."

"Begin at the beginning. With *him*." She nodded at the portrait.

"The beginning… okay." He was up again, moving away to sit in a chair near the hearth. Facing her but far enough away so they didn't touch. Hands together, leaning forward, he frowned as if struggling to get his thoughts into some kind of order. He took a deep breath.

"Heinrich Wilhelm von Dorff left Austria to escape being arrested for sorcery." As she started to speak, he held up a hand. "I'm not asking you to believe he was a wizard or anything, only that he was accused of being one." Lisa nodded and he went on, "Since he was minor nobility and also as well-educated as one could be back then, he ran afoul of his village's council on several occasions. They were looking for an excuse to get rid of him. When several local women disappeared, they got it. One of them was found alive and she accused Heinrich of holding her captive and attempting to offer her to a demon he'd summoned. That was all they needed to go after him."

He said it without any emotion, as if repeating something from memory.

"He managed to get away with his wife and servants and a small fortune, boarded a ship to Savannah, then used some of the money to buy the island."

"That's terrible," Lisa broke in. "To be unjustly accused like that."

"That's the thing…it wasn't unjust. It was true." She frowned as he went on, "Part of it, anyway. You see, Heinrich had this belief there were creatures in space, so far away they were beyond the outermost star. They'd gotten to Earth somehow and were followed by their enemies who imprisoned them in various places…in the deepest part of the ocean, in remote deserts, in the Antarctic…"

"Oh, come on, Drex." She gave a shaky laugh. "I thought you were going to be serious."

"Damn it, Lisa, I *am* serious." He shook his head. "This was a mistake. I should've known bringing you here would make you see too many things you'd ask about and then refuse to accept."

"I'm sorry." His distress got to her. *Can he really believe this?* "Go on." When he continued to stare at her, she said, "Please."

"Heinrich was certain there was a device enabling him to communicate with them. A Star Stone, and he spent years searching for it. He found it shortly before he had to run away. He…The story goes that he contacted the beings…the Great Old Ones…and he promised them one of his blood would be the means by which they'd be freed. In return, they agreed to give him untold power."

As he stopped, Lisa forced a laugh. "But it's just a story, right?" *Why did I say it like that? Of course it's only a story.* "One everyone here has been taught to believe? You, included?" He nodded. "Then surely…" She paused, taking a deep breath. "What does this have to do with those graves?'

"Plenty. After Heinrich's first wife died, he married twice more. To make sure he had sons to fulfill that promise."

Lisa felt a sudden pity for those women. *How could they love a lunatic like that?* She hoped Drex wasn't going to follow his ancestor's footsteps in that direction.

"Neither of them lived long, and neither of them had children…there was no one of Heinrich's blood to help free the Old Ones. In between marriages, and probably during them, he used village women to make certain his bloodline continued. Most of those offspring didn't survive, either and the ones who did…were…marked."

""You mean like Hansi and Isak."

He nodded. "Wife Number Four finally gave him a son who was only too glad to do as his father wanted. And so on."

"So each master of Land's End…"

"They all seemed to prefer village women." Drex gave a short laugh. "My father…After I was born, he never touched my mother again…and she was eternally grateful for that."

Looking too agitated to sit still, he began to pace before the hearth. Heinrich's painted eyes seemed to follow his movements.

"I was about six when I realized he hated her….around the same time I learned the other red-haired children here, the ones I wasn't allowed to play with, were his but not hers. She was from the mainland

and he seemed to be contemptuous of her because of that. I wondered why she married him in the first place, and once got up enough nerve to ask her. Know what she said?"

Lisa shook her head, realized he didn't see the movement and stayed silent.

"*He was different. He intrigued me.*" He shook his head. "The intrigue died fast once she got here and after that, she tried to lose herself in caring for me. That was the only time she spoke of their early life together."

The need for movement spent, he dropped into the chair again.

"When I was twelve, my father became obsessed with my virility. *Got to get the kid fucked* was how he so genteelly phrased it. He made three attempts to take me to a woman in the village but Mother managed to thwart him." His laugh was rueful. "I guess if she'd had her way, I'd still be a virgin." His voice dropped to a whisper. "Two years later, she died and Dear Old Dad wasted no time pushing me into the nearest bed. I spent the day of her funeral having sex with a woman he'd given the honor of *breaking me in*…that was how he put it." When Drex looked at Lisa, his eyes were dark, voice shaking with an anger surviving sixteen years.

"The following year, I ran away to my mother's people who'd been trying to stay in touch with me though Father intercepted all their letters. They sent me to a college far enough away that no one could find me, or so we thought." Drex sighed. "For four years, I had the most wonderful, normal life. Then…just before I graduated, Rustin showed up. He said my father was sick and needed me. So I let myself get conned into coming home."

"What happened?"

"Isn't it obvious? I never left again. After that, we survived in an atmosphere of continual hate, mainly because I did nothing to ensure the continuation of Heinrich's bloodline. One of his milder comments was that he had a eunuch for a son. I was ready to kill either myself or him."

"Why didn't you leave?"

"I wanted to, believe me. He told me if I did, he'd make sure Mother's relatives paid for helping me. He'd kill them all. They think I abandoned them for my father's wealth when I actually saved their lives by staying here. He never missed a chance to remind me of that, either. He laughed at me, told me I'd never get away. I swear if it hadn't been for Aura, I'd…"

Drex dropped his head into his hands. Lisa felt a sudden stab of jealous. *Does he love her? He didn't seem to when we were in the village.*

"I seduced her, Lisa, got her pregnant. I admit it. I was still naïve enough to expect to marry her but he told me that was out of the question. A von Dorff didn't wed a peasant…Father was furious when the baby was stillborn. He acted as if I caused it. Deliberately. He couldn't urge us to try again fast enough. The night Joshua was born, he got drunk on Heinrich's brandy, yelled at me, *You've finally proven you've got balls.* I was going to kill him." He got to his feet, hands clenched into fists. "As it turned out, I didn't have to. He fell down the staircase that night and broke his neck. We don't have phone service here and he wouldn't allow anyone to have a cell, so I had to drive for a doctor but it was too late."

Lisa placed a hand over his, pulling him to sit beside her. She felt his fist relax.

"And so I became master of Land's End." He gave her a brief smile. "First thing I did was buy everyone on the island a cell phone."

"You should get away from here, from these memories." She parroted what Halyard had said.

"That's just it. I can't. Not now. I don't think I could survive in the outside world. Here at least, I'm master..." He laughed. "Like Lucifer...ruler of my own private Hell." His smile was grim. "*You* can leave though. Do you want to? Now that you know all the family secrets? Shall I have Rustin bring the car around?"

"I'll leave if you go with me."

"What about the Chief?"

"What about him?" She hated his referring to Dan Walker like that.

"I know how he feels about you...and how you feel about him."

"What I feel for Dan Walker doesn't matter. Not now."

"Does that mean what I think it does?"

"It depends on what you think it means."

"You'll stay?" For a moment, he stared at her, as if hearing what she wasn't saying. "In spite of all I've told you?"

"I don't believe in blaming someone for what his family's done, or for something happening in the past."

Let Dan Walker do that. He seems to be good at it. "All I want to know is…Do you still love Aura?"

"I don't think I ever really did."

"You two had another child. That had to mean something," she persisted.

"It means I was searching for someone to ease my unhappiness and she was there. I can't forget we had two children together and lost one, but we don't love each other. Not now. The only one I love…is you, Lisa."

"And I love you, Drex." *She didn't care what anyone thought, especially Dan Walker. She'd been attracted to Dan, might've eventually convinced herself she loved him, but now…she knew…she loved Drex.*

To her surprise, Drex didn't have a smart comeback to that. Squeezing the hand resting in his, he touched her cheek, then kissed her. Out of the corner of her eye, she saw something glitter. She caught his hand, pulling it down, staring at the ring on his finger. Gold and ornate, with a green stone. "Is that…"

"I inherited it along with everything else." He touched it and looked at the portrait. "If it'd fit you, we could use it for an engagement ring."

I don't think I want to wear that thing. It was a polished baroque stone, irregularly cut and as green as Drex's eyes. She brushed a finger across the smooth surface. "Oh…"

"What is it?"

"The ring…when I touched it, there was a spark."

"Couldn't be…You imagined it. See?" He held up his hand, showing how the stone didn't reflect light.

She knew she hadn't imagined it. She'd seen light gleaming in it as he touched her face. "What kind of gem is it?" she asked.

"It's a chip from Heinrich's Star Stone."

"You mean the thing really exists?"

"Didn't I say he found it?" He gestured toward the desk. "See for yourself."

On it was a large piece of glass, something else Lisa hadn't noticed. *Either I'm completely unobservant or I was more upset than I thought when we came in here.* She got up and walked over to the desk, looking down at the Star Stone. It was beautiful, translucent green with opaque shafts of jade buried within it. The surface was chipped and cracked as if tremendous heat had once engulfed it. It was vaguely egg-shaped, resting in a carved wooden cradle.

"Malachite?"

"I think it's green milk quartz. There's the place where the piece for the ring was removed." He indicated a small hollowed-out spot on the top. "It's said those with whom the Stone has ties can see things in it."

"Have you ever seen anything?" Surely Drex would have the strongest ties of all.

He shook his head. "Never had the pleasure."

"Mind if I take a peek?" Intrigued by the stone, she peered into the green crystal. "Maybe I'll see our future." Leaning over it, she looked through the green depths into its heart…a cold, gleaming fire burned…swirling clouds of milky emerald, streaks of pale jade. Lisa tried to look away. Couldn't move. She saw wavering figures, faces obscured. A brilliant flash of light illuminated the scene…

Gasping, she raised her head.

"What did you see?" he asked eagerly.

"I'm not sure." She tried to move away but he caught her arm, keeping her at the desk. "Myself? A child...my baby..."

"Did you see me?" He sounded if he were pleading.

"No, you weren't there...Drex, what was that?" She looked from the stone to him, ready to become frightened if he said the wrong thing. *I'm letting my imagination run away with me. Did I or didn't I see something? My God, it's no wonder they think Drex is weird. It's a miracle he's not raving if he's had to live with things like this.* "What did I see?"

"You didn't see anything." He laughed, a brief look of betrayal disappearing behind his smile. "You're too suggestible, Lisa. I'm sorry." He kissed her forehead, hugging her gently. "I shouldn't have told you any of that. Not after all you've been through."

"But it seemed so real."

"That's enough." Catching her around the waist, he swung her off the floor, planting a quick kiss on the side of her neck. "Set the right mood and some people'll believe anything. It's like UFOs or Bigfoot."

"So all of that was just a bunch of hoo-hah?"

"A lot of bullshit and a little truth...I was miserable while my father was alive, I did try to get away and failed and Joshua's my son. The rest? Like you said. Hoo-hah. Don't worry about it."

"You know what we need?" Lisa laughed a little shakily, forcing herself to change the subject.

"A couple of hours of good old-fashioned bed-bouncing? I'm for that."

"Some light." She gave him a glance saying, *You're incorrigible*, though she doubted he thought so. The room seemed to have gotten darker as they talked. Outside, shadows hid the yard and the trees. "What time is it anyway?"

"Search me." He glanced out the window. "From the length of those shadows, I'd say about ten o'clock." He touched a switch on the wall. Light flooded on overhead. "Would you like to know what I think?"

"If you repeat yourself, I may hit you."

"I think it's time for you to be in bed." He put his arms around her, kissing the tip of her nose, then leaned back. "Alone. I promise. Damn it."

~ * ~

Outside her door, he kissed her on the forehead. "There, is that chaste enough? For now? Lisa, are you going to make me behave until we're actually married?"

"I imagine so." She ignored his plaintive tone. "One of us has to observe propriety."

"Why? When misbehaving is much more fun." He looked upward beseechingly. "Oh God... Did you do the same to your first husband?"

"He didn't seem to mind."

"Right. I'll bet he went through a lot of cold showers and a good bit of tool-pulling every time he left you."

Lisa turned her head to hide the shock of that statement. Truthfully, she'd never thought of what Robin might've suffered from her continual refusals.

"If he managed it, I'll try to. Good night, sweetheart. Comfortable dreams." Before she could answer, he walked to his own room. At the door, he paused. "Remember. The adjourning door's locked, and you have the key." He winked. "If you change your mind…use it. I'll be receptive."

She was tempted…to go inside, put on a nightgown, and find that key and open the door. The way she felt just then…she'd never experienced such an emotion for a man before…not Robin, certainly not Dan Walker. The complete and near-overwhelming hunger rushing through her made her want to run after Drex and drag him back into her room. *Better not. I'm still shaken by what I thought I saw, by everything Drex has told me. Right this minute, all I want is for him to hold me…and then… The safest thing I can do right now is to get into that big bed and go to sleep.*

~ * ~

The sheets had been turned back, the bed looking cool and inviting. As soon as she saw it, exhaustion hit like the proverbial ton of bricks.

Her clothes had been unpacked, a white nightgown lying across the foot of the bed. *Who did that? Ursula?* The thought of the housekeeper handling her things didn't sit well.

Nevertheless, as she lay in bed, the entire afternoon in all its oddity came back, parading through her mind. *And I came here to relax? When I compared Drex's family to the Addamses, I was kidding. Tomorrow I hope everything's back to normal…* she was asleep before she could finish the thought.

~ * ~

Lisa…Lisa…we're waiting…

"Who are you?" The voice sounded near but she couldn't see anything. Everything was hazy, as thick as black cotton packed against her eyes.

You're not ready to see us yet. Just as you weren't ready to see Him, but we've seen you. We're watching you.

"When will I see who you are? When?"

Soon. Where sea and earth and sky meet, that's where we'll be. We're waiting for you there...

Chapter 20

"Most of the island's marsh so it's uninhabitable," Drex said. "Some of it's dangerous because there are hidden bogs. Therefore, we're confining our rambles to the north end where we live."

They set out walking along the little path worn into the sandy soil. Sometimes they held hands. For a little while, Drex walked with his arm about her, holding her close against his side.

Even in the morning warmth, he was wearing a sweater, its turtleneck collar rolled high under his chin though the sleeves were pushed up to his elbows. With a stab of envy, Lisa noticed no freckles marred the evenness of his skin, not like the spattering of brown flecks on her own cheeks and shoulders. *His skin's smooth as satin.* She wondered what the body beneath those clothes looked like. *Better stop that kind of thinking*, she told herself. *Unless you plan on finding out in the very near future.* It sounded like something to look forward to.

"I suppose I should get you an engagement ring," he said. "Do you want to pick it out or do you trust my judgment?"

"You mean I don't get some treasured heirloom…your great-great-great-great-grandmother's betrothal ring or something?"

"Sorry. As far as I know, that was buried with her, and I really don't think you want me trying to retrieve it." He paused, giving her a raised brow. "Do you?"

"Please." She shuddered then looked coy. "Besides, who says I'm going to marry you?"

"You did." Briefly, he looked uncertain. "Didn't you? At least that what I thought you said last night."

"Loving you and marrying you are different things," she teased.

"Lisa…" For a moment, he appeared stricken.

"If I do marry you, it has to be with the promise you're never going to mention your crazy ancestors again," she said, wanting to get that look off his face.

"You've got it." He relaxed.

"In that case…a nice little solitaire will be fine…and I'll let you pick it out. Surprise me." She hugged him. "Why am I so happy?"

"Because you've found another man who loves you…and is going to take care of you," he told her, kissing her cheek. "And your baby."

"Is the baby going to make a difference?" A little late to worry about that now.

"I'll say the same thing I said the last time you asked that," he replied. "Of course it will. I'll have a ready-made family…and I intend to add to it after little *whatever-you-decide-to-call-him* gets a little older."

"So you want a large family?"

"Not too large. We're already proven we can both have children, so I think we should do it together and give your child a sibling, don't you?"

Her expression changed slightly as he said that. She didn't like being reminded about Joshua or that little grave.

"Hey...don't look that way." He caught her chin, thumb caressing gently. "Joshua's always going to be part of my life. I'll never deny him, and your baby'll be told he has a half-brother, but it's over between Aura and me. You don't have to worry about me straying, Lisa. I'll be faithful, I promise."

He hugged her again, kissing her a little forcefully as if to prove it. She snuggled her head against his chest, arms tightening around his waist.

"All I want is to be happy again, the way I was with Robin." She looked up at him. "You needn't worry that I'll snub Joshua. He's a darling little boy and I'll include him in our family...if Aura allows it." She wondered why she added that.

"She will." He said it confidently, then a little quieter, "She'd better." Looking up, he gestured at the trees. "Hey, I thought we were supposed to be exploring. Believe it or not, for an island, this place has a lot to look at. We'd better get to it." He looked down at her again. "Unless you'd rather find a quiet spot somewhere and indulge in a little premarital nookie?" He waggled his eyebrows, leering comically.

For two seconds Lisa didn't answer. Then she pulled from his embrace and caught his hand, tugging on it. "Let's explore."

"I was afraid you'd say that."

As they walked along the path, she saw things she hadn't noticed the night before. The scenery was completely different from the mainland, having a starved depleted look. The soil was soft and sandy, typical beach land, yet there seemed to be a *drained* quality to it, as if all the nutrients had somehow been sucked out of the earth. As at the Manor, most of the trees were pines, slender and twisted, bark dried and covered with gray lichens and sickly white moss. Surprisingly, there were wildflowers, untouched by whatever had stricken the trees. Lisa released Drex's hand. She wandered a bit farther, exclaiming over the leaves of a creeper curling around the trunk of a tree, and then stared at the sky where it was visible through the treetops.

"What's this?" she asked, pointing to a bright yellow vine encircling a row of huckleberry bushes. "It's practically strangling those poor bushes."

"That's exactly what it's doing," he told her. "It's a parasite. Wraps itself around other vegetation until the host dies from being enveloped. Come on." He caught her hand.

"That's horrible." Lisa looked back at the plant, entwined through the bushes like a tangled ball of yellow yarn. "What's it called? The Strangler Vine or something?"

"Actually, it's *cadena de amor*…chain of love."

"Hah. A misnomer if ever there was one. Love isn't like that."

"Isn't it?"

"Don't be cynical." She hit his shoulder. He winced and began to rub it in exaggerated pain. "You know it isn't."

"Well…"

"Love is great. It's fantastic."

"Why don't you show me exactly how fantastic?" He spun her around, arms tightening. He kissed her, tongue pressing against her lips, invading just enough to flick at her own before he raised his head. "Nice. For *Introduction to Love 101*. I'm ready for more advanced studies." He dived in for another kiss.

"What's that?" Lisa backed out of his arms, spotting another vine. "Those yellow flowers?" She pointed to tiny blossoms strung along slender green tendrils stretching from the branch of one tree to another.

"That's wild jasmine." He started walking again. "And here's the beach."

The path rose over a mound of a hill. From the other side came the sounds of waves, the pounding of surf, and a breeze carrying a salty sea-smell. To the roar of waves clashing against the rocks, they came out of the woods and onto the shore.

~ * ~

The ocean lay at the end of an expanse of dazzling sand, blinding after the darkened shadows of the woods. It was littered with bits of driftwood and pine needles blown from the surrounding trees. At the moment, the surf was out, waves splashing at the shoreline. It tossed broken bits of shells, making ripples in the wet sand as it receded. On either side of where they stood, a curved border of stone lay tumbled about as if a giant played with them, tossing and then abandoning them. It looked secluded, private, and very lonely.

Taking a deep breath, Drex paused to let Lisa catch up with him. The wind blew his hair off his face, sending it into gleaming copper tangles reflecting the sunlight glowing on his skin. Where his clothing didn't touch, Drex shone like a bolt of sunshine.

"How do you like it?" He waved a hand at the ocean as if he'd created the scene especially for her benefit. "What do you think?" He didn't give her time to answer. Catching her hand, he began to run across the dunes.

The sand was brilliantly white. Washed by the relentless movement of the surf, that below the tideline was damp and gray. Like straw-colored thickets, clumps of sea oats topped little hillocks of sand, making slender wavering shadows. Patches of bronze and yellow gaillardia added splashes of color. The damp sand squeaked under their running feet.

Stopping in front of a clump of sea oats, Drex dropped onto the sand. "Here, sit down."

Looking at the space he indicated, Lisa brushed at it with her hand, peering intently.

"What are you doing?" He squinted at her against the sunlight.

"Looking for ants," she said, her own eyes twinkling. "Don't want to get ants in my pants."

"It's not ants you have to worry about," he said, pulling her down beside him.

Sighing, she leaned her head against his shoulder. It felt good when he put his arm around her waist and rested his cheek against her hair.

"All this is yours?"

"The beach is. I can't lay claim to the ocean, I'm afraid. Not yet, anyway." He studied the water, whitecaps breaking beyond the rocks protruding through the choppy surface. "This is the only beach on the island. The rest of Land's End simply drops away into the sea. Maybe someday all of it will." He pointed past the breakers. "The boats used to anchor out there because of the underwater rocks. The landing-boats had a hard time getting in."

"It's beautiful."

"And peaceful. I used to come here to get away from my father. I'd bring Aura here and we'd..." He shook his head. "Sorry..."

"It's all right. She was part of your life, and you're bound to mention her, just as I'll occasionally say something about Robin. I can understand why you brought her here. This is your haven, isn't it?"

"When I'm here, I can forget everything. This place feels so isolated." He resumed what he'd been saying. "It's as if the water and the sky and the beach all come together and melt into each other to form a new world....another dimension."

Lisa looked out over the ocean. He was right. The little crest of land seemed to blend into the sea, the blue of the sky meeting it. Sea and earth and sky meeting...She frowned. *Where have I heard that? Sea and land and sky...*

Drex fell quiet, watching the water. Lisa studied his profile against the background of dazzling sand. He seemed so at home in this little stretch of land, more than anywhere else she'd seen him.

Wind blowing off the water ruffled the waves. Lisa brushed a stray lock of hair from her forehead where it clung, damp from the moisture in the air. "It looks so cool. Wish I could just jump in."

"Why don't we?" He smiled at her.

"For one thing, we didn't bring suits."

"So?"

"Swim without them?" She dropped his hand, staring at him. "Is this some of that premarital...uh...nookie...you mentioned?"

"You'd better believe it." He barely paused before adding, "I hope."

"Don't tempt me."

"That's exactly what I plan to do, sweetheart. Definitely."

"Can anyone see?" She tried not to look as eager as she felt. To be with Drex in that cool, white-foamed water...naked...

"Not a chance." He got to his feet, brushing sand from his jeans. With a broad gesture including the scene before them, he went on, "No one trespasses here. We can do as we like." He began to roll up the hem of his sweater, revealing a tanned midriff. "Fact is, I don't even own a swimsuit. I've skinny dipped here all my life."

With Aura? She didn't say it aloud, that jealousy she'd sworn she didn't have springing to life. She caught his arm, stopping its movement. "You can't undress out here in the open."

"Didn't you hear what I said?" He pulled the sweater up and over his head, dropping it to the ground. Lisa took a deep breath, gaze skittering over his chest before she forced it back to his face. "This is my land, Lisa. I do what I want here." His hands went to her shoulders, caressing. "Come on...you know you want to." She didn't move. "If you insist on modesty..." He turned her around so she faced the sea oats. "Get behind those and shuck your clothes, lady." He gave her a little push, then unsnapped his jeans.

As Lisa stumbled toward the little hillock, she heard the rasp of his zipper. Safely behind the sea oats, she began to unbutton her dress, slipping it off her shoulders and over her hips and dropping it to the sand. Bra and panties followed.

From the other side of the sea oats, there was splashing.

"I'm ready," she called.

No answer. Peeping from the security of the reeds, she said, "Drex?"

Still no answer. She came from behind the barricade.

"Come on in…the water's fine."

Chapter 21

Against the water's darkness, Drex's red hair was a glowing flame. Pushed by his paddling hands, waves rippled around him in little circles. Automatically, Lisa's hands came up, one spread over her breasts, the other across her thighs.

"Too late," he called. "I've seen it all."

"Did you like what you saw?" Feeling brazen, she dropped her hands, putting them on her hips as if challenging him.

"Definitely. Get with grabbing range and I'll show you how much."

Taking a deep breath, she sprinted across the stretch of beach to the water's edge. A wave rushed to meet her, the water cold. She hesitated, then splashed into the surf until it was up to her knees, fell forward and began to swim.

The current changed to a pleasant warmth. She was acutely aware of water moving against her breasts, encircling her, swirling around her legs, tickling upward between her thighs.

"Took you long enough." He reached for her, ducking her. Then he swam away laughing as she surfaced spluttering, to paddle after him.

He kept it up, splashing and diving until Lisa was soaked, water dripping from her hair into her eyes while she laughed the whole time. Taking a deep breath, Drex dived. The surface rippled and smoothed. Something brushed her ankle.

She kicked, laughing. "Hey, stop it."

A few yards away, more ripples appeared and Drex surfaced, slinging water from his eyes.

"Very funny. We are not amused." She paddled, treading water. "I didn't like that...grabbing my ankle and then swimming away."

"What are you talking about?" He looked puzzled. "I didn't do anything."

"Oh, sure." Something touched her again, sharp and rough this time, giving a quick tug. She sank into the water, bobbing. Water splashed, sand swirled, clouding the water as if something churned the ocean bottom. There was a fumbling scrape against her calf, her leg was seized and jerked downward. Water splashed into her mouth and she began to strangle, coughing. "Drex..."

"Take it easy." He swam toward her, managing to float while he caught at her waist, pulling her toward him and holding her head above the water. Lisa clutched at him, splashing water on his face. He turned his head, dodging. "Calm down."

"Something grabbed my ankle." Wiping at her face, she took a deep breath and huddled against him. "There's something down there." There was pressure on her ankle as if a sharp and scaly hand held it. She glanced around frantically, visions of that terrible attack scene from *Jaws* flashing through her mind. "There's something down there!" This time it came out in a squeal.

Everything Drex said about the ocean came battering back. An imprisoned sea god ...*it carried Heinrich away... Full fathom five... Sea-change... changeling...* the pressure tightened. Lisa began to struggle, clinging to Drex, fighting against the thing seizing her.

"Lisa, let go." He caught her hands, pushing them away. "You're going to drown us both." He shook her as he said it, sending water roiling. Swimming backwards, he dived while Lisa splashed in a frantic circle, kicking wildly.

This time when something caught her ankle, she recognized it as a human hand. The pressure lessened. She waited anxiously, moving her feet just enough to keep her head above water. When Drex reappeared, she went so limp, she sank. A small wave splashed her face. He swam away from her, standing upright and wading into the shallows, motioning for her to join him. He was looking at something in his hand. Lisa swam toward him. As soon as her feet touched bottom, she stood up.

"Here's what frightened you." Drex thrust the thing he held toward her. A rope of barnacles cemented together by sand onto a piece of seaweed.

"It...pulled my leg," she protested. "I felt it."

"A very long strand of seaweed caught in some rocks. You got tangled in it. When you kicked, it felt like it was pulling." It sounded so reasonable. She gave a trembling laugh to hide her embarrassment. He held it out to her. "Souvenir?"

"No." Pulling the string of shells from his hand, she threw them as far away as she could. They hit the water and sank. Behind her, she heard Drex splashing toward the beach.

When she turned, he was almost out of the water. He looked back. The sun struck the waves, sending a mass of writhing sunlets dancing around him. He was a dazzling marine creature…hair plastered to his shoulders like the fronds of a vivid sea fern. Rivulets streamed down his arms and chest, dripping back into the swirling water. The sea light reflected in his eyes, casting brazen shadows onto his skin, carving his face into a copper mask.

Vision overwhelmed by the dancing reflections, Lisa caught her breath. For an instant, he was alien, beautifully inhuman. *If there's a sea god here, it's Drex, and he isn't a* cetto thlot-lo. She blinked, was rewarded with dancing black afterimages before her eyes.

"Like what you see?" As if suddenly aware she was watching him, he threw her own question back at her.

"No, darn it. The sun's in my eyes." She realized she was standing waist-deep in the water, her own wet hair the only thing hiding her bare breasts from him. She began to swim.

He met her in a few strokes, lifting her out of the water. Hands on his shoulders, she looked down at him, smiling. Her hair floated over them, mingling with his own.

"Getting tired?"

She nodded.

He started to drop her back into the water, then pulled her toward him instead, so her breasts touched his chest. He leaned toward her…and Lisa brought up both hands, launching a cascade of water over his head. Laughing, she pushed away and splashed toward shore.

Wiping water from his eyes, Drex started after her. Lisa clambered out of the water and ran across the beach. Behind her, she heard Drex do the same. He caught her by the ankle. She stumbled and they both fell to the sand, still laughing. Then he was kissing her again, body pinning her to the sand. His hand slid from her waist to her hip, traveled across, pressing against her thighs, fingers seeking upward.

A twig snapped. Lisa jerked away. "What was that? Is someone…"

"Better not be." Drex looked up the slope, searching the shadows under the trees. "Who is it? Who's there?" He got to his feet, erection springing upward. *When did he get so aroused?*

"There's someone there. Someone's watching us." Lisa scrambled to her feet also.

They could hear someone running through the underbrush, trampling leaves as he crashed through the bushes. Drex turned as if he could see the runner, eyes seeming to following the sound.

His back was to her, that startling hard-on hidden. Once more the brightness of sun against sand dazzled her eyes. She put up a hand to shade them as she stared at Drex's back. *What's the matter with it?* She could see a faint pattern on the tanned skin…almost like…scales? Light stung her eyes. She blinked and he turned to face her as the sound of the retreating footsteps died away. His arousal was lessening.

"Lisa…"

She didn't answer, didn't say a word as she ran for the safety of the sea oats, snatching at clothing and brushing at sand sticking to her wet skin.

When she emerged, clothed but damp. Drex had dressed also. He zipped his jeans as she reached his side.

"That definitely wasn't the way I wanted this to end." He gave it a comic inflection though his expression said he was furious.

"It's a good thing we were interrupted... I think this was wrong."

"That's crap." He closed the waistband snap, reaching for her. She dodged, keeping far enough away he couldn't touch her. "What's the matter?"

Looking down, she saw the bosom of the dress gaped. A button had been overlooked in her haste. She fastened it. "We shouldn't have done that, Drex." Her voice was muffled, spoken into the fabric of her dress.

"Hell, Lisa." He caught her by the shoulder, pulling her around so roughly she glared at him.

"You were enjoying it...I know I certainly was. We're both adult and we both know the score...and we're engaged now, so why was it wrong? Because someone saw?" His eyes glittered furiously, jade fire in their depths. "If I ever find out who, he'll regret it."

"I thought I had the whole thing settled." She pushed away, shaking her head and brushing a hand across her eyes. *What if it wasn't a 'he'? What if it was Aura?* "It's been pointed out to me very plainly I shouldn't have come here. I've been a widow four months and I had no right to do what we just did...nearly did."

"Is that really it?" Now it was he who wouldn't look at her. "Because if it is, it's the biggest bit of bullshit I've ever heard." He stared at the water. "It's the baby, isn't it?" When she didn't answer, he snapped, "Come on, Lisa, You know damned well if you were merely a widow…four months new or not, you'd have absolutely no qualms about being here with me…swimming naked or having sex or doing anything else. If you weren't pregnant." He took a deep breath, stopped, and, as if making a decision turned back to face her. "Sit down." She didn't move. He pushed her toward a nearby rock. "*Sit.*"

Obediently, she sank onto it. For several minutes, Drex paced in front her without speaking. At last, he stopped.

"It was supposed to turn out differently. I was going to make love to you, and…" He looked down at her. "The first time I saw you, I knew there was something special about you. Even in the hospital, you looked so…" he paused.

"What are you talking about?" She frowned. It sounded so much like what Dan had said, she was shaken. *This is no time to think of Daniel Walker.* No time to think of refusing his phone calls, and sending him away when he stopped by or of what she'd said to him the last time she saw him.

"It's…when I came to see you, I knew how the Chief felt. Anyone with eyes would've. I wasn't sure I had a chance. I wanted to do this fair and square, then I had to go away, and realized when I came back, he'd had plenty of time to work his own magic… So I was going to bring you here…and…get you on the beach and…" His voice trailed away. Dropping to his knees beside her, he seized her hands. "Last night, you said you loved me. Do you still mean that?"

"Of course. You don't think I'm going to fall out of love because a Peeping Tom spied on us, do you?"

"In that case, let's make it official…I mean *really* official…Lisa, will you marry me?" She didn't answer, just stared at him for so long he demanded, "Well?"

"I thought that was a given. As of last night." She laughed, and it was a nervous little sound. "All right…official…Yes, Drex, I'll marry you."

"Great. We'll drive into Temple and have whatever tests need to be done. I'm not up on that but I suppose someone at the hospital can tell us, and we can be married as soon as we get the results and apply for a license…"

"Hold on, Romeo," Lisa interrupted. "I can't marry you *now*."

"Why not?" Sheer petulance touched his face. "Do you have something better to do? Not wanting to point out the obvious—"

"Then don't," she retorted.

"—but I'd think you'd be glad to get a ring on your finger before the blessed event," he went on as if she hadn't spoken.

"Why should I do that? I had a husband when my baby was conceived. I don't have a thing to be ashamed of." *Much.* She ignored that thought. "We'll get married, Drex, but it'll be afterward."

"Why would you possibly want to wait…?"

"Because this is Rob's baby." She didn't give him time to finish. "It's all I have left of him and it's going to be born with his name, not his stepfather's." Drex looked as if he disagreed with that. She held up a hand. "No argument."

His sigh told her he accepted that, surprising her. She'd expected more. "The next five months are going to be the longest of my life."

"It won't be so bad." She put her arms around his neck, swaying against him. He pushed her away.

"Stop it." He didn't look angry, however. "That's the kind of temptation I don't need right now." Contradicting his words, he swung her around. "Do you know what touching you does to me?"

"I'm getting a pretty good idea." She could feel his arousal pressing against her thighs, rigid and persistent. *My God, if he gets excited this easily, I may find myself pregnant on my wedding night.* Gently easing out of his arms, she managed not to glance down.

"None of this is turning out as I expected."

"Quit complaining. You're getting what you wanted," she told him.

I always get what I want.

"Just not when I want it," he pointed out. "I'll have to remind myself of that when I start jerking off into a towel." Hooking fingers into his trainers, he whirled and started up the beach. Lisa watched him a moment, then picked up her own sandals and ran to his side. She caught his hand. With an exaggerated groan, he reached out and drew her close, one arm going around her shoulders. She leaned into his side as they walked along the shore. The tide was coming in now and the gently approaching water lapped at their bare feet.

When they reached the rocks, Drex dropped onto a long low boulder that looked chiseled to form a bench. Lisa sat beside him. For a long time, neither spoke as they watched the sun's bright ripples sink into the waves. At last, Lisa sighed and dropped her head to his shoulder. Without speaking, he put his arms around her.

"I said I'd be faithful to you, Lisa, and it starts now." He didn't look at her but kept his gaze on the incoming water. "But I don't intend to be celibate until we're married."

"What does that mean?" She looked up at him.

"It means you should give up and accept the fact that somehow I'm going to get you into bed and keep you there…until the day you're too big for me to get near." He pressed a kiss against her temple and returned to watching the water.

When at last they left the beach, the sun was making blood red splashes on the sea. Their walk back was a very quiet one.

Chapter 22

Rustin was still nowhere in sight so Ursula had to serve the meal from the massive mahogany sideboard, muttering under her breath the entire time. She'd set the table as if royalty were visiting, with gleaming china and clear delicate crystal which looked to be very old.

"Will Mrs. Chambers have wine, sir?" she asked, not looking at Lisa. She picked up a bottle that had been opened and set on the buffet to breathe.

"One glass," Drex answered, surprising Lisa as he looked at her. "That's right, isn't it?"

She nodded, remembering how she and Dan had argued about that. *Someone's been doing a little prenatal reading. And told Ursula, too.*

As the housekeeper approached Lisa's place to pour the wine, he went on, "Ursula, I've some good news for you."

"Yes, Mr. Drex?" She reached for Lisa's goblet.

"In a few months, Land's End will finally have a mistress. Mrs. Chambers has consented to marry me."

The neck of the bottle jerked. Wine splashed onto the snowy tablecloth, narrowly missing Lisa's hand.

"E-excuse me…" Ursula was immediately apologetic. She hurried to the sideboard, taking a napkin from those folded there and began to mop at the stain. "I'm so glad, sir…Mrs. Chambers." She flicked a bare glance including Lisa.

Why do I think you're anything but?

"Don't worry about the stain," Drex said, impatiently.

Nodding at each in turn, she stepped back, once more the proper servant, composure regained. "Will that be all, sir?"

"I believe so," Drex said. "Mrs. Chambers and I can serve ourselves."

Ursula paused in the doorway, looking back at Lisa. Her expression held hate so virulent and obvious Lisa drew in her breath. The housekeeper turned and went out.

"She certainly didn't seem overjoyed by the news." *That is an understatement.* Lisa didn't look at the wine stain. It was too much like a splotch of fresh blood on the purity of the white cloth. Trying to be as nonchalant as possible, she dropped her napkin over the spot.

"Ursula has run this household for sixteen years." Drex set down his wine glass and concentrated on cutting his steak. "I guess she decided I'd never marry. Now, I tell her she's got to become merely a housekeeper again." He studied the morsel of beef on his fork. "Give her a little time to get used to the idea."

"Granted she's been running the show for all that time," Lisa answered, stabbing into her salad. For a moment, she wished it were Ursula's flat chest. That startled her. *Since when did I get so vindictive? She didn't really intend to spill that wine on me.* "But you're only…what… thirty-one?"

"Thirty," he corrected, sticking the bit of steak into his mouth.

"That's nowhere near an age for her to assume you're going to be a lifelong bachelor." She ate the forkful of lettuce and tomato. "Are you sure she isn't going to put arsenic in my chocolate mousse or something?"

He laughed. "I'm sure. Ursula's going to be as concerned for your welfare as I am. If she knows what's good for her." His smile softened the implied threat in his words, making them into an ironic statement but there was something in his expression saying differently. He raised his wineglass. "To the future Mrs. Von Dorff."

Lisa raised her own glass, taking a sip of the wine. It was surprisingly mild, with a faint cherry flavor. She drank slowly, the housekeeper's expression lingering in her mind.

~ * ~

Later, Drex walked her to her room as he had the night before. "If you hear strange sounds outside tonight, don't be afraid."

"What kind of sounds?"

"It's All Hallow's Eve. The villagers'll be celebrating."

"All Hal...You mean Halloween? Is today October 31st? How could I forget that? What'll they be doing?"

They'll build a bonfire and have a party. I imagine a few'll get drunk. They usually get a little noisy."

"Sounds like fun. I remember Aunt Allie and my mother always took me Trick or Treating." She wondered if Drex had ever done that. She tried to imagine him as a little redheaded ghost or goblin, going from door-to-door in the village with a shopping bag holding his treats. *Everyone on the island is living the*

Addams Family Dream, *remember? Why would they pretend to be supernatural creatures for a silly holiday?* "Will the children be there?"

"The children aren't allowed at the celebration. They stay at home, out of harm's way." He smiled as if in apology. "I'm afraid we're not invited, either. It's a private party."

"I'm not disappointed. I doubt if I could stay awake." As if to prove it, she blinked and yawned. "For some reason, I'm really tired. Must've been the swimming. When I was small, I had to take a nap after I came back from the pool." She stood on tiptoe and gave him a peck on the lips. "Good night, Drex. Trick or treat."

"Don't tempt me...I've a treat I'd really like to give you." He returned the kiss, making it more than a peck. "Good night, Lisa."

~ * ~

Lisa shut the door and turned to find Ursula standing by the bed.

"Mrs. Chambers...I...you startled me." The housekeeper's hand went to her chest as if clutching her heart.

"I'd think it ought to be the other way around," Lisa answered. "What are you doing here?"

"I was bringing an arrangement for your room. I thought I'd have it ready before you..." Under Lisa's unconvinced stare, Ursula gestured at the vase on the bedside table.

Dark purple blossoms, blue petals, pale lilies filled the vase. Lisa walked over to look at it.

"It's lovely." The arrangement truly was. "Thank you." She hoped she didn't sound ungrateful. She looked a little closer. *Wait a minute. Those flowers aren't lilies.* They were white and trumpet-shaped with delicate lavender veins. "Is this Jimson weed?"

"Yes, madam." Ursula was over her fright now, voice very precise. "It's sometimes called thorn-apple. It grows wild here."

And everywhere else in Georgia.

"And this is foxglove," the housekeeper went on as she indicated the purple cup-shaped flowers hanging from a tall stalk. "These are from the flower garden."

"What are the blue ones?" Lisa's curiosity got the best of her though she felt she should be exclaiming in horror instead. *Who grows foxglove in a flower garden? Morticia, Morticia...how does your garden grow...?*

"Monkshood."

Monkshood? That's wolfsbane...or I don't know my werewolf movies.

"Aren't they poisonous?" Lisa thought of what she'd said to Drex about arsenic. She didn't touch the flowers. *Can poison be transmitted by touch?* She noticed Ursula didn't touch them either.

"Only if they're eaten, madam." Ursula smiled as if she sensed Lisa's distrust and was amused.

"They're certainly a fitting bouquet for tonight, aren't they?"

"You know about tonight?" Ursula took a step backward, her face becoming even more colorless.

"Drex told me," Lisa said. Why did that upset her so? "About the Halloween bonfire, and the party..."

"Halloween. The party." The housekeeper relaxed. "Yes."

"Are you going to the celebration, too?" She was tired of standing there, wanted the housekeeper to leave.

"No madam." Ursula's answer was stiff, almost insulted. "I have other duties to attend to." Her tone implied she considered the villagers' little pleasures beneath her notice.

"Too bad." Lisa yawned openly, hoping she'd get the message. "It sounds like fun."

"I imagine it will be…for some of them. You must be tired, madam. I'll leave now."

"Thank you for the flowers." Lisa blinked. *I can hardly keep my eyes open.*

As Ursula went out, Lisa bent over the vase. There was a faint lily-like fragrance coming from the Jimson weed. She thought about that specific plant. Loco weed. *How can something smelling so good be so deadly?* A swirl of dizziness swept over her. *I'm so tired. Better get into bed before I fall down.*

No sooner had she settled herself in the four-poster than she was asleep.

~ * ~

What…what is it? Lisa struggled awake.

In spite of being so warm during the day, it was cool when she went to bed and someone…Ursula…had closed the shutters against the sea air. *Thanks for that, anyway.*

The scent of the flowers was stronger. *Was that what woke me?* She had a sense of someone standing close to the bed. Opening her eyes, Lisa stared into the darkness. There was a full moon and in the light filtering through the windows, she could see a dark outline…a figure between her and the window.

"Drex? Is that you?"

Yes. His whisper came from the shadows.

"What is it? Is something wrong?" She struggled to sit up, pushing back the sheet. "How did you get in? I thought you said the door was locked."

It is. I'm not really here, Lisa. You're merely dreaming I am.

"Sure I am. You think I can't tell a dream from being awake?"

You haven't been able to so far. What about that business with my roses...at the hospital? And after you went home?

"Those were...just dreams...this is...Wait a minute...how did you know..." She sensed, rather than saw him move toward the bed, gliding like a shadow. He touched her cheek, bending to kiss her gently.

It doesn't really matter what I know or how I got here. What's important is that I'm here... like you want me to be...

"I don't..."

Unh-uh... don't lie...you didn't want me to walk away when we were outside and you don't want me to leave now. He didn't raise his voice from that soft whisper. The hand on her cheek slid downward. It caressed her throat, resting against her breast covered by the soft fabric of her nightgown. *Just as you want me to do this.* Deft fingers plucked open the bow, pushing aside the cloth.

Lisa didn't move, didn't do anything to stop him. It was true. She *did* want him...even if he were nothing more than a voice in the darkness, a voice and bodiless hands, touching, caressing.

He seized the front of the gown, ripping it apart. The sound of tearing cloth was loud in the quiet of the room. She should've cried out, protested the violence. Instead, she shivered and stayed silent, breasts and belly gleaming palely in the shuttered moonlight. She trembled as a hand cupped her breast, stroking the nipple, didn't make a sound except for a faint shudder of pleasure.

I told you I wasn't going to give up. She felt his smile as she responded, nipple peaking into a hard little nub under his stroking fingers. He bent, taking it into his mouth, tongue laving cold against her suddenly heated skin. Without warning, he was gone.

With a whimper, Lisa leaned forward, her own hands wavering, trying to find him. She wanted to hold his head against her breast, feel him suck her nipple, wanted her flesh damp from his tongue.

With a flutter of curtains the windows swung outward, shutters crashing against the sides of the house. His shadow blocked the moon, a monstrous splotch of darkness framed in the window, floating over the sill.

Come with me, Lisa. Come with us…the thought was in her mind. His hand…many hands…reached out to her. *We're waiting. I'm waiting… Come to our party… Help us celebrate.* The wind whipped the shadows about him into an obscuring cloak…like wings…

Lisa slid out of bed. Her bare feet made no noise as she ran to his shadow. She was caught in invisible arms, pressed against an unseen body.

Don't be afraid. The words brushed her mind, soft as the wind blowing against her flesh as it curled inside the torn nightgown and wrapped around her.

With a single motion, he raised her to stand beside him on the windowsill. Mist crept off the sea, covering the lawn, floating upward, billowing white and soft. Through the open window she could see the yard two stories below. If they fell, they'd die. She tried to pull away.

Don't be afraid. You're with me...with us...

"Yes," she whispered. "I'm with you, Drex. Nothing else matters."

The mist curled closer, caressing their faces.

Are you ready?

Holding Drex's hand, she stepped into the mist...

Chapter 23

...onto sand soft and warm under her bare feet, sifting between her toes. She stumbled slightly, felt Drex pull her forward. His hand on hers, she followed obediently until he stopped and the mist began to fade, the moon shining through it.

They were in the little cove again, on the beach bounded by the high boulders. Except for the darkness and the mist, it was as it had been earlier...quiet...isolated...

We're here. I've brought her. He released her hand and stepped away and Lisa faltered. She felt adrift, as if he'd set her into an swiftly-moving stream, sending her floating away from him. With one hand, he swept back the mist as easily as a white curtain, sending it rolling over the water, swirling and creating an avenue to the shore.

Moon-glimmering water swayed and rippled, movement in its depths. Darkness floated to the surface, became scale and weed-draped forms, slime-coated and long submerged. Sea changelings rose from their ocean slumbers, wading to the shore, lumbering onto the sand, leaving foam-rippling wakes as the mist parted before them...

...and Lisa stood, unmoving and unafraid, watching the creatures kneel before her on the silver sand.

Behind them a fire burned. Untended, the villagers' bonfire blazed. A log crackled and exploded, shooting cinders into the air. Sparks gathered, forming pulsing globes of color. They shimmered, collided, and coalesced, creating a gigantic fireball searing across the sky.

The creatures' scaly paws caught at her nightgown, plucking it from Lisa's shoulders. They did the same to Drex's robe, pulling the garments from their bodies. They faced each other naked in the fire's glow. Lisa felt no shame standing before him...or those unblinking creatures...all she could think was how beautiful he looked in the gleam of the firelight...his skin highlighted by the flickering of the flames, hair brilliant as the fire itself. His face reflected the light, nipples gleaming copper, belly and thighs lustrous, his erection a darker spear...

The beings crawled nearer, touching foreheads to the sand...

Our worshippers... our slaves.

Drex dropped to his knees, wrapping his arms around her waist, pressing his mouth against her thighs. His tongue probed and delved and as Lisa gasped, he pulled her down beside him onto the sand. He kissed her, tongue claiming hers. With dismaying eagerness, Lisa welcomed its invasion.

The sand was rough and coarse under her shoulders. From beyond the fire, a frog called out and another answered from the trees. A whippoorwill shrieked. Drex's weight covered her. Taking her in his arms, he kissed her again, lips traveling to the hollow of her throat, breath warm against her neck. Trapped beneath him, crushed into the sand, she was touched by a hundred hands, her breasts caressed by thousands of fingers, sliding between her thighs, moving upward, inward, pushing inside her....

His skin was warm against hers. She felt the brush of the hair on his chest and groin against her breast and thighs. Felt the growing hardness captured between them. Heat...pulsation...rigid flesh becoming even tighter. She pressed her face against his shoulder, stifling a near sob as he forced her legs apart and thrust into her.

It hurts... He was massive... Her body stiffened in protest. *This has happened before.* The heavy body pinning her down. *When, where... Fire, fire, burning right*...it was cold, so cold, the wind from the sea blew out the fire and everything was freezing...the mist came smothering down as he began to move inside her. She was falling...the sky whirling...

Night voices swept through her mind, rending the white veil, singing in unison with each thrust and stroke. They replaced the beat of her heart...all senses, all thought. The need to be possessed sent her body arching to meet his, moving to receive and entrap. She clasped her legs around his hips, holding tightly, forcing him further inside her...*I'll never let him leave me*...Pale fingers talon-curved raked golden shoulders crimson...

Lisa opened her eyes as the globe hovered above them, swelling and widening like a grotesque canopy. Its slender tentacles reached downward, grazing Drex's heaving shoulders. They attached themselves to his skin, pulsing deep red, paling to bloodless white, color shifting to the beat of his thrusts, gorging itself on his passion.

Drex cried out in orgasm and lay still, body dead-weight on hers, his breathing deep and slow against her breast. Her hands caught and stroked the hair tangled on his shoulders. The mist covered them, hiding him from her sight.

Surging upward, the creature thrust its tentacles into the white layer, wrapping them around his neck. Drex's body was slung away, the formless orb taking his place. It shuddered and coalesced into a vague man-shape, twisted and massive. Her hands touched scales and stiff, thick hair as it shoved itself inside her.

You're mine...not his...nor the shaman's...only mine...promised to me. A caricature of Drex's face stared into hers. It shuddered, vanishing in a spiral of sparks. The sky was empty, the ocean silent. She lay alone on the sand, hands outstretched...crying, *Come back...*

Which one was she reaching for?

~ * ~

"She should be mine." *M'AneseNebh* growled at his brother. "*I* speak for the Old Ones. *I* deliver their words. She should be given to me."

"In that case," he was looked at contemptuously. "You can have her...the day you walk among them undetected...as I do."

With that, he stalked away, leaving his twisted and less-than-human sibling crouched there.

I hate him. It isn't fair. Why should his brother, his oh-so-perfect brother...in outward appearance so like the humans be the favored one? *M'AneseNebh* hated him but they were tied together, by birth and their respective fathers who were different while still being One.

One day, one day soon, it'll be my turn. Wait and see.

~ * ~

With a gasp, Daniel Walker forced himself upright, eyes staring, hands clawing at the slimy blackness threatening to smother him. As full consciousness returned, he realized how ridiculous he must look, sitting naked in the middle of the bed, arms fending off nothing.

With a groan, he fell back onto the pillow, the sweat-soaked cotton clammy against his neck. He forced his breathing to quiet, waiting for his heart to stop trying to batter a hole through his ribcage.

What a dream. So bad the chill was still with him. What was it about? Lisa…something to do with Lisa. He was certain of it. What—

A familiar constriction in his groin cut into his thoughts, causing him to look down. The sheet across his hips tented dangerously. *Shit! I've a hard-on. Turned on by a God-damned dream?* That hadn't happened since he was a freshman in college. He'd thought he was over that particular sensation forever, especially since he was getting satisfaction from another woman…That brought guilt by the bushels. How much satisfaction was it, really? He was using Mud and he knew it, but she knew it too, as plainly as he. Two consenting adults… He should do something about that, stop it and soon, but she kept his mind from Lisa…except for tonight, when he'd decided to go home instead of staying…and now, alone, he dreamed…

If it affected him that way, why couldn't he remember what it was about? Something sensual…it had to be, but also deadly.

Pulling the sheet free, he touched the rampant column of flesh angrily. *Fuck, I don't need this.* Worry about the dream disappeared as a more pressing need asserted itself. *I refused to start jerking off at this stage of the game.* Game? What game? If this were a game, he was already the loser. Lisa wouldn't answer his calls, ignored his voice mails, wouldn't even let him into the house. And that day he'd seen her at the hospital…

He couldn't understand it. They'd seemed to be getting along. Was she having problems with her pregnancy? He'd tried to get information from Brad in a way not raising suspicion. All his friend would tell him was that she was progressing as well as expected. As the former attending physician, that was all he'd get, because he had no right to any more information, because he couldn't come out and declare himself in love with her. He might be emotionally entitled to know more about how she and her baby were faring but that was all. No one but a relative by blood or marriage could be told what was happening and he was neither. Alice could tell him but there was always the chance Lisa would find out if he spoke to her. Besides, hadn't she forbidden him talking to her aunt?

Why is she avoiding me? The hard-on was raging, getting so stiff it hurt. He felt as if the skin were about to split. *Forget Lisa. Right now, you're got something more important to tend to, Danny Boy. Something's got to give… and fast.*

Swinging his legs over the side of the bed, he headed to the bathroom at a jerky little run, groping in the darkness for the shower fixtures. There was the spatter of water on tile. It struck his bare feet like bits of sleet.

Okay, Doc, get in there and do some sexual healing. With a sigh, he walked into the rain of icy water.

Which did nothing. He was so damned tight and so ready, he came before the water could hit...*a seize and a squeeze*, two more, and he was adding his own liquid, thick as it was, to that pouring out of the showerhead. Four violent spurts striking the tiles and dripping down it, intense and draining but such a relief. He reeled, falling against the shower stall wall, clinging to the grab bar until his legs could hold him up again.

When he returned to the bedroom, shivering, all desire as well as flesh successfully wilted, he didn't bother with a towel. The sheets were already damp, a little clean water wasn't going to make them any wetter. Thank God the air conditioning hadn't decided to kick in.

Pounding the pillows into a mass under his back, he rummaged in the bedside table for a cigarette, lit it and leaned back, coughing a lungful of smoke into the darkness. Odd how using worry about Lisa as his excuse to resume the vice now seemed to bother him, especially after his abortive attempt to quit.

He was calm now and completely awake. *Got to think... remember that damned dream before consciousness does away with it entirely, and why it affected me so.* It definitely wasn't like the ones he used to have as an adolescent. Those were wholly enjoyable, even when he woke to a very messy bed, and completely memorable if he jerked off just *after* awakening. He inhaled again, breathed out smoke without coughing this time, and stared at the ceiling as he concentrated.

Darkness. That's a start...

~ * ~

In the dream everything was dark. Someone—some *thing*—hovered near his shoulder. He could feel it touching him, light as a brush of air. He turned his head, bracing for what he might see but it didn't frighten him. It was as if he'd expected it, knew all along what was there.

Floating at shoulder-level...a groping, writhing mass of tentacles half the size of a man. It glowed palely with a crimson flow of inner light, as if whatever life sustained the creature also illuminated it. One tentacle slithered toward him. It rested on his shoulder and he accepted its touch. He knew he should back away in disgust but he didn't move.

Dan...

A few feet away, Lisa stood wrapped in darkness clinging like a black blanket. *Her stomach's flat... she had her baby... when?*

Arms outstretched, she walked toward him, and light poured upward through the ground, a wall of sunlight making a circle around them. She put her arms around his neck, waiting for him to kiss her but as Dan leaned forward, he felt the creature move, its arms tightening around him, pressing against his back, sucking, drawing against his skin as if draining his emotions.

I don't care. Let it. He had Lisa. It could do whatever it wished. Tentacles encircling both, it drew them together, pushing them into each other's' embrace. He felt her body pressed against his, nipples hard and driving into his chest, belly soft and grinding against his erection... He leaned toward her.

His love disappeared as the creature absorbed the last of it...

...and she was snatched away, arms reaching for him as her body hurtled backward into the darkness. *Dan... Dan, help me!*

The creature followed, floating before her, one arm caressing her face. Lisa turned her head, closing her eyes. She struggled, pushing at the tentacle encircling her waist, while a third wound itself around one thigh. He couldn't move, could only watch that thick snake-like appendage creep between her thighs, jelly-blob crimson against her pale skin, forcing itself inside her.

Lisa screamed.

The creature pressed against her. He could see Lisa through it, struggling to escape, held as immobile as he. The thing swelled and shrank and became man-shaped, joined to her by that single tentacle now become a gigantic penis, thrusting into her. It shuddered, glowing deep red. Sluggishly sated, withdrawing into itself, that single tentacle invading Lisa's body, contracting into a normal human penis as the body became a normal human male's...and then changed again...scaled, furred...claws instead of hands...

With a scream, it writhed and vanished.

Pale and unmoving, Lisa floated above him. Her body changed, belly swelling and grotesque, skin rippling. *She can't get any bigger, she'll burst.* Her head fell back. A trickle of blood ran down the inside of her thigh, followed by another and another until a scarlet river poured from her.

You can't help her.

Dan turned his head, blinking away his fear. *Who...*

Someone stood beside him. His head was shaven except for a narrow strip roached and stiffened with red Georgia clay into a four-inch brush. Two feathers were secured by a seashell comb. There were tattoos on his cheeks and chest, blue dye rubbed into the skin. One hand held a stone club. Around his neck was a rawhide thong from which hung a small clay disk. Except for a wide band of leather wrapped around muscular hips, he was naked, not even wearing moccasins.

"Katsal-Ka? Old Father?" He didn't realize he'd spoken out loud.

I tried to warn them but no one listened. Now no one believes. Catē-Hvse-Hoktē *can't be saved.* Cetto-Honvnwv *has her now...*

Abruptly Dan could move. His hand went to the medallion around his own neck. *Thank God I have it back again.* Gripping it tightly he took a step toward Katsal-Ka. There was so much he needed to ask and he knew he had little time. "Please, tell me..."

The creature was on him, wrapping around his throat...

~ * ~

...and he woke up, fighting and choking.

What does it mean? Dan stubbed out his cigarette. *Does it have a meaning, or is it merely my frustrated libido giving me Hell?*

A hundred years ago, he'd have asked a *dream-skeare* for the answer. Today? A shrink'd probably be the modern equivalent but he thought he preferred the Creeks' method. *All it means is that I want a woman I've lost and I refuse to accept that fact.* He touched the clay disk. Settling himself against the pillows, he tried to sleep again, still clutching Katsal-Ka's medallion.

Chapter 24

When Lisa awoke, the shutters were open with the sun streaming into the room. Stretching luxuriously, arms embracing the world, she sat up.

Ummm. I feel good. A few more nights like this and I'll pass my next check-up with flying colors. She got out of bed, reaching up to pull apart the bow at the neck of her nightgown. It was already undone, the neck gaping. *Guess I was so tired last night I forgot to tie it.*

Pulling the gown over her head, she tossed it to the foot of the bed. Something fluttered to the carpet, a tiny speck of red. She picked it up. A petal. A piece of gaillardia, like those growing on the beach. *How did it get here? Did I bring it in on my sandal?*

Dropping the torn bit of flower into the little wastebasket by the bed, she brushed her hands together to rid them of the sand clinging to them.

Dressed at last, Lisa stood before the mirror combing her hair. *Feels as if it has a ton of sand in it.* She'd have to wash it tonight or it'd look like a haystack for the rest of her stay. She'd never realized swimming in the ocean would make it so stiff, but why hadn't it felt that way earlier? Giving her hair a final pat, she put down the comb and left the room.

She was halfway down the stairs when she heard Drex's voice. It was raised in anger, his words coming clearly to her.

"...dare spy on me. Do you know what I ought to do to you for that?"

Lisa stopped, gripping the banister.

"Please, Master Drex...I only wanted to see her. How could I know you'd be..." The cringing tone changed to an eager question. "Is she truly the one?"

"Are you calling me a liar now?" Drex snapped.

"And the child?"

"Don't worry. I'll claim the child, too."

He sounded so confident Lisa felt her skin chill before her surprise was replaced with anger. *You're wrong, Drex. He's Robin's and he'll stay that way no matter what you say.*

"Master, please forgive me."

"I suppose I should be lenient," Drex's tone took on a thoughtful quality. "I can understand your curiosity, but..."

"It won't happen again, I-I swear." The fear in the man's voice was real.

"It'd better not." He said it softly but the threat was there. "Remember...when the Doorway opens, faithful servants get what's coming to them...but so do disobedient ones."

"Please master, I swear..." Whatever that meant, the man was plainly frightened.

What can Drex do to him that'd terrify him so? What the heck is the Doorway? She had a feeling it wasn't what it sounded like.

"See that it doesn't, Rustin." His answer was cold and final.

"Rustin? The missing manservant? He was the Peeping Tom? The one who ran away after disturbing them on the beach? Remembering how angry Drex had been, she thought it was no wonder the man was frightened. *And now I have to go downstairs and face him.* Would he be as unfriendly as Ursula? How would he look at her? With a smirk whenever he thought Drex wouldn't see, a smugness, saying *Aha... Caught you letting the master screw you, didn't I?*

She couldn't stay on the stairs forever. Taking a deep breath, Lisa called out, "Drex? Good morning," and went down the stairs, making as much noise as possible.

He turned as she left the last step into the foyer. Did she imagine it or did the happiness on his face at seeing her replace a darker more deadly expression? It went so quickly she wasn't certain.

"Lisa." He held out his hand and she put her own into it. "I was about to have Ursula call you. Did you have a good night? No dreams or anything?"

"Uh...no...I slept like a baby..." She thought he looked disappointed in her response. Was there some hidden meaning in his question?

"Lisa, this is Rustin." He looked back at the servant, pulling her forward.

"Hello, Rustin." Lisa held out her hand. "I'm glad to meet you at last."

Whatever she'd expected, it wasn't this very frightened, very small man who didn't look at her but kept his gaze on the floor. At his sides, his hands kept clenching into fists then relaxing, as if that movement alone was keeping him from bolting through the nearest door. Remembering what she'd said about the Addams Family, Lisa wrote off Rustin as being a Lurch-clone. She was also relieved to see he didn't have red hair or resemble Drex in the least. If Ursula reminded Lisa of a snake, however, Rustin had an odd batrachian quality about him. She could imagine him as a very small, very harmless little tree toad.

When Rustin didn't respond or take her hand, she dropped it to her side. *Was that the wrong thing to do? I don't know how to act around servants.*

"If you'd been here last night," Drex told him. "You'd have heard my announcement to Ursula. Mrs. Chambers and I are going to be married."

Rustin still didn't respond. He continued to study the parquet under his feet.

"Look up when you're spoken to!" Drex rapped it out so loudly both Lisa and the servant jumped.

Obediently, Rustin looked up but it was a furtive, frightened glance. His eyes swept over Lisa before going to Drex as if begging. "My best wishes, master. I-if you'll excuse me, sir? I've chores to attend to."

Impatiently Drex waved him away, ignoring the haste with which Rustin disappeared. His attention was all on Lisa.

She was watching the little man's frantic exit, however. "Do you always treat him like that?

"He was insolent. He deserved it."

"But to treat him as if he's a...a..."

"A what? A servant?" He laughed. "That's exactly what he is. An inherited one, too. His great-great-great-great-grandfather was Heinrich's manservant. You've

272

got to be strict with servants, Lisa. It keeps them efficient."

"I hope you aren't going to treat me that way," she dared say.

"You? Of course not. You're much more precious." His manner changed, becoming serious. "There's something I need to ask you."

"Oh?" It was the same tone he'd used when they were in the study, when he told her about Joshua and his family's secrets.

"About yesterday."

"Which part of yesterday?" she asked lightly.

"When we were swimming. It's a little embarrassing." His laugh was self-conscious.

"But pleasant," she added.

"It could've been a lot more pleasant, if we hadn't been interrupted."

She waited for him to tell her Rustin had been the cause, was surprised when he didn't.

"That part of yesterday's not what I mean, however. Let's not talk here in the foyer." He pulled her into the library.

~ * ~

As soon as she stepped through the door, he turned away, leaning against the desk. "Lisa, yesterday at the beach, did you see my back?"

"Your back?" Why did that question make her stomach quiver? She had looked at his back while his attention was on the mad scramble through the underbrush but she couldn't really see because of the sun's glare. "Why do you ask?"

"It's nothing." His expression said the opposite. "I've some scars...I'm a little sensitive about them." He laughed again, tone slightly sheepish. "You made me forget all about them for a little while." He sounded rueful.

"How did you get them?"

"I was thrown into some barbed wire by a horse. They don't hurt but they're not pretty."

"You ride? I thought animals didn't like you."

"They don't. That's why the horse threw me." He looked away from her. Lisa put her hand on his shoulder. She was unprepared for the way he flinched.

A tiny pinpoint of red appeared, spreading and spotting the white cloth of his shirt.

"You're bleeding. What..."

"Don't worry." He turned toward her, catching her hand. "Sunburn. Believe it or not, I've very thin skin. Most people tan...I bleed."

When she started to protest that, and point out what a smooth tan he had, he kissed her. She knew it was to distract her, but...*what a way to have my attention diverted.*

"I'm glad that's all it is," she murmured as he released her. "Anything else you want to tell me?"

"No, but there are a couple of things I'd like to ask."

"What would those be?" Watching his face, she could see his mood lightening.

"Still going to marry me?"

She nodded.

"Are you happy?" When she nodded again, he went on. "Great. Let me run upstairs and change shirts, and we'll have breakfast."

Chapter 25

"Tomorrow you'll be back in Temple."

Drex opened his eyes, looking up at her.

They were on the beach, watching the morning sun play across the water. He'd spread a blanket on the sand and Lisa sat on it, legs curled under her. Drex lay beside her, coppery head resting in her lap. She was wrapping and unwrapping a strand of bright hair around her finger.

"Next time you come back here, it'll be as mistress of Land's End."

Mistress of Land's End. Lisa looked away, eyes going to the horizon. Would she ever feel she belonged in that ugly old house?

There was a ripple under the water, sun casting shadows below the surface, making it seem some gigantic shape floated there. She shivered, looking down and meeting the green eyes regarding her so solemnly. She bent to kiss him.

A hand touched her neck, pulling her down against him. Once again, she felt the urgency and demand behind his kiss. So far, he hadn't pressured her, but each time they neared each other, whether in a kiss, an embrace—and there had been plenty of both—or simply walking side-by-side, she felt the desire he was so carefully holding in check. It trembled below the surface, shivering likes that underwater shadow, transmitting itself through his touch, as it did now. *Go with it. Let him have his way.* With a sigh, she gave in to the feeling surging through her, pressing against him.

He pushed her away and sat up.

"I guess we'd better not." He looked at the water as if he could see whatever was hiding beneath it. "In spite of what I said, it's time for me to start practicing fortitude…a little, anyway. Making out with you on the beach isn't the way to do it. Besides," he got to his feet and pulled her up beside him, scooping up the blanket. "For all I know, our mysterious peeper may still be lurking, wanting another free show."

*But it was Rustin…*she didn't dare say that. She wasn't supposed to know. Could there be someone else, too? If so, surely he wouldn't dare try it again.

"Come on." Shaking the sand off the blanket, he folded and tucked it under his arm. "Let's go home."

Lisa knew it'd be a long time before she thought of Land's End as home.

~ * ~

"I've got to go into the village," Drex told her when they arrived back at the house. "Why don't you take a nap while I'm gone?"

Though that was the last thing she wanted, Lisa agreed, then stood at her window, watching him walk down the road leading to the village. She felt restless, the sensation kicking in as soon as she set foot inside the Manor. She had to get outside again. Opening her door, she went down the stairs.

"Did you need something, madam?" Ursula was in the foyer, carrying packages down the hallway leading to the kitchen.

"Not really, Ursula." *I hope he didn't tell you to keep an eye on me.* She'd hate to have an argument with the housekeeper about leaving the house. "It's so nice out I can't stay inside." That sounded better than *I'm going to jump out of my skin if I don't get out of here.* "I think I'll walk around outside while Drex is in the village. Will he be gone long, do you think?" She'd forgotten to ask him.

"Several hours, I imagine." That response surprised her. "If you plan on leaving the house grounds, don't get off the road. Marsh soil can be treacherous for a newcomer." She smiled slightly as if the idea of Lisa bogged to her knees in quicksand was a pleasant thought.

"Don't worry, I'll be careful." *Can that grimace be her version of a friendly smile?* Lisa escaped through the front door as fast as she could.

Outside, she paused, undecided. Which way to go? *Should I stick to the road as Ursula advised, or strike out on my own?* She was certain she could find the beach again, but she didn't want to go there without Drex, especially if Rustin hadn't been the one watching them and that unknown person was still lurking. Besides, they'd been there for several hours this morning. She decided to follow the road.

Heading for the driveway, she turned left and walked in the direction of the village. The soil was so soft she could see Drex's footprints in it. *Perhaps I'll meet him on his way back.*

~ * ~

The village was farther away than she thought. As the sun beat down, Lisa's pace slowed. At last, she stopped, sinking onto a nearby tree stump, puffing and fanning herself with one hand.

I could've sworn we were only minutes away. It seemed we left it and immediately were at the house. Where is it? Surely I'm not lost.

There was a vaguely familiar look to the spot where she now sat. Behind her, a deep ditch separated the road from the nearby woods, a pine tree leaning over it. The tree was tilted and bent, a gash in its side, bark crushed and twisted where something heavy had crashed against it. The grass around the tree was scorched and blackened, the ground broken by two deep scars gouged into the dirt as if a large object had fallen, clawed into the soil and burst into flames…

With a gasp, Lisa got to her feet, staring at the blackened branches of the damaged pine. *This is where our car left the road*…diving nose-first against the trunk of the pine, where Robin died and she didn't…

She began to run, not looking where she was going, wanting to get as far away from that spot as she could. Dodging between trees, blundering through bushes and shrubs…they caught at her skirt, tried to stop her. She was out of breath and there was a stitch in her side. Clutching her ribs, she leaned against a tree, gasping. She had no idea where she was. She kept running until the trees thinned into a little clearing.

A look around told her the place had been cleared by someone. The lack of trees and stumps wasn't natural. Brush had been cut away and the soil looked as if it had been swept clean. In the center of the clearing stood a ring of large gray boulders like those on the beach, placed end-to-end so they formed a circle. At one end, two upright tabby pillars disrupted the circle, oyster halves, crushed cowry, and coquina visible in the weathered mortar. Balanced across them was a third stone, forming a doorway through which she could see another stone slab.

It was large and rectangular, like an altar.

Stepping beneath the archway, Lisa walked into the circle. There was a faint humming in the air, like the singing of old telephone wires in the wind. She remembered hearing such a sound when she visited her grandparents at their farm but there were no wires strung above the clearing. *Don't they put cables underground nowadays?* Hadn't Drex said his father didn't allow anyone to have phone service? She hadn't seen a telephone in any of the rooms at Land's End, but she was certain Drex had a cell.

First thing I did was buy everyone a cell phone. Was that the only communication with the mainland? They had electricity. Perhaps they had some type of wireless service. He'd called her so many times…

From somewhere came the call of a bird. One of those whippoorwills. It was answered, then another sounded, until the air was alive with their cries. *Where did they come from?* She'd never realized they were so plentiful in this area.

The humming grew louder. It sounded like words.

It's speaking to me. If I listen closely, I'll understand. Lisa leaned forward, placing both hands on the flat top of that gigantic stone. She looked up at the sky. Clouds scudded by, faster and faster. *Yes? I'm listening.*

The cloud began to whirl. The whole world spinning. In a moment, she'd hear plainly, she could feel it. The birds sang louder, almost a single voice, shrieking, ear-piercing. *Her name.* Lisa's eyes rolled upward...

"Lisa!"

She was seized roughly, jerked backward.

The sky stopped moving, the birds fell silent, the voices disappeared. Stumbling, she turned, her head spinning. *I'm so damned dizzy.* She looked up at Drex.

"Why did you do that?" Angrily, she struck at him, furious he'd interrupted what the voices were about to tell her. "I almost understood!"

Her knees buckled and he scooped her into his arms, running back through the arch and out of the circle. The world began to move again and Lisa shut her eyes, hiding it from her sight.

"Damn it, Lisa! You shouldn't have gone out alone."

Why is he so angry with me?

"I saw the spot where we...I had to get away. I heard them...I couldn't understand." She opened her eyes, peering over his shoulder. Everything was too bright, too gleaming. She put a hand to her head. "I'm so dizzy..."

The sun got even brighter. A loud ringing encircled her, drowning everything else as she plunged downward into a deep and darkened well.

~ * ~

Water poured over her. She gasped, forcing her eyes open as it struck her. She was lying in a bathtub, faucets flooding icy liquid.

"My head hurts so." It was the whimper of a sick child.

"You got too much sun." Drex dipped a cloth into the water, pressing it against her forehead, splashing water on her temples. "Try to relax."

Obediently, she closed her eyes. The water felt so good, so cold. It stopped flowing. She floated, on the verge of sleep. She could hear Drex speaking but she wasn't listening. She was too tired.

"Why the Hell did you let her go off like that?"

"I-I thought she'd be all right, Mr. Drex." Ursula's voice shook. "I didn't think she'd go to the Ring."

"*You didn't think.*" Drex's mockery was sharp as a knife. "She *heard* them. What if something happened? If she fell and lost the baby? Where would we be then, you stupid bitch?" There was the loud, sharp sound of flesh striking flesh. Ursula gasped. "Damn it, I ought to take you to the Ring and let *him* have you. If anything happens to Lisa, that's exactly what I'll do."

Ursula's wail of terror was cut off by the slamming of a door.

~ * ~

Lisa slept.

She had a vague memory of the housekeeper reappearing, helping her climb from the tub, wrapping her in a thick towel, and assisting her in putting on her nightgown. When she again awoke, it was morning and Drex was standing by the bed, telling her it was time for her to get ready to go back to Temple.

Chapter 26

Drex didn't take her directly home. Instead, he insisted she see Dr. Halyard.

"Just to be safe. I've already called his office. They said they'd fit you in." His tone implied they'd better. She wondered if he'd made a scene on the phone as she'd been told he did in the ER.

~ * ~

Dr. Halyard didn't appear worried.

"A little too much sun, perhaps a little more exercise than you're accustomed to, especially now, combined with the shock of finding the accident site." He smiled. "I said *have fun,* not *get too much sun.*" He smiled at his little joke. "Your friend did the right thing with cold water and bed rest. That's exactly what I'd have prescribed."

"But the voices…"

"A symptom of fainting." He brushed it aside. "Blood leaving the brain makes ringing in the ears. Sometimes it sounds like someone speaking. You overdid it a little, Lisa. That's all." He said it as if it were a magic formula guaranteed to reassure her.

"The baby's all right?"

She was told everything was fine.

~ * ~

At home they had to go over the entire episode again. After Drex left, extracting a promise to call if she

282

needed him, Alice attempted to put her to bed and keep her there. Instead Lisa planted herself stubbornly at the kitchen table and drink a cup of coffee with little enjoyment but great determination.

"How did your week go?" Conceding defeat, her aunt sat down and picked up her own cup. "Other than baking your brain in the sun?"

"That's not fair." Lisa set down the coffee cup with exaggerated gentleness. It was either that or throw it at her aunt. "I walked a little too fast and got a little tired."

"We won't argue." Alice looked as if she wanted to. She took a deep breath. "About Drex..." She waited until Lisa again took a sip of her coffee before she went on. "From the way he was fussing around you, I'd say he's very much in love with you. What are you going to do about it?"

"For goodness sake, Aunt Allie." This time, Lisa set down her cup so violently the coffee splashed onto the counter top. "Look what you made me do."

Getting up, she took a sponge from the sink and began to wipe the brown spatters from the tile.

"Are you going to treat him like you did Dan Walker?"

For a moment, Lisa thought her aunt was hoping she'd say she was.

"I'm going to tell you what I told Drex." She tossed the sponge into the sink, dropping back into her chair. "I'm sorry, Aunt Allie. I'm a little on edge after what happened."

"What did you tell Drex?" her aunt persisted.

Lisa didn't answer, studying her coffee cup.

"Lisa?"

"He…kind of asked me…to…"

"He asked you to marry him?" Alice finished the sentence in disbelief. "And you said…"

"I said *yes*." Lisa's reply was defiant. "I told him after the baby's born, I'll marry him.

"Is it so important to have the baby first?"

"Why does everyone keep asking that?" She struggled to keep from shouting. "Wouldn't it be more of a scandal if I don't? I imagine having a wedding so soon after…everything…will be one anyway." She paused. "Why can't anyone understand? This is Robin's child, Aunt Allie. Boy or girl, it has to be born with his name. Robin Chambers." She sighed and her next words were a whisper. "All I want to do is have my baby and then…then I'll think about getting married again."

"Drex agreed to wait?"

She nodded.

"He must really be in love with you." Alice shook her head as if she didn't understand his patience. "Where does this leave Dan?"

"I wasn't aware he was being left anywhere." Lisa didn't want to think about Dan. She didn't want to think about *anything* just then. "It looks like both you and Dan saw a lot of things that weren't there." *That's right. Take that attitude, keep pretending nothing existed and soon it'll be so.*

"Did we? He's a good man, Lisa. You didn't have to hurt him. I…" Alice didn't say any more. She raised her cup, taking a quick swallow of coffee.

"I didn't intend to. It's too bad you and he both misunderstood the way I felt." Lisa stood up. "I think

I'll lie down after all. Suddenly I'm a little tired." Her voice was brusque, a hair short of angry.

For the last five days, she hadn't thought of Dan Walker, and she wasn't going to think about him now.

Chapter 27

Winter succeeded in driving away autumn. Winds began to blow, preluding cold, bleak days as they finished removing the rest of the leaves from the trees. The temperature dropped so low dew froze into hoar-frost, icy stalagmites projecting from the soil.

The season wasn't the only thing changing. Lisa's body thickened as the child within her grew and nourished itself. She moved slower and more carefully. She couldn't walk far without having to stop for extra breaths. Sometimes the baby's vigorous activity left her gasping.

Other than attending her pre-natal classes, she rarely went out, sudden shyness because of her ungainliness overcoming her desire for company. She'd be the first to admit winter wasn't the best time for a pregnant woman to be up and about, with the danger of a fall on icy streets. A couple of college friends drove to Temple to see her, but soon most visits were made by phone, those out of the city keeping in touch through Skype.

Alice appeared to be settled in for the duration. She'd spent a very long hour on the phone speaking to the Dean of the college, arranging for an extended leave of absence, and getting assurances her job would be there when her niece was ready to be on her own again. At the moment, Lisa wondered if her aunt would be the one deciding that or if she'd have the freedom to declare her own independence once the baby was born.

Dan Walker was conspicuously absent. Since her return, he hadn't called or appeared at the house again and she hadn't seen him at the hospital when she went for her check-ups. As far as Lisa was concerned, he was out of her life. If she thought about him at all, it was in the moments before she slept at night or perhaps in her dreams where no one but she would know.

Drex, however, was very much in attendance, seeing her several times a week and calling when he wasn't there in person. He also gave Lisa a number he said was for the Manor though she never used it. Why should she, when he called her at least once a day when he was absent? He was considerate, caring, but very proprietary and didn't mind telling Alice or anyone else who happened to be around.

If Lisa worried that his attitude might continue after they were married, she didn't show it. As she'd told Alice, her main concern was getting her baby born.

~ * ~

The gas logs sputtered cheerfully in the fireplace. It was the second week of December, nearing midnight when the doorbell routed Lisa from her chair.

Lumbering to the door—and that was the only way to describe how she moved these days—she opened it to find Drex standing there. She hadn't seen him for two days. When they'd spoken earlier, he'd been busy with business calls, but he hadn't mentioned coming to town, so she was surprised to find him dressed for traveling, in heavy overcoat and leather gloves.

"Come in before you get blown away."

On cue, the wind gusted into the doorway, whipping his hair into wild elflocks about his face.

"I can only stay a minute," he explained as he obeyed, gesturing outside.

"Are you going somewhere?" Looking past him, she saw a car parked at the curb. Not the Jag, a larger one with Rustin standing beside it. He was also bundled in a thick coat and gloves but he was blowing on his hands and looking anxiously toward the house. Lisa pushed the door shut as the wind aimed another icy blast through it.

"Those damned phone conferences didn't clear up a thing. So now..." He looked angry. "I have to fly to New England. Of all the times of the year to go, this is the very worst."

"How long will you be gone?" Her heart did a nosedive at the thought he might not be around when the baby came. She wondered exactly what type of business those northern holdings involved.

"At least until March."

"You won't be here for Christmas?" She didn't mean to say it so sharply. Somehow the fact of the holiday made it worse of a disappointment. "I haven't got your gift yet, but..."

"Don't worry about that." He touched her cheek, the leather of his glove chill against her skin. "The only present I need is you."

"Where are you going?" For once, she decided she wanted to know exactly where he'd be and not merely some vague northerly direction.

"A place called Colfax Harbor."

She shook her head. It wasn't familiar.

"Near Arkham?" He supplied.

"I've never heard of either."

"I wish I hadn't." He looked through the glass in the door and shivered. "It's going to be snowing up there. Damn it, if I had my way I'd never leave Land's End, or you." His hands went to his head, brushing back his hair. Then he placed a finger under her chin, tilting her head as he brushed his lips against hers. Releasing her, he reached for the door.

"Call me if you have a free minute."

"Won't be able to." That earned another angry look. "Place where I'm going is a dead zone. Not even landlines."

"Go on." She laughed. "Nowhere like that really exists."

"Trust me, it does, in rural Massachusetts." He looked serious. "Listen Lisa, if you need me…if anything happens…call the Manor. Rustin has orders to get in touch with me…somehow. I'll come back immediately."

"Drex, the only time I might really need you is when the baby comes. If that happens before you get back, I don't think I can wait while you make flight arrangements."

"Oh…right." He nodded his agreement, then burst out, "Damn it! I don't want to go but I've got to." He pulled open the door. The wind rushed in, whistling around them. "Confound it, Lisa, when I see you again, you may be a mother."

She caught his chin, holding his head in imitation of the gesture he'd made. "Hurry back. I'll miss you."

Drex nodded and hesitated as if he wanting to say something more. Turning up his collar, he went down the steps. "Damned Yankees...damn winter solstice..."

At least that's what Lisa thought he muttered. "What? What did you say?" she called after him.

"Never mind." He looked back at her. "'Bye, sweetheart. I love you."

She watched him run across the lawn to the car, head down against the wind. Rustin opened the back passenger door for him. Drex looked back and waved, then slid inside. Rustin slammed the door and got back under the wheel. Above the wind, the engine roared as the car sped away from the curb.

Hurry back. I love you. Lisa continued waving though she knew Drex couldn't see.

Chapter 28

Without Drex, each month seemed even longer. Christmas came and went and December gave way to January. Lisa saluted the New Year with a glass of warm milk and a piece of fruitcake, as she watched watching the televised New Year's celebration from New York City. That had always been a tradition in her family. She'd watched it with her parents, then only her mother, then Aunt Allie, and at last Robin. She'd hoped to do it this year with Drex, disappointed because she knew he couldn't be there. Alice wasn't a good substitute, going to bed an hour earlier and leaving Lisa alone in the living room determined to sit there until it was a different year.

When the phone rang at one minute to midnight, she was startled.

"Happy New Year!" His voice sounded very far away and lightly trembling as if he were shivering.

"Drex?" She barely kept from squealing with happiness. "You're one minute early. It's still 2013."

"Damn…and I thought I had this timed perfectly." Behind him there came a high-pitch wailing.

"Where are you calling from? Are you back home?" She hoped. "Is that wind I hear?" She glanced toward the television as she spoke. The big glittery ball of light was sliding down the pole.

"No such luck, sweetheart. I managed to get into town. I'm calling from a little Mom and Pop store called the *Four Corners Shoppe*...that's with a *P-P-E* on the end of it. Yes, that's wind. We're in the middle of a blizzard." There was a long pause. "I miss you, Lisa. I wanted to be there, drinking champagne—well, me drinking champagne, anyway—as we rang in the New Year."

"And we are...ringing it in, at least." The ball struck the base. From the television came the announcer's voice, declaring, *It's 2014!* "Happy New Year, Drex."

"Happy New Year to you, too, sweetheart." Behind the whistle of the wind, she thought she heard someone say something. "Got to go. My ride's getting antsy. I'll be counting the days until I can leave here."

There was a click and he was gone.

Dropping the phone back into its cradle, Lisa reached for her glass, toasting the television screen and its montage of celebrants. "And a Happy New Year to me."

~ * ~

"Fifteen minutes to go." Dan kissed Myrtice lightly, then raised his glass in a toast.

Since that first night, he spent more and more time at his cousin's. First a couple of nights a week, now almost every night, especially after he'd heard the rumors of Lisa Chambers' engagement to Drexl von Dorff. They'd leave the office, make rounds, then go to Myrtice's where she'd cook dinner and then...usually they ended the night in bed where Dan made frantic love to her, then snuggled her close and fell asleep.

Myrtice ignored the fact that he never seemed to enjoy it. He was still clinging to Lisa Chambers, she told herself. Nevertheless, he didn't stay away. *If she's marrying Drexl von Dorff, he'll have to give up, and then we can be happy.*

~ * ~

"The same to you." She looked thoughtful. "You know, they say whatever you do on New Year's Eve, you do the rest of the year, too."

"Did you have anything planned?" He didn't look particularly interested, refilling his glass. He'd already had several drinks and the bottle wobbled slightly as he poured. "If not, I'd better stop right now or I'll find myself drinking away the New Year." He returned the bottle to the upright antique chest Myrtice used as a liquor cabinet.

"Now that's where you're wrong." Taking the glass from his hand, she set it on the coffee table and led him into the bedroom. She ignored his less-than-enthusiastic expression. *I'm not going to lose you, Danny.*

"I don't know, Mud." He hung back slightly. "I think I've had a little too much celebration already…"

"I can fix that." Pushing him onto the bed, she caught the tab of his zipper. He fell backward and didn't move, lying passively as she reached into his fly.

Thanks to her, Dan and 2014 came at the same moment.

Chapter 29

Filled with cold and rain, bleak and dreary February blew away. March arrived with a promise of cool sunlit days fading into warm spring.

Prenatal classes were over. Lisa was now seeing Dr. Halyard once a week. *Zero Hour* was rapidly approaching with apprehension and joy, and Drex still hadn't returned.

Lisa walked to her car, coat buttoned tightly as she fought the wind for control of the scarf she was attempted to wrap around her neck. *Why didn't I do this while I was inside?* Slow. Clumsy. Heavy. *I thought I was big at Christmas time. I feel like I've been pregnant forever. Step right up, see Lisa, the Baby Elephant. The little Tub. The Barrel with legs.*

Alice hadn't wanted her to drive herself to the doctor. Independent to the last, Lisa thrust out her chin and lumbered out the door.

Abandoning the scarf for a moment, she smiled as she looked down, searching for her feet. *Poor things. I'll have to be reintroduced to you after this is over.*

The wind whipped one end of the scarf out of her hands. She clutched at it, hair flying.

"Lisa?"

Someone hurried toward her.

Dan. In the small space the baby left for it, Lisa's heart sank.

"Hi." Out of breath, he stopped in front of her. The wind whipped his dark cheeks into a glowing crimson. She had to admit the color it gave his face looked good, as did the way his hair was tossed into a mass of unruly waves.

"Hello, Dan." *Be cool but friendly, that's best. Not as if several months ago you told him to get lost.*

"Can we talk a minute?"

"I don't have time. Aunt Allie's waiting." She wished now she'd let her aunt drive her.

"I think your aunt can wait a little longer. Where is she anyway?" He looked around. "She didn't let you drive here alone, did she? You don't look as if you can fit behind the wheel of a car."

"You're such a flatterer."

"Come on." He caught her arm. "Let's get out of the wind. Go have a cup of coffee."

"Really, Dan. I don't have time." He didn't release her so she had to go with him or be dragged into the shelter of one of the pillars at the hospital's entrance. There was a bench there and he pushed her onto it. "Before you say anything, I suppose I may as well tell you now…"

"Tell me what?"

"I'm…after the baby's born, I'm marrying Drex."

It probably would've been better if she'd slapped him, striking out with real blows instead of words. He released her, stumbling backward, then shook his head.

"I hoped it wasn't true…" He looked stunned. "Thanks for sugarcoating it, Lisa." He spoke tightly, as if choosing each word with care. "I didn't want to do this but I think there are some things about Drex you need to know."

"Like what?" she asked with a sigh.

"There've been other women…"

"I know about Aura," she interrupted. "Joshua, too. Drex told me."

"Did he tell you about the rest of them?" When she looked surprised, he went on in apparent satisfaction, "About how Aura and I were engaged, until he showed up and seduced her? Guess not."

"So you let someone else make you forget Kathy Halyard?" She made it an accusation. "I'm sorry you struck out twice…" *Three times if you count me, too.* "I don't want to hear any more, Dan." She struggled to her feet. "I don't believe we've anything else to say to each other."

"Sit down. I'm not finished." Shoving her back onto the bench with no pretense of gentleness, he went on, "You need to know this and you're going to sit and listen."

"All right. Tell me." His roughness startled her. "So I can get out of this wind."

"Aura was one of the luckier ones," he went on. "Another girl had a miscarriage. The fetus was abnormal." He didn't look at her as he said it, as if remembering the dangers still threatening her own baby. "A third had a stillbirth. It was just as well. The baby had no arms or legs."

Lisa winced.

"The night Joshua was born he wouldn't let them take her to Temple. He sent that manservant of his to bring a doctor to the village. I was pulling night ER duty but when I found out who the man was and what he wanted…I know I'm not an obstetrician, but all the others were busy, so I got permission to leave the hospital and go with him." He stopped as if seeing again the pale struggling girl, and her parents, grim with fear. "The baby was breech. Aura nearly died. I managed to keep them both alive but Joshua's leg was twisted, his hip dislocated."

Dan looked down at her with a fierceness making her cringe. Lisa shook her head, remembering how the little boy had limped across the village road beside his mother.

"For four years now I've treated that child, while his father's never lifted a finger to help him. He refused to waste money on a cripple." He pulled her off the bench, hands gripping so tightly they hurt. "Lisa, the man's evil. It marks his children." His fingers bit into her arms. She winced.

"Let me go."

"He took Aura from me, Lisa. I'm not going to let him take you, too."

"That's enough," she shouted the words, wrenching herself out of his grasp. Even as she did it, she remembered Drex's words… *Looks like I was wrong and that doctor was right*. "I'm leaving. I won't tell Drex about this. It'd only make things worse between you two and…I really don't want that, Dan."

"Isn't there anything I can say to make you change your mind?" He looked as if he knew the answer before she spoke.

"Nothing," she said stiffly. "Except goodbye."

"No." He shook his head. "I'll never say that."

"Then *I* will. Please don't bother me again." Lisa pushed past him, hating herself for hurting him, hating him for making her do it.

"Lisa, don't walk away from me."

Did she hear that or not? She didn't look back.

~ * ~

She's walking out of my life, leaving me forever. Dan watched her retreating figure. *There's nothing I can do to stop her.*

His face was wet. The wind stung icily as he wiped the back of his gloved hand across his eyes. He was thankful it was still winter and the street was fairly deserted so no one could see his shame or his fear.

~ * ~

The man's evil. It marks his children.

All she could think about were Dan's words. They weren't true. He was jealous, a rejected lover's spite. That wasn't right. He'd never really been a lover, had he? She hadn't let him. She'd never imagined Dan could be so shaken or raise his voice in such anger. He was always so quiet, so reserved. Like Robin.

She blinked as the truth came to her. After all this time...even in the hospital she saw the resemblance and refused to recognize it, except in her subconscious. Hadn't the man in her dream told her the person she was describing was her husband? *He reminds me of Robin. In that case, why isn't he my choice?*

Lisa stopped the car for a red light, staring ahead without seeing. The light changed. Impatient to get moving, the driver in the car behind her leaned on his horn. *Honk... honk... honk...* She pressed the accelerator, driving at a lessened speed the rest of the way home, trying not to think, not *wanting* to think.

Automatically, she slowed the car and flipped on the turn signal as she rounded the curve into the driveway. *Stop the car, set the break.* Lisa leaned forward, eyes closed, resting her forehead against the steering wheel. She could barely touch it. *Dan's right, I really shouldn't be driving.* She raised her head. *Please,* she breathed. *Don't let me have chosen the wrong one.* A tear crept from under her lashes and slid down her cheek.

Hastily she brushed it away, pulled the key from the ignition and struggled out of the car.

Chapter 30

Inside the stone ring in the little clearing, Lisa stood by the altar. In the cold cottony dark, someone knelt beside it.

A tiny figure lay on the ground, whimpering softly. *My baby.* Lisa bent and picked it up only to have it plucked from her grasp by a pair of hands coming out of the dark.

Lisa, Lisa, don't let them harm my child. A few feet away, a shadowy figure floated in the mist.

"Robin?"

Don't let them. The dark surged red, closing around him. Smoke billowed. She heard the crackle of flames.

The figure at the altar got to its feet, holding something against its chest. Drex looked down at her, but he was changed, his body hunched and twisted. Above him the air seethed and writhed with shadowy shapes. A pulsing gray mass hovered, reaching for him.

Lords... Great Ones. His voice thundered through her mind. *The Doorway opens. I've obeyed your commands. Enter.* The words echoed into the air and the mist cleared and Lisa could see the thing he held.

Her baby.

There was a chubby body, but its face was a smooth flat surface topped by a crest of red curls. Projecting from the pink flesh were wriggling slender threads, stretching and coiling as it balanced itself in Drex's hands.

It can't be her child. *It can't!*

Lisa screamed and kept on screaming. The sound flew around her, trapping her inside her own voice. She began to run, not toward her baby but away...

~ * ~

...Lisa found herself sitting upright, hands over her open mouth, stifling the screams filling her lungs. With a gusty sigh, she realized she was in her own bed.

Oh God. Inside her, the child gave a sleepy kick and rolled over as if resenting having his slumbers disturbed. *Okay... all right... I'm sorry.* She lay down, punching the pillow into a circular shape as she attempted to go back to sleep. From the foot of the bed, Timothy raised his head, blinked sleepily and gave an irritated mew. He resented having his nights disturbed, also.

"Oh shut up," she muttered. "You don't know what I'm going through."

No one did.

Chapter 31

March the Lion puffed itself into a ewe lamb and trotted away. Grass changed from brown to green, trees began to sprout tiny leaflets though the nights were still chill and the waters off the coast churned gray.

~ * ~

"I'm home, Lisa." Alice called from the back door. Daily shopping done, she deposited the bag of groceries on the table and made a return trip to the car for the second one. As the door opened again, Lisa heard her say, "Move, Timothy."

There was a loud screech and an even louder crash.

"Aunt Allie?" Dashing for the safety of the stairs, Timothy leaped past Lisa as she headed to the kitchen. She found Alice on the floor in the midst of cans and scattered food packages, "What happened?"

"I tripped over Timothy," Alice's reply was embarrassed. "It was bound to happen one day, the way he's always underfoot."

"Can you get up? Here, let me help you." Lisa knelt bulkily, putting an arm across Alice's back only to be shoved away.

"Don't even try lifting me, not in your condition." Alice struggled to push herself into a sitting position. She fell back with a yelp. "Lisa, I think my leg's broken."

"Lie still." Clinging to the kitchen counter, Lisa got to her feet. "I'll call 911."

While her aunt reclined on the floor, muttering more in anger than pain, she made the call. As she set down the phone, Alice, still practical even in a prone position, ordered, "Put the groceries away while we wait."

Obediently Lisa gathered the frozen food packages and put them into the freezer, stacking the canned goods in the pantry. As she stuffed the torn grocery bag into the trashcan, they heard the ambulance's approaching scream.

~ * ~

Insisting Lisa ride in the ambulance with her, Alice was taken to Temple General's emergency room. She now rested behind one of the curtained-off exam rooms.

Lisa was shuffled out of the way as the doctor on duty checked Alice. She found herself in the visitor's waiting room in a too-soft chair. It made her back ache. *I need more support. What kind of hospital makes their chairs so damned soft? How long have I been waiting, anyway?*

A glance at the wall clock told her it'd only been half an hour. A nurse stopped by, reporting Alice was resting comfortably and they were waiting for the orthopedist's arrival. She was also refused permission to see her aunt.

Movement in the doorway made her look up. A tall figure in surgical greens stood here. She lurched to her feet as Dan came into the room.

Of course he'd be the one called for a broken bone. Temple General might have other orthopedists from surrounding cities on its staff but Lisa should've known Alice would ask for Dan.

"Lisa." He acknowledged her presence, nothing in his voice or look indicating the antagonism of their last meeting. She saw there was a surgical mask hanging around his neck and the front of the green smock had a fresh-looking red smear.

"It took you long enough." She decided not to give him a chance to say anything personal. "My aunt has a broken leg or something and you've been…"

"…in surgery," he cut in. "I wasn't notified until I finished. Brad Halyard."

"Dr. Halyard?" That cut short her tirade. For a moment she forgot about her aunt. "What happened?"

"He drove his car off the road on the way home last night. Went through a guardrail." Saying that seemed to be an effort. There was weariness in his expression, taut lines around his eyes and mouth.

"Will he be all right?"

"He's in pretty bad shape. It took me six hours to get the pieces back together but he'll be back on the golf course eventually, not any time soon, however. About your aunt…" He got back on subject. "She has a fractured hip. How'd it happen?"

"She tripped over Timothy."

"I thought perhaps she fell down some stairs. That sort of injury…never mind. She's signed all the forms, so we're ready to go. They're prepping her for surgery and I need to do the same thing." He started out, then paused as if remembering something. "How are you?"

"I'm fine." She didn't say any more, didn't want him starting to pry or preach or say anything else personal.

"Good. Well…I…" He shook his head. "Surgery's on the fourth floor. Why don't you go to the waiting room there?" He turned and went out.

Sighing, Lisa walked down the hall to the elevator. At this stage, it was more of a waddle than anything else. Dan was nowhere in sight. He'd probably taken the staff elevator.

On the fourth floor, the volunteer at the nurses' station directed her to the waiting room where she settled herself into another too-soft chair, trying to find a comfortable spot as she sat back to wait…and wait…and wait…

Chapter 32

At eleven that night, Lisa was still sitting there, having left only long enough to get a sandwich from a vending machine in the little snack bar on the first floor and wash it down with a can of soda, before hurrying back to wait some more, on a couch this time. As she was checking the clock again, and wondering if the dining room was closed or if she should leave and get some dinner elsewhere, Dan reappeared. Though the fatigue in his face was more pronounced, Lisa was relieved to see he was wearing a different smock and it wasn't bloodstained.

She didn't move as he sank down beside her with a sigh and gently collapsed, head resting against the back of the sofa, eyes closed.

"Alice is going to be fine." He didn't open his eyes. "I had to do a total hip replacement. That's what took so long. The joint was too shattered to rebuild, but she'll be all right."

"How long have you been here?"

"Since around eight this morning when I got the call about Brad." He raised his head, smiling tiredly. "It took about four hours to get him stabilized before I could do my part… I'd just stepped out of surgery when they called me about your aunt, so I went right back in. Hope to God no one else gets hurts today."

"Would you like some coffee?" She didn't want the conversation to lull, didn't want him having a chance to talk about her and Drex, although from the way he looked, Dan was too tired to think straight, much less harass her with questions. She hoped no one else needed him. He didn't look fit to operate again.

"Please." He managed a smile. "If you've got breakfast and lunch tucked away somewhere, I'll take that, too."

"You do have a habit of skipping meals, don't you?" She went to the automatic coffee maker on the little counter at the end of the room. Selecting two cups, she filled them and returned, handing him one as she sat down again.

He took a deep drink from the cup, then set it on the flat of the sofa's arm. Leaning forward, elbows resting against his knees, he pressed his hands to his head.

Without speaking, Lisa sat looking at him. In that moment, he seemed very vulnerable. She wanted to place a comforting hand on his shoulders. The way they drooped sent pity rushing through her. She didn't move. *I don't have the right to do that. Not now. He needs someone. Just not me.* Hadn't there been a rumor about him and his nurse? She'd refused to let Alice tell her.

"Why are you still here?" Dan straightened, hand going across his eyes as if to brush away the tiredness hovering there. "It's nearly midnight. I gave orders you could see Alice in the morning."

"Not to me you didn't. No one said anything, so I've been sitting here waiting."

"Damn it. I specifically told them at the nurses' station…"

"There's been a lot of activity out there." Four times, she'd seen nurses rushing past the open door, several gurneys carrying patients rolling past. "Maybe they were so busy they forgot. They'll probably get around to it after everything settles down." She tried to downplay that oversight. He didn't look like he had enough energy to get angry just then.

"You need to be home, Lisa. Get some sleep. Alice is still in Recovery and she won't be conscious enough to see anyone until tomorrow...shit, it's tomorrow already." He glanced at his watch. "...this morning."

"In that case, I'll go home," she told him. "Except I don't have a way." She hesitated, then said, "Call me a cab?"

"If you insist...you're a cab." He was almost too tired to respond to the old joke.

She remembered the night at his apartment, when he said that.

"Look. Let me get cleaned up and I'll take you home." His expression told her he remembered, too.

"Don't you have reports to dictate or something?" Still feeling she didn't have the right, she didn't want to take him away from his duties.

"I can do those tomorrow." He got up and started out, not waiting to hear if she agreed.

~ * ~

Fifteen minutes later, they were in the Mercedes.

"Will you be all right alone?" he asked. "When's your baby due?"

"Any minute now." She raised a hand to stifle the protest she expected. "Don't worry. Mrs. Campbell's across the street and she still drives, if I need someone."

There was a car in front of the house, a big black one. Lisa's heart sank as she recognized it as the one Drex had ridden in to the airport.

"Who's that? Were you expecting company?" Dan stopped the Mercedes behind it. They could see someone at the front door. He turned away, saw the car and came toward them at a fast walk.

"Drex…" In spite of Dan's presence, Lisa couldn't hide her delight. She opened the car door. "When did you get back?"

"Just now." His hand was on the door handle before she finished speaking, jerking the door further open and pulling her from the car. "What's happened? Why are you with him?"

Dan drew in a sharp breath. Hoping to forestall the argument she saw coming, Lisa told Drex about Alice's accident.

"That damned cat. Is she all right?"

"She'll be fine," Dan answered. By this time he was out of the car, coming around it to stand behind Lisa. "I made sure of that."

Drex's eyes flicked past her to Dan. "Guess this is one time I can appreciate you upholding the family tradition, Medicine Man."

"Don't push it, von Dorff." Dan may have spoken quietly but there was no mistaking the threat in his words. Lisa had a feeling his fatigue, coupled with anything Drex might say, could tip him into the violence she was certain seethed beneath that tired exterior. "I've spent the past sixteen hours putting my best friend back together and making certain Lisa's aunt will walk again and I'm no mood to take any of your shit."

"Then I won't bother giving it to you. You can't stay here alone, Lisa." Lisa blinked slightly at Dan's profanity, as Drex promptly ignored him. "Pack a bag. You're coming home with me."

"With you? That's the last thing she needs to do."

"What would you have her do? Spend the night with *you*? You'd like that, wouldn't you?" Drex put his arm across Lisa's shoulders. She allowed him to pull her away from the car. "Guess it's a good thing I told Rustin to come by here instead of waiting until I got home to call." He guided Lisa toward the walk.

"Hold it right there." Dan caught Drex's arm, spinning him around. He raised his right hand, balled into a fist.

"Don't try it." Drex smiled. "I got the best of you a long time ago." Shrugging off the detaining hand, he turned his back on Dan and hurried Lisa across the lawn.

"Please, Dan." Lisa looked back. "Just go…"

"If you need me…" He didn't finish, turned and went back to his car.

Taking the keys from her, Drex opened the door. Behind them came the screech of tires against pavement. "Get some things together and let's go."

"Did you have to bait him like that?" She felt she had to say it.

"I don't want him around you, Lisa. Even professionally." His manner changed, the little triumph over Dan forgotten. "Sorry, sweetheart, guess I'm naturally jealous." He kissed her forehead. "Even when I've no reason to be." He quirked a smile, looking down at her. "Do I?"

"Of course not." Pulling away, she went inside.

~ * ~

Lisa dozed as they drove. She now had a headache to go with her backache. Once or twice, she moved uneasily as a twinge of pain touched her. She barely remembered arriving at Land's End or being half-carried up the stairs. There was a hazy memory of someone helping her undress, turning out the lights and closing the door but she wasn't certain who. All she remembered was wanting to sleep and doing just that.

Chapter 33

A loud knock on the bedroom door woke her.

Struggling upright, Lisa stared around in surprise. *Where am I?* As the memory of Alice's accident returned as well as its aftermath and the trip to Land's End, she glanced at the little antique clock on the bedside table. Eleven o'clock.

"Who is it?"

The knocking continued.

"Come in."

The door opened. Ursula, holding a tray, stood there. "I've brought you breakfast, madam."

"Thank you," Lisa muttered. "Though it's more like brunch, isn't it?" She plumped the pillows and tucked the sheets around her waist as the housekeeper set the tray across her knees. "Why didn't someone wake me before now?"

"Mr. Drex gave orders you weren't to be disturbed," the housekeeper explained. "I came up on the chance you'd awakened."

What would she have done if I was still asleep?

"If you need anything else, just ring the bell." She indicated a braided silk rope hanging by the bedstead.

As Lisa looked at the bell-pull, Ursula went out. She hadn't noticed that before, didn't think such things still existed. There seemed to be a lot of things on this island not found anywhere else.

After finishing breakfast, she gave the white cord a tug. Within minutes, Ursula appeared. When questioned about Drex's whereabouts, she explained he was in Temple on business. "He'll return when needed, madam."

Lisa showed her disappointment at that. "I'd like to call the hospital and ask about my aunt."

Ursula looked startled.

"You do have a telephone here, don't you?" It came out sharply.

"Of course." The housekeeper appeared insulted. "Mr. Drex had one installed after his father..." Her voice trailed away, as if bringing up a forbidden subject. "It's in Mr. Drex's study."

"In that case, as soon as I get dressed that's where I'll be," Lisa gave a loud sigh of annoyance, suddenly seeing no need to be polite. "And no...I don't need any help getting dressed," she went on as it appeared the housekeeper was about to ask that.

Nodding, Ursula took away the tray.

Lisa dressed leisurely, feeling no hurry to do anything. The ache in her back was gone but once she was on her feet, it returned. She blamed it on the feather mattress.

When she left her bedroom, however, she found herself clinging to the top edge of the carved wooden wainscoting. She felt so clumsy and slow she didn't want to fall. Besides, the pain was getting progressively worse and seemed to be travelling downward into her hips.

~ * ~

The door to the study was unlocked. Nevertheless, in Drex's absence, she felt like a trespasser as she went inside.

"If there's a phone in here, I sure don't see it." She looked in the places she'd expect a telephone to be...on the desk...on a small chairside table...All she saw was what *wasn't* there. The Star Stone was gone. Where the wooden cradle had rested was a large bare spot.

"All right." She was talking to herself, like someone trying to bolster courage. Whistling in the dark...*why? What do I have to be afraid of?* "If I were a telephone, where would I hide?" She began to inspect the bookshelves. "Perhaps it doesn't look like a phone?"

She'd seen phones fashioned like books, opening to reveal a handset inside, M&M characters...even a Darth Vader. Surely Drex didn't go in for novelties like that? He didn't strike her as the type. If he had a phone, she was certain it'd be something costly and very noticeable.

Watched by Heinrich's painted eyes, she inspected the leather-bound books in the shelves on each side of the fireplace. Some appeared incredibly old, most titles were in German, a few in English...*Secrets of the Elder Gods...Cultes des Coules...De Vermis Mysteriis...A Treatise on Certaine Prodygies Super-Naturall*...She smiled at the archaic spelling and, intrigued by the title, slid the last volume off the shelf.

It was so heavy she had to grasp it in both hands to keep from dropping it. Lisa carried the book to the desk, opening it. The pages were thick and fine-grained. They had to be *real* parchment and not paper. A frontispiece illustration caught her eye and she smoothed the page, studying it closely. A second later, the book fell to the floor.

The pages fanned, opening to the picture she'd seen. A woodcut…a large, amorphous *thing* floating in the air. From its body protruded appendages, some short stumpy blobs, others serpentine and sinuous. They reached out of the picture toward her, seeking…grasping…the thing she'd seen in her nightmare hovering over Drex.

Clumsily, Lisa ran from the study to her bedroom, slamming the door and leaning against it. Gasping from the exertion, she tried to slow the pounding in her chest, heart beating so fast it hurt. A violent stab tore through her. Not like the aches she'd felt all morning, this one was different, its deep intensity made her recognize it for what it was.

I'm going into labor.

Opening the door, she hobbled to the head of the stairs. Now it hurt to walk. She felt her thighs cramping.

"Ursula? Ursula!" It hurt to speak, too. She hoped she could make the housekeeper hear. *I don't think I can manage the stairs alone.*

"Madam?" Ursula appeared, looking up at Lisa expectantly. "Is something the matter?"

"Y-you've got to find Drex…" She broke off as another contraction made her catch her breath. "I-I'm having labor pains…"

"I'll find him immediately, madam." There was more emotion on the narrow face than Lisa had ever seen. "Perhaps you should rest until he gets here."

Without answering, Lisa went back into the bedroom. She didn't lie down, however, but stood by the window, looking out at the rapidly deepening afternoon. The pines were beginning to throw their shadows across the lawn. *I hope Drex hurries.*

From outside, she heard footsteps. As she turned toward the door, they stopped. The doorknob turned slightly and there was a click.

Lisa caught the doorknob and twisted it. It didn't move. *I'm locked in. Ursula locked me in. Why?* Abruptly she saw again the way the housekeeper looked the day Drex told her they were to be married. *She doesn't intend to call Drex. She isn't going to do a thing...but he'll come back...so why...*

That might not be for hours.

I have to get to the hospital, call Dr. Halyard... Wait... he can't help, he's a patient, too. Why did he have to wreck his car just now? Dan, I'll call Dan... he delivered Aura's baby, he can deliver mine, too... She didn't dare think Dan might not be so cooperative. *I've got to get to Drex's study and find that phone, but how?*

The windows? They were two stories above the ground. Tying bed sheets together? *I doubt I could tie a knot that'd hold my weight. Besides, there's no way I can get out one of them, even if I were in good shape and at present, I'm definitely not.*

In frustration, Lisa beat her fist against the windowsill. Looking out across the yard, she saw someone emerge from the road between the trees. Aura, carrying a basket of laundry, headed toward the servants' entrance at the back of the house.

"Aura...Aura!" It was a stage whisper, Lisa not daring to call louder in case the housekeeper was lurking outside the door.

Unheeding, Aura neared the house. She didn't look up. Lisa glanced around the room for something to attract the girl's attention. Her gaze fell on the bedside clock. Without a thought of the damage to the object, she hurled it through the window.

It fell directly at Aura's feet. The girl jumped, stared at it a moment, then looked up. Lisa waved frantically.

"Miss Lisa? What—" Lisa pressed a finger to her lips. "Why did you throw that clock? What is it?" She set down the basket.

"You've got to help me." Lisa leaned out, clinging to the window frame. "I-I think Ursula's gone crazy. She's locked me in...the baby's coming..."

"What can I do?" Aura made a helpless gesture. "If they don't want you to leave...I can't help you."

"What are you talking about? If who doesn't want me to leave?" Lisa gripped the window sill as another pain struck. "Drex is in the village. Didn't you see him? Tell him to come home."

"I-I have to go..." Picking up the basket, Aura ran around the corner of the house, stopping as Lisa called out.

"Please, help me. I'm having my baby. I know how bad it was for you when Joshua was born." She took a deep, pain-relieving breath, leaning forward slightly as a cramp seemed to cut off her air supply. Aura skidded to a stop. "D-don't let that happen to me. Please." The girl looked up at her. Lisa took a deep breath. "I-I need a doctor...Call Dr. Walker...Tell him...tell him I need him..." Another pain shot between her legs, accompanied by a trickle of liquid. "P-please." She nearly shrieked the word. The liquid became a flood, spattering the carpet.

Looking from Lisa to the trees as if she wanted to bolt for their shelter, Aura made her decision. "I'll do what I can." She ran back the way she'd come.

Lisa watched her go. *I can't wait. I've got to do something...get out and meet Dan.* If Drex got back before that happened...*I hope to God they don't fight.*

Again, she looked at the locked door, then around the room. *If only I had a key...*her gaze fell on the door connecting the two bedrooms. Once again, she saw Drex making an elaborate show of locking that door, dropping the key carelessly on the dresser. "The key. Where is it?

Hurrying to the dresser, she searched its cluttered top, scattering brushes and bottles. She pulled out drawers, feeling in the empty spaces. Tears of frustration stung her eyes as she turned toward the bed, and then...she found it...in the back of the drawer of the bedside table.

Pulling out the key, she thrust it into the lock. It stuck...turned...slowly the door opened.

Lisa hurried through, heading for the opposite doorway, not bothering to look at the room she'd entered. She pulled at the knob. The door came open easily but she felt as if she were barely moving, the weight of the child making her awkward and clumsy. *I'm moving as fast as I can, but I'm not getting anywhere.* Her legs felt so thick and heavy, and damp. It hurt to lift them.

She was in the hall now, but the lights were off. *When did it get so dark? It's only late afternoon...* She realized she didn't know what time it was. The entire house was dark. Feeling for the banister, Lisa gripped it tightly as she started down the stairs. She had no idea where the light switches were, carefully brushing her feet over the steps before taking each one.

The front door was open. Moonlight was shining in, bright enough that she could see. Someone stepped into the doorway, blotting out the moon. It went dark so suddenly Lisa stumbled, catching the banister to keep her balance. A silhouette threw a long shadow across the foyer floor.

"Drex?" She stepped from the stairs, stumbling toward him, feeling her legs go jelly-like with relief.

"I'm here, Lisa."

"I'm so glad...The baby's coming. I told Ursula and she locked me in my room. She wouldn't call you."

"It's all right now." He didn't appear upset by her accusation.

"Let's go." She caught his hand, fingers brushing his sleeve. The fabric was soft and thick. "We've got to get to the hospital—" Lisa looked down. Now that her eyes were becoming accustomed to the semi-dark, she saw he was wearing a long flowing garment, like a...robe? "What are you—?"

"We aren't going anywhere, sweetheart. Your baby'll be born where it's supposed to be."

"What do you mean? I need a doctor."

"It's certainly not going to be Brad Halyard." His laugh was so low and deep it sent a chill through her. "Not after all the trouble I had putting him out of commission. Making his car run off the road wasn't easy. Your aunt was even more difficult. That damned cat fought me. He dislikes me so." He shook his head. "You really should get rid of that animal, Lisa."

"What are you talking about?"

"Did you actually believe they were accidents?"

"You mean you caused them?" She couldn't believe it. "That's not funny, Drex."

"It wasn't intended to be."

"How could you? You were nowhere around."

"Wasn't I?" He gave a short, satisfied laugh. "Dan Walker gave me the most problems, though, but he was the one I enjoyed most."

"What did you do to Dan?" She caught his arms, shaking him.

"I didn't do anything to him." He didn't move, except to put a hand over hers, holding it so she couldn't pull away. "You did it all. Remember telling him you never wanted to see him again?"

"But…" All she could do was stand there and shake her head. *Is he saying* he *made me say those things to Dan?*

"I had to make sure you two were completely finished, that you were alone, so you'd come with me. You had to be at Land's End when the child's born. And now…here you are." He gestured and she heard the smile in his voice though she couldn't see it.

"Don't joke like that. I know you don't like Dan, but…" His words made her feel faint. Behind her, another door opened. She didn't turn around, didn't want to see who stood there.

"I'm not joking." He sounded insulted she might think that. "When Ursula gave me your message, I was busy with preparations."

"What kind of preparations?" That didn't sound good. She took a step backward.

"I didn't intend for her to lock you in. You might've hurt yourself trying to get out." Anger flared briefly. "Sometimes I think that woman's too stupid to live…but what can you expect from one of *them?*"

"Them? What…Never mind. Let's get to the hospital, and…after the baby's born, after things have settled down, we'll talk about all this."

"Aren't you listening?" His voice rose. "Haven't you heard anything I said? *You aren't going anywhere.*"

"You're wrong…" Lisa took another step away from him. "I'm getting out of here." Clumsily, she whirled…and ran directly into Rustin's arms.

"Let me go." Lisa beat against his chest, twisting away to claw at him. He dodged, seized her wrists and forced her battering hands to her sides. The manservant might be small, but he was strong.

The dizziness was back, more powerful than before. The darkness was ablaze with pinwheels of light. The strongest contraction yet twisted inside her. From far away she heard Drex shout. "Don't let her fall, you idiot!" She was aware of being lifted into the air and that was all…

Chapter 34

The phone's strident shrilling roused Myrtice, who jerked it off its cradle. *Quiet, damn it, don't wake Danny.*

"Hello?" she whispered, voice fuzzy with sleep. *What time is it?* She glanced at the clock. The luminous dial told her it was a little after ten. "Who is this?" *Please, please don't let it be an emergency.*

"Miss Williams?"

"Yes?" She thought the voice sounded familiar.

"This is the switchboard at Temple General. I've received a call for Dr. Walker and he isn't answering his own phone…"

Of course he isn't, Myrtie thought. *I switched it off as soon as he went to sleep.* She glanced at Dan's phone and watch lying on the bedside table. Tonight, she'd been determined they weren't going to be disturbed. She realized she couldn't simply set it on *vibrate,* however. He'd programmed himself to wake even if it gave the slightest buzz, so she deactivated it. In the morning, if he managed to get to it before she did, she'd say he did it himself and didn't remember… and she'd be so convincing he'd believe he'd done just that.

"…and he left your number as a relay."

Damn it, no. Myrtice didn't answer.

"I'm sorry to bother you," the operator plowed on into the silence. "But it's so unusual for him not to answer…"

"No, no…that's all right." A deep inhalation, almost but not quite a snore made Myrtice look back at the bed and Dan's sleeping profile. "As a matter of fact, Dr. Walker's phone's been on the fritz all day—battery's going, I think—so I'm his answering service tonight." It was all she could do to keep from biting off the words she was so angry. "Who's the message from?"

"It's from an Aura Edenfield."

"Oh?" *Who's Aura Edenfield?* Myrtice scowled. Wait a minute…that girl from the island. The one Danny thought he was going to marry until…she sat up a little straighter…that von Dorff character took her from him, too. He hadn't been as broken up about her as he was about Lisa Chambers, though that was little comfort. *Danny didn't come to me after he lost that one.* Myrtice was wide awake now. "What did she want?"

"It's a rather strange message and I hope I got it right."

"Tell me and I'll let you know." She snapped the words, managing to soften them with, "Please."

"She said…" There was a pause as if the operator were reading something written down, probably from one of those *While You Were Out* pads. "*Mrs. Chambers is in labor. Needs you.* I know that's a bit odd. I mean, Dr. Walker isn't OB and I'm not sure I got the message correctly. She must've been using a cell phone because it kept cutting out and then went dead in the middle of our conversation." She paused to take a breath.

"It must be a mistake," Myrtice agreed. "We don't know anyone named Edenfield and Dr. Walker certainly wouldn't be seeing an OB/GYN patient." Myrtice tapped an impatient finger against the tabletop. "Frankly it sounds like a crank call."

"We do get those occasionally," the operator admitted. "That always makes me so angry, especially when it disturbs a doctor for no reason. Still, I had to report it, so…"

"You did the right thing. Thanks." She hung up before the operator could say more.

"Mud…?" The conversation, though in whispers, awakened Dan. "Who was that?"

"Just a wrong number… Go back to sleep…"

"C'mere…" He pulled her toward him.

Rolling over, she rested her head against his chest as Dan put his arms around her.

Chapter 35

She was staring up at stars spangling the sky above her, something cold and solid under her. She lay on a large square block. *It's that stone in the ring in the woods. How can that be?* Turning her head, she saw the shadows of the trees surrounding the Ring. Ropes crossed her chest, looping through holes drilled into the stone, tying her to it. Her dress was gone. She was wrapped in a robe like the one Drex wore.

It was quiet except for a soft crackling and...chanting...The sounds floated to her. Lisa raised her head. A few feet away a fire burned in a hole dug into the dirt and between it and the altar were three figures. Two knelt, heads bowed, faces hidden inside deep cowls. From their size, she guessed they were Ursula and Rustin, and the third... She'd know that tall figure anywhere, though he was standing with his back to her.

Raising his hands, Drex spoke aloud the words they were whispering, "*Ey-hr Yog-Sothoth, nyrl lwa ectra otwa...*" Those eldritch words she remembered from her dream.

"Drex?" Her call cut into the chant, making him whirl around. "I thought you loved me. Why are you doing this?"

"I do love you, sweetheart." He sounded hurt, as if he couldn't believe she'd doubt him. He came toward the altar. "I'm doing this because I love you."

There was something in his hand, a knife, its blade reflecting the fire. He lay it beside her on the altar. Lisa shrank as far as the ropes let her. Another pain stabbed through her, and she gasped.

"Don't be frightened." He mistook her cry for fear. "Lie still. I'm not going to hurt you." He sounded so apologetic she might've believed him if he'd made any move to untie her. "I'm afraid I lied to you, Lisa. About some things...several things, in fact...but now I can tell you. Now that you're about to become one of us."

"What are you talking about?" She shook her head.

"You see..." His tone was so conversational and calm all she could do was stare at him. "The power from the stars is very real. So is the promise Heinrich made to the Old Ones. Then his wife died and he had no sons to fulfill that promise. The village women didn't conceive so there were no more of his bloodline...and then..." Drex laughed and the sound was so harsh it grated like a rasp against stone. "The Old Ones made him an offer...and the old bastard accepted...and condemned us all." His voice rose, overflowing with that hatred she'd heard before but now it was so much stronger, so high and sharp it seemed to burn her ears.

"What do you mean? Lisa cowered against the stone, wishing she could escape that hate.

"They sent their servants...female creatures from the sea. That's why there aren't any graves for his other wives, Lisa. They all returned to the sea to die." Drex looked up, gaze seeming to search the stars. "With one of those creatures, Heinrich got the son he wanted but he wasn't truly human. They were all that way…deformed…twisted…We've waited so long for a perfect one …but they were all disappointments…Isak…Hansi…even *I* didn't escape."

"What are you talking about? There's nothing wrong with you."

"Isn't there?" For a moment his smile was ironic, mouth twisting.

I've some scars…

"When my father came along, he briefly preferred humans, so he beguiled my mother and brought her here." He looked away, saying in a rush, "There *is* a god imprisoned under the sea, Lisa…*Tschenebhua*…On my parents' wedding night, he sent his spirit to possess my father and together they sired the sons he needed." He laughed but the sound was cold and angry.

"Sons? You mean you have a brother?" *Where is he? Is he one of those birth-crippled villagers?*

"Of sorts…*M'AneseNebh*…stupid fool. Don't ask to meet him, Lisa. He's not very pretty." For a moment, his voice held sarcastic pity. "Takes after *his* father…I'm afraid…

Evil marks his children. Dan told her that. *Why didn't I listen?*

"Don't worry about our child…he's going to be perfect."

"*Our* child?" That jerked her attention back to him. "What are you talking about? We don't…"

"Don't you understand?" He was petulant now, like a child telling something and no one listening. "Haven't you figured it out by now? That's my child you carry."

"No…oh no…" She began to shake her head.

"It was mid-summer eve, the night of total power." He was speaking words she didn't want to hear. "I looked into the Star Stone and the message was there…*she's coming. Even now he's bringing her to you.*"

Robin, saying, *Come on, Lisa, we're going for a drive.*

Dan asking, *Did your husband often do things on the spur of the moment, Mrs. Chambers?*

"I sent the others away and waited. I thought it'd be one of the village women…but no one came…so I returned to the Manor. I was crossing the road when that car appeared…"

What's that in the road?

"It was *you?*" Again she saw that dark thing, something like wings flapping behind it. Drex in his robes, running in front of the car.

"It nearly ran me down." His eyes were frozen, staring at an image only he could see. "I wasn't going to stop…I could always discover the wrecked car later, but then I saw you…and I knew you were the one sent to me…I got you out of the car and…did what I had to…"

No, no, I don't want to hear this. Lisa struggled against the ropes. *If only my hands were free, I'd put them over my ears, shut out his words. It isn't true.*

"I had to hurry. The seed had to be planted before one of the villagers saw the fire and overcame his fear."

"No…" Lisa screamed, shutting out his voice, drowning the words proving what her mind had known all along…*it had happened. It had been real.*

"You fought me. Even as broken as you were, you didn't submit easily." Drex shut his eyes and the vicious pleasure on his face sent fear slicing into her. "Not like those weak villagers. I had to hold you down."

Funny thing about those lacerations. They look like fingernail scratches. Five crescent-shaped marks on each wrist.

"Then *M'AneseNebh* showed up and we fought over you...but I got the better of him because I'm stronger. Because I'm almost human. I bested him like I did the Shaman." The words were wrenched from him. He leaned against the stone, hands touched her shoulder, caressing.

Cruel hands. Murderer's hands.

"Don't touch me." She tried to pull away. The rope cut into her breasts. "Why didn't you save Robin? Why didn't you get him out, too?" Tears of hatred burned her eyes as she flung the words at him.

"He was in the way." He was calm again. "I'd have to get rid of him later. It was easier this way."

"Murderer!" she screamed, hands arched into claws, trying to reach him. The ropes held, making her cry out as they scraped her wrists.

"Lisa, lie still." There was genuine concern in his voice but there was also madness. Not foam-flecked lunacy but colder and more deadly, generations of madmen held in check, finding release in the man hovering above her like a giant bird of prey.

"Drex, please don't hurt my baby." She was sobbing now. "You've killed his father, please don't hurt him, too."

329

"Didn't you hear what I said?" he asked, patiently. "It's *my* baby."

Shaking her head, she shut her eyes. She didn't want to look at him, couldn't bear to see the man she thought she'd loved, who'd just confessed to rape and murder. Something touched her feet, making her open them again. Ursula was folding back the hem of the robe Lisa wore.

"Well?" Drex turned toward her.

"Soon now." A hand touched Lisa's bulging stomach, pressing inward.

"Drex, please," Lisa tried once more to get past the madness. "Get me to a hospital."

"Don't worry." He soothed. "Ursula's skilled in childbirth."

"I don't want Ursula!" Lisa struggled frantically. Jerking against the ropes, she kicked at Ursula who jumped back as she shrieked, "I need a doctor."

Dan, help me. Oh God, why didn't I listen to you? Another pain coiled within her and struck.

~ * ~

Rolling over, Dan opened his eyes. "Did I hear the phone ring earlier?" For a moment, Myrtice didn't answer. "Mud?"

"Wrong number..." she mumbled. She stayed on her side, away from him so he couldn't see her face. "Some drunk."

"Thank God...though I'm surprised I haven't gotten at least one call. What time is it anyway?"

"A little after ten."

"That early? I must've been more tired than I thought. Damn, it's been a pretty long time since I've gotten to sleep before eleven." He yawned and stretched, then lay there staring at the ceiling for a moment. "Hand me my phone, will you?"

"Why?" She didn't move.

"Because I want to make sure the battery isn't dead. I've haven't had a night without at least one call since I took over the practice, especially a week-end one."

"You don't need to check it. It hasn't rung." She rolled over, pressing herself against him and kissing his mouth. "Why don't you relax and enjoy it?"

It was the wrong thing to do. He pushed her away, then lay there staring at her. "Hand me the phone."

"Danny…"

He held out his hand. Reluctantly, she picked up the cell and placed it on his palm. He tapped it. The screen stayed dark. "What… Who turned it off. Mud?"

"I wanted you to get some rest," she said defensively. "I wanted us to have one night without some patient dragging you back to the hospital."

He didn't answer. Activating the phone, he checked his voice mail, seeing immediately the call from the switchboard. Tapping the icon, he sat up as the voice mail message played. *I've a call from an Aura Edenfield. It was a very bad connection and the line went dead while we were talking. I couldn't call her back because the number was blocked but I understood her to say Mrs. Chambers is in labor and needs to be taken to the hospital. I'll also try the contact number you have listed.*

"Contact number? Did the switchboard call you?" The way Myrtice avoided looking at him gave him his answer. "When were you going to tell me?"

"She's hurt you enough, Danny. Why drag you into this now? Let her have her baby wherever she can."

"Damn it, Mud." He pressed *Recall*, waited a moment, then snapped, as he was connected to Temple General's switchboard, "This is Dr. Walker. I understand you had a message for me earlier? Unh-huh…how long ago? She said what? Thanks." Deactivating the phone, he slid out of bed, dropping it onto the table.

"What are you doing?" Myrtice gave a cry of despair.

"Getting dressed." He was picking up scattered clothing as he spoke, shrugging into his shirt, pulling on trousers without bothering with underwear. "I'm leaving."

"Where are you going?" *Why am I even bothering to ask?*

"Where do you think?" he answered so sharply Myrtice flinched. "To Land's End. To get her."

"You'll need a nurse…" Maybe she could make it up to him if she acted concerned now. She threw her legs over the side of the bed. "I'll…"

"Don't bother." He didn't give her a chance to finish. "If you want to be useful, call an ambulance and have them meet me at the Land's End island bridge."

With that he was gone, leaving Myrtice sitting there. As she heard the door slam and the sound of the Mercedes' engine, she began to rock, wrapping her arms about herself and sobbing in her misery. *Now I've lost him…Why did I do it?*

It was fifteen minutes before she was calm enough to call 911. Tears still rolled down her cheeks as the operator answered. "Nine-one-one…what is your emergency?"

Chapter 36

Motioning to Ursula, Drex ignored Lisa's outburst. The housekeeper got to her feet, picking up a small clay bowl sitting on the ground beside her. She held it out to him. He dipped two fingers into the liquid and began to stroke Lisa's forehead.

"What are you doing?" She tried to dodge. There was nowhere to go.

"You have to be marked with the sacred symbols before the child's born. To solemnize our marriage." He spread the cold liquid across her cheeks and chin.

"We aren't married. We never even..." She broke off as he smiled, eyes glittering with a half-light of madness.

"Of course we did. Remember Allhallows' Eve?"

"That was a dream."

"Hardly. My people witnessed it. And now..." He looked around, as if speaking to an audience. "Hear me O Ancient Ones, you who would again enter this world and regain what was long ago lost. I've brought you the Mansion, who carries within her the Doorway and the Door. I've kept to the bargain made by my ancestor. Tonight I claim her as promised." He slid the green-stoned ring from his finger. Taking Lisa's hand, he placed it on her wavering left hand. The metal was warm from contact with his skin. It seemed to shrink until it fit her finger, too tight to remove. "Now you're truly mine, Lisa."

Above them a light flared. The Star Stone lay across the lintel of the pillars forming the gate. By some trick of refraction, it caught the moonlight, throwing the rays onto the altar like a spotlight, encircling Lisa's body in a green glow.

Wind sprang out of the trees. It blew Drex's hood from his face, ruffling his robe, making his body a dark shape silhouetted against the firelight. He gave a short, sharp cry and stiffened. Backing away from the altar, he fell into a crouch, arms clasping his chest.

"No…damn it…it isn't fair…" His words were gasped, as if he could barely get enough breath to speak. "I'm…sorry, Lisa…" He cried out, face contorted. "I-I…guess you're… going to meet…M'AneseNebh after all."

He placed a hand on the altar, clutching at the stone as if to pull himself upright. The hand was clawed and scaled. It scratched at the altar. A claw snagged Lisa's robe, shredding it.

Drex fell to his knees, forehead pressed against the stone. Body heaving, he clung to the altar, his voice dying to a pain-filled whimper. His visible hand was almost a paw now, scaly and furred, fingers stubbed into claws gouging furrows into the stone.

"Drex? What…"

With a lurch, he pulled himself to his feet, straightened and raised his head, pushing back the cowl. Crimson-slitted irises gazed down at Lisa out of a twisted caricature of Drex's face. Thick hunched shoulders thrust his head forward. The wind shipped the heavy copper mane running down his spine.

"At last...so glad to meet you...my dear Lisa..." The words were garbled, coming from a throat not built for human speech. "My brother's had you...to himself...much too long." The paw covered her hand as he bent over her, the other swiping the hair out of his face. M'AneseNebh smiled, lips drawn back from protruding fangs. "Now...it's my turn."

Lisa screamed. The sound rose, hovering above them, and an answering wail came from beyond the trees.

A siren.

It shrieked again, then died away. Car doors slammed. Voices sounded within the trees. M'AneseNebh forced himself upright, gesturing. Rustin disappeared into the dark. In a few minutes, he was back, calling in a loud whisper, "It's the doctor. He's brought an ambulance. He—" His whisper broke off as Dan called out Lisa's name.

"Dan...I'm here..."

The creature's hand went over her mouth, stifling her words. She turned desperate eyes toward him.

"Be quiet," he rumbled. "Rustin, see to them."

They were moving through the trees, voices going away from the Ring and toward the Manor. *I've got to warn Dan, call them back.* She might die, her baby might die but she couldn't let Dan be harmed... Jerking her head sideways, Lisa pulled away from M'AneseNebh's grasp, sinking her teeth into the side of his paw.

"Damn it..." With a snarl, he released her, and Lisa gave vent to a scream stopping the retreating searchers.

It seemed only seconds before Dan was in the clearing, two uniformed EMTs behind him.

"Stop them." The creature growled the command and Rustin obeyed.

From somewhere, he produced a pistol, firing as the three men leaped over the stones. Without hesitation, one of the EMTs rushed him. Swinging the medical kit he carried, he aimed it at the gun, knocking it from Rustin's hand. The manservant fell to the ground, scrabbling for the weapon, taking the Med-tech with him. The gun fired, the shot striking the dirt harmlessly as they grappled for it.

With a shriek, Ursula launched herself at the other officer. Past the trees, a flash of lightning cut the air, followed by a rumble of thunder. The wind began to blow over the treetops. Dan ran to the altar. Turning his back on the robed figure, he attempted to untie Lisa.

"Don't touch her. You won't take her away."

Claws raked Dan's shoulder. He was spun around and struck, sent reeling against the altar. They swayed against the stone, two dark shadows grotesquely elongated by the firelight. Though his body was twisted, Drex's twin was strong. Hauling Dan to his feet, he released him, paw swinging out. There was a solid impact against flesh as Dan went down, rebounding off the altar as he fell.

Above them the sky came alive, clouds flowing and colliding, small explosions of light within it as faint booms of thunder grew louder and louder.

M'AneseNebh seized the knife Drex placed on the altar. He held it aloft. "Hear me Old Ones. Destroy this intruder. Help me, I command you." His voice was caught by the wind and flung at the stars.

The wind blew harder. From beyond the trees came the cry of whippoorwills. As if in answer to M'AneseNebh's call, a streak of lightning escaped the clouds, splitting the darkness. It seared the sky bright as daylight, sending fragments of cloud scattering. The sky itself ripped apart as the beam of light aimed itself toward the tabby lintel.

The bolt plunged into the Star Stone. Instead of shattering, the green crystal caught and captured the light. Imprisoned within that green heart, the lightning glittered and churned, crackling and hissing as it tried to escape.

Green mist bled out of the hole in the sky, thickening and widening until it covered the entire Ring. From the altar, Lisa twisted, looking around. *Can't they see? Why don't they stop him?*

Movement inside the mist froze while above them there was frenzy. Through the gaping wound, creatures pushed and crowded, each struggling to be first re-entering the world. Dark formless shapes gibbered and screeched as they fought to go through the tear. The shrilling of the birds grew louder, the wind adding its own shriek.

Leading them was the creature from Lisa's nightmares, tentacles thrust before it like reaching arms. It wavered, as if its first glimpse of Earth in a thousand, thousand years struck it momentarily blind. It recovered, gaining strength. The arms thrusting and curling through the tear began to twist like the blood-threads dripping from the roses in her dreams. They coiled and hovered, seeking…reaching…moving toward the immobile humans below.

One of the medics stood at the outer edge of the circle, frozen in his struggle with Rustin. He was looking upward at the sky but not seeing. The other held Ursula. Her mouth was open, teeth bared in silent rage, like a snake poised to strike.

No one moved. No one saw…except Lisa…

…and M'AneseNebh, who looked up at the blood-red tentacles aiming themselves toward Dan. "No…no…" The words were growled in disbelief. "You can't abandon me. I've been faithful. I've done all you asked…"

Dan turned his head…and smiled. M'AneseNebh's cry died in mid-sentence.

The tentacles dropped to Dan's unresisting shoulders. They rested there, encircling his neck, sucker-tips caressing his temples. The birds' calls fell to a steady trill.

"G'en 'st nga-nga ul orta sa." Dan's hands came up, thumbs touching. He held them before his face as if to hide M'AneseNebh from his sight. One rested above the other, palms outward, fingers stiff and spread. The upper one clenched itself into a fist.

"I won't let you." M'AneseNebh's cry was a mixture of desperation and fury. He rushed Dan, upswung blade glittering.

The Star Stone shattered into emerald fragments, spewing lightning outward. The beam of light plummeted toward the knife blade, struck it…and M'AneseNebh.

In a brilliant flare, he was surrounded by a jagged green halo. M'AneseNebh stiffened, transfixed by the green corona as lightning coursed through his body, impaling him on the beam of light. In the next moment, he was flung backward as the light died away.

Fire flared and faded. Wreaths of smoke curled from the charred form. With a single shriek, the chorus of birds became as quiet as the dying away of the wind. There was a single loud crash like the slamming of a heavy door and the sky cleared, the rip in the firmament healed.

In the silence, movement returned.

Another cry rent the air. Aura, unnoticed until that moment, ran through the entrance, falling on her knees beside M'AneseNebh's body. She placed a hand on the smoldering shoulder, then dropped her head, her own shoulders shaking.

Dan's hand went to his head. He bent to pick up the knife lying on the ground, nearly dropping it as the heat of the handle burned his hand. Gripping it gingerly, he staggered to the altar, slicing through the ropes. One cheek was splotched and purple, blood trickling from the corner of his mouth. Putting his arms around Lisa, he leaned against the altar, panting.

She pushed him away, pointing at Aura. Reluctantly, he released her and went to Aura. Bending over the body, he rolled it over. Drex's eyes, open and blank, stared up at him. He felt inside the neck of the robe, searching for a pulse, then shook his head. He straightened, pulling Aura to her feet. "No one could've lived through a jolt like that."

By now, the medics were moving also. The one subduing Ursula produced a pair of handcuffs, snapping them around her wrists. His face was scratched and bleeding. The housekeeper had put up a fight before he'd gotten her arms behind her.

"You little bitch." She shot Lisa a venomous glare, then looked past her to Drex's body. "He's dead...and so are our hopes...I begged him, *take me*...but he had to have *you*. Now we're lost..." The rest of her words trailed away into a high-pitched wail.

"You saw what he was going to do." Lisa slid off the altar, leaning against it for support. "Why didn't you stop him?"

"Ma'am?" The medic stared at her.

"You saw it," she repeated.

"Saw what, ma'am?" He frowned, shifting attention from Ursula. The housekeeper's cries died to a piteous whimpering.

"Drex..." But it hadn't been Drex. Had it? "That creature...he was going to stab Dan. You could've stopped him. Then the Star Stone wouldn't have aimed lighting at him..." She realized she was gabbling but couldn't stop the furious rush of words. The medic began to shake his head. "The mist...those creatures..."

"Mist...creatures? Lightning came out of the sky and hit that fella. That's all I saw." His face was concerned but more at her distress than what had happened to Drex.

"But the light... M'AneseNebh saw it..."

"Who?"

"What do you mean...who?" She nearly shrieked the word. "M'AneseNebh."

"I think Mrs. Chambers is in shock." Dan's fingers on her arms, digging into her flesh, stopped her. His voice overrode anything else she might say.

Why does he sound so hollow? Like he's far away? Oh no... She was going to faint.

"And if I'm not mistaken, she's in labor."

"That's what we're here for." The medic looked around at his partner. "We'll secure these two in the ambulance and get a stretcher." He headed back through the stone entrance, dragging Ursula with them. The other followed with Rustin. The housekeeper's whimpers trailed behind them until they died away completely.

~ * ~

Dan waited until they were alone before he released her, bending close so Aura couldn't hear. "Keep quiet. I'll take care of everything." They should've been calming words. Instead they sent a shiver through her. She continued to tremble and he put his arms around her. "Shh...there now, it's over..." His voice changed, no longer empty and lifeless. Now it was normal and full of concern. "Can you walk?"

"She shouldn't try." Aura put a hand on his arm. "His child's going to be born here, as he wished."

"*His* child?" Dan stared at her. "What do you mean?"

"He knew this was going to happen," she went on as if he hadn't spoken. "He told me she didn't see his image in the Star Stone. He knew he wouldn't live to see his child. Now the birds...they've been fed. They caught his soul."

"Lisa, do you know what she's talking about?"

"Drex...he..." Dan told her he'd take care of things. Now he was acting as if he didn't know anything. She couldn't tell him, didn't want to repeat what Drex or M'AneseNebh, or whoever or whatever that creature had been, said to her.

"Never mind." Dan brushed away her stammers. "We can talk about it later. Right now, I need to get you to TempeGen." He looked toward the trees. "What's keeping those techs?"

When she started to take a step, however, the pain returned...in the small of her back, grabbing and twisting, circling around to crush muscles in her thighs into immobility. She crouched, hands pressing against her pelvis. "I can't..."

Her legs gave way. Lisa went down and was hauled upright as Dan caught her.

"It's too late," Aura exclaimed.

There was movement within the trees. One of the medics appeared pushing a gurney. He struggled to maneuver the wheels over the uneven ground.

"Bad news, doc."

"What do you mean?"

"Lightning must've hit the engine." He looked back, nodding in the direction he'd come. "There's a burn hole in the hood and the block is cracked. We're not going anywhere." He gestured at the gurney. "I can get her back to the ambulance. At least we can tend her there a little better than here."

"She needs a bed." Aura spoke up.

"What about the other two?" Dan's attention was on the ground inside the Ring, as if looking for something.

"They're not going anywhere either." The medic managed a laugh. "My partner's got them handcuffed to one of the support rails in the cab. He's standing guard."

"Is the radio working?"

"Checked it. Yes."

"Go back to the ambulance and call the sheriff's department." Dan bent, picking up the medical kit dropped during the fight with Rustin. "Have them send out another, pick up those two and take you back to the hospital."

"What are you going to do?" The medic asked. "If she needs…"

"We'll take her to the village," Aura said. "To my home."

He hesitated. "Do you need one of us to go along?"

"I think it'd be better if the two of you stay with your prisoners," Dan decided. He held up the bag. "I've got this and unless something unexpected happens, I think I can handle a simple delivery."

"Right. In that case…" Nodding, the medic wheeled the gurney around and headed it back toward the trees.

"Get on her other side, Aura." Dan didn't wait for him to disappear. With Aura's help, he half-carried Lisa out of the Ring.

Chapter 37

It was slow going. Lisa could only take a few steps at a time before she had to stop and rest, biting her lip to keep from crying out.

"I'm sorry…" It came out as a tear-filled whimper.

"It's all right. Just take it easy. Deep breaths. We've still got plenty of time."

He was so calm and soothing it made the guilt she felt even worse. She wanted to tell him it wasn't the fact that she couldn't move fast that she was sorry for. It was the things she'd said to him, what she'd done to hurt him…the way she'd been such a fool, getting herself into this mess in the first place…She wanted him to know that…and he was being so understanding and…

A light shone ahead of them. A figure carrying a flashlight appeared.

"Aura?" The light was turned on her. "We saw the lightning flashes. What happened? Was something hit?"

"You know you're not supposed to be out alone." Aura looked past him. "Why didn't Isak or some of the others come with you?

"They're all hiding behind their doors." His voice held contempt. "I decided someone had to find out what's going on. What happened?"

"The…" Aura hesitated, swallowing loudly as if to keep from bursting into tears. "H-he's dead, Papa…Master Drex…"

"Dead?" For a moment he appeared confused. "I don't understand."

"Drexl von Dorff was struck by lightning, Mr. Edenfield," Dan spoke up. "He's dead."

"Daniel?" The light swung toward Dan. "You're here?" He turned the beam on Lisa. She leaned against Dan, closing her eyes against the light. "Is that the Mansion?"

"Mansion?" Dan asked. "What do you mean?"

"She's about to give birth," Aura said. "I'm taking her to our home."

"No, you're not." Ignoring Dan's question, Edenfield took a step toward them, raising his hands as if to prevent their coming any further. "We're free now and I won't have any more demon spawn born in my house."

"Papa, it isn't her fault." Aura's flinch at those words was visible even in the dim light.

"She isn't going there." The light swept back to Lisa's face, blinding her. She put up a hand to shield her eyes. "She slept with him. Let her lie in his bed and have his bastard there!"

"Mr. Edenfield, I understand how you feel but don't take it out on Lisa..." Dan broke off as Aura's father snapped off the light so quickly the darkness was a shock.

"I won't let her in," floated back to them as he started back into the woods, feet crushing the grass as he stalked away. "Neither will the others."

"I'm sorry." Aura looked at Dan

"Never mind." He was tight-lipped with anger. Lisa gasped and bit her lip as another contraction twisted through her. He hugged her. "It's going to be all right, sweetheart…we'll go there."

"Where?"

"To the Manor." Tightening his arm around her waist, he turned. "Come on."

With Aura between them, they started toward the path leading to the darkened house.

~ * ~

As they reached the steps, Lisa's legs finally gave way.

"I can't go any further," she murmured, shaking her head. "I'm sorry, Dan. I just can't."

"You've got to," he told her. "Take this." He thrust the medic's bag at Aura. Bending, he hefted Lisa's weight and staggered up the steps.

Clutching the bag, Aura ran ahead, opening the door. She slapped at a switch and the foyer flooded with light.

"Do you know your way around this place?" At her nod, he went on, "Find me a basin, some alcohol or antiseptic, and several clean towels."

She started through a nearby door, flinging over her shoulder, "The bedrooms are upstairs." She disappeared into the darkness.

"They would be." He looked from Lisa to the staircase. *I'd better start thinking a little clearer.* "We'll never make it up that. I'm not even going to try." He turned toward the open door on his right.

~ * ~

It was a parlor, filled with furniture belonging several centuries back.

Dan assessed their usefulness. Chairs, a loveseat... nothing big enough for a woman about to give birth to lie on comfortably.

Where to put her? Got to find somewhere before I drop her. Her body was like lead on his arms. His shoulders were starting to ache, biceps cramping from holding up so much extra weight. *Damn it, I'll lay her on the floor if I have to.*

Then he saw it...a fainting couch...one of those chaise lounge-type things all Victorian homes used to have. *Couldn't be more appropriate.* He stumbled toward it, depositing Lisa as gently as possible. She moaned and tried to sit up.

"Be still." He pushed her against the curled backrest, grateful when she didn't argue. His hand was hurting. A glance at it told him the knuckles were swollen. *Oh God, did I break it? Please, not that, not now. I need both hands.* Flexing his fingers, making certain he could still move them, he decided nothing was fractured. *Better remember to have it x-rayed it later.*

He began pulling cushions from nearby chairs, piling them behind Lisa so she was sitting up. "There. That comfortable?"

"As comfortable as it can be, I guess." She puffed out an answer, managing a bare smile. As he patted her shoulder, the smile turned rueful. She managed an expression completely devoid of anxiety...for a moment. "Before we go any further..."

"Hell of a time to say that." Thinking she was going to make some tearful apology, he hurried on, "Whatever it is, it can wait."

"I don't think it can."

"All right, go ahead." His fingers went to her wrist. *Pulse a little rapid but nothing out of the ordinary...yet.* "But hurry."

"Drex raped me the night he pulled me from the car. He told me tonight. This is his baby, not Robin's." As if saying that exhausted her, she fell back, eyes shut.

"That son of..." Dan took a deep breath. "We'll talk about it, later, Lisa." He didn't want to take time to process that just now. Nevertheless, he felt an icy stab of rage cutting the pit of his stomach, a spark of savagery deep inside blazing to life. *The lightning was too quick. He should've died very slowly.* "Right now, we've something more important to tend to."

As if in answer, Lisa cried out, short, sharp, quickly bitten off.

"Okay, sweetheart..." He knelt by the couch, pulling up the skirt of her dress. "Damn it, Lisa, this is something I've wanted to do, but not like this." With that, he hooked fingers into the waistband of her panties, pulling them down.

She groaned a protest.

"No time for modesty now, sugar."

"And I thought it was bad having to ask for a bedpan..." Somehow, she managed a sarcastic snort dissolving into a gasp. "Oh God, that was the worst one yet." She struggled to raise her hips, letting him pull the panties completely off. Dan tossed them into the chair from which he'd taken the cushions. He turned back to her, pushing the skirt higher and stopped, staring in disbelief at her swollen body, distended nakedness rising grotesquely.

My god, she's huge. Too big. Lisa's body seemed dwarfed by her belly, as if she'd been invaded by a gigantic leech intent on internally engorging itself. He thought of the other children Drex had sired. If what she says is true… *What kind of monster did he put into her?*

Balancing a basin in one hand and the medical bag in the other, Aura came through the door. Several towels and a bottle of rubbing alcohol were tucked under one arm. She set the basin on a small table near the couch.

Glad of something to do to distract his thoughts, Dan checked what she'd brought before taking the kit from her and opening it. She placed a couple of clip clothespins on the table next to the basin and set down the other items she held.

"What are those for?" He reached into the bag.

"Umbilical clamps." She went to the mantel, taking down a glass and a large decanter. As she came back to where he knelt, he saw it was filled with dark liquid.

"And that?"

"Brandy. I thought you might need it."

"No thanks." He managed a smile. "I need a clear head right now."

"Not for you." She gave him a look holding surprising pity. "For her. I doubt if that medical kit's got anything strong enough to kill her pain."

"Good thinking." He took the decanter from her, pouring some into the glass, sniffed at it and recoiled, coughing. "How strong is this stuff?" He poured a little more, handing the glass to her as he set the decanter on the floor. "Give her this."

"Is that enough?"

He shook his head. "Too much could slow her contractions. I don't think any of us want that to happen."

Supporting Lisa's shoulders, Aura pressed the tumbler to her lips, saying gently, "Drink, Lisa." Lisa exhaled, coughed and strangled as the liquid fire burned its way down her throat. "That's right. A little more." Aura continued pouring the liqueur into her mouth.

"God, Aura…that's strong," she gasped.

Removing his jacket, Dan rolled up his sleeves. From the kit, he took a pair of stainless steel scissors, setting them on the table, then saw the spool and the needle Aura had stuck into it, already threaded. "Are you expecting me to do an episiotomy or something? No sutures, please."

"What's an episiotomy?" Lisa asked.

"Never mind." He pulled out a stethoscope, putting it around his neck. Next came a blood pressure cuff. Dan wrapped it around her arm.

"You don't need that. I can tell you," she muttered. The words came out in a slur as the brandy took effect. "It's sky-high."

"I doubt that," he said. He squeezed the pump, saw her grimace as it tightened, then pressed the stethoscope against the vein in her elbow. "Not too high." He looked at Aura. "I don't suppose you know how to take blood pressure readings?"

"Where would I learn that?"

"It was worth asking. Here." He readjusted the cuff, leaving it around Lisa's arm and handed her a small electronic thermometer. "Check her temperature.

Aura activated the unit, pressed it into Lisa's ear and got another grimace. "99.7," she announced.

"By my estimation, those contractions are less than two minutes apart now. Right, Lisa?" He got a grunt in answer. "If I have time, I'll monitor her blood pressure. Aura, at intervals, check her temperature. If it gets over 100.4, let me know. We might have a problem if that happens..."

"Will...you...please stop talking about me...as if I'm not here?" Lisa forced out. "Ohhh...it hurts so..."

"Probably going to hurt a lot more before we're through," Dan said.

"Don't sound so cheerful about it."

He reached into the kit again, bringing out hand sanitizer and latex gloves. "Open the alcohol," he ordered, rubbing the sanitizer over his hands. As Aura obeyed, he held his hands over the basin, "Okay, pour it on my hands."

"But you just..."

"Extra precaution. I don't really trust sanitizer."

She splashed alcohol liberally, then held up a towel, helping him dry away the excess. Dan snapped on the gloves and turned around. "Okay, sweetheart. Not much longer now. Just relax and show me how well you learned your lessons."

Lisa didn't answer. She was in a half-stupor now, the brandy affecting her more than he expected. She barely saw the two figures hovering over the couch, didn't care that she lay half-naked and exposed, blood and birth-fluid staining the couch's striped satin upholstery. All her concentration was on the center of the pain inside her, caused by the creature Drex planted within her, the thing even then trying to tear its way free.

"My baby…Robin's…" The words were gritted out. *But it isn't Rob's baby…it's Drex's.* She could see Isak's cleft lip, Hansi's beautiful, vacant face…what monstrous thing grew from Drex's wicked seed? She strained, forced contracting muscles to push the thing from her body.

"Lisa, not yet. Save your strength."

"Hold my hand, Lisa," Aura whispered.

Fingers touched hers. She seized it, squeezing, hearing Aura gasp. Outside the window, the birds began to chirp again.

"Don't they ever shut up?" Dan exclaimed.

"They're waiting," Aura told him.

"For what?"

"For The Doorway and the Door."

"For what?" He snapped it in exasperation. "For God's sake, what's with all these weird words?"

"It's…" Lisa began an explanation. It ended in a scream as the worst pain yet shot through her.

…the way they'll enter… She could see Drex's hand marking her forehead, placing the ring on her finger. His face in a halo of fire…so handsome but as internally twisted as the others…*why did you do it?*

"I love you, Lisa."

Who said it? They both had. Neither lied. It was all a lie. What's true? She tried to sit up.

"Lisa, lie down."

"…got to get the marks off…" She slapped at her forehead.

"Aura, see what you can do. I'm going to need all the help she can give me."

Lisa felt the cool sting of alcohol on her forehead as Aura scrubbed at it with a towel dipped into the basin. It came away tinged with red as the marks disappeared.

Dan's hand touched her stomach. "Push, Lisa. A big one. The baby's coming. Aura, I need you. Now."

Aura dropped the towel. He began giving her instructions.

"Put your hand here, under the neck...don't let the head drop. Now, Lisa...bear down..."

Lisa obeyed. Hands gripping the edges of the couch, she opened her eyes. The ring on her finger glittered, the light within it winking like a heart beating in time to the birds' shrieks. She tugged at it. *I can't get it off!*

"Lisa...did you hear me?" Dan's shout cut into her thoughts. "Push!" She forgot about the ring, forgot everything except to obey. Straining until she thought she'd force out her insides as well...grunting with the effort, she screamed...and felt the child leave her body.

She was empty...part of herself missing. Her hand fell over the edge of the couch and the ring slid from her finger. The soft sound of it striking the carpet was lost in the baby's cry.

The birds fell silent. This time there was no single chorus of shrieks. They simply...stopped.

Through half-closed eyes, she saw Dan lift the wet and bloody creature...it was so tiny, barely longer than the width of his two hands. It look so helpless as it lay in those hands, fragile chest heaving with the effort of its first breaths, still attached to her by the throbbing cord.

~ * ~

"Hand me those scissors, Aura." Dan looked at the child, eyes scanning the tiny body.

Alive…male…unmarked…*normal*. "Oh God, oh God, oh God, oh God." He whispered the two words over and over like a prayer, relief so intense he felt faint. He didn't hesitate as he took the scissors from Aura's hand.

"No, Dan. No…" Lisa misunderstood what he intended.

"Calm down." He cut the cord. If there'd been any question of the child's humanity, he'd have used the scissors a different way. Pinching shut the clipped umbilicus, he passed the baby to Aura, pulled the needle from the spool and stitched the stump closed, clipping a clothes pin in place before turning his attention to Lisa. "Towel."

Aura thrust one into his hands.

"Dan…"

"Just a minute, sweetheart…one more thing to do." He tugged on the remaining bit of cord. The afterbirth came slithering out, gray and silvery, streaked with ruptured veinlets. He caught it in the towel, folded it and dropped it to the floor. He leaned toward Lisa. She was pale, eyes shut. "Lisa?"

"Tell me you didn't hurt him…tell me he's all right…" The words escaped from barely-moving lips.

"Of course I didn't. See for yourself."

Aura placed the towel-wrapped thing on her stomach. She opened her eyes, looking down at the little bundle. She didn't touch it, afraid to push the blanket aside.

"How…Dan, what does he look like?"

"Like a baby, Lisa. Your baby." He pulled the towel open.

The crown of a tiny head, plastered with damp red curls moved from side to side. Freed from the towel, tiny fists waved in the air. A healthy infant protest rose from a little throat.

"Shhh." Lisa placed her hand on the baby's chest, patting it gently. Such smooth soft skin. *My baby... here... alive...* Love banished fear. "Shhh, darling."

From outside, another sound replaced that of the now silent birds. The wail of an ambulance.

Chapter 38

The sun shone brightly through the hospital window. The walls were white, pinpoints of light reflecting off the crystal vase holding six pink roses. There was no pain in this room, only joy.

Martha had been in twice that morning, *oohing* and *ahhing* and generally acting as idiotic as any adult who loved babies. Alice had been notified she had a great-nephew in the maternity wing.

The baby was sleeping, comfortable in the sensation of being held by the person he already recognized as the supplier of warmth, nourishment, and love. He'd been fed, bright eyes peering over the curve of her breast, tiny fingers kneading gently as he nursed.

Lisa was content to hold him and do nothing else. She'd counted fingers and toes, kissing each one. Touched delicate fingernails, marveling at the brightness of the fluffy curls on the little head and the blueness of his eyes. She'd looked long into those eyes, struggling to detect a glint of green in them, convincing herself they'd never change.

A knock at the door distracted her. It slid open, Dan's dark head appearing around it. "Want a visitor?"

"You bet."

He looked pretty beat up. The bruise on his cheek had faded to a pale green. A scab held the corner of his mouth together where his lip had been torn. One hand was bandaged and splinted. He'd cracked two knuckles in his fight with Drex.

"How's the new mother?"

"The same as yesterday when you asked me that. She's fine."

"And our young man?"

"He's beautiful. The most beautiful baby in the whole world."

Both looked at the sleeping infant.

"About Drex." Dan broke the silence. "I know you don't want to hear this but... There's going to be an inquest."

Her reaction to that was to look down at the baby.

"The autopsy was completed this morning." He'd heard even the medical examiner was shocked by the findings. He hated mentioning anything about what had happened but there were questions he had to ask. "Lisa, did you ever see his back?"

She remembered the day on the beach, of Drex also asking her that, and his admission at the altar. *I was marked*...

"Please, honey." Dan misunderstood her silence. "I don't want to know anything that went on between you two. I just want to know...There were heavy weals, almost scales. His back looked like a snake's skin."

Cetto-Hanhkv...snake monster man...a creature beneath the sea...his father...*cetto thlot-lo*...

"Forget I asked." He snapped the word. "I know enough." He placed a hand on hers, fingers tightening. "I know it's going to be tough, but try to forget it...all of it. We won't talk about it again. Let it be buried with Robin and Drex."

"Easier said than done," she muttered.

"You can do it. Remember, you've got your son to live for."

"Whose son?"

"Does it matter? He's here, he's alive, and..."

"...and he has red hair."

"So does his mother. Don't condemn the poor kid for that." He smiled and she surprised herself by smiling back. "No matter who his father was, he's your child, too, Lisa. Love him for that." He paused, then added, "*I* will."

"I do love him," she admitted. "That's why it hurts me so." She thought of Aura and Joshua. "What's going to happened to the islanders?"

"Nothing. They haven't broken any laws. In fact, now that they realize there's no one to intimidate them, several have already left the island." He shook his head. "Drex was insane, Lisa. He had to be, to do what he did. From what I've heard, the father and grandfather weren't too stable either. Guess it was inherited insanity. The von Dorffs were as nutty as a bunch of fruitcakes and that's all there is to it."

Lisa didn't answer. *That's the heritage my child's going to have. Dan, how can you think I'll forget that?*

"I'm afraid there's going to be a lot of publicity about this," he went on. "The remaining islanders are willing to talk to whoever'll listen. The networks have gotten wind of the whole thing in spite of the sheriff trying to keep it quiet." He realized he was still holding her hand and awkwardly released it. "The doctor filling in for Brad tells me you should be able to go home tomorrow. "

"I know. Think there'll be reporters camping out on the front lawn?"

"If there are, I imagine Alice can handle them."

She managed a slight laugh.

"I guess you'll want to get away from here for a while." His tone said he hoped she'd contradict him.

"I'm not sure. Look what happened last time I tried that. I guess I *should* leave. Until things die down, anyway. Maybe I'll go home with Aunt Allie."

"Will you be coming back?"

"Of course." She seemed surprised he'd ask. "After all, there's a doctor here who's taken a more than professional interest in me." She looked up, meeting his gaze. "Hasn't he?" She put her hand behind his neck, whispering, "Better say yes."

"Lisa…" His expression was too solemn. "After all that's happen, I can't say anything else—" The rest of the sentence was muffled as Lisa pulled his head down, mouth striking his.

Between them, the baby awoke, waving his fists and complaining. Dan pulled away, glancing down. "Quiet, young man. You'd better get used to seeing me kiss your mother. I'm going to be doing a lot of it." He straightened. "Guess I'd better be going for now, though. Got my own patients to see."

At the door, he looked back.

"I'll be back…later." He went through the door.

For several minutes, Lisa sat looking at the door. She felt happier than she had in some time. *It's time for a new life.* With her baby, with Dan…but it was going to take a long time to forget. No matter what Dan said, she'd seen the terrifying reality of the Old Ones and their world, and she knew they existed.

How did the line from that Kipling story go? *A bit of the dark world got inside his head and crushed him to death*...something like that. Drex's dark world had destroyed him and nearly killed her, too, but now, it was over. Shivering, she looked down at the baby.

He was wide awake, making loud sucking noises against one fist.

"It's all right," Lisa told him, smiling. "It's going to be all right."

The baby's eyes met hers. For one heart-stopping moment, they were old and knowing. Lisa felt her heart clutch. Then his gaze softened and the blue eyes slid sideways into the cross-eyed stare of a newborn. The translucent eyelids blinked and closed.

Drex's son slept.

~ * ~

Outside in the corridor, Dan stopped as the door swung shut behind him. There were going to be a lot of changes in his life, he realized. That morning, Myrtice had turned in her resignation, telling him she was leaving Temple and returning to Americus. He felt guilty about that. Because he'd used Mud but...*she used me, too, and her jealousy could've harmed Lisa and the baby.* He salved his conscience with that thought.

The baby... Lisa was going to call him Robin. He'd already shortened that to Robbie. He started to smile but all expression faded from his face as his thoughts disappeared.

Pity the good son had to die but M'AneseNebh disobeyed once too often... falling in love with the woman when she was intended for his brother... they had to rid themselves of him... unfortunately, when one died, the other did, too... Besides, Drex couldn't have dispatched her when the time came... I'll be stronger... Lisa trusts me, she won't question... and when the time's right, I'll take the boy to the Ring and together, we'll do what has to be done...

Dan stumbled slightly as his thoughts seemed to swirl inside his brain. He put a hand against the wall, steadying himself. *Whoa... I must've gotten a harder hit on the head than I thought. For a minute, I completely spaced out... that's the second time that's happened. One more episode like that and I'd better have someone in Neurology check me out. What was I thinking? Oh yeah... Lisa... Lisa and the baby... and me...*

Smiling, he started down the hall.

~ * ~

Had they waited thousands of years merely to wait longer? So be it. They could be patient. Again banished, once more confined... They would wait.

What was Time, when an eon was no more than the blink of an eye? They'd seen the Other World again, for seconds felt it within their grasp when the barrier between them was torn away. Seen it snatched away a second time as the tear once more closed.

The child was alive and normal and they would wait. This time, the years would pass swiftly.

How long does it take for a little boy to grow into a man?

The End

Trademarks Acknowledgement

The author acknowledges the trademarked status and trademark owners of the following wordmarks mentioned in this work of fiction:

Nicorette CQ
Mustang
Barbie
Jaguar
The Leaper
Mercedes C63
Escalade
Prius
Hallmark Moment
Seven-Up
Scarlett O'Hara
Mutt & Jeff
African Neptune
Ziemia Bialostocka
Sidney Lanier Bridge
Ford F-150
Lucy Lewis
Dracula
Cliff Notes
Jaws
The Addams Family
Morticia
Itt
Lurch
Cousin Fester

Gomez
Caller ID
Skype
Cultes des Coules
De Vermis Mysterii
M&M
Corian Sandalwood
Darth Vader

Quote from the Hippocratic Oath taken from
The History of the Hippocratic Oath: Outdated,
Inauthentic, and Yet Still Relevant
Raphael Hulkower
Albert Einstein College of Medicine
2010

About Toni V. Sweeney

Toni V. Sweeney has lived thirty years in the South, a score in the Middle West, and a decade on the Pacific Coast. Now she's trying for her second thirty on the Great Plains. An accomplished artist as well as writer, she has a degree in Fine Art and a diploma in Graphic Art.

Since the publication of her first novel in 1989, Toni divides her time between writing SF/Fantasy under her own name and romances often set in the South under her pseudonym Icy Snow Blackstone. She's been associated with the *South Coast Writer's Association,* the *Pink Fuzzy Slipper Writers,* many writing groups, *myspace, Facebook,* GoodReads, Twitter, and LinkedIn. In 2013, she also became a reviewer for the New York Journal of Books. She is now promotion/publicity manager for Class Act Books (US) and Double Dragon Publishing (Canada).

Currently, Toni has had sixty-three novels published.

Other Titles by Toni V. Sweeney

Serpent's Tooth
Wizard's Wife
Blood Bay
The King's Swordswoman
The Rose and the Dragon
Dragon in Chains
My Lord Ax
The Seventh Mothman
Bride of The Beast
For the Love in Adler's Brain
Spacedogs' Best Friend
That Demon in Blue Jeans
The Eclectic Paranormal Reader
Variation on the Theme of Man

Available from www.classactbooks.com

*We invite you to visit
our website for more great
fiction*